Disney

DONALD QUEST

HAMMER OF MAGIC

Facebook: **facebook.com/idwpublishing**
Twitter: **@idwpublishing**
YouTube: **youtube.com/idwpublishing**
Tumblr: **tumblr.idwpublishing.com**
Instagram: **instagram.com/idwpublishing**

ISBN: 978-1-63140-912-7   20 19 18 17   1 2 3 4

COVER ARTIST
ANDREA FRECCERO

COVER COLORS BY
DISNEY ITALIA

SERIES EDITOR
SARAH GAYDOS

ARCHIVAL EDITOR
DAVID GERSTEIN

COLLECTION EDITORS
JUSTIN EISINGER
and ALONZO SIMON

COLLECTION DESIGNER
CLYDE GRAPA

PUBLISHER
TED ADAMS

Originally published as DONALD QUEST issues #1–5.

Ted Adams, CEO & Publisher
Greg Goldstein, President & COO
Robbie Robbins, EVP/Sr. Graphic Artist
Chris Ryall, Chief Creative Officer
David Hedgecock, Editor-in-Chief
Laurie Windrow, Senior VP of Sales & Marketing
Matthew Ruzicka, CPA, Chief Financial Officer
Lorelei Bunjes, VP of Digital Services
Jerry Bennington, VP of New Product Development

Special thanks to Eugene Paraszczuk, Julie Dorris, Carlotta Quattrocolo, Manny Mederos, Chris Troise, Roberto Santillo, Camilla Vedove, and Stefano Ambrosio.

Written by
Stefano Ambrosio, Davide Aicardi,
and Chantal Pericoli

Art by
Andrea Freccero, Paolo De Lorenzi,
Francesco D'Ippolito, Stefano Zanchi,
and Vitale Mangiatordi

Colors by
Disney Italia with Travis and Nicole Seitler
and Erik Rosengarten

Letters by
Nicole and Travis Seitler

Dialogue by
Pat and Carol McGreal

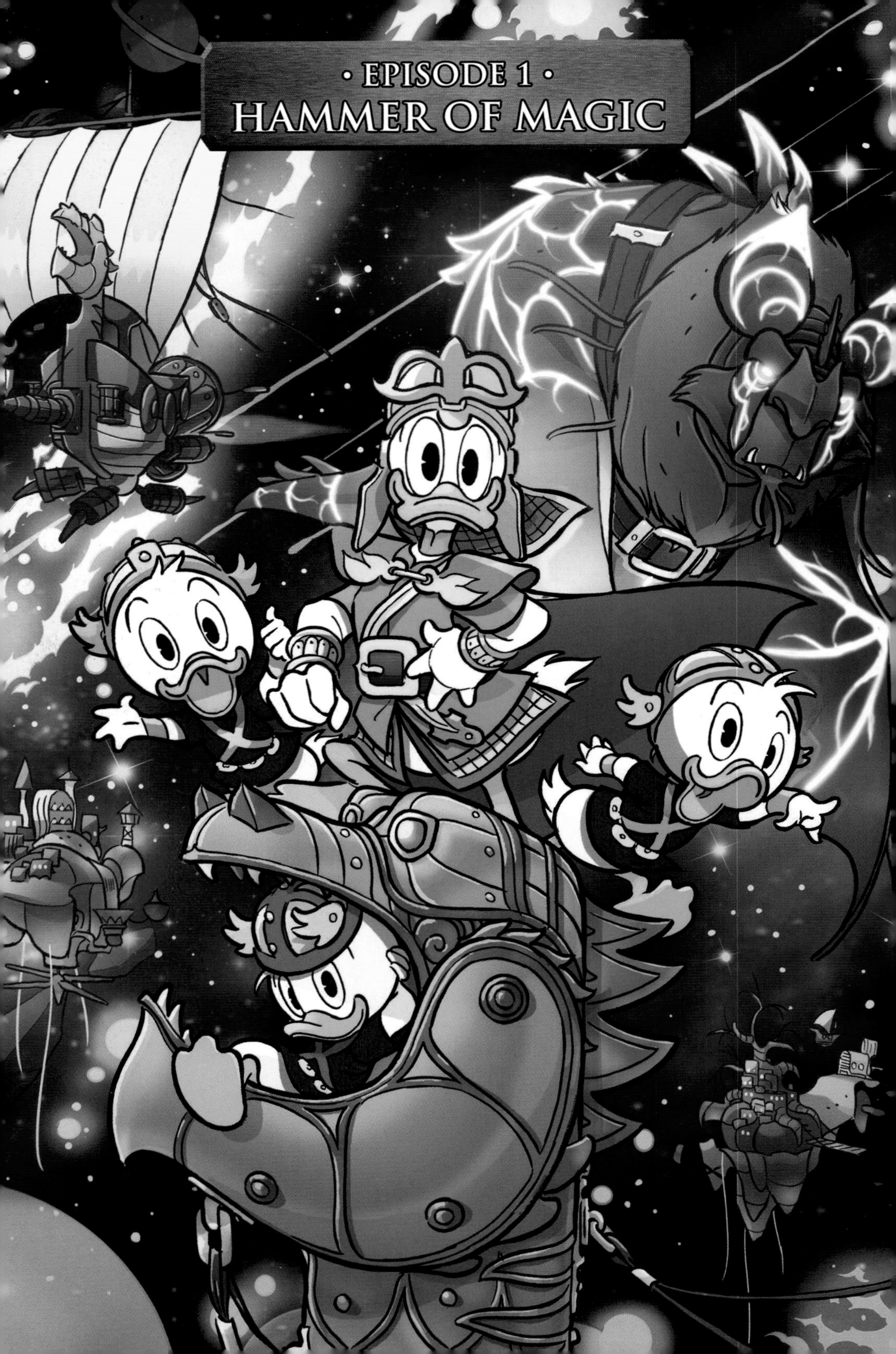
• EPISODE 1 •
HAMMER OF MAGIC

Prologue:
HOW IT ALL BEGAN

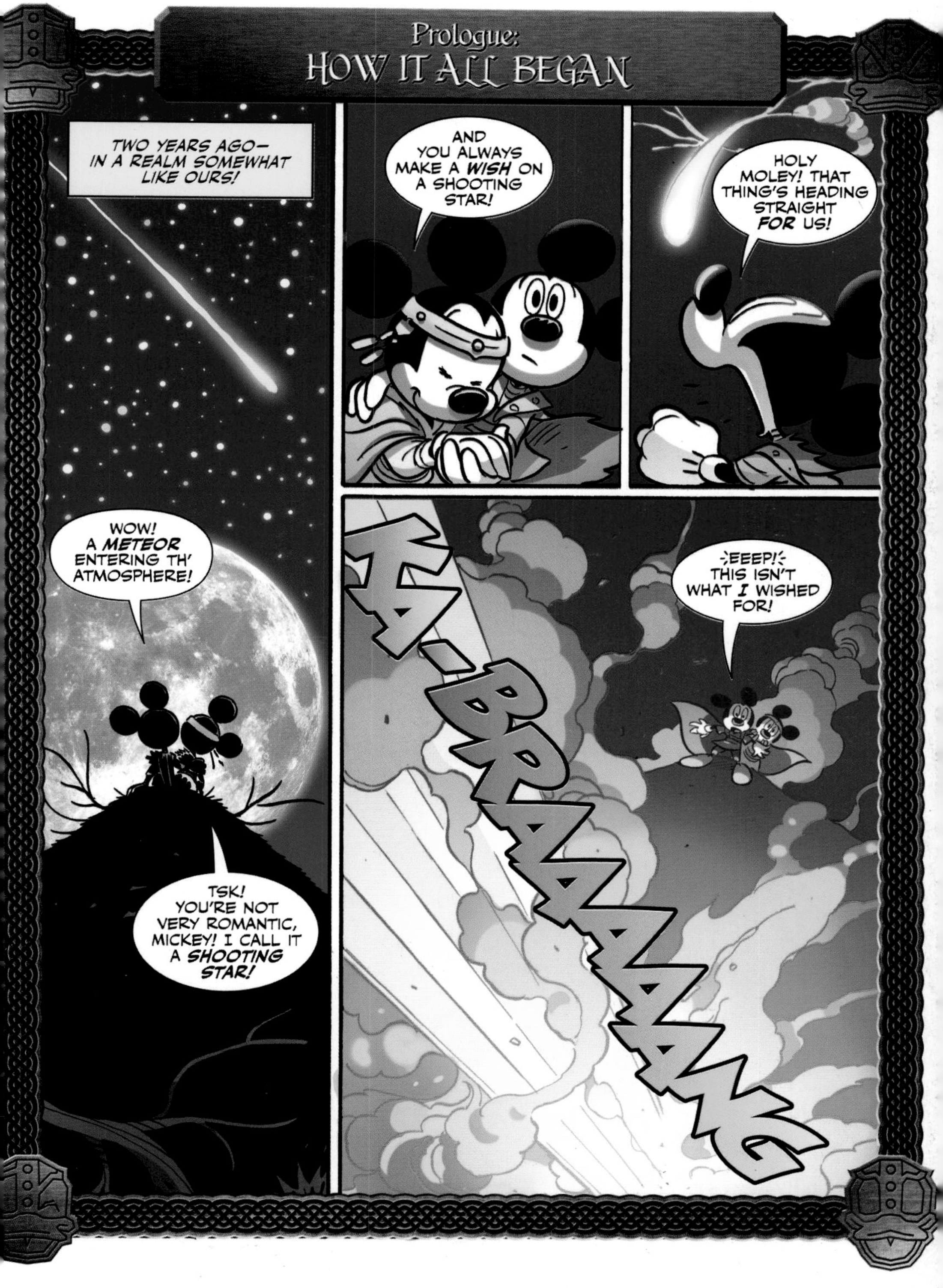

TWO YEARS AGO— IN A REALM SOMEWHAT LIKE OURS!
WOW! A METEOR ENTERING TH' ATMOSPHERE!
TSK! YOU'RE NOT VERY ROMANTIC, MICKEY! I CALL IT A SHOOTING STAR!
AND YOU ALWAYS MAKE A WISH ON A SHOOTING STAR!
HOLY MOLEY! THAT THING'S HEADING STRAIGHT FOR US!
KA-BRAAAAAANG
EEEP! THIS ISN'T WHAT I WISHED FOR!

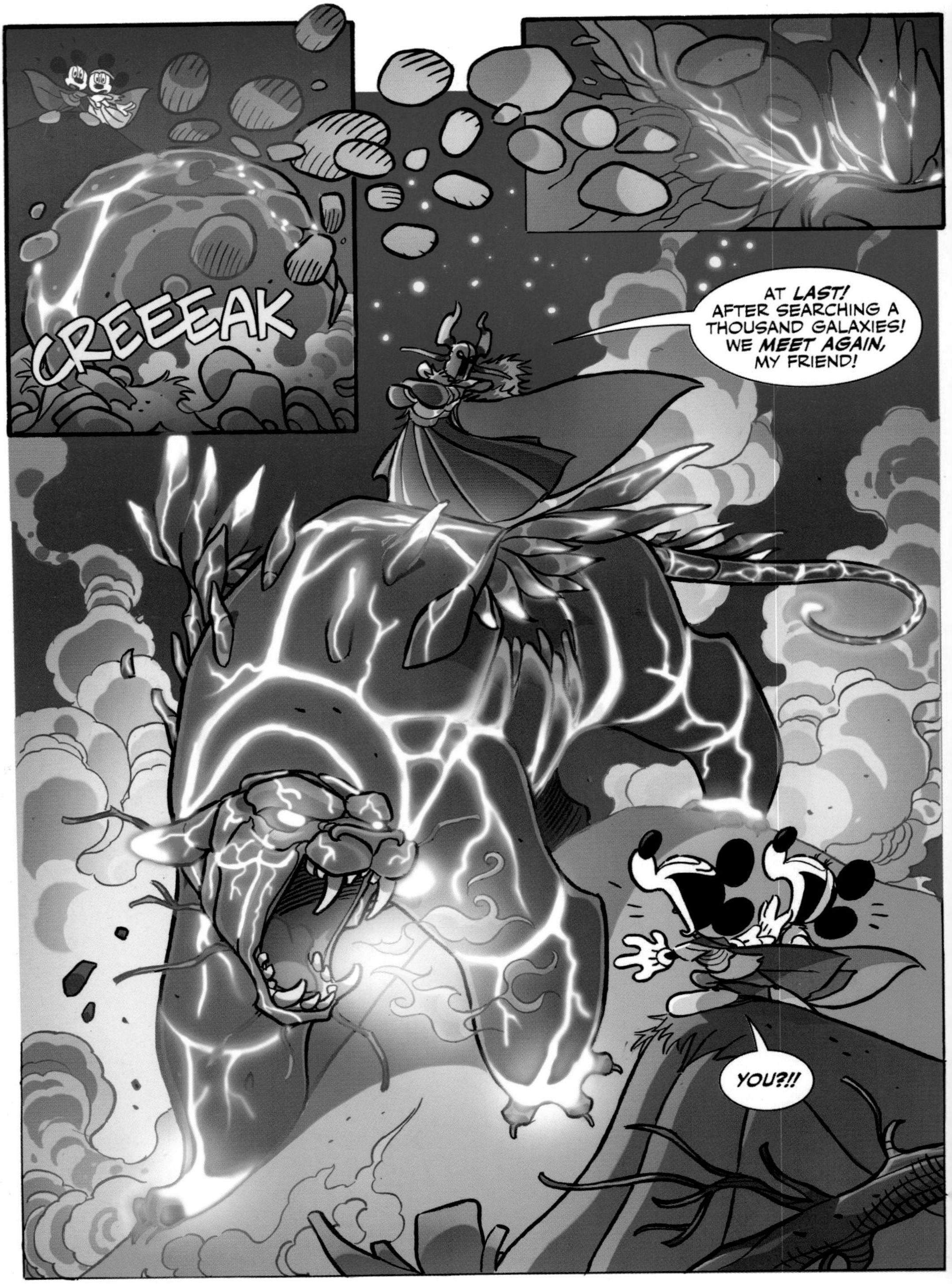
CREEEAK
AT LAST! AFTER SEARCHING A THOUSAND GALAXIES! WE MEET AGAIN, MY FRIEND!
YOU?!!

Chapter 1
IN SEARCH OF A HERO!

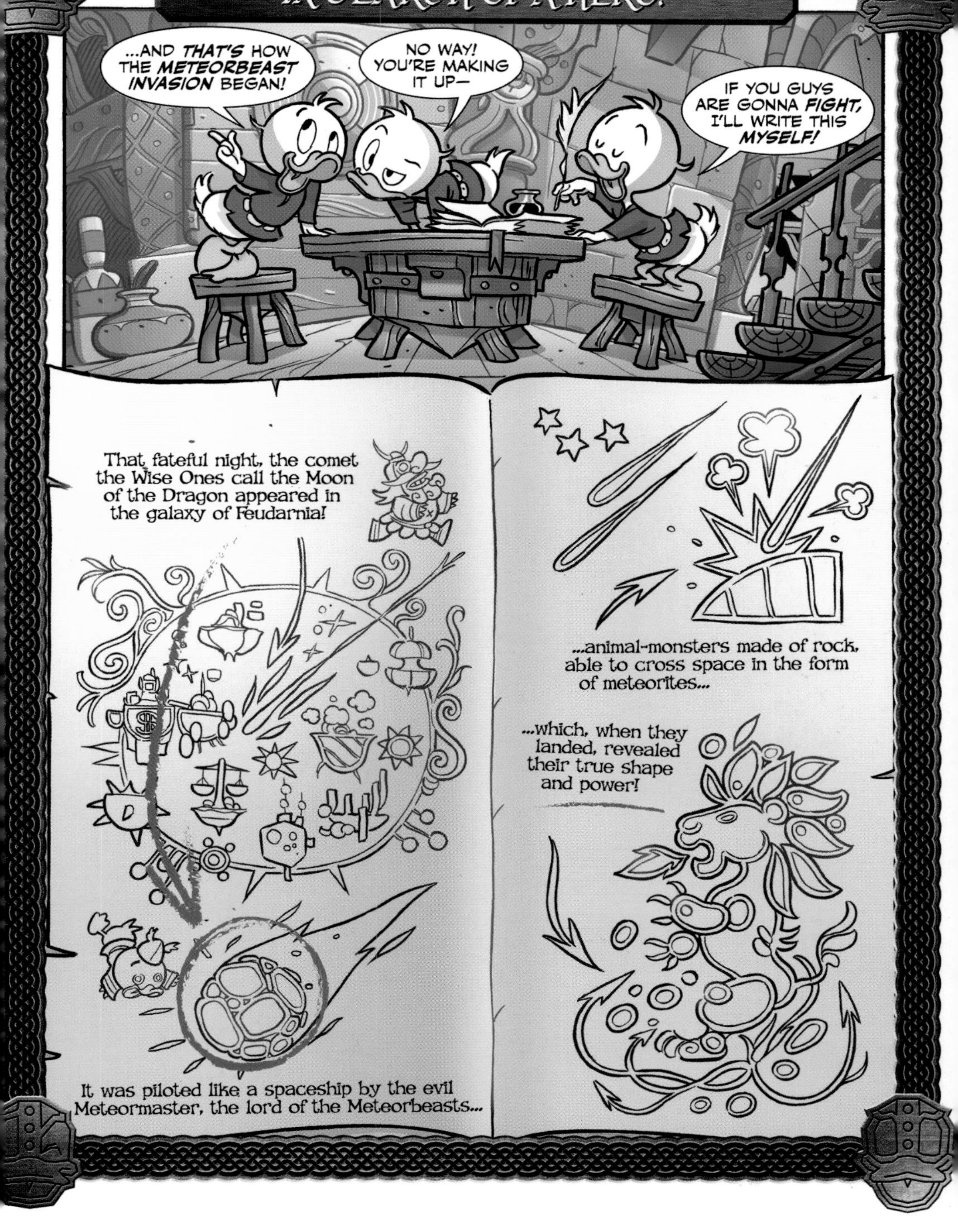

...AND *THAT'S* HOW THE *METEORBEAST INVASION* BEGAN!
NO WAY! YOU'RE MAKING IT UP—
IF YOU GUYS ARE GONNA *FIGHT*, I'LL WRITE THIS *MYSELF!*
That fateful night, the comet the Wise Ones call the Moon of the Dragon appeared in the galaxy of Feudarnia!
It was piloted like a spaceship by the evil Meteormaster, the lord of the Meteorbeasts...
...animal-monsters made of rock, able to cross space in the form of meteorites...
...which, when they landed, revealed their true shape and power!

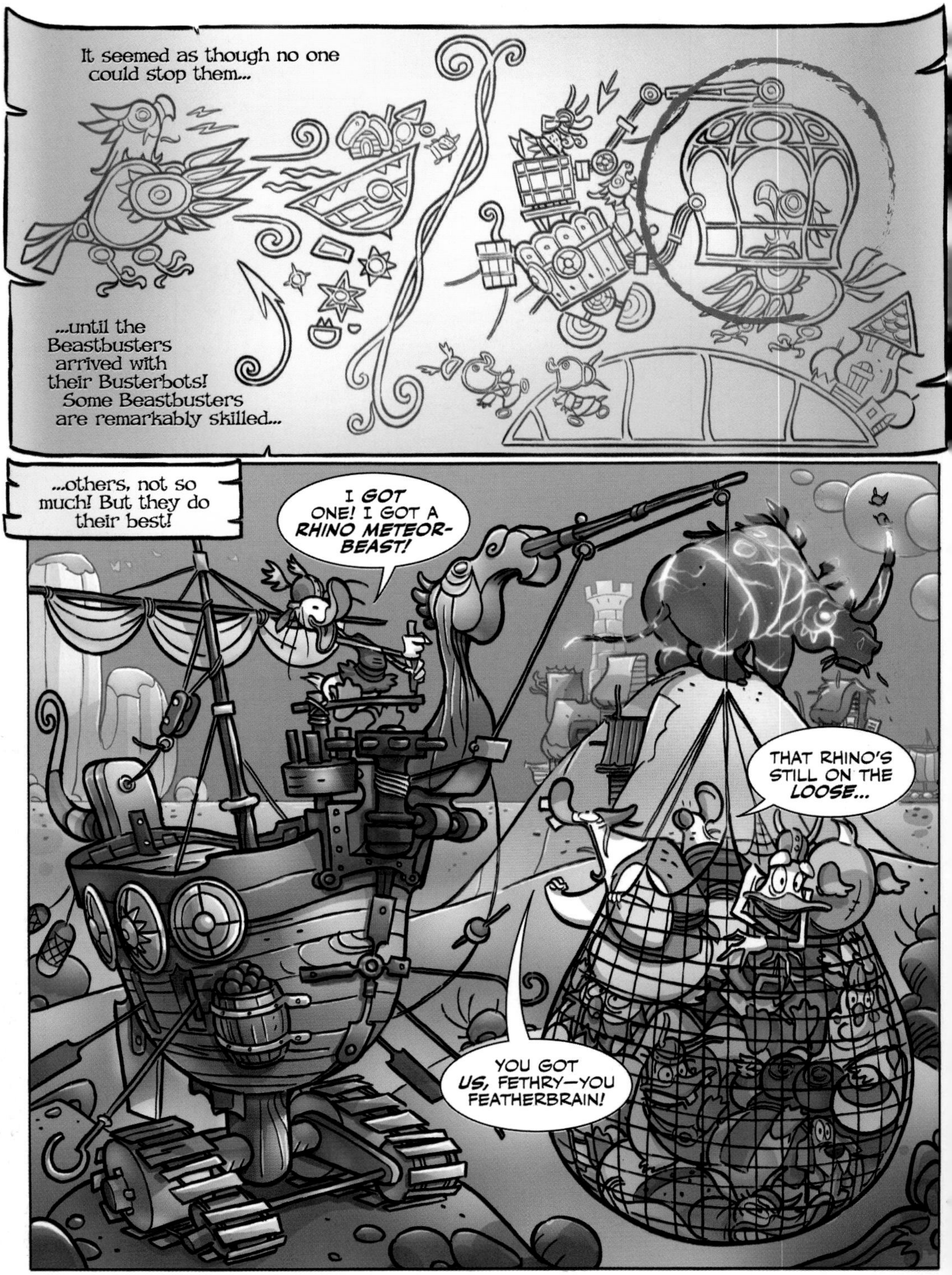
It seemed as though no one could stop them...
...until the Beastbusters arrived with their Busterbots! Some Beastbusters are remarkably skilled...
...others, not so much! But they do their best!
I GOT ONE! I GOT A RHINO METEOR-BEAST!
THAT RHINO'S STILL ON THE LOOSE...
YOU GOT US, FETHRY—YOU FEATHERBRAIN!

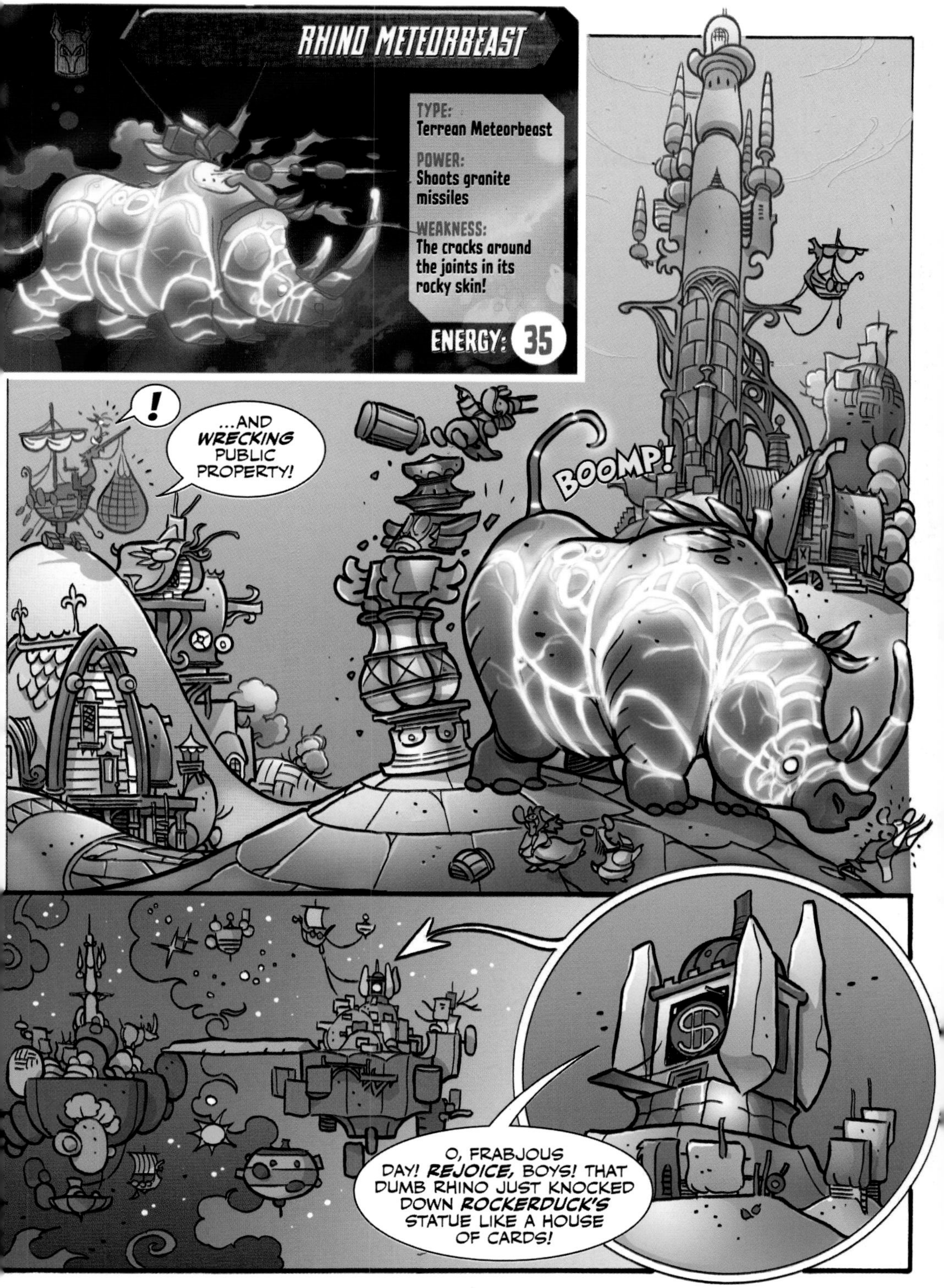
RHINO METEORBEAST
TYPE:
Terrean Meteorbeast
POWER:
Shoots granite missiles
WEAKNESS:
The cracks around the joints in its rocky skin!
ENERGY: 35
!
...AND WRECKING PUBLIC PROPERTY!
BOOMP!
O, FRABJOUS DAY! REJOICE, BOYS! THAT DUMB RHINO JUST KNOCKED DOWN ROCKERDUCK'S STATUE LIKE A HOUSE OF CARDS!

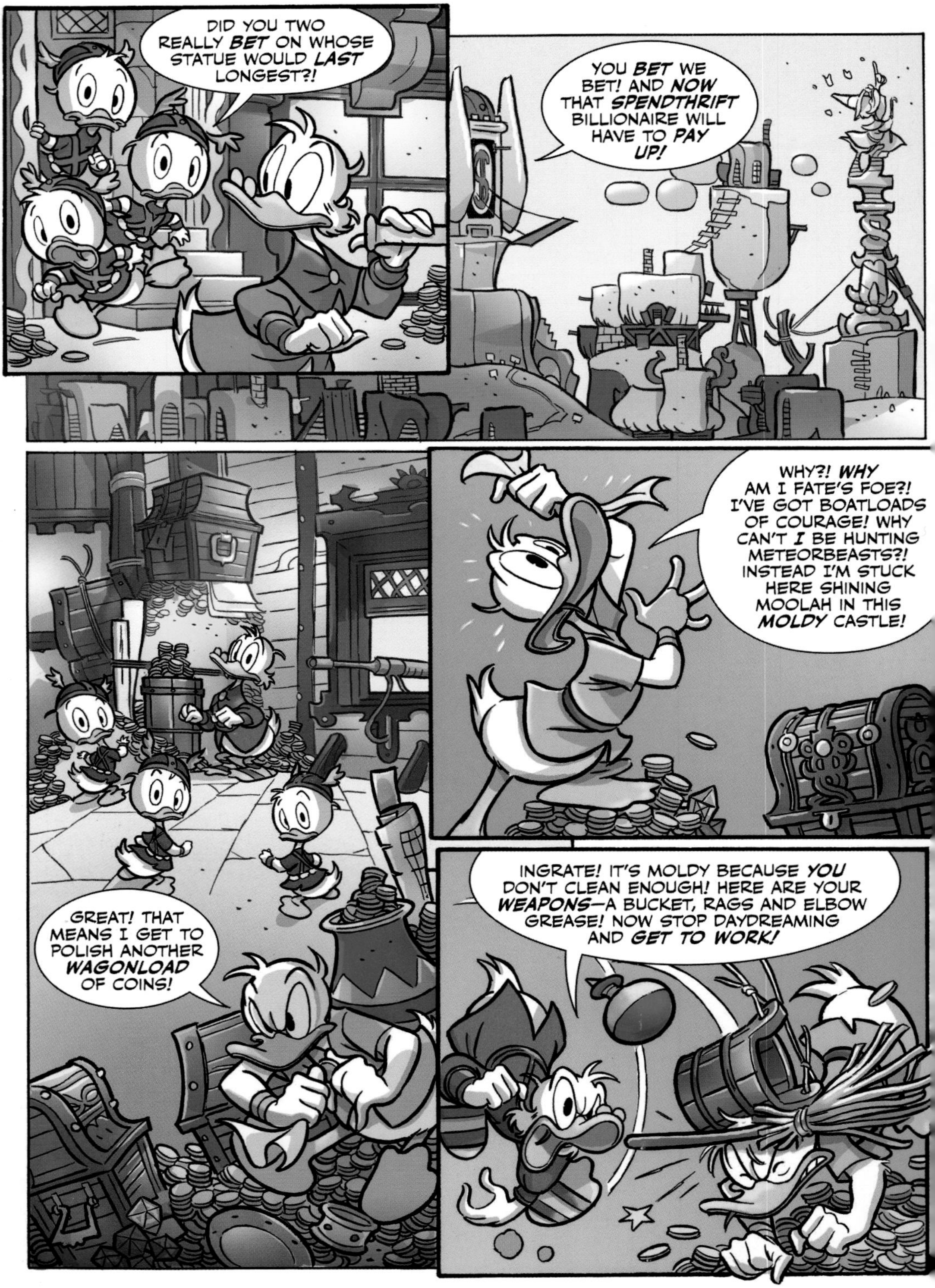
DID YOU TWO REALLY BET ON WHOSE STATUE WOULD LAST LONGEST?!
YOU BET WE BET! AND NOW THAT SPENDTHRIFT BILLIONAIRE WILL HAVE TO PAY UP!
GREAT! THAT MEANS I GET TO POLISH ANOTHER WAGONLOAD OF COINS!
WHY?! WHY AM I FATE'S FOE?! I'VE GOT BOATLOADS OF COURAGE! WHY CAN'T I BE HUNTING METEORBEASTS?! INSTEAD I'M STUCK HERE SHINING MOOLAH IN THIS MOLDY CASTLE!
INGRATE! IT'S MOLDY BECAUSE YOU DON'T CLEAN ENOUGH! HERE ARE YOUR WEAPONS—A BUCKET, RAGS AND ELBOW GREASE! NOW STOP DAYDREAMING AND GET TO WORK!

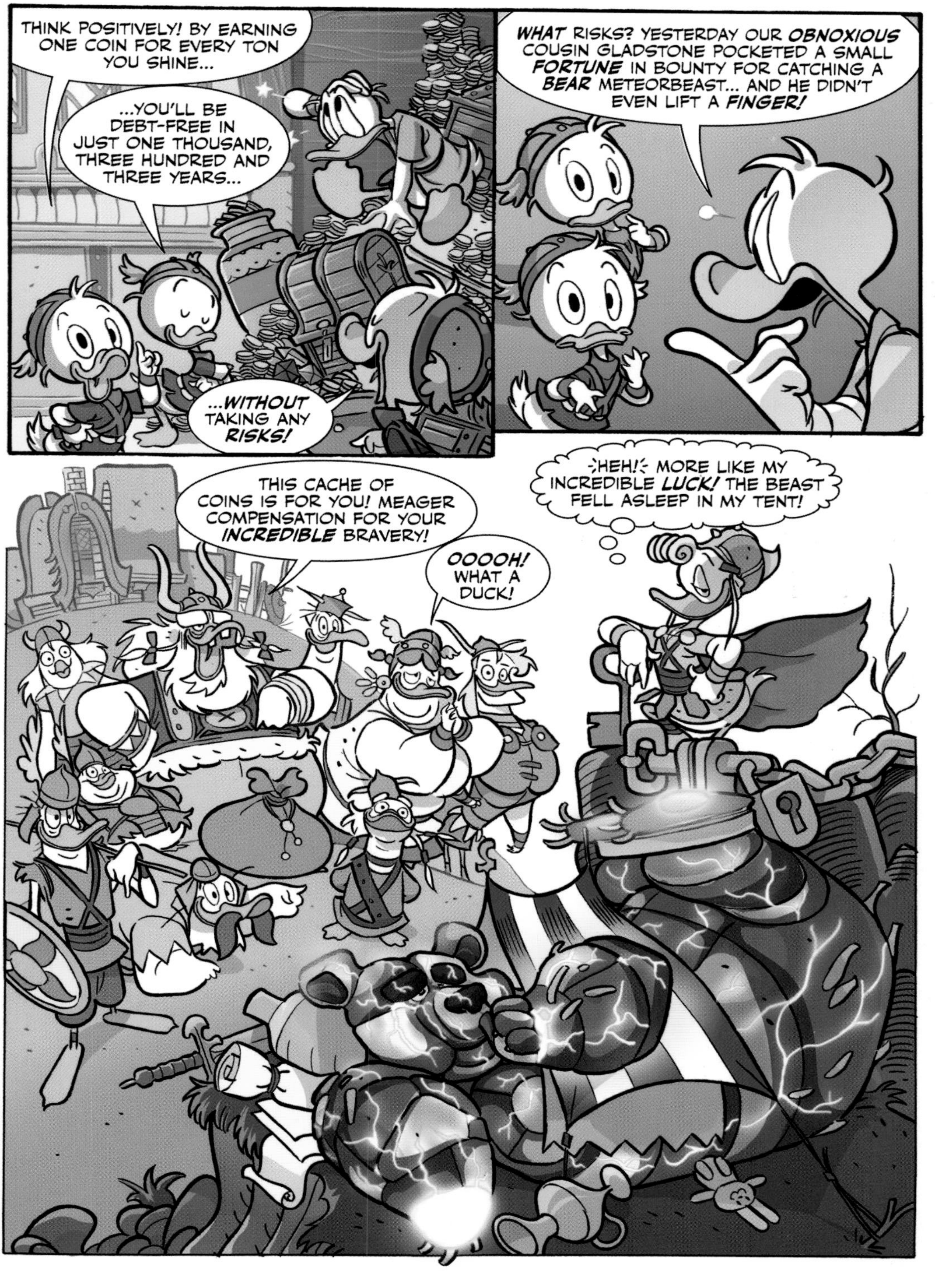
THINK POSITIVELY! BY EARNING ONE COIN FOR EVERY TON YOU SHINE...
...YOU'LL BE DEBT-FREE IN JUST ONE THOUSAND, THREE HUNDRED AND THREE YEARS...
...WITHOUT TAKING ANY RISKS!
WHAT RISKS? YESTERDAY OUR OBNOXIOUS COUSIN GLADSTONE POCKETED A SMALL FORTUNE IN BOUNTY FOR CATCHING A BEAR METEORBEAST... AND HE DIDN'T EVEN LIFT A FINGER!
THIS CACHE OF COINS IS FOR YOU! MEAGER COMPENSATION FOR YOUR INCREDIBLE BRAVERY!
OOOOH! WHAT A DUCK!
HEH! MORE LIKE MY INCREDIBLE LUCK! THE BEAST FELL ASLEEP IN MY TENT!

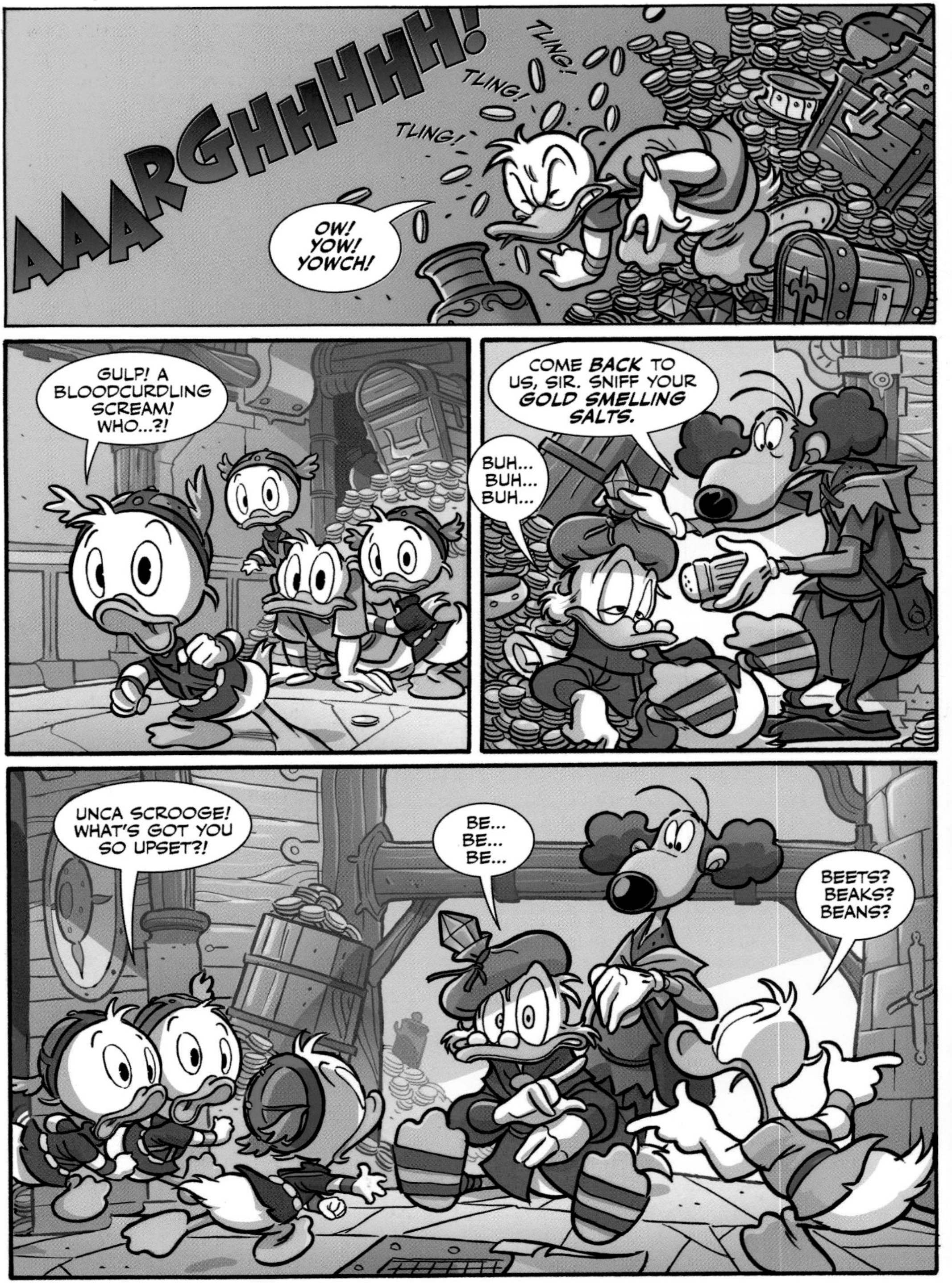

AAARGHHHHHH!
TLING!
TLING!
TLING!
OW! YOW! YOWCH!
GULP! A BLOODCURDLING SCREAM! WHO...?!
COME BACK TO US, SIR. SNIFF YOUR GOLD SMELLING SALTS.
BUH... BUH... BUH...
UNCA SCROOGE! WHAT'S GOT YOU SO UPSET?!
BE... BE... BE...
BEETS? BEAKS? BEANS?

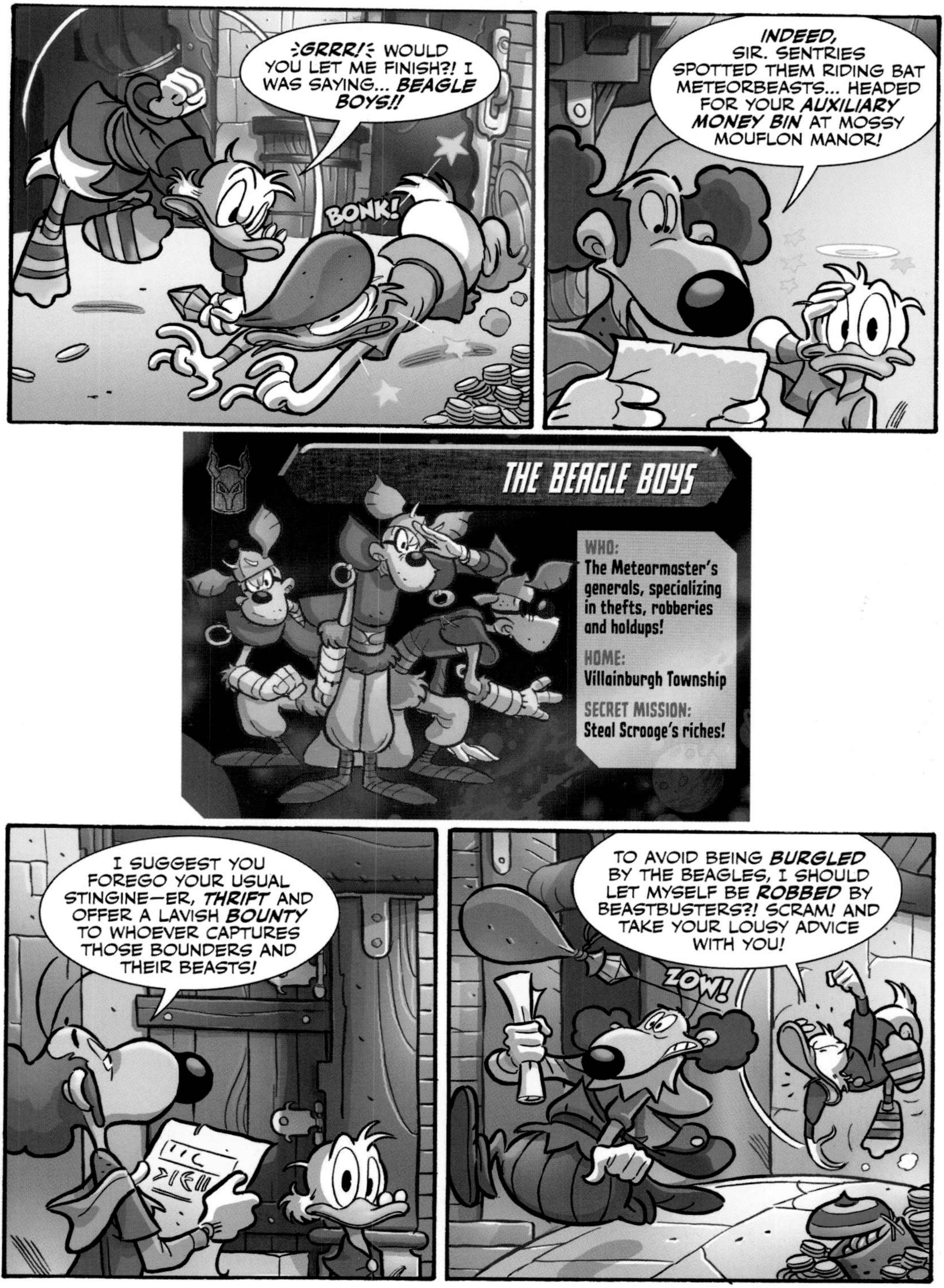
GRRR! WOULD YOU LET ME FINISH?! I WAS SAYING... BEAGLE BOYS!!
BONK!
INDEED, SIR. SENTRIES SPOTTED THEM RIDING BAT METEORBEASTS... HEADED FOR YOUR AUXILIARY MONEY BIN AT MOSSY MOUFLON MANOR!
THE BEAGLE BOYS
WHO:
The Meteormaster's generals, specializing in thefts, robberies and holdups!
HOME:
Villainburgh Township
SECRET MISSION:
Steal Scrooge's riches!
I SUGGEST YOU FOREGO YOUR USUAL STINGINE—ER, THRIFT AND OFFER A LAVISH BOUNTY TO WHOEVER CAPTURES THOSE BOUNDERS AND THEIR BEASTS!
TO AVOID BEING BURGLED BY THE BEAGLES, I SHOULD LET MYSELF BE ROBBED BY BEASTBUSTERS?! SCRAM! AND TAKE YOUR LOUSY ADVICE WITH YOU!
ZOW!

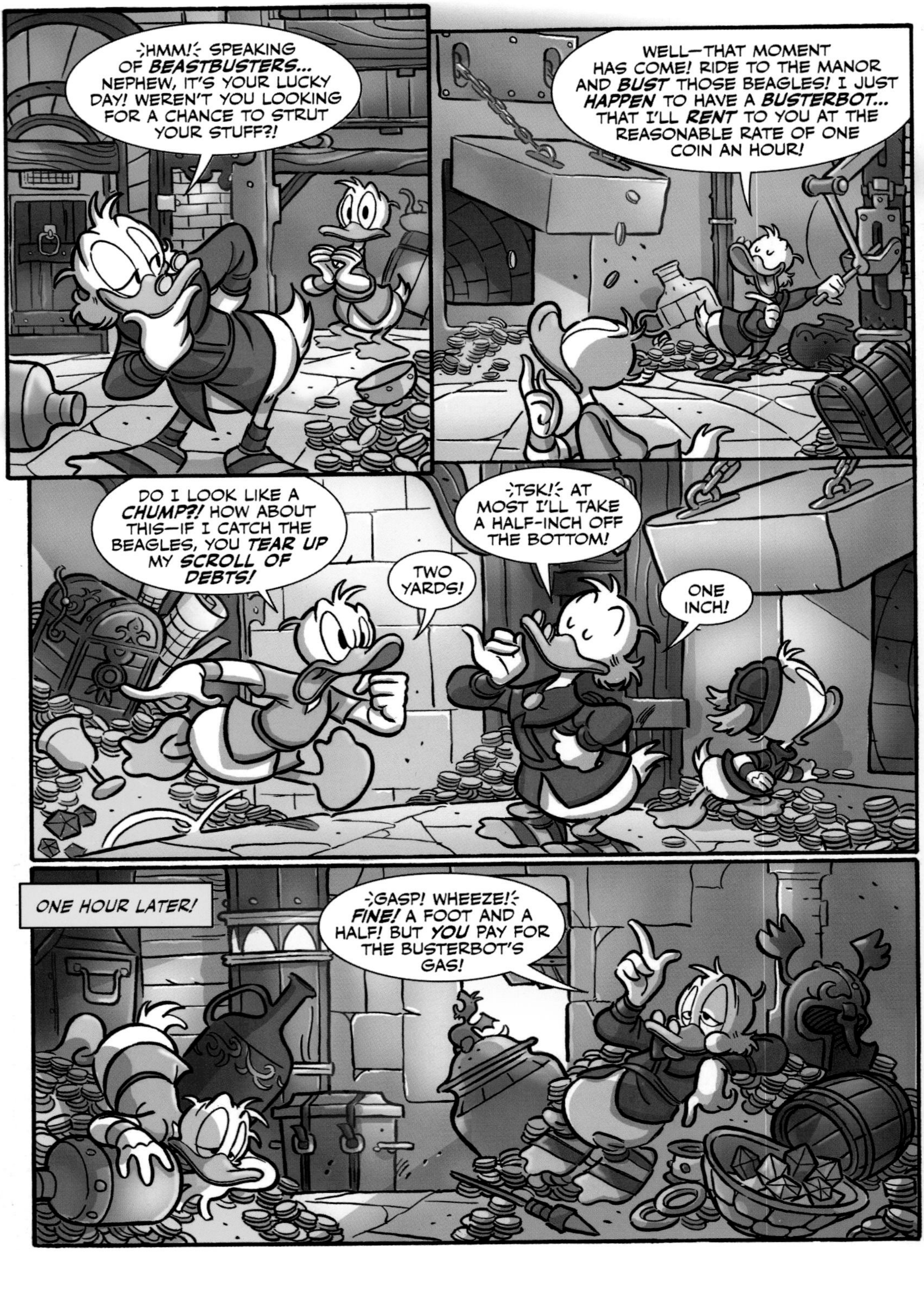

HMM! SPEAKING OF BEASTBUSTERS... NEPHEW, IT'S YOUR LUCKY DAY! WEREN'T YOU LOOKING FOR A CHANCE TO STRUT YOUR STUFF?!
WELL—THAT MOMENT HAS COME! RIDE TO THE MANOR AND BUST THOSE BEAGLES! I JUST HAPPEN TO HAVE A BUSTERBOT... THAT I'LL RENT TO YOU AT THE REASONABLE RATE OF ONE COIN AN HOUR!
DO I LOOK LIKE A CHUMP?! HOW ABOUT THIS—IF I CATCH THE BEAGLES, YOU TEAR UP MY SCROLL OF DEBTS!
TSK! AT MOST I'LL TAKE A HALF-INCH OFF THE BOTTOM!
TWO YARDS!
ONE INCH!
ONE HOUR LATER!
GASP! WHEEZE! FINE! A FOOT AND A HALF! BUT YOU PAY FOR THE BUSTERBOT'S GAS!

Chapter 2

THE BATTLE OF THE MANOR

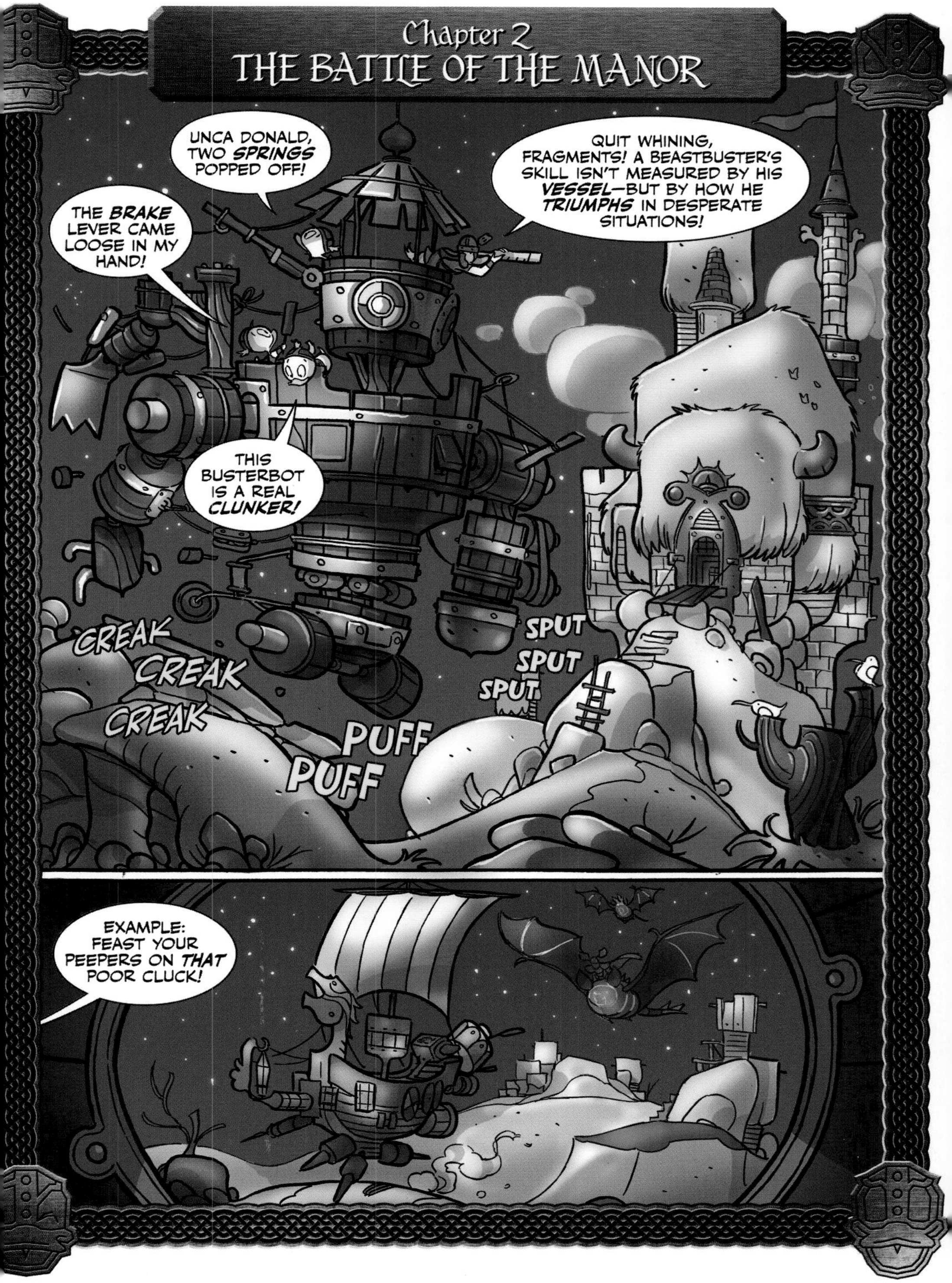
UNCA DONALD, TWO SPRINGS POPPED OFF!
THE BRAKE LEVER CAME LOOSE IN MY HAND!
QUIT WHINING, FRAGMENTS! A BEASTBUSTER'S SKILL ISN'T MEASURED BY HIS VESSEL—BUT BY HOW HE TRIUMPHS IN DESPERATE SITUATIONS!
THIS BUSTERBOT IS A REAL CLUNKER!
CREAK
CREAK
CREAK
SPUT
SPUT
SPUT
PUFF
PUFF
EXAMPLE: FEAST YOUR PEEPERS ON THAT POOR CLUCK!

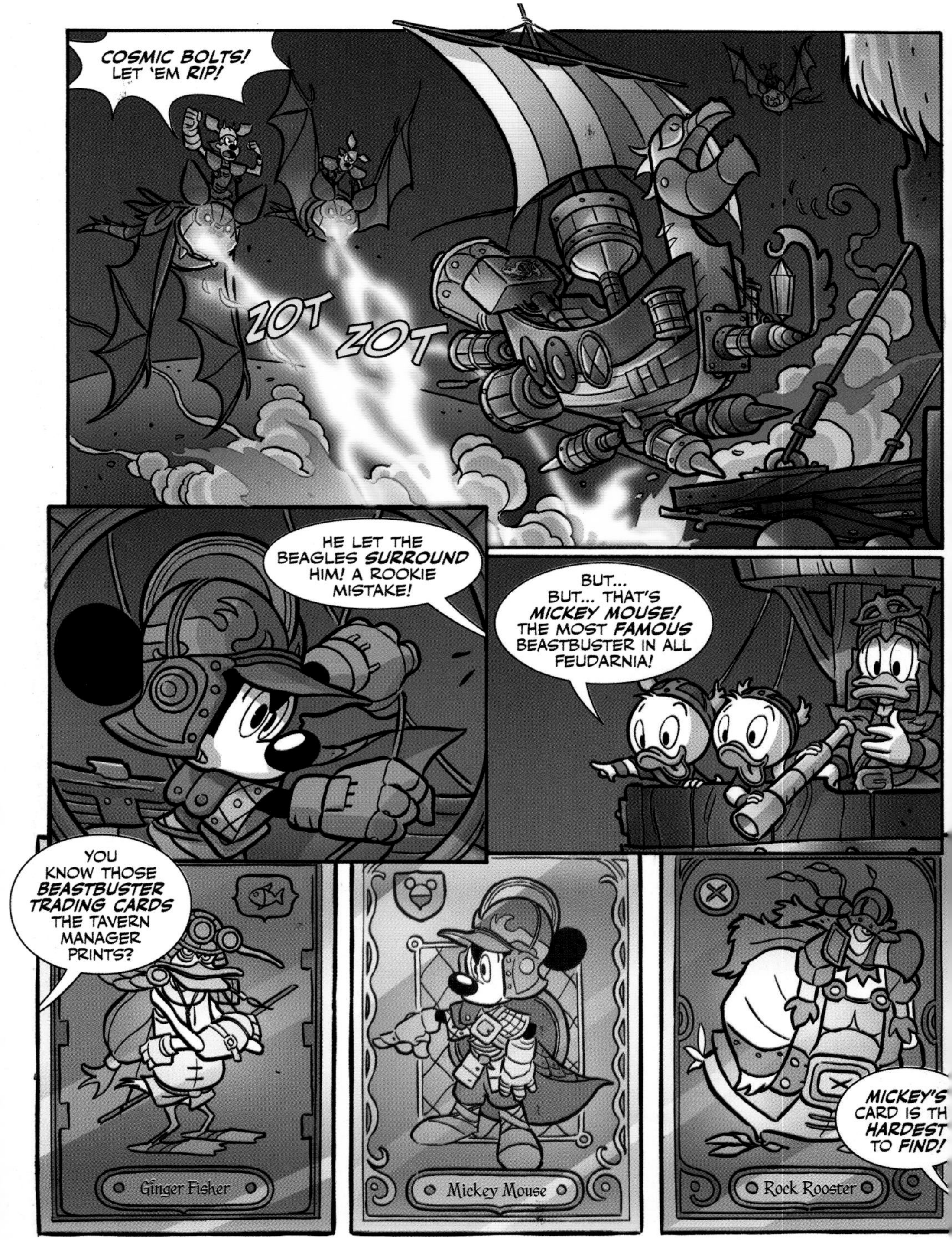
COSMIC BOLTS! LET 'EM RIP!
ZOT
ZOT
HE LET THE BEAGLES SURROUND HIM! A ROOKIE MISTAKE!
BUT... BUT... THAT'S MICKEY MOUSE! THE MOST FAMOUS BEASTBUSTER IN ALL FEUDARNIA!
YOU KNOW THOSE BEASTBUSTER TRADING CARDS THE TAVERN MANAGER PRINTS?
Ginger Fisher
Mickey Mouse
Rock Rooster
MICKEY'S CARD IS TH HARDEST TO FIND!

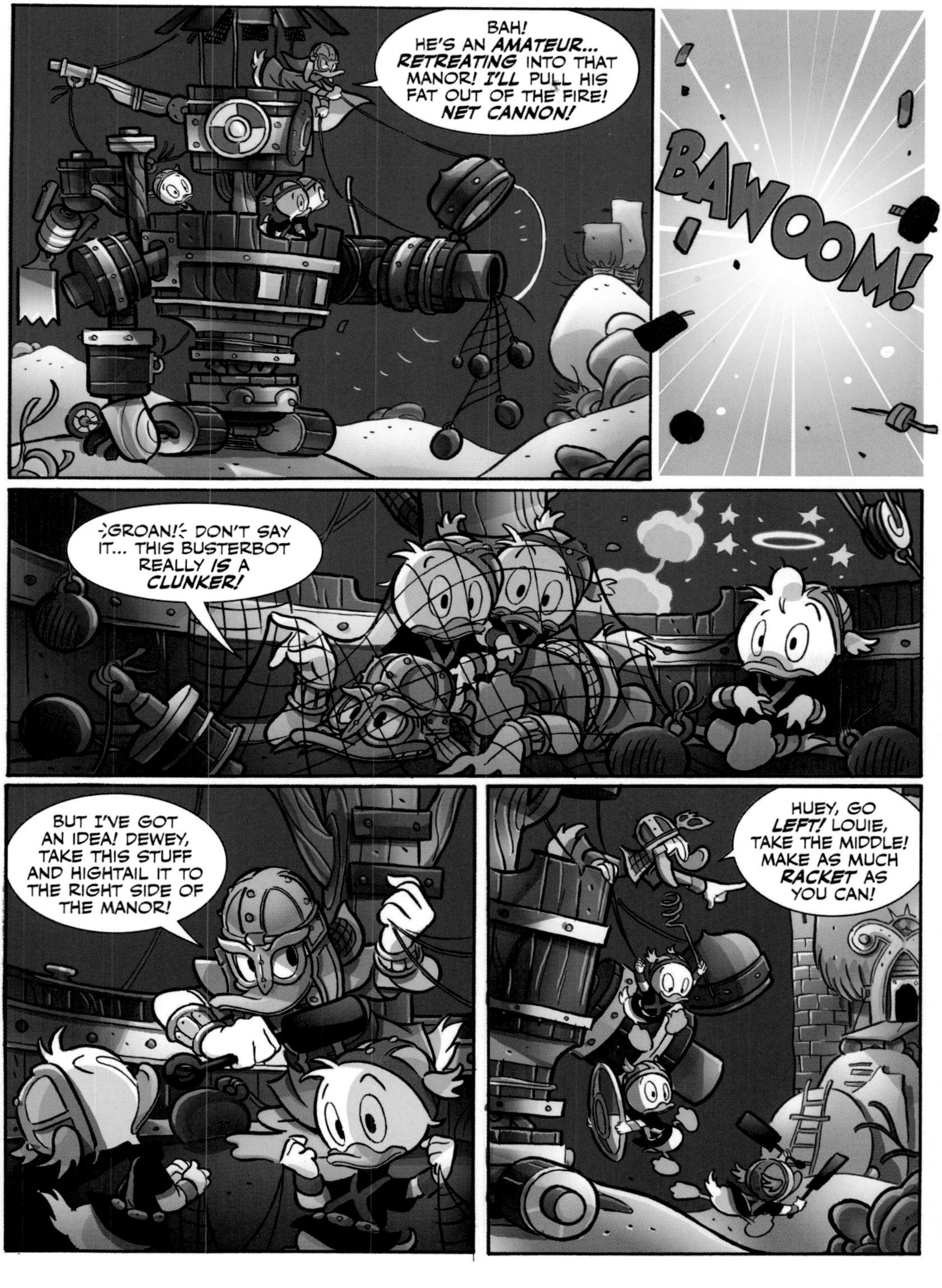
BAH! HE'S AN AMATEUR... RETREATING INTO THAT MANOR! I'LL PULL HIS FAT OUT OF THE FIRE! NET CANNON!
BAWOOM!
-GROAN!- DON'T SAY IT... THIS BUSTERBOT REALLY IS A CLUNKER!
BUT I'VE GOT AN IDEA! DEWEY, TAKE THIS STUFF AND HIGHTAIL IT TO THE RIGHT SIDE OF THE MANOR!
HUEY, GO LEFT! LOUIE, TAKE THE MIDDLE! MAKE AS MUCH RACKET AS YOU CAN!

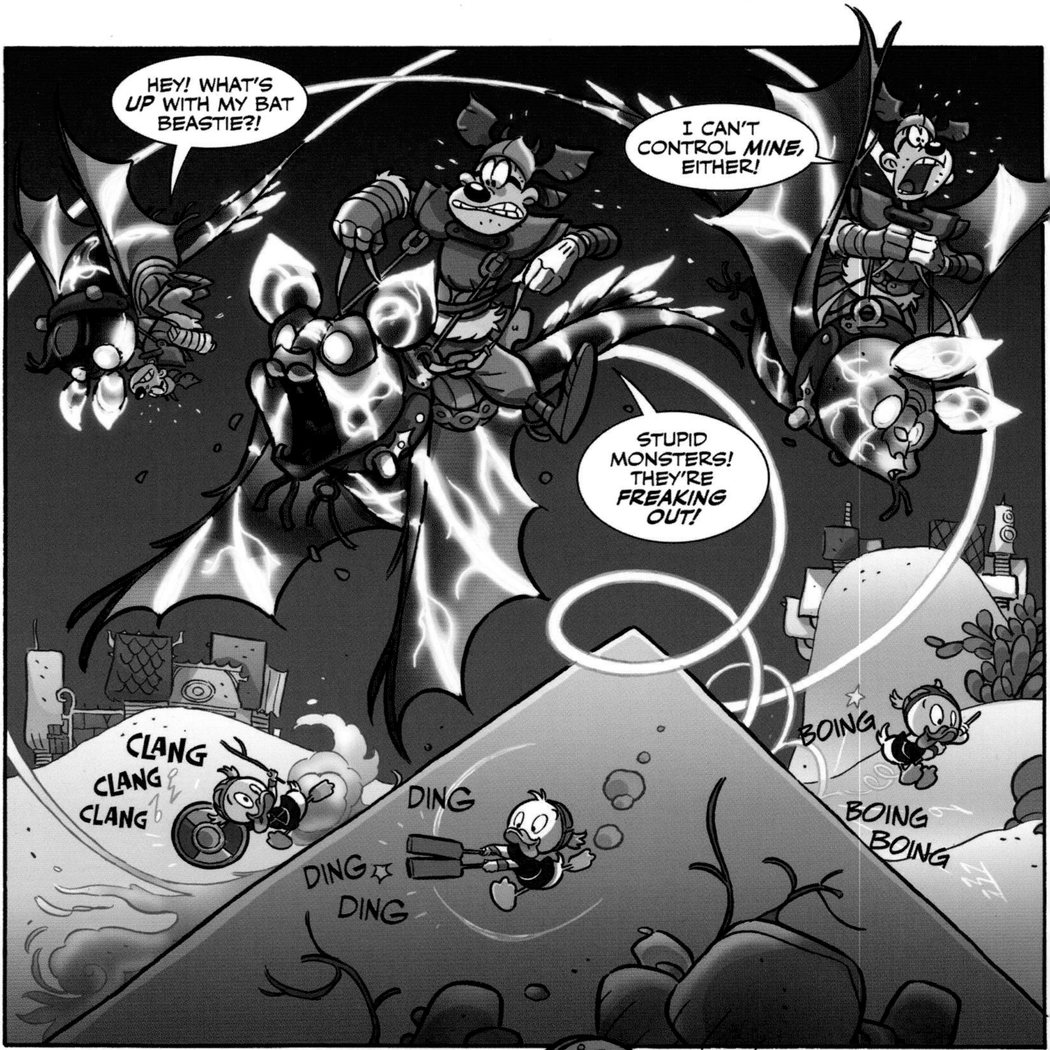
HEY! WHAT'S UP WITH MY BAT BEASTIE?!
I CAN'T CONTROL MINE, EITHER!
STUPID MONSTERS! THEY'RE FREAKING OUT!
CLANG
CLANG
CLANG
DING
DING
DING
BOING
BOING
BOING

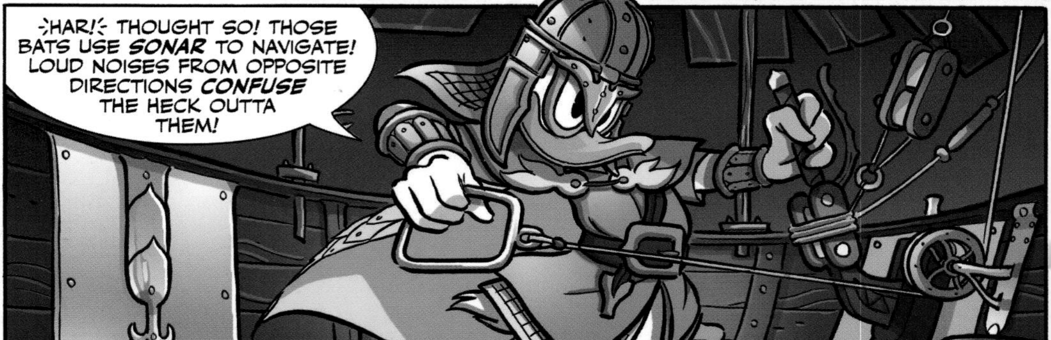
HAR! THOUGHT SO! THOSE BATS USE SONAR TO NAVIGATE! LOUD NOISES FROM OPPOSITE DIRECTIONS CONFUSE THE HECK OUTTA THEM!

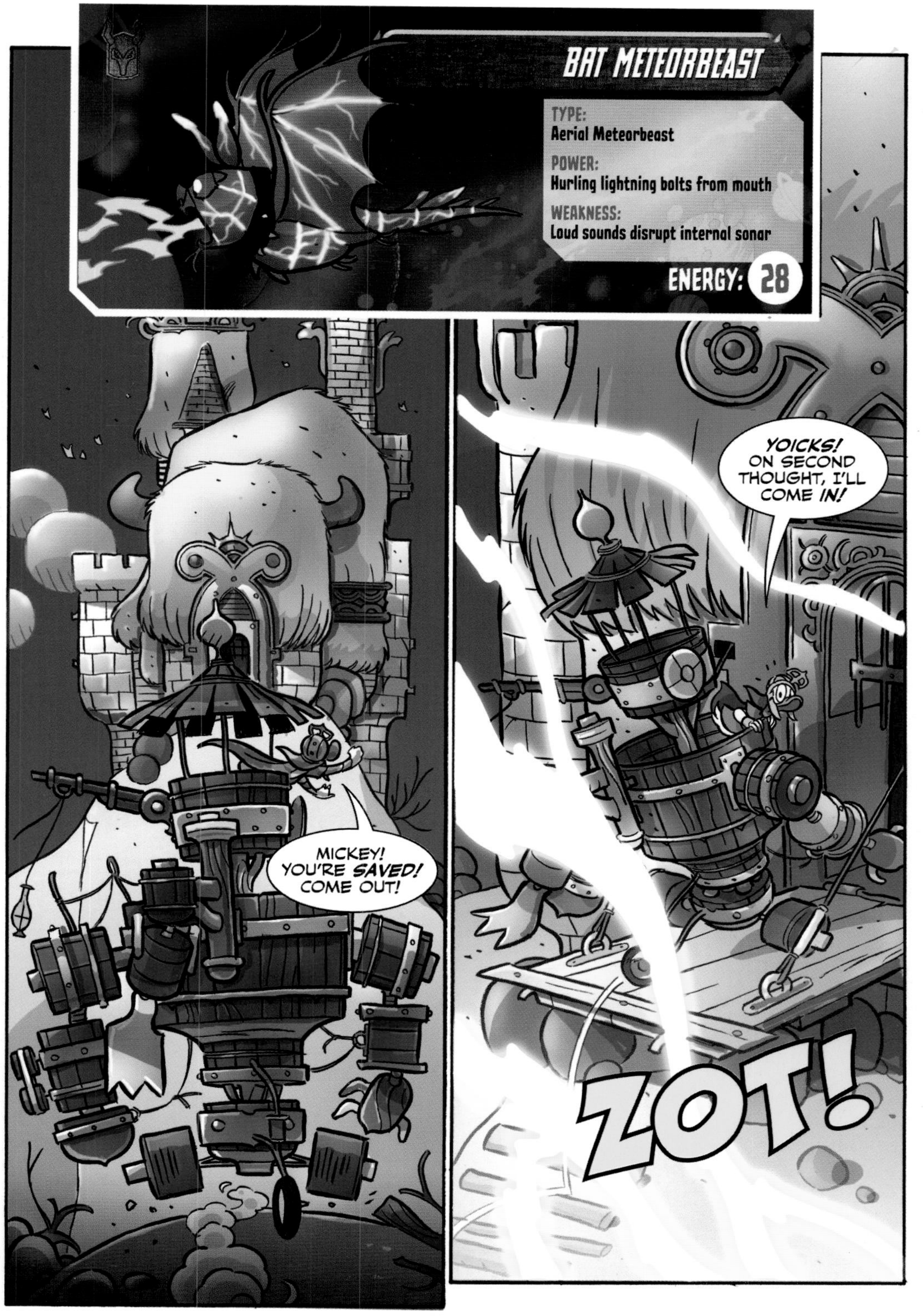
BAT METEORBEAST
TYPE:
Aerial Meteorbeast
POWER:
Hurling lightning bolts from mouth
WEAKNESS:
Loud sounds disrupt internal sonar
ENERGY: 28
MICKEY! YOU'RE SAVED! COME OUT!
YOICKS! ON SECOND THOUGHT, I'LL COME IN!
ZOT!

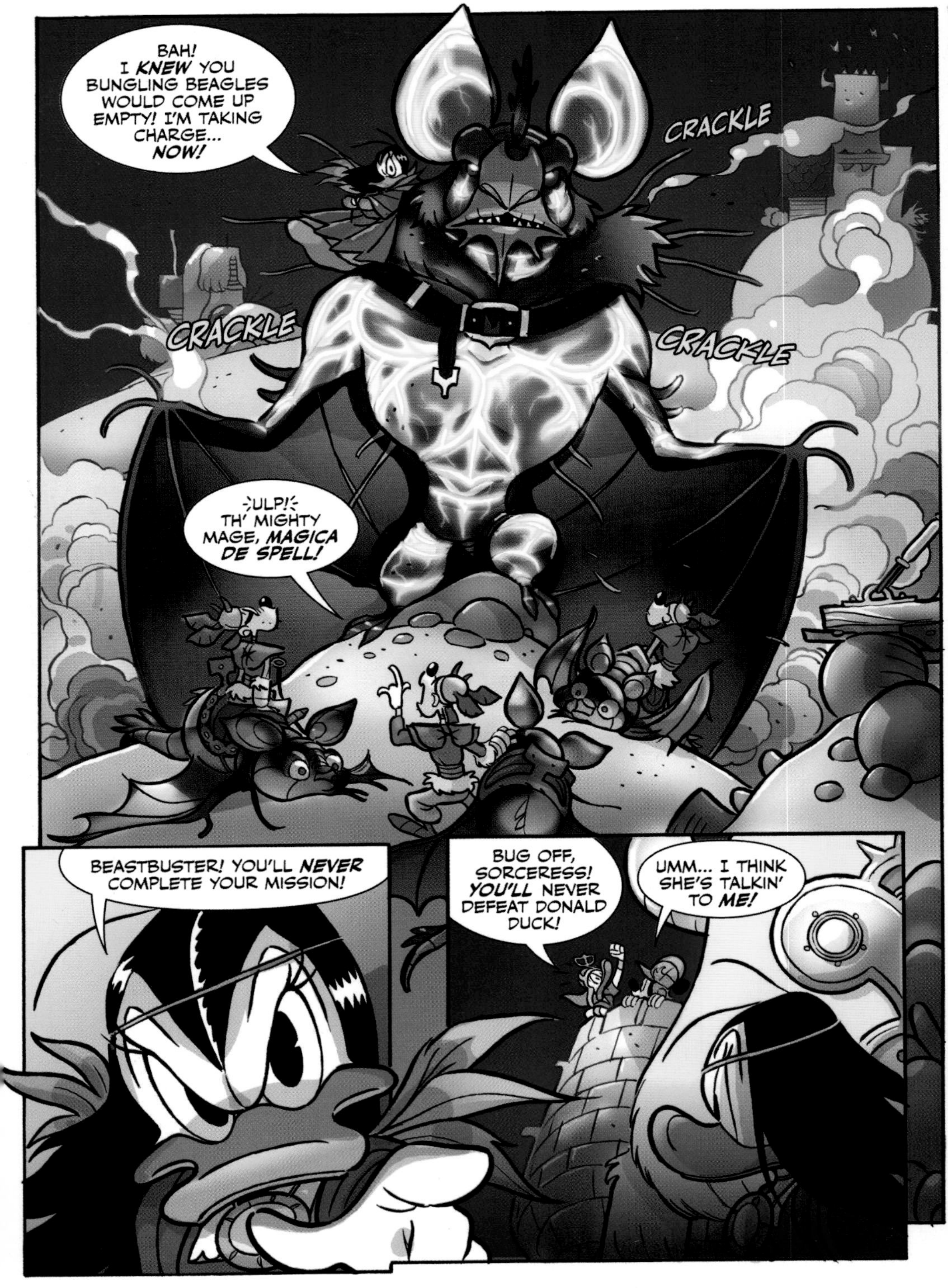
BAH! I KNEW YOU BUNGLING BEAGLES WOULD COME UP EMPTY! I'M TAKING CHARGE... NOW!
CRACKLE
CRACKLE
CRACKLE
-ULP!- TH' MIGHTY MAGE, MAGICA DE SPELL!
BEASTBUSTER! YOU'LL NEVER COMPLETE YOUR MISSION!
BUG OFF, SORCERESS! YOU'LL NEVER DEFEAT DONALD DUCK!
UMM... I THINK SHE'S TALKIN' TO ME!

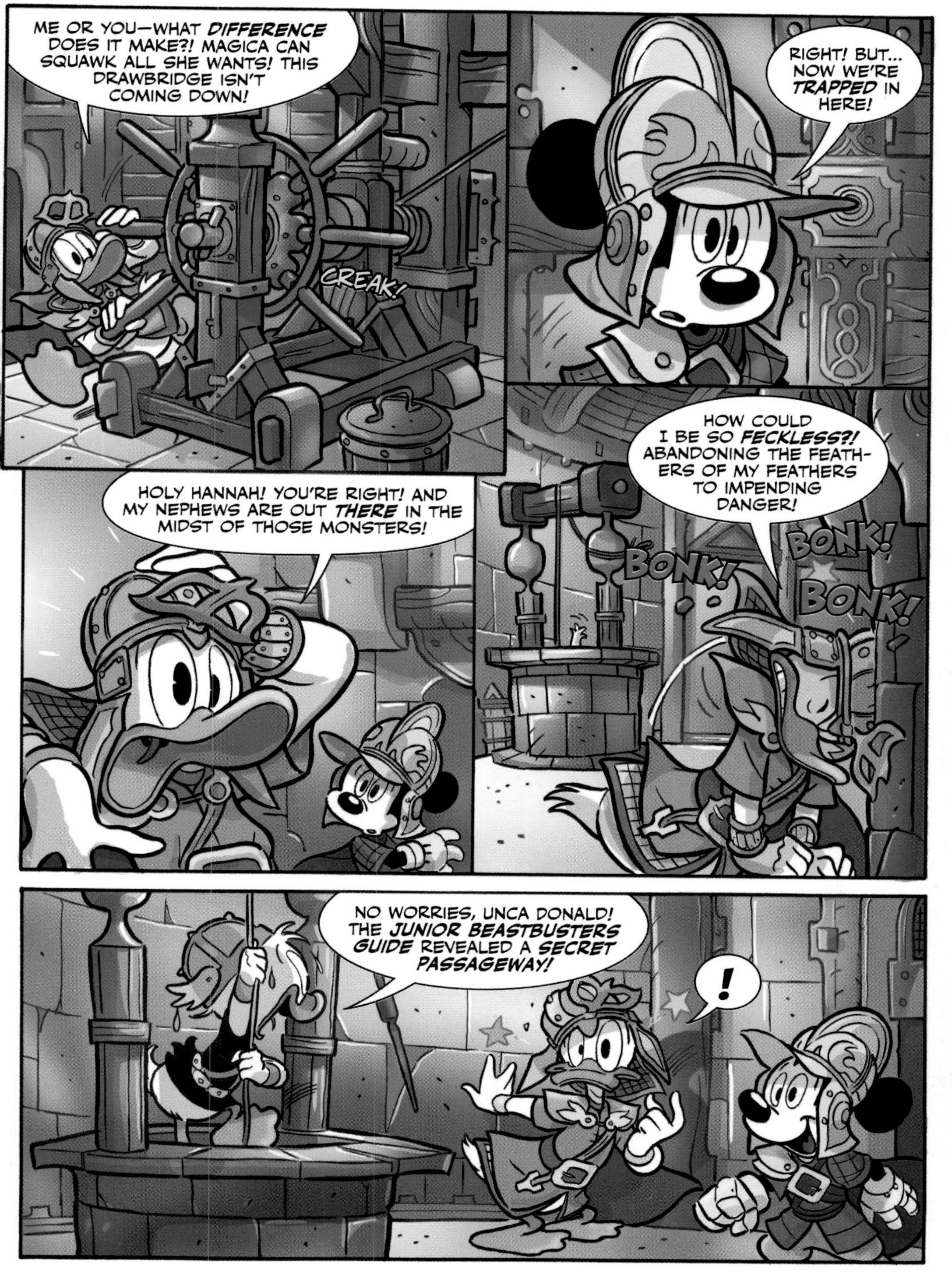
ME OR YOU—WHAT DIFFERENCE DOES IT MAKE?! MAGICA CAN SQUAWK ALL SHE WANTS! THIS DRAWBRIDGE ISN'T COMING DOWN!
CREAK!
RIGHT! BUT... NOW WE'RE TRAPPED IN HERE!
HOLY HANNAH! YOU'RE RIGHT! AND MY NEPHEWS ARE OUT THERE IN THE MIDST OF THOSE MONSTERS!
HOW COULD I BE SO FECKLESS?! ABANDONING THE FEATHERS OF MY FEATHERS TO IMPENDING DANGER!
BONK!
BONK!
BONK!
NO WORRIES, UNCA DONALD! THE JUNIOR BEASTBUSTERS GUIDE REVEALED A SECRET PASSAGEWAY!
!

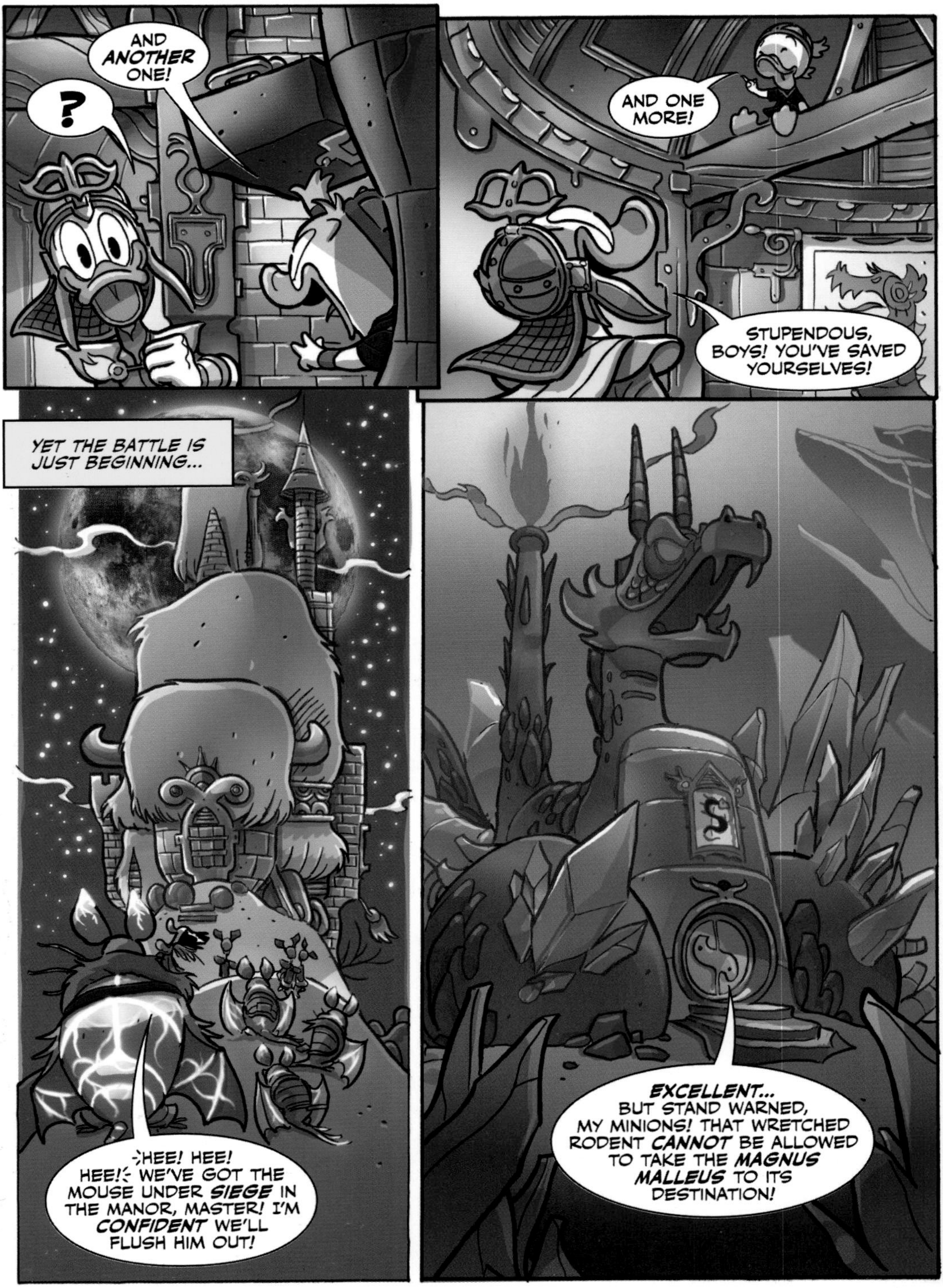
?
AND ANOTHER ONE!
AND ONE MORE!
STUPENDOUS, BOYS! YOU'VE SAVED YOURSELVES!
YET THE BATTLE IS JUST BEGINNING...
HEE! HEE! HEE! WE'VE GOT THE MOUSE UNDER SIEGE IN THE MANOR, MASTER! I'M CONFIDENT WE'LL FLUSH HIM OUT!
EXCELLENT... BUT STAND WARNED, MY MINIONS! THAT WRETCHED RODENT CANNOT BE ALLOWED TO TAKE THE MAGNUS MALLEUS TO ITS DESTINATION!

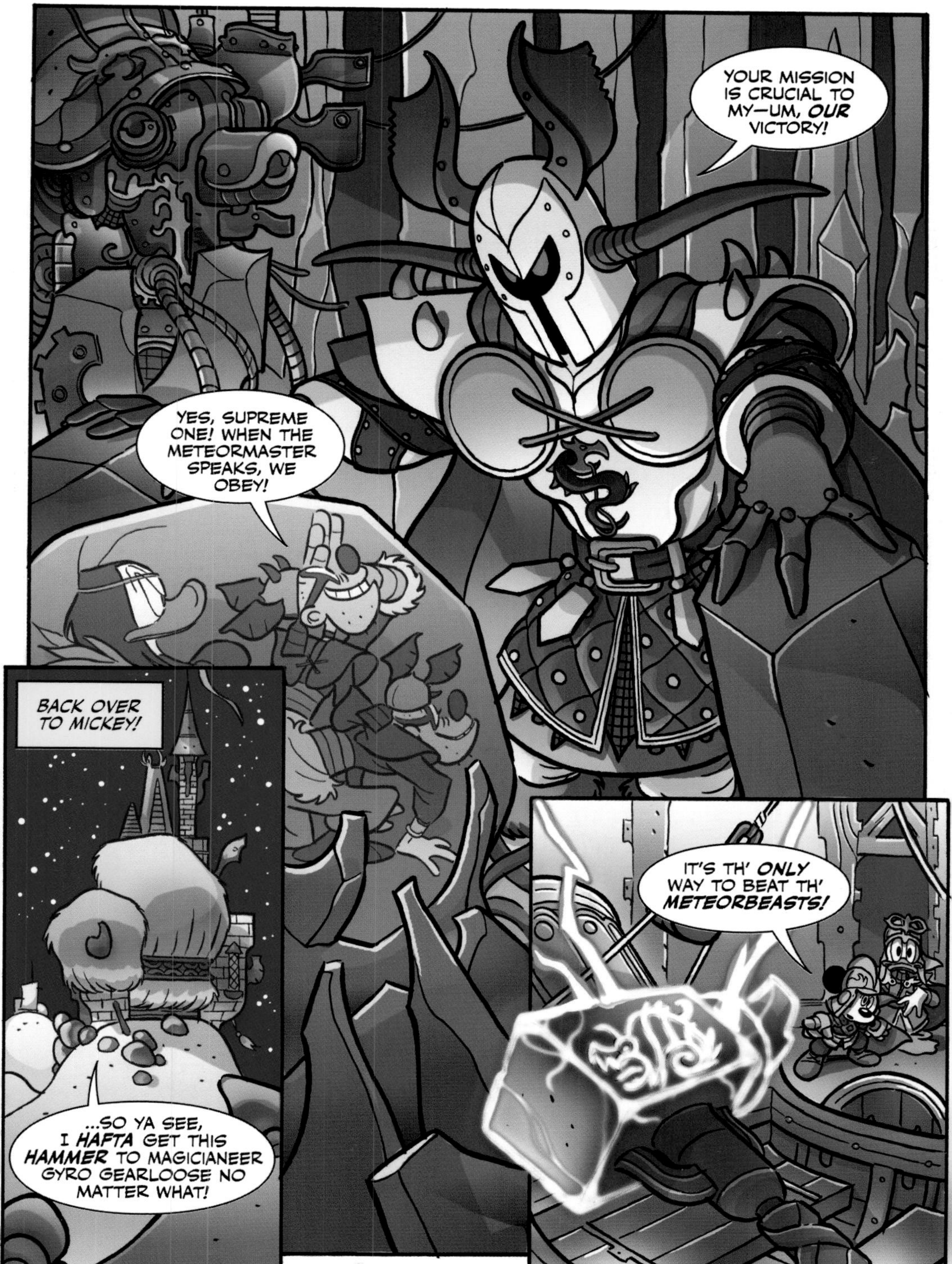
YOUR MISSION IS CRUCIAL TO MY—UM, ***OUR*** VICTORY!
YES, SUPREME ONE! WHEN THE METEORMASTER SPEAKS, WE OBEY!
BACK OVER TO MICKEY!
...SO YA SEE, I ***HAFTA*** GET THIS ***HAMMER*** TO MAGICIANEER GYRO GEARLOOSE NO MATTER WHAT!
IT'S TH' ***ONLY*** WAY TO BEAT TH' ***METEORBEASTS!***

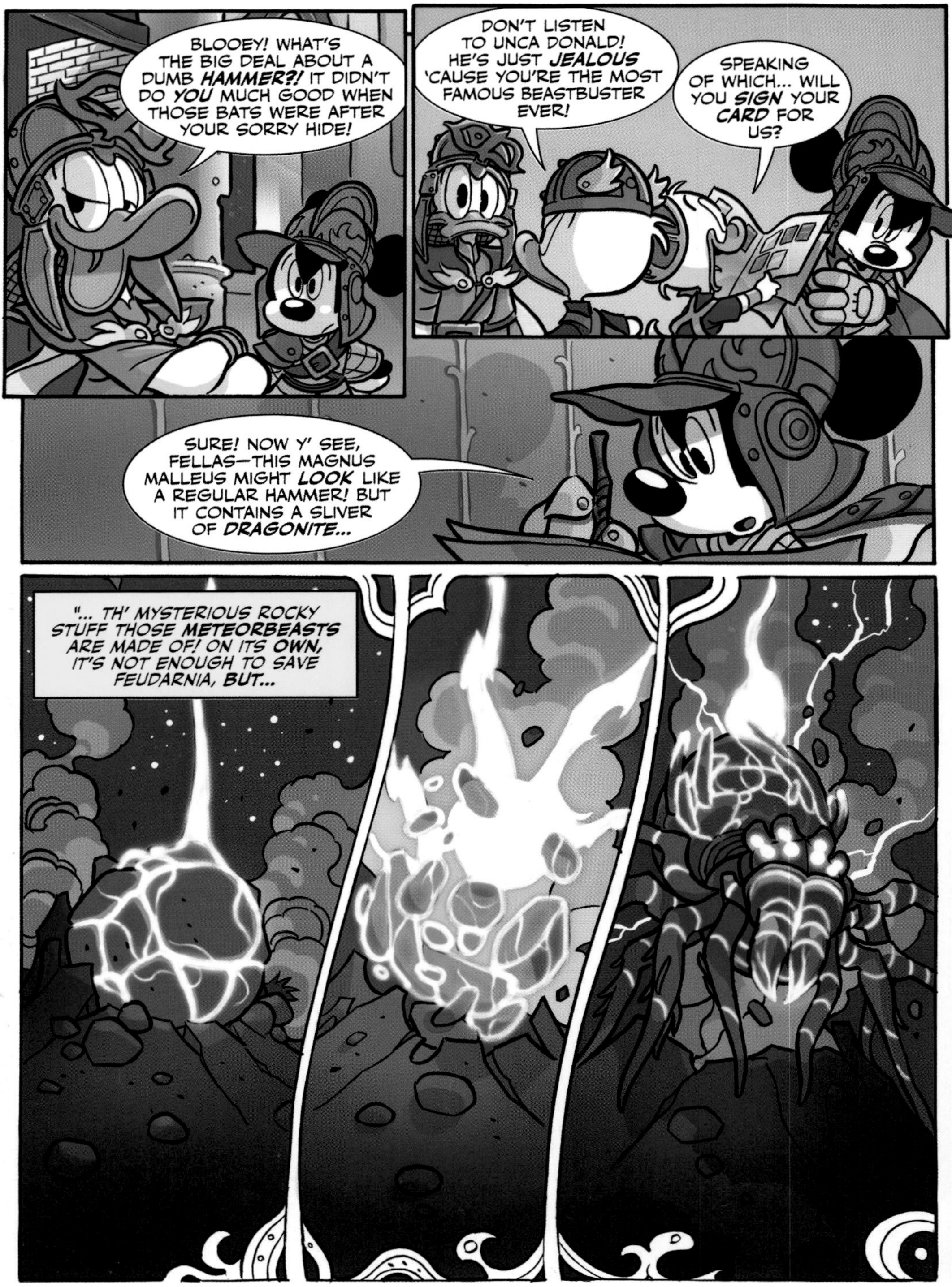
BLOOEY! WHAT'S THE BIG DEAL ABOUT A DUMB HAMMER?! IT DIDN'T DO YOU MUCH GOOD WHEN THOSE BATS WERE AFTER YOUR SORRY HIDE!
DON'T LISTEN TO UNCA DONALD! HE'S JUST JEALOUS 'CAUSE YOU'RE THE MOST FAMOUS BEASTBUSTER EVER!
SPEAKING OF WHICH... WILL YOU SIGN YOUR CARD FOR US?
SURE! NOW Y' SEE, FELLAS—THIS MAGNUS MALLEUS MIGHT LOOK LIKE A REGULAR HAMMER! BUT IT CONTAINS A SLIVER OF DRAGONITE...
"... TH' MYSTERIOUS ROCKY STUFF THOSE METEORBEASTS ARE MADE OF! ON ITS OWN, IT'S NOT ENOUGH TO SAVE FEUDARNIA, BUT...

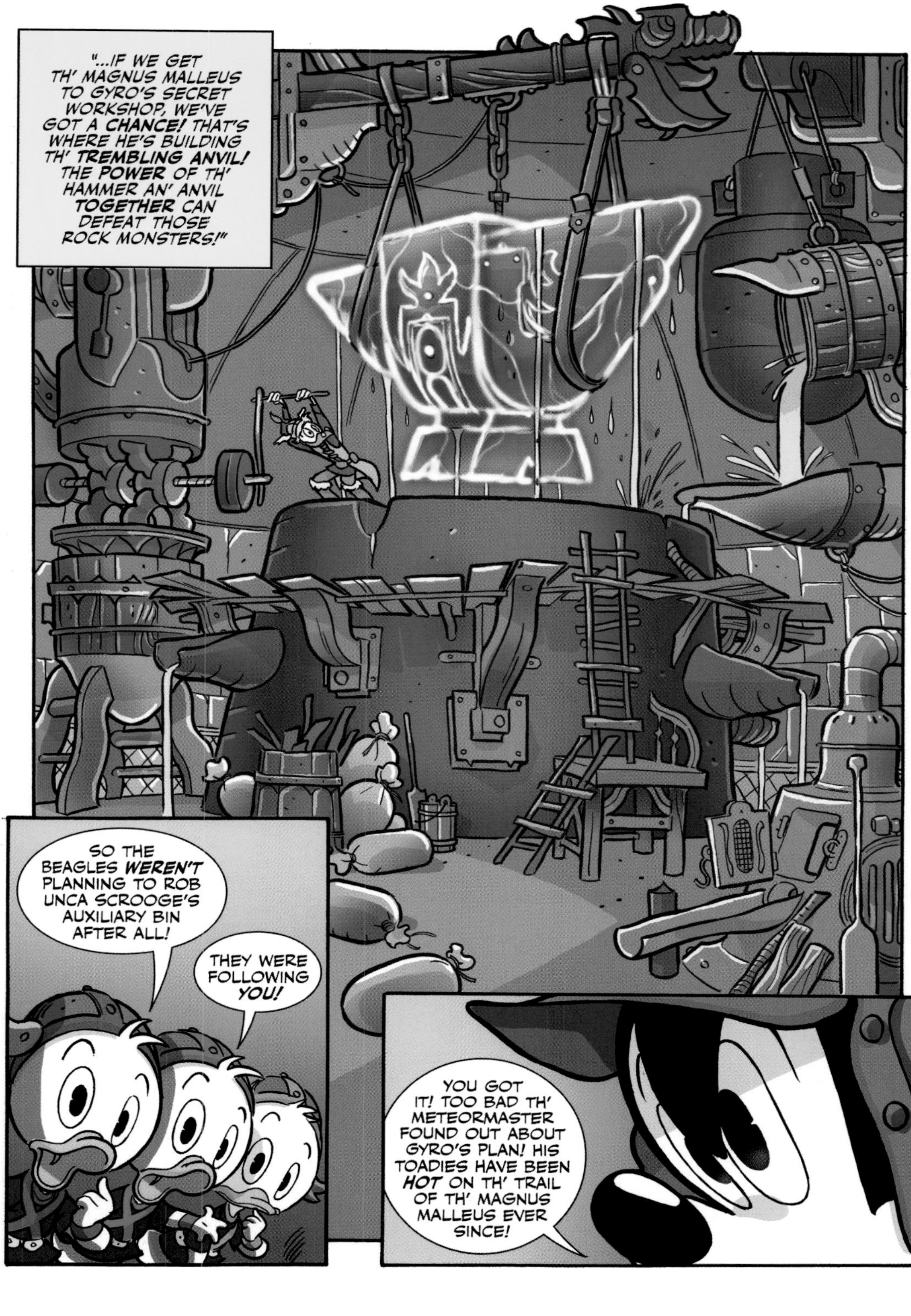
"...IF WE GET TH' MAGNUS MALLEUS TO GYRO'S SECRET WORKSHOP, WE'VE GOT A **CHANCE!** THAT'S WHERE HE'S BUILDING TH' **TREMBLING ANVIL!** THE **POWER** OF TH' HAMMER AN' ANVIL **TOGETHER** CAN DEFEAT THOSE ROCK MONSTERS!"
SO THE BEAGLES ***WEREN'T*** PLANNING TO ROB UNCA SCROOGE'S AUXILIARY BIN AFTER ALL!
THEY WERE FOLLOWING ***YOU!***
YOU GOT IT! TOO BAD TH' METEORMASTER FOUND OUT ABOUT GYRO'S PLAN! HIS TOADIES HAVE BEEN ***HOT*** ON TH' TRAIL OF TH' MAGNUS MALLEUS EVER SINCE!

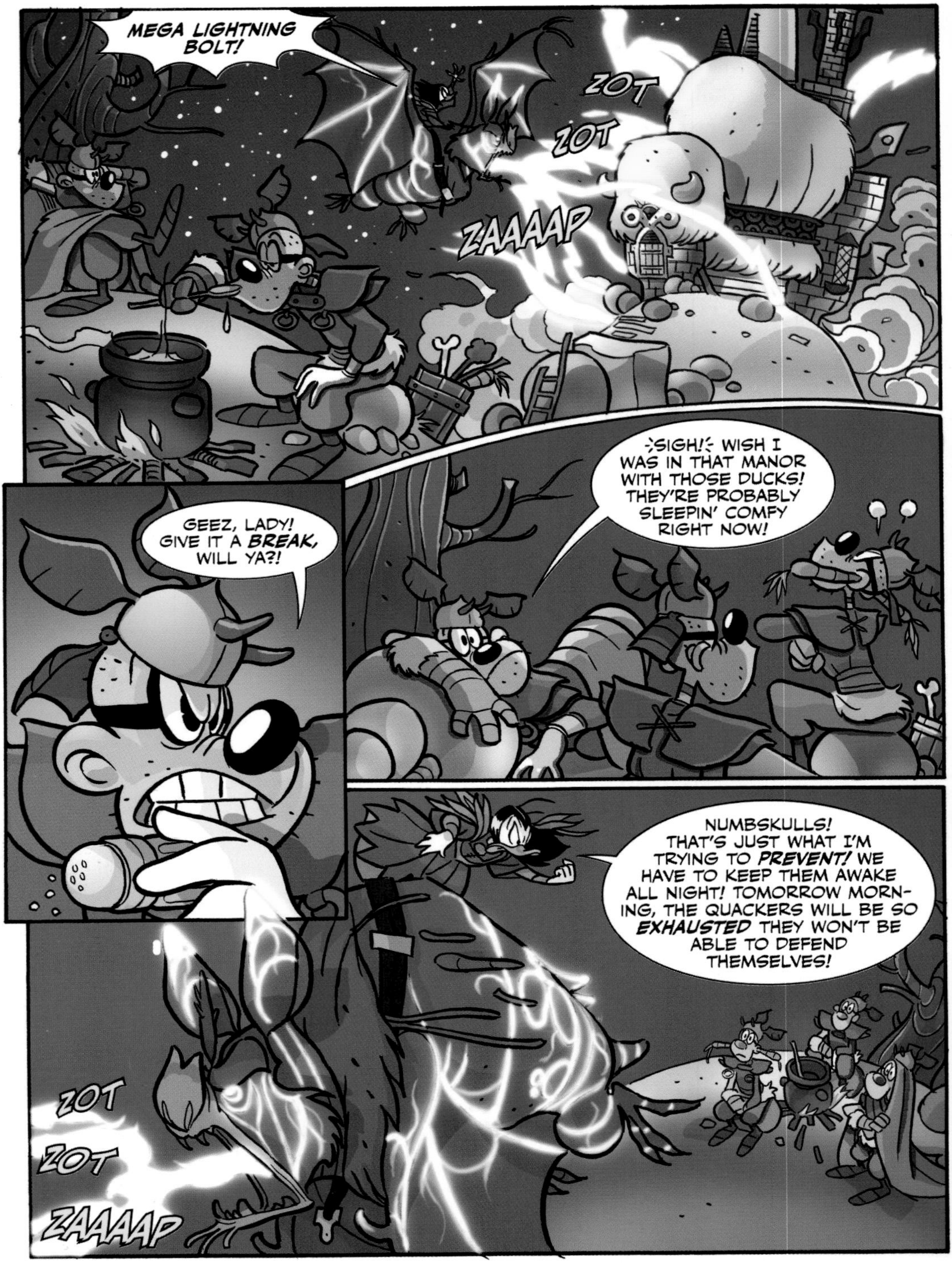
MEGA LIGHTNING BOLT!
ZOT
ZOT
ZAAAAP
GEEZ, LADY! GIVE IT A BREAK, WILL YA?!
SIGH! WISH I WAS IN THAT MANOR WITH THOSE DUCKS! THEY'RE PROBABLY SLEEPIN' COMFY RIGHT NOW!
NUMBSKULLS! THAT'S JUST WHAT I'M TRYING TO PREVENT! WE HAVE TO KEEP THEM AWAKE ALL NIGHT! TOMORROW MORNING, THE QUACKERS WILL BE SO EXHAUSTED THEY WON'T BE ABLE TO DEFEND THEMSELVES!
ZOT
ZOT
ZAAAAP

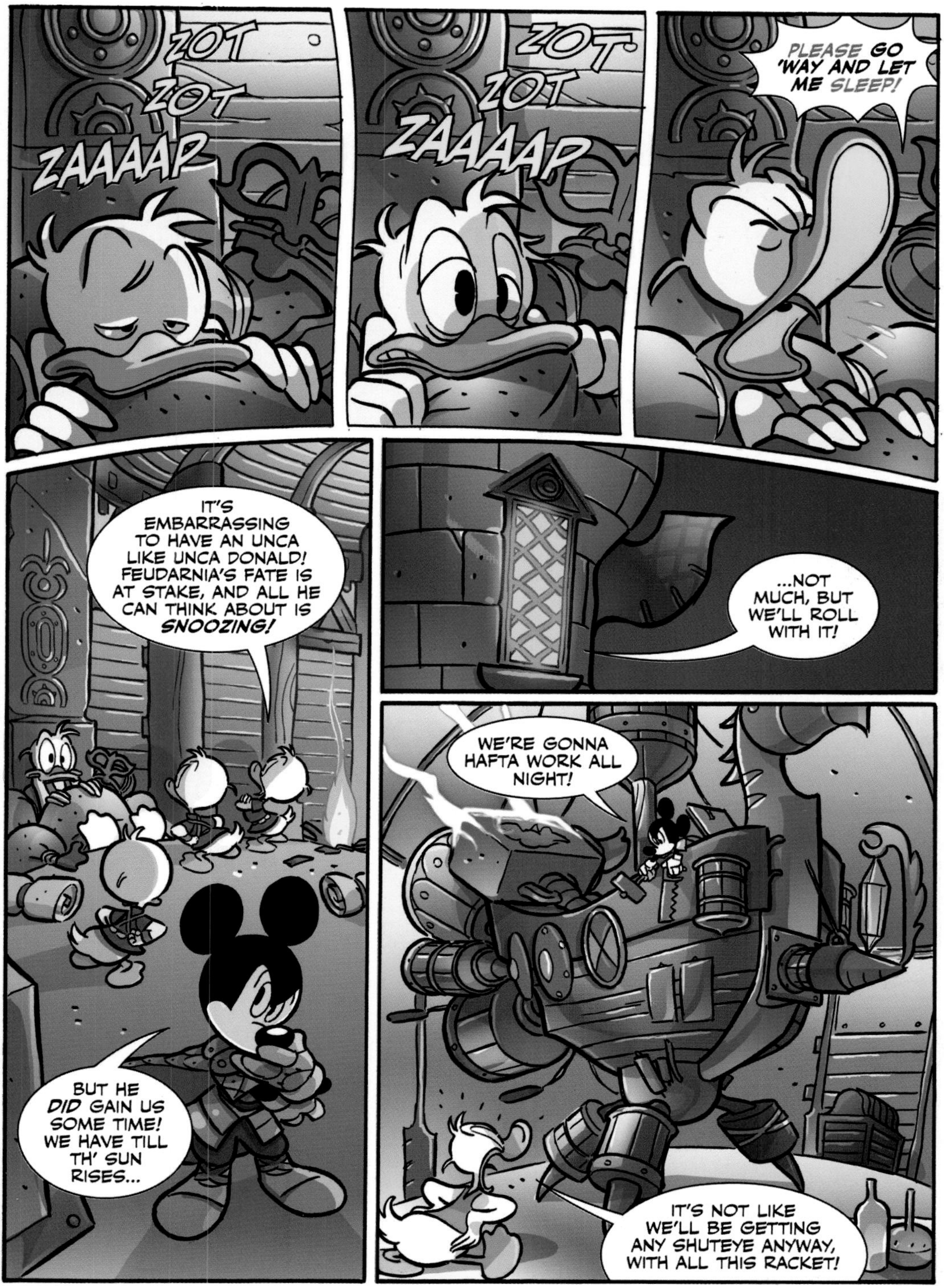
ZOT
ZOT
ZAAAAP
ZOT
ZOT
ZAAAAAP
PLEASE GO 'WAY AND LET ME SLEEP!
IT'S EMBARRASSING TO HAVE AN UNCA LIKE UNCA DONALD! FEUDARNIA'S FATE IS AT STAKE, AND ALL HE CAN THINK ABOUT IS SNOOZING!
BUT HE DID GAIN US SOME TIME! WE HAVE TILL TH' SUN RISES...
...NOT MUCH, BUT WE'LL ROLL WITH IT!
WE'RE GONNA HAFTA WORK ALL NIGHT!
IT'S NOT LIKE WE'LL BE GETTING ANY SHUTEYE ANYWAY, WITH ALL THIS RACKET!

Chapter 3
THUNDER AT DAWN

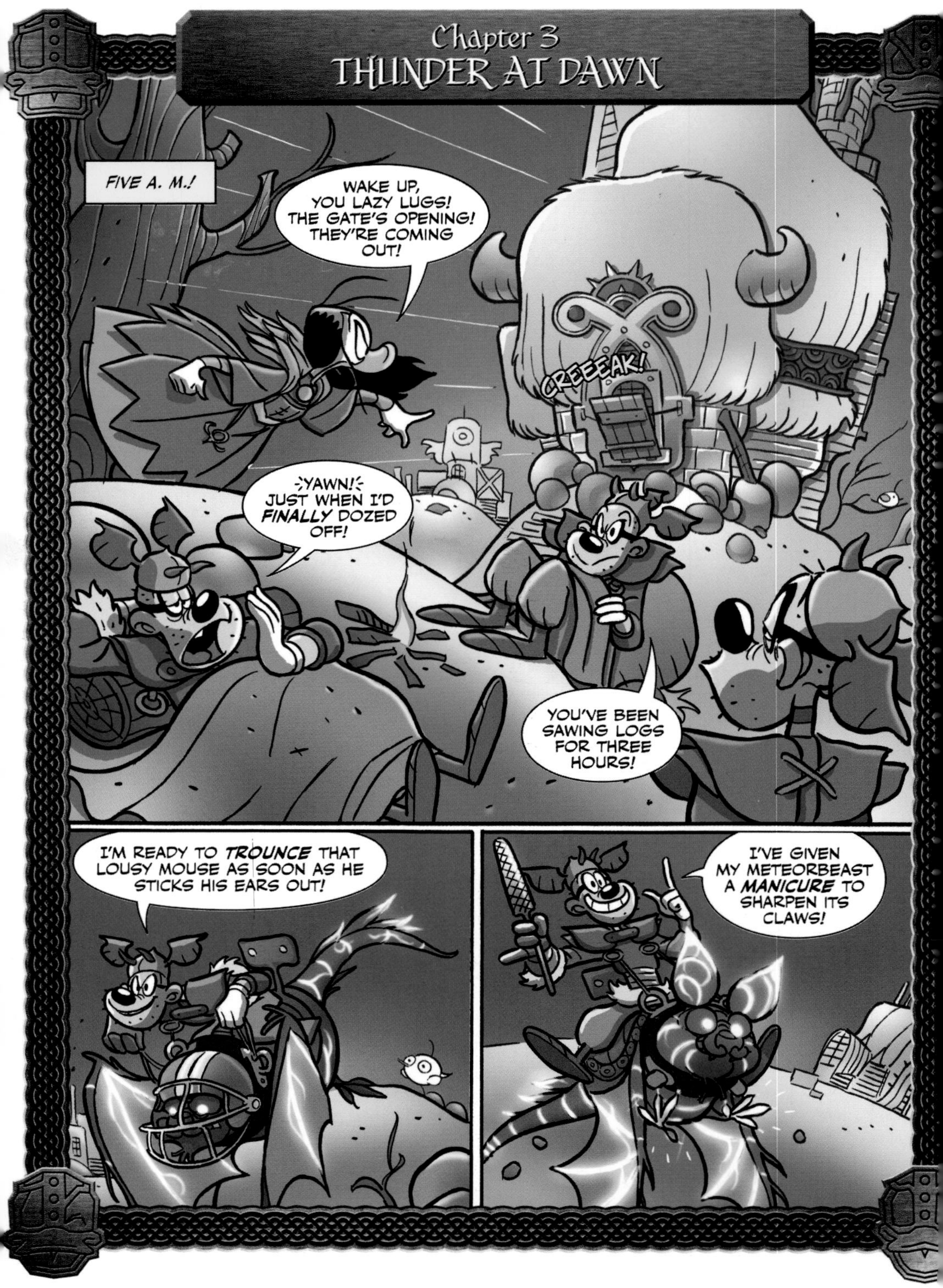
FIVE A. M.!
WAKE UP, YOU LAZY LUGS! THE GATE'S OPENING! THEY'RE COMING OUT!
CREEEAK!
YAWN! JUST WHEN I'D FINALLY DOZED OFF!
YOU'VE BEEN SAWING LOGS FOR THREE HOURS!
I'M READY TO TROUNCE THAT LOUSY MOUSE AS SOON AS HE STICKS HIS EARS OUT!
I'VE GIVEN MY METEORBEAST A MANICURE TO SHARPEN ITS CLAWS!

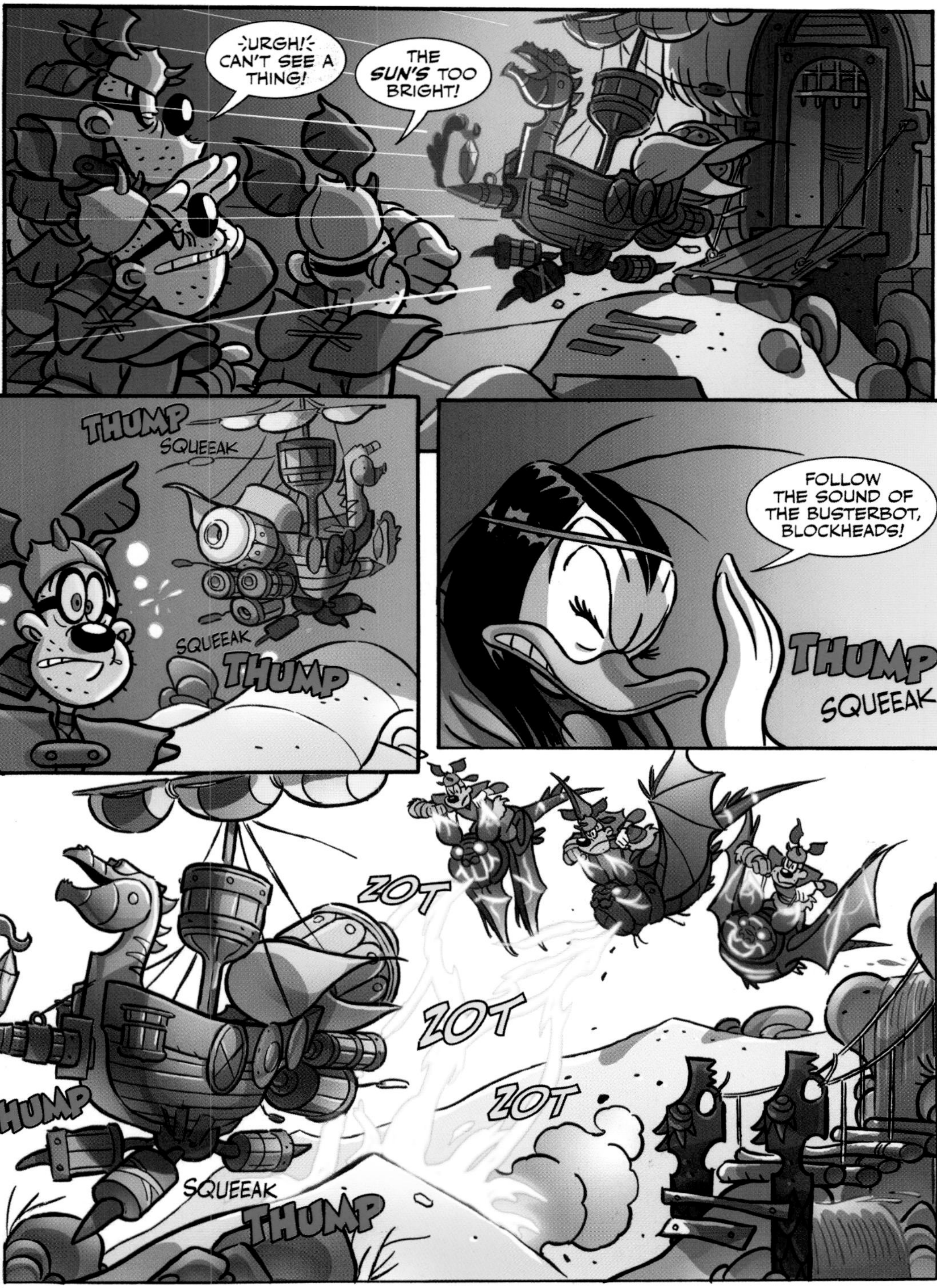

URGH! CAN'T SEE A THING!
THE SUN'S TOO BRIGHT!
THUMP
SQUEEAK
SQUEEAK
THUMP
FOLLOW THE SOUND OF THE BUSTERBOT, BLOCKHEADS!
THUMP
SQUEEAK
ZOT
ZOT
ZOT
HUMP
SQUEEAK
THUMP

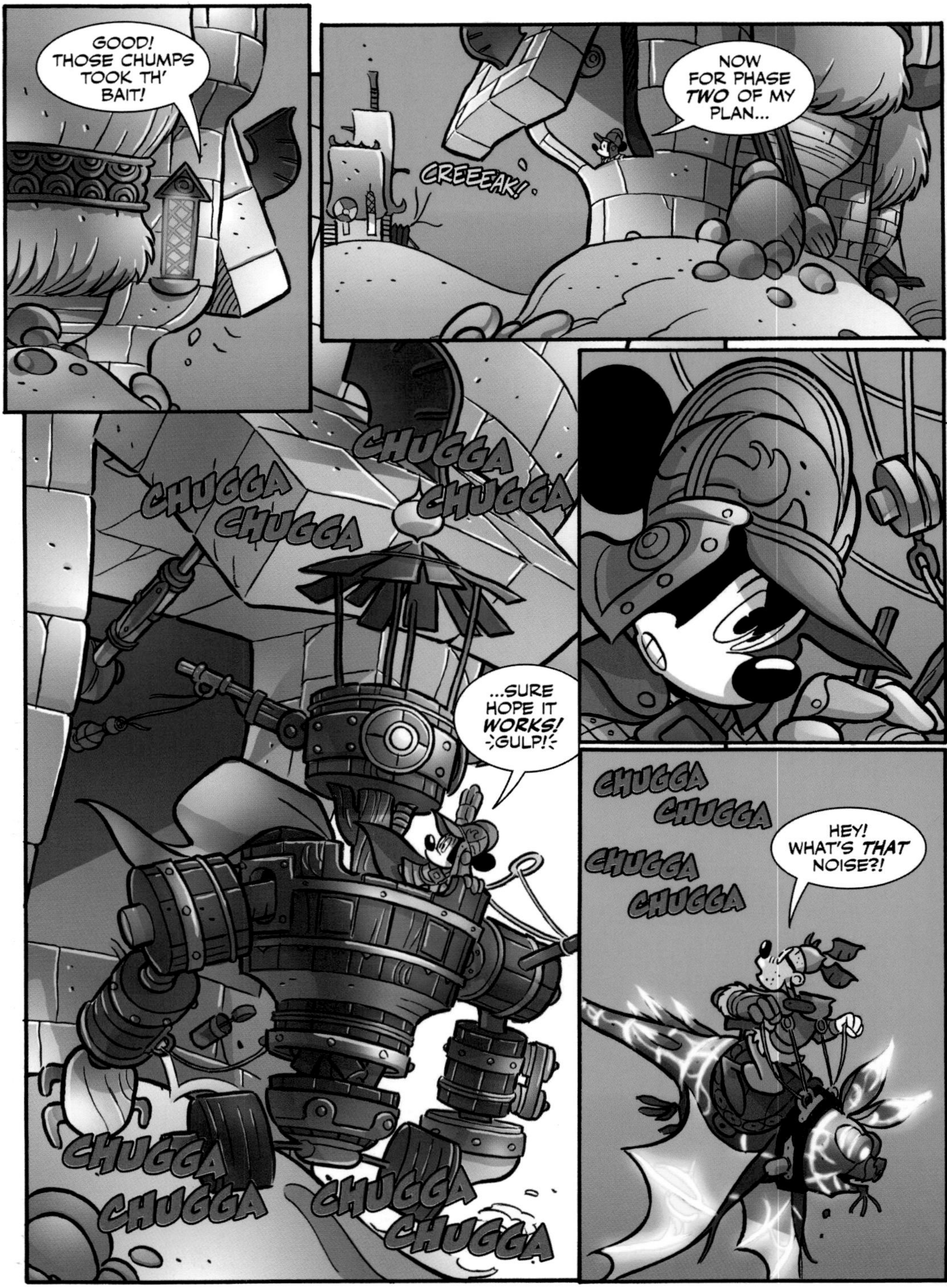
GOOD! THOSE CHUMPS TOOK TH' BAIT!
CREEEAK!
NOW FOR PHASE TWO OF MY PLAN...
CHUGGA CHUGGA
CHUGGA CHUGGA
...SURE HOPE IT WORKS! GULP!
CHUGGA CHUGGA
CHUGGA CHUGGA
CHUGGA CHUGGA
CHUGGA CHUGGA
HEY! WHAT'S THAT NOISE?!

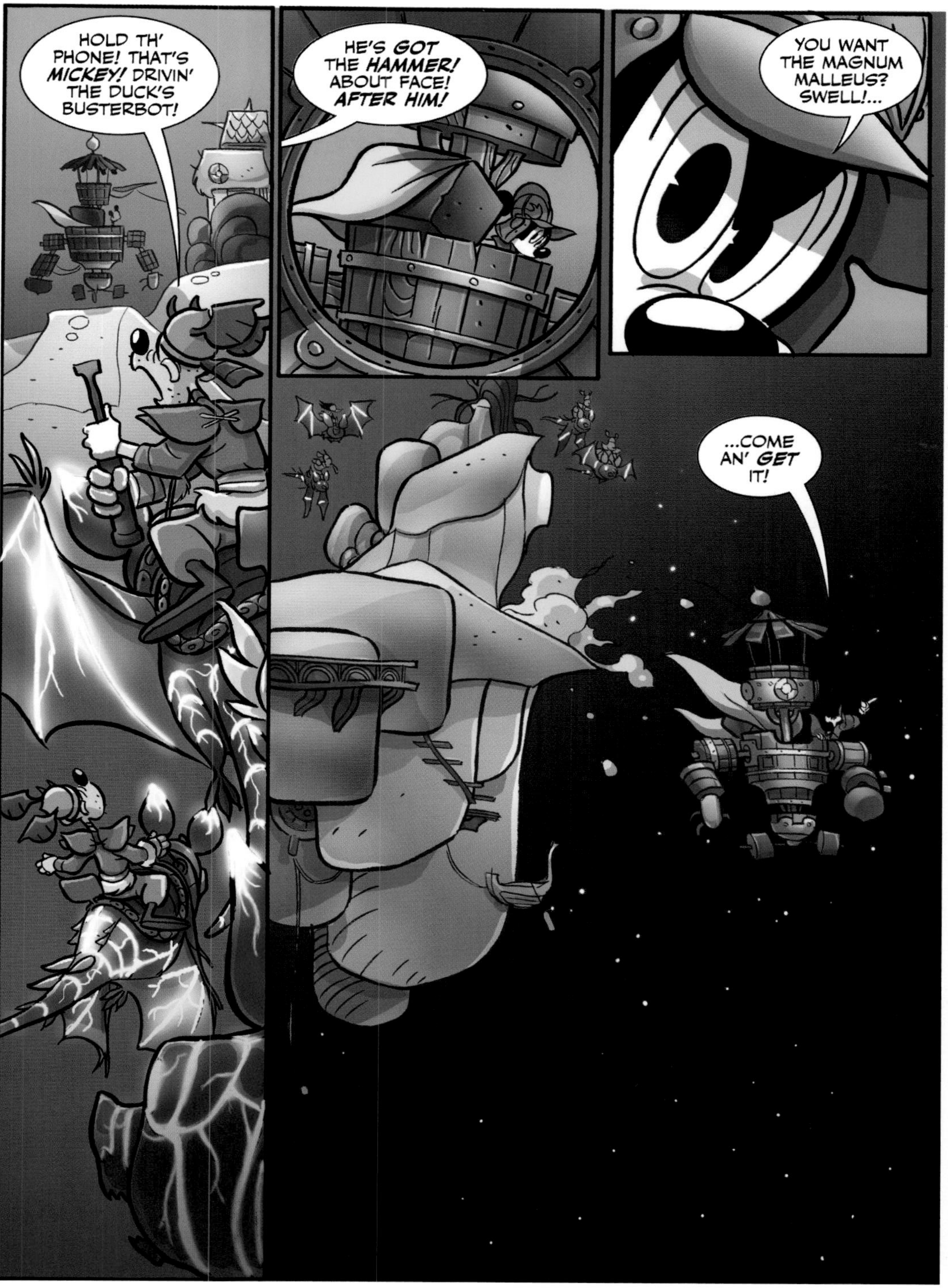
HOLD TH' PHONE! THAT'S MICKEY! DRIVIN' THE DUCK'S BUSTERBOT!
HE'S GOT THE HAMMER! ABOUT FACE! AFTER HIM!
YOU WANT THE MAGNUM MALLEUS? SWELL!...
...COME AN' GET IT!

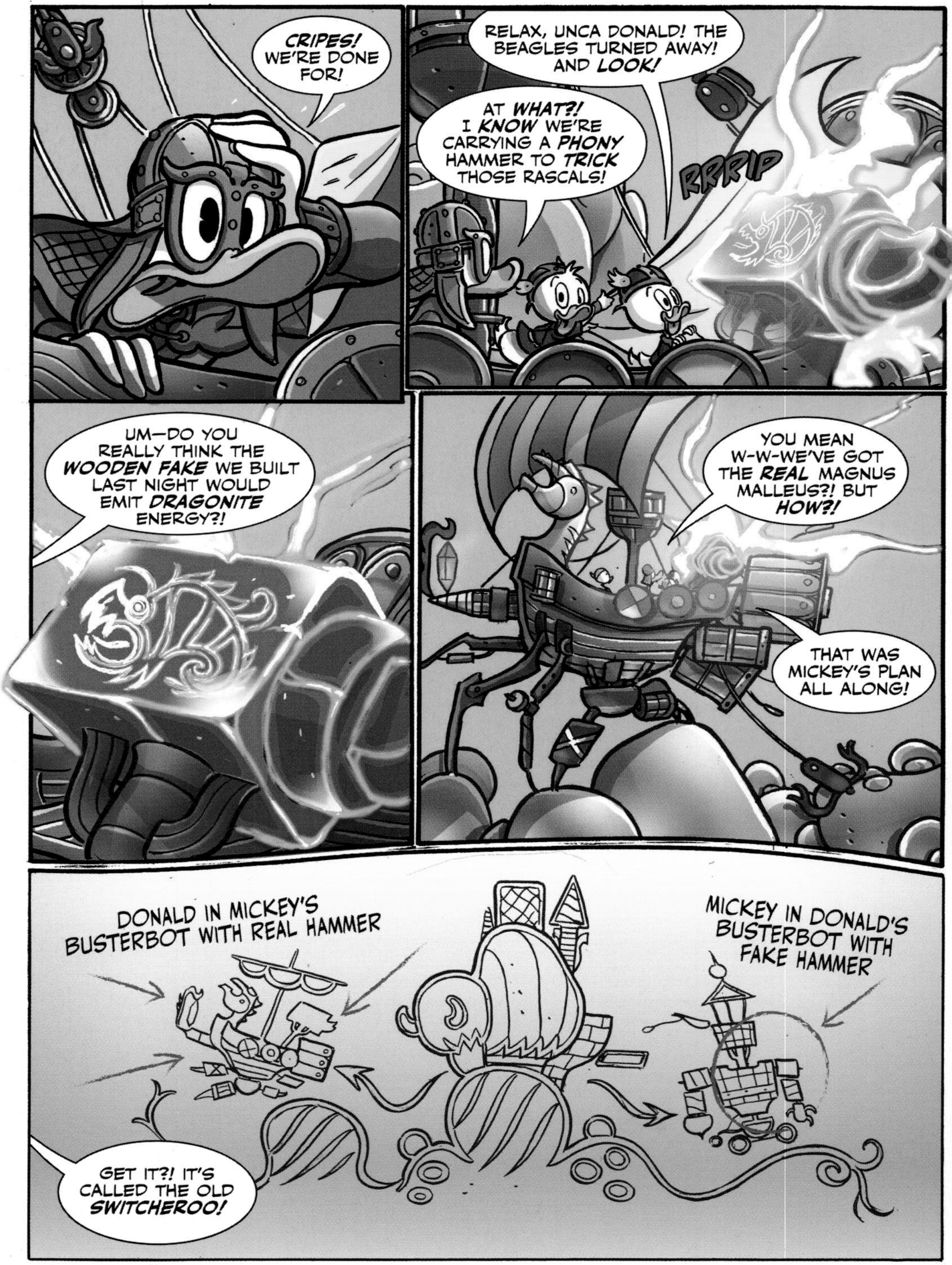
CRIPES! WE'RE DONE FOR!
RELAX, UNCA DONALD! THE BEAGLES TURNED AWAY! AND LOOK!
AT WHAT?! I KNOW WE'RE CARRYING A PHONY HAMMER TO TRICK THOSE RASCALS!
RRRIP
UM—DO YOU REALLY THINK THE WOODEN FAKE WE BUILT LAST NIGHT WOULD EMIT DRAGONITE ENERGY?!
YOU MEAN W-W-WE'VE GOT THE REAL MAGNUS MALLEUS?! BUT HOW?!
THAT WAS MICKEY'S PLAN ALL ALONG!
DONALD IN MICKEY'S BUSTERBOT WITH REAL HAMMER
MICKEY IN DONALD'S BUSTERBOT WITH FAKE HAMMER
GET IT?! IT'S CALLED THE OLD SWITCHEROO!

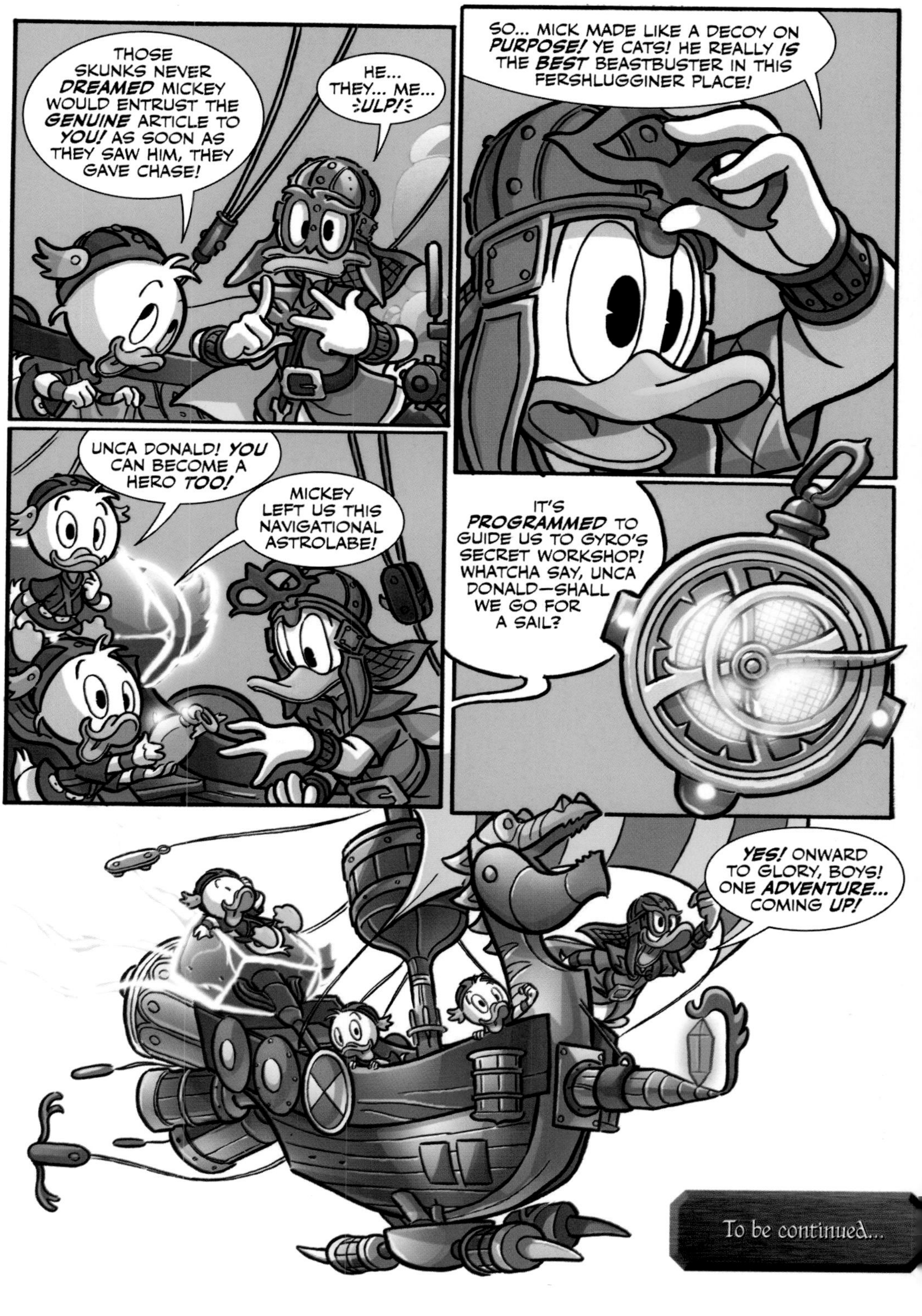
THOSE SKUNKS NEVER *DREAMED* MICKEY WOULD ENTRUST THE *GENUINE* ARTICLE TO *YOU!* AS SOON AS THEY SAW HIM, THEY GAVE CHASE!
HE... THEY... ME... *ULP!*
SO... MICK MADE LIKE A DECOY ON *PURPOSE!* YE CATS! HE REALLY *IS* THE *BEST* BEASTBUSTER IN THIS FERSHLUGGINER PLACE!
UNCA DONALD! *YOU* CAN BECOME A HERO *TOO!*
MICKEY LEFT US THIS NAVIGATIONAL ASTROLABE!
IT'S *PROGRAMMED* TO GUIDE US TO GYRO'S SECRET WORKSHOP! WHATCHA SAY, UNCA DONALD—SHALL WE GO FOR A SAIL?
YES! ONWARD TO GLORY, BOYS! ONE *ADVENTURE...* COMING *UP!*
To be continued...

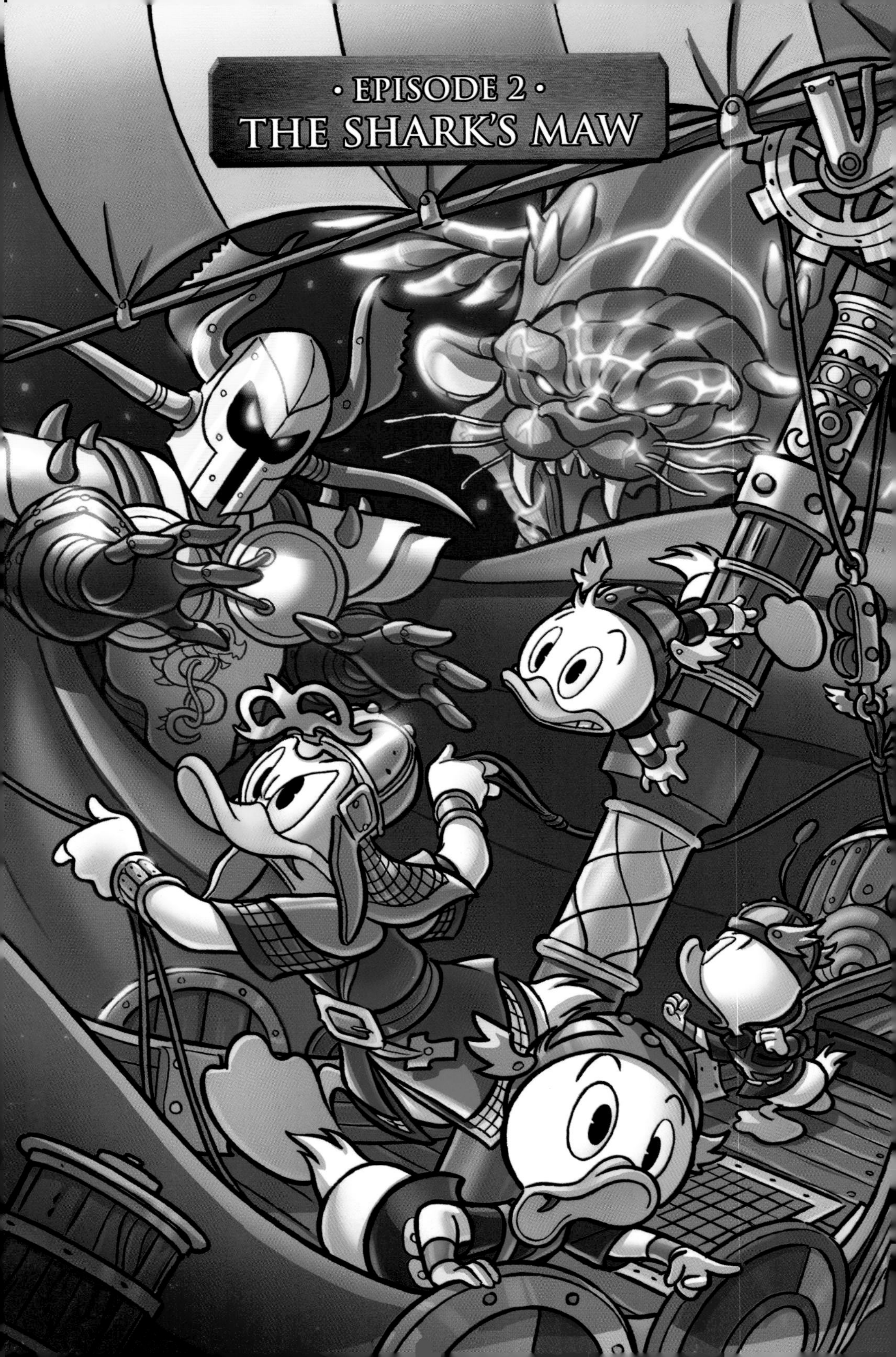
• EPISODE 2 •
THE SHARK'S MAW

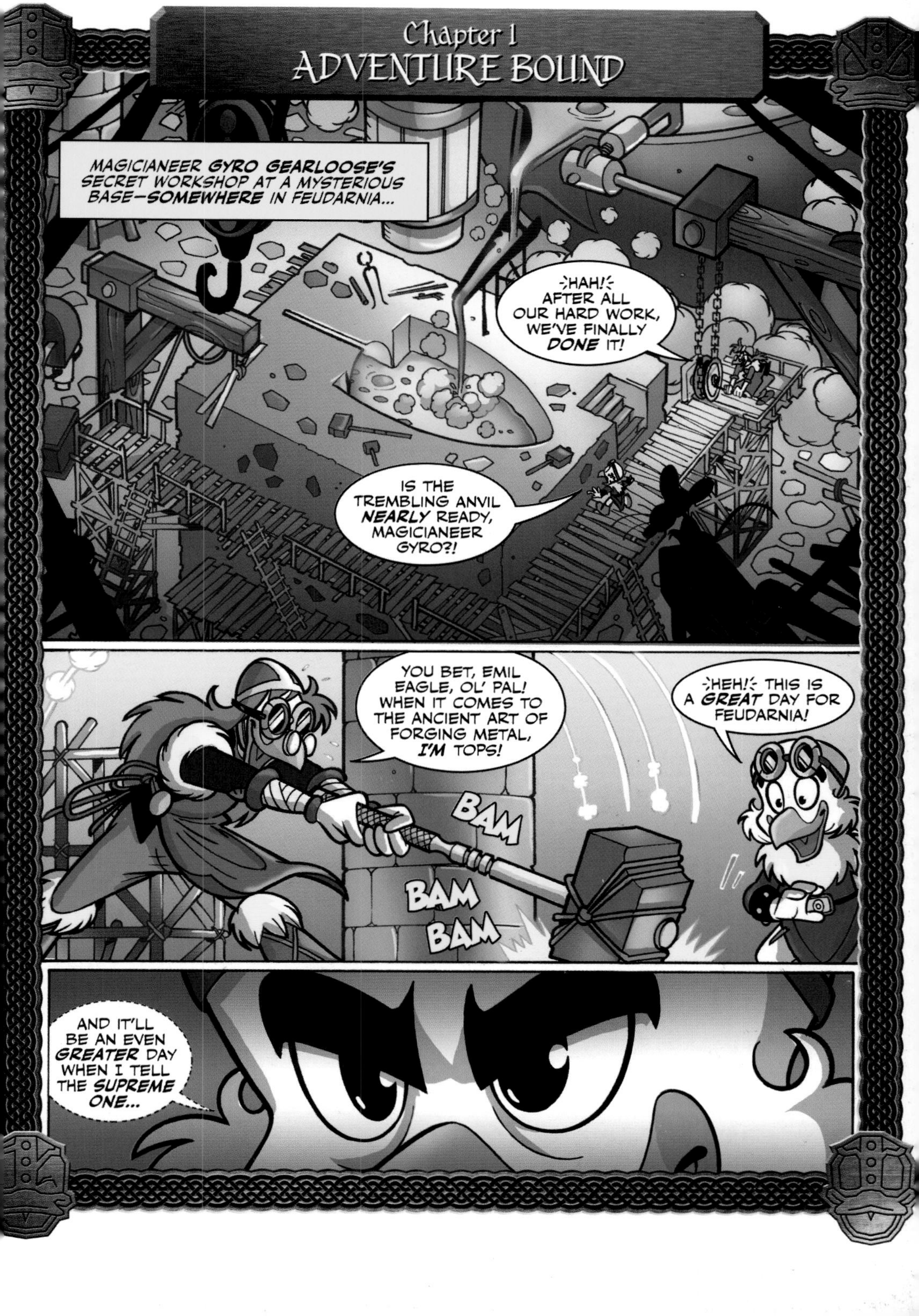

Chapter 1
ADVENTURE BOUND
MAGICIANEER GYRO GEARLOOSE'S SECRET WORKSHOP AT A MYSTERIOUS BASE—SOMEWHERE IN FEUDARNIA...
HAH! AFTER ALL OUR HARD WORK, WE'VE FINALLY DONE IT!
IS THE TREMBLING ANVIL NEARLY READY, MAGICIANEER GYRO?!
YOU BET, EMIL EAGLE, OL' PAL! WHEN IT COMES TO THE ANCIENT ART OF FORGING METAL, I'M TOPS!
HEH! THIS IS A GREAT DAY FOR FEUDARNIA!
BAM
BAM
BAM
AND IT'LL BE AN EVEN GREATER DAY WHEN I TELL THE SUPREME ONE...

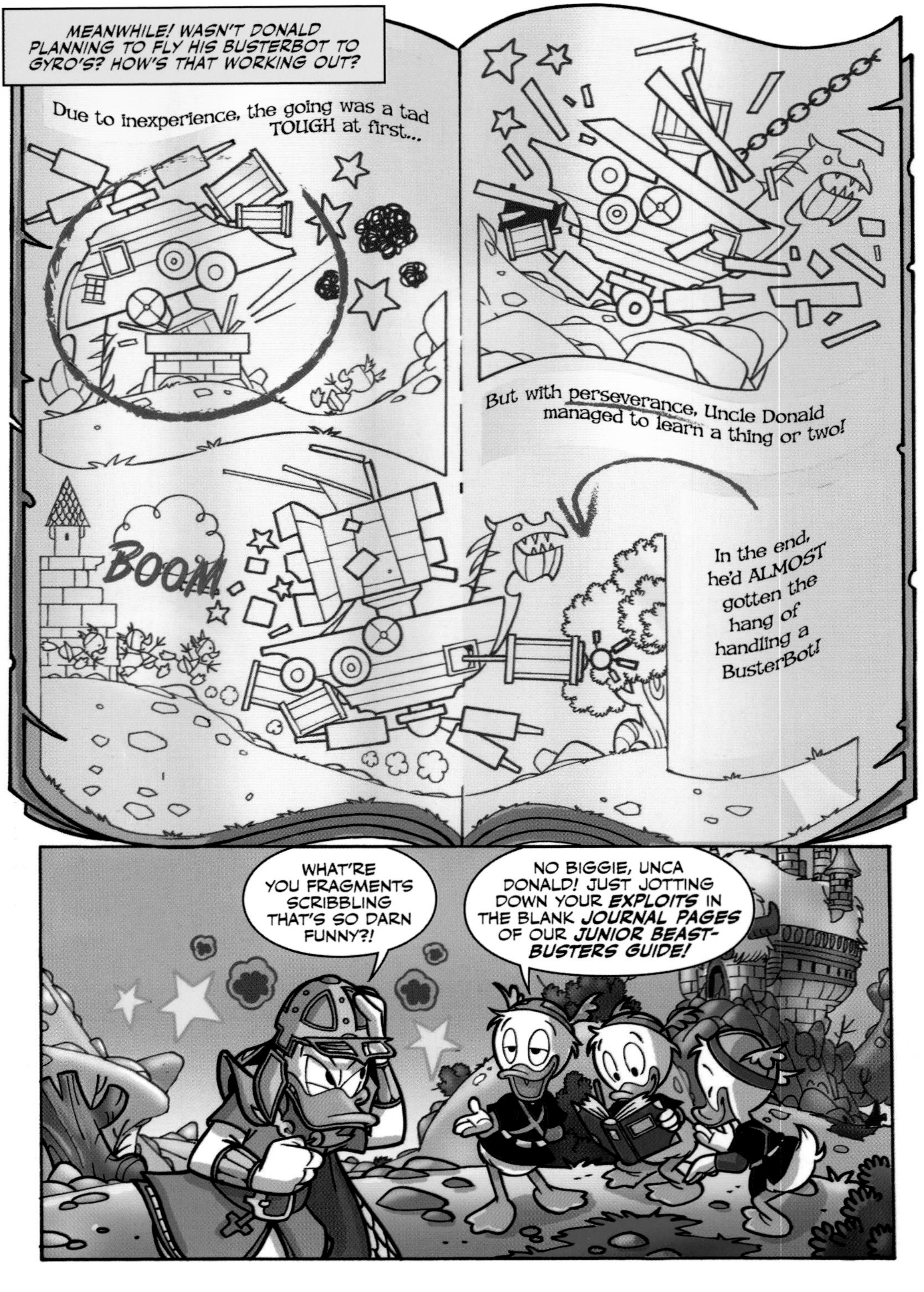
MEANWHILE! WASN'T DONALD PLANNING TO FLY HIS BUSTERBOT TO GYRO'S? HOW'S THAT WORKING OUT?
Due to inexperience, the going was a tad TOUGH at first...
But with perseverance, Uncle Donald managed to learn a thing or two!
BOOM
In the end, he'd ALMOST gotten the hang of handling a BusterBot!
WHAT'RE YOU FRAGMENTS SCRIBBLING THAT'S SO DARN FUNNY?!
NO BIGGIE, UNCA DONALD! JUST JOTTING DOWN YOUR EXPLOITS IN THE BLANK JOURNAL PAGES OF OUR JUNIOR BEAST-BUSTERS GUIDE!

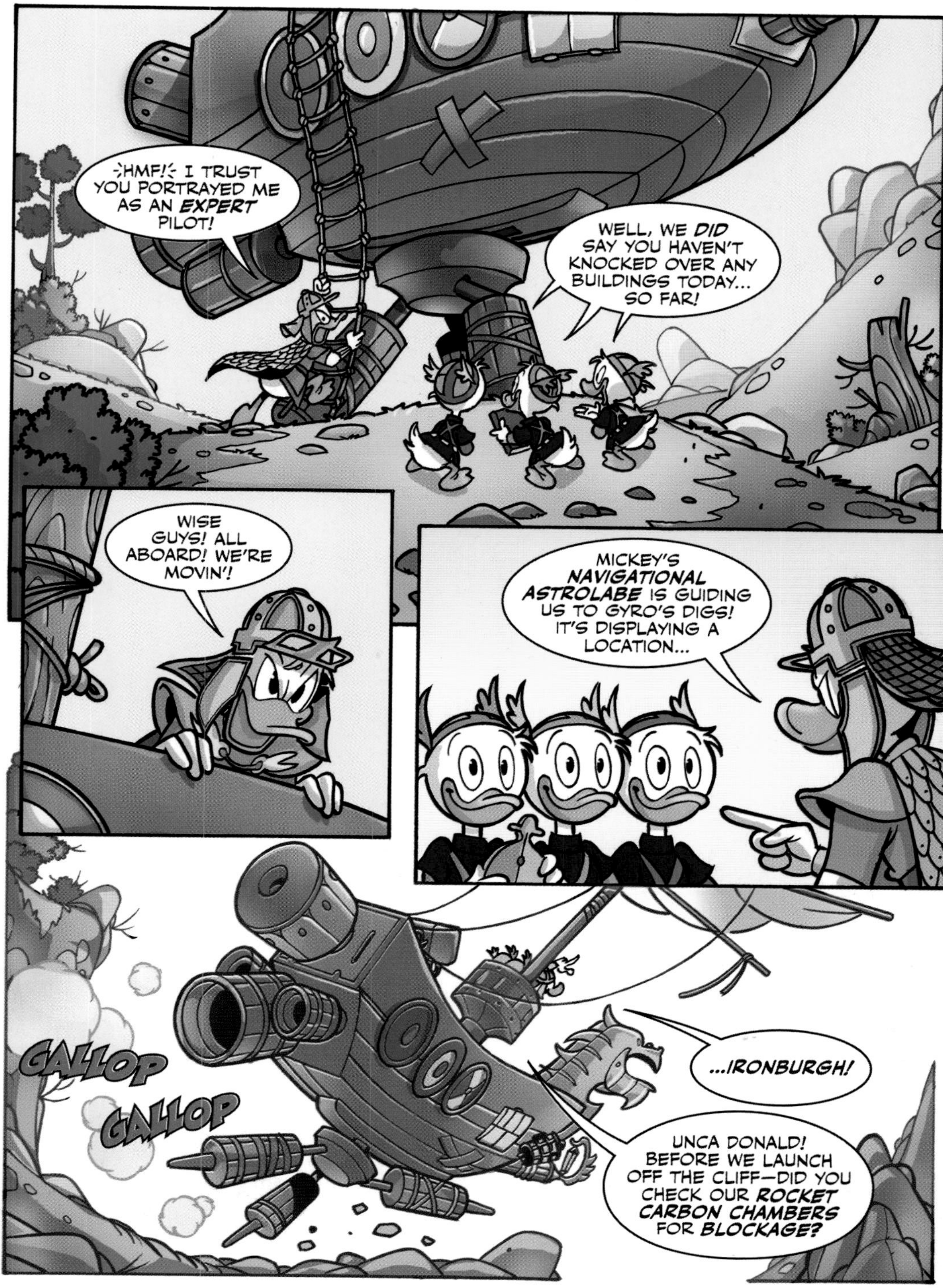

HMF! I TRUST YOU PORTRAYED ME AS AN EXPERT PILOT!
WELL, WE DID SAY YOU HAVEN'T KNOCKED OVER ANY BUILDINGS TODAY... SO FAR!
WISE GUYS! ALL ABOARD! WE'RE MOVIN'!
MICKEY'S NAVIGATIONAL ASTROLABE IS GUIDING US TO GYRO'S DIGS! IT'S DISPLAYING A LOCATION...
GALLOP
GALLOP
...IRONBURGH!
UNCA DONALD! BEFORE WE LAUNCH OFF THE CLIFF—DID YOU CHECK OUR ROCKET CARBON CHAMBERS FOR BLOCKAGE?

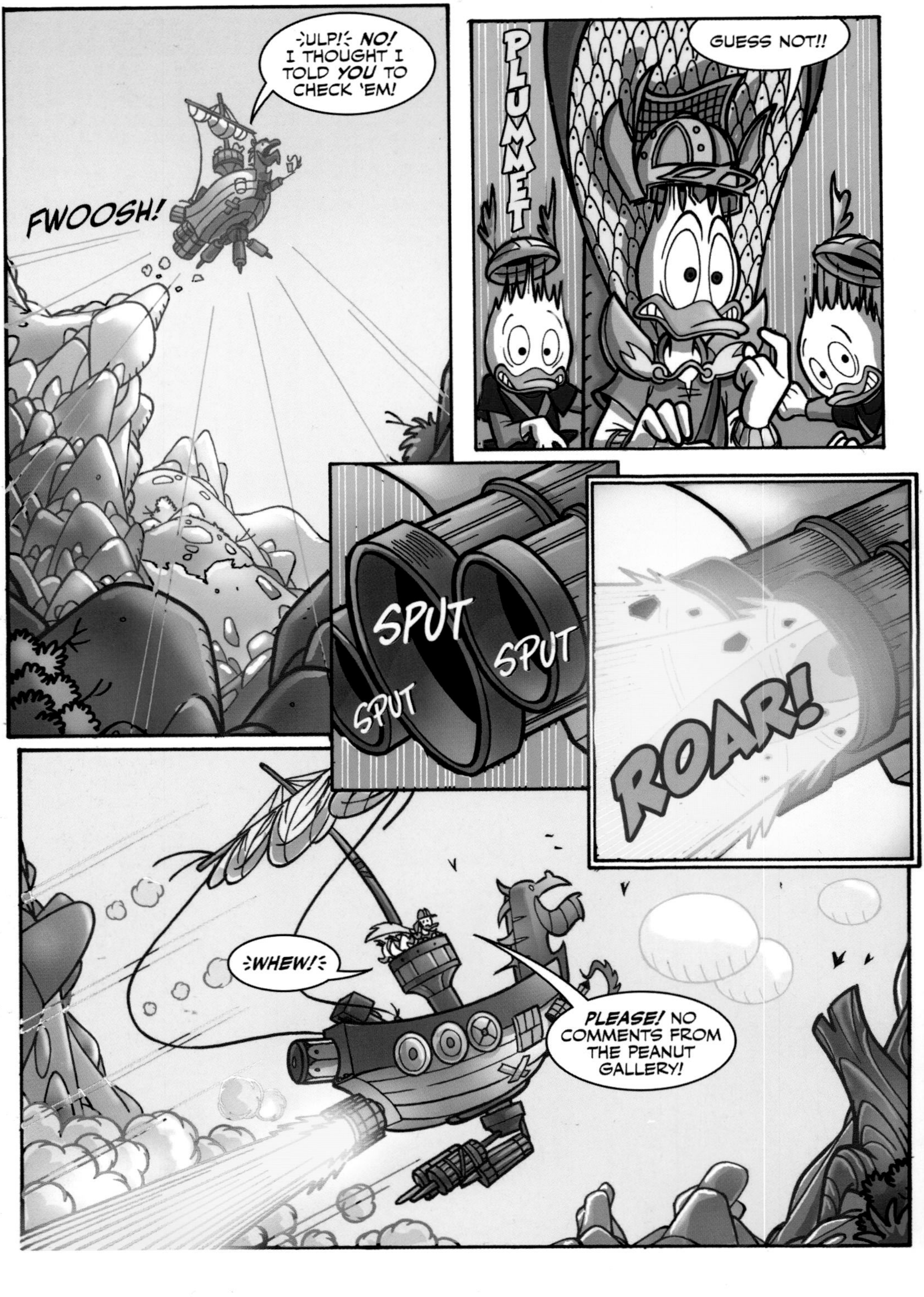

ULP! NO! I THOUGHT I TOLD YOU TO CHECK 'EM!
FWOOSH!
GUESS NOT!!
PLUMMET
SPUT
SPUT
SPUT
ROAR!
WHEW!
PLEASE! NO COMMENTS FROM THE PEANUT GALLERY!

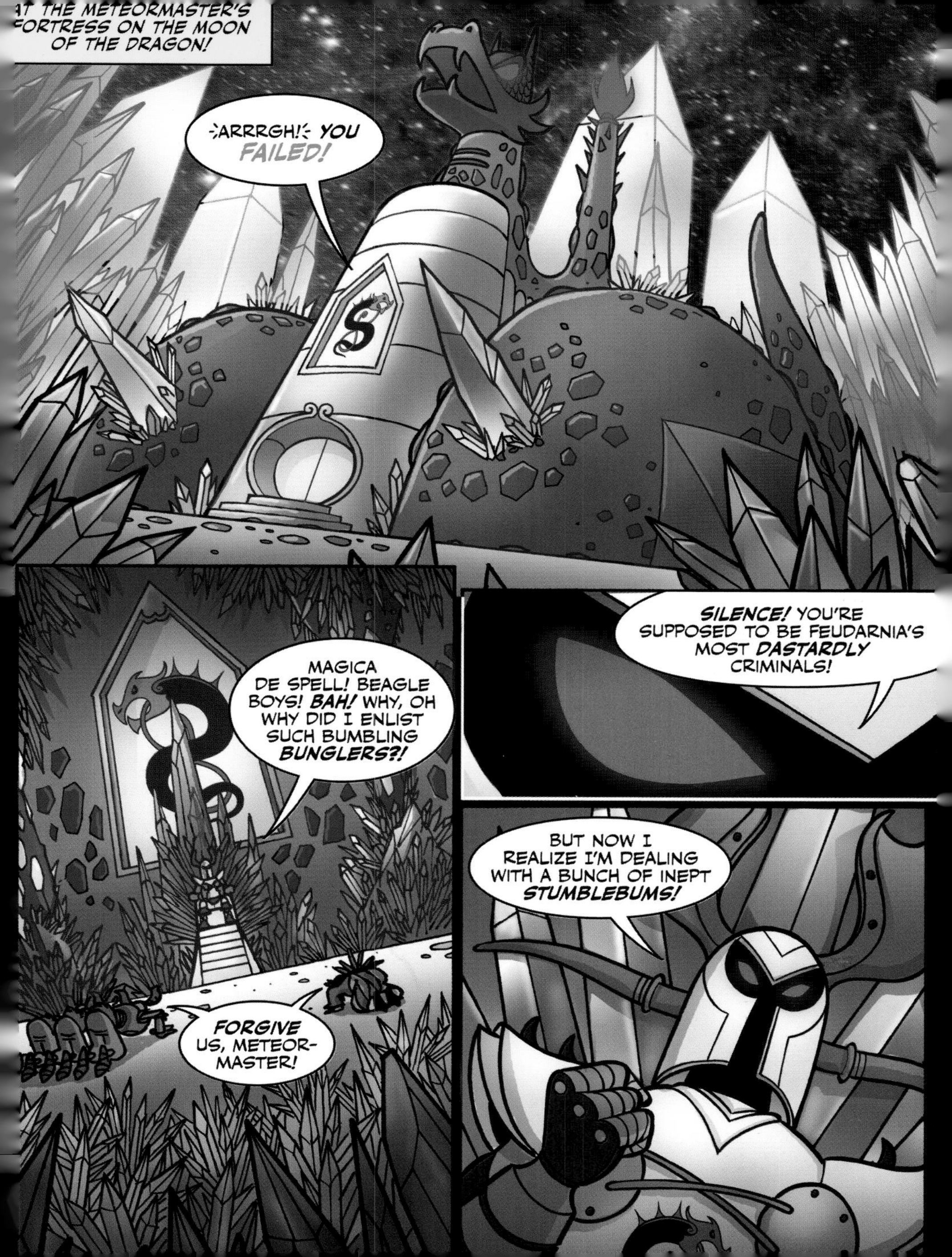
AT THE METEORMASTER'S FORTRESS ON THE MOON OF THE DRAGON!
ARRRGH! YOU FAILED!
MAGICA DE SPELL! BEAGLE BOYS! BAH! WHY, OH WHY DID I ENLIST SUCH BUMBLING BUNGLERS?!
FORGIVE US, METEOR-MASTER!
SILENCE! YOU'RE SUPPOSED TO BE FEUDARNIA'S MOST DASTARDLY CRIMINALS!
BUT NOW I REALIZE I'M DEALING WITH A BUNCH OF INEPT STUMBLEBUMS!

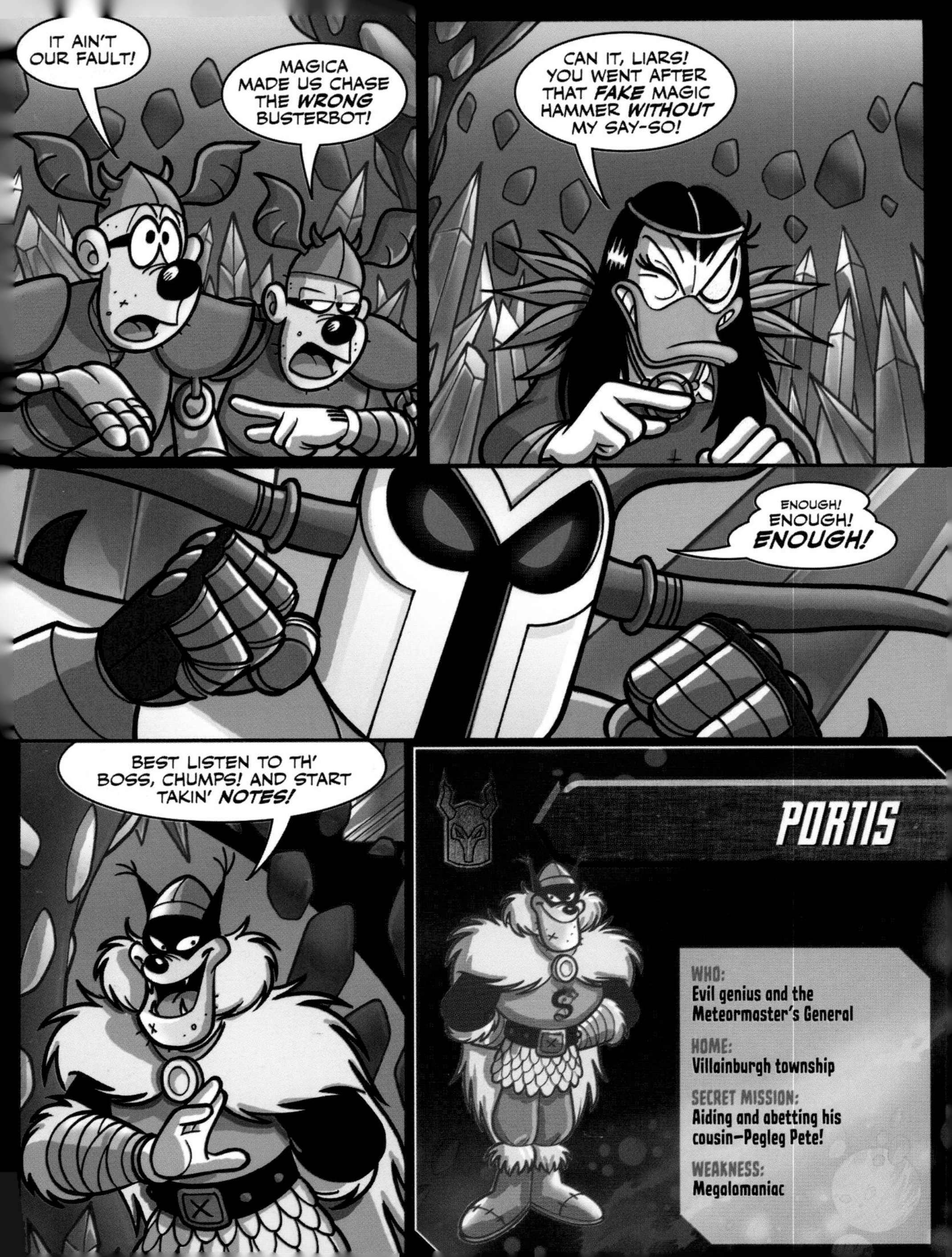
IT AIN'T OUR FAULT!
MAGICA MADE US CHASE THE WRONG BUSTERBOT!
CAN IT, LIARS! YOU WENT AFTER THAT FAKE MAGIC HAMMER WITHOUT MY SAY-SO!
ENOUGH! ENOUGH! ENOUGH!
BEST LISTEN TO TH' BOSS, CHUMPS! AND START TAKIN' NOTES!
PORTIS
WHO:
Evil genius and the Meteormaster's General
HOME:
Villainburgh township
SECRET MISSION:
Aiding and abetting his cousin—Pegleg Pete!
WEAKNESS:
Megalomaniac

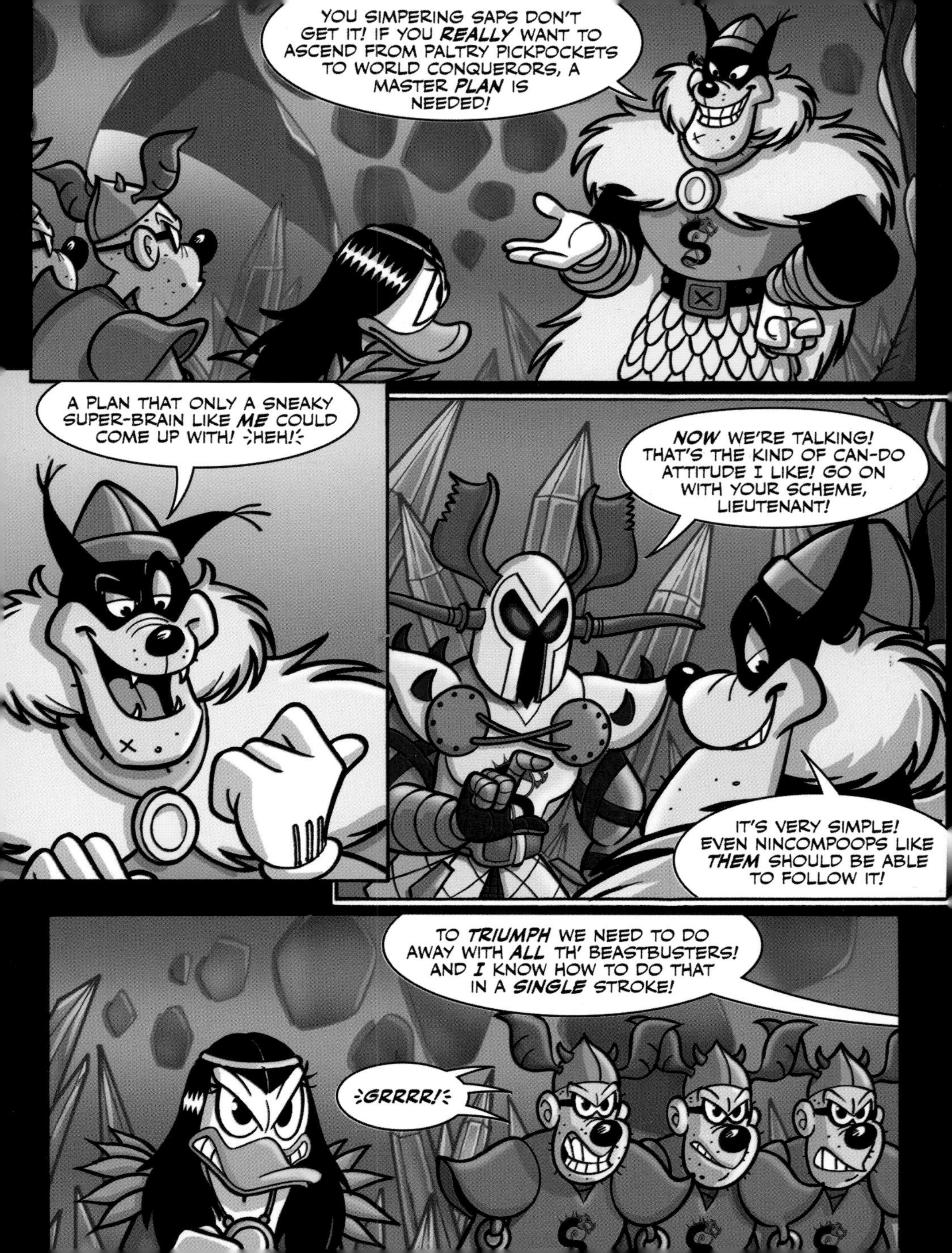
YOU SIMPERING SAPS DON'T GET IT! IF YOU REALLY WANT TO ASCEND FROM PALTRY PICKPOCKETS TO WORLD CONQUERORS, A MASTER PLAN IS NEEDED!
A PLAN THAT ONLY A SNEAKY SUPER-BRAIN LIKE ME COULD COME UP WITH! HEH!
NOW WE'RE TALKING! THAT'S THE KIND OF CAN-DO ATTITUDE I LIKE! GO ON WITH YOUR SCHEME, LIEUTENANT!
IT'S VERY SIMPLE! EVEN NINCOMPOOPS LIKE THEM SHOULD BE ABLE TO FOLLOW IT!
TO TRIUMPH WE NEED TO DO AWAY WITH ALL TH' BEASTBUSTERS! AND I KNOW HOW TO DO THAT IN A SINGLE STROKE!
GRRRR!

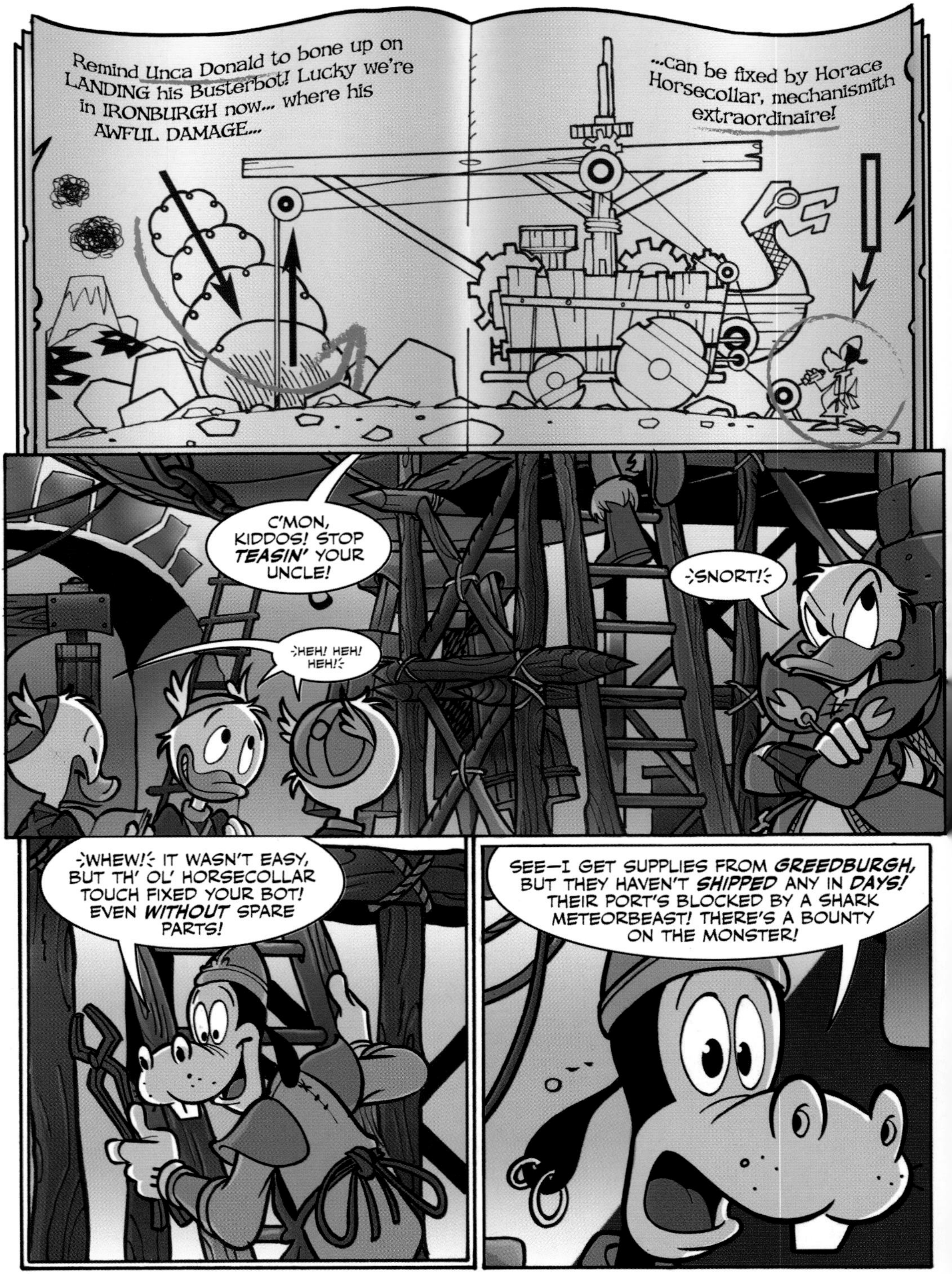
Remind Unca Donald to bone up on LANDING his Busterbot! Lucky we're in IRONBURGH now... where his AWFUL DAMAGE...
...can be fixed by Horace Horsecollar, mechanismith extraordinaire!
C'MON, KIDDOS! STOP TEASIN' YOUR UNCLE!
SNORT!
HEH! HEH! HEH!
WHEW! IT WASN'T EASY, BUT TH' OL' HORSECOLLAR TOUCH FIXED YOUR BOT! EVEN WITHOUT SPARE PARTS!
SEE—I GET SUPPLIES FROM GREEDBURGH, BUT THEY HAVEN'T SHIPPED ANY IN DAYS! THEIR PORT'S BLOCKED BY A SHARK METEORBEAST! THERE'S A BOUNTY ON THE MONSTER!

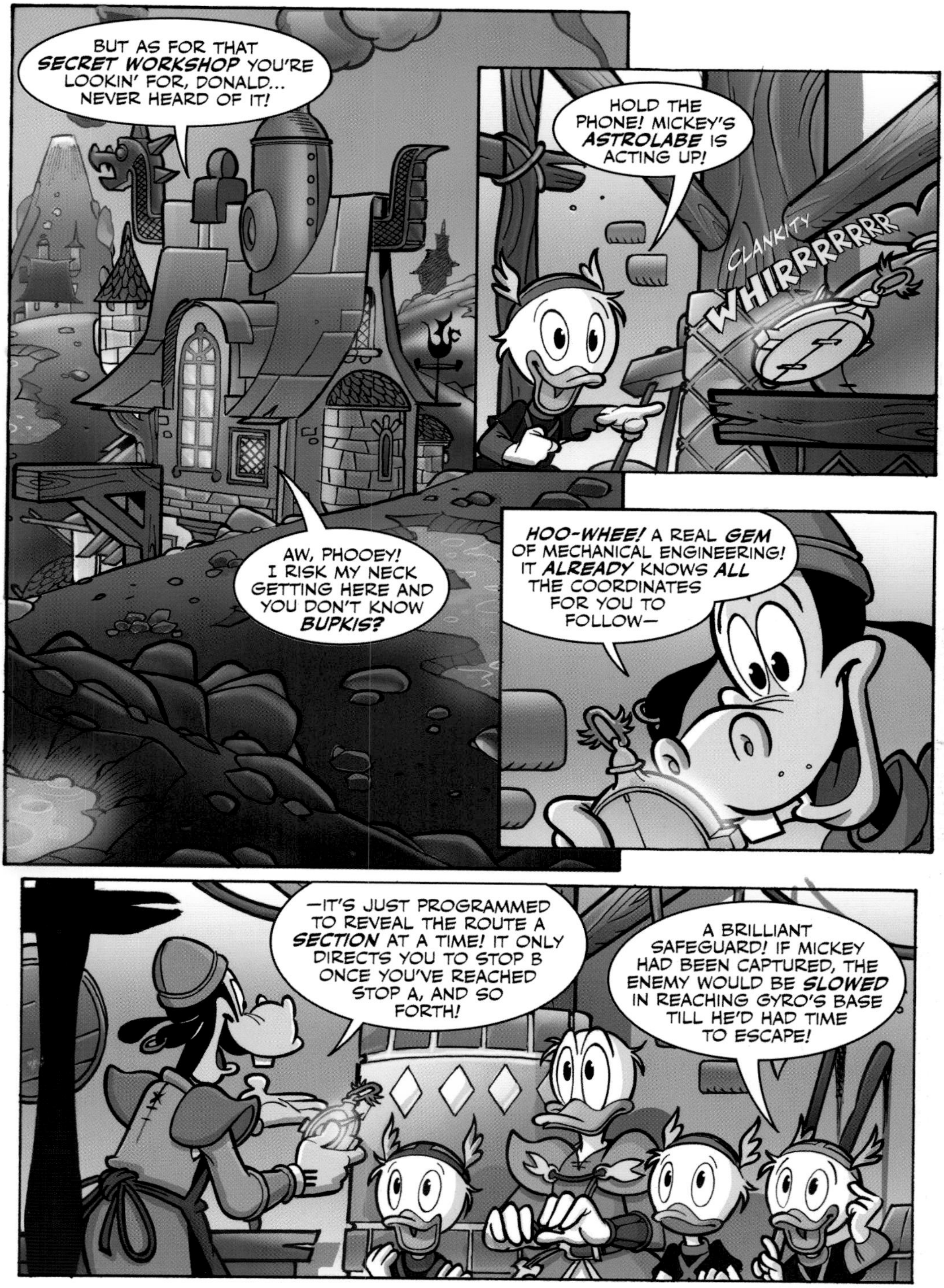
BUT AS FOR THAT SECRET WORKSHOP YOU'RE LOOKIN' FOR, DONALD... NEVER HEARD OF IT!
HOLD THE PHONE! MICKEY'S ASTROLABE IS ACTING UP!
CLANKITY
WHIRRRRRR
AW, PHOOEY! I RISK MY NECK GETTING HERE AND YOU DON'T KNOW BUPKIS?
HOO-WHEE! A REAL GEM OF MECHANICAL ENGINEERING! IT ALREADY KNOWS ALL THE COORDINATES FOR YOU TO FOLLOW—
—IT'S JUST PROGRAMMED TO REVEAL THE ROUTE A SECTION AT A TIME! IT ONLY DIRECTS YOU TO STOP B ONCE YOU'VE REACHED STOP A, AND SO FORTH!
A BRILLIANT SAFEGUARD! IF MICKEY HAD BEEN CAPTURED, THE ENEMY WOULD BE SLOWED IN REACHING GYRO'S BASE TILL HE'D HAD TIME TO ESCAPE!

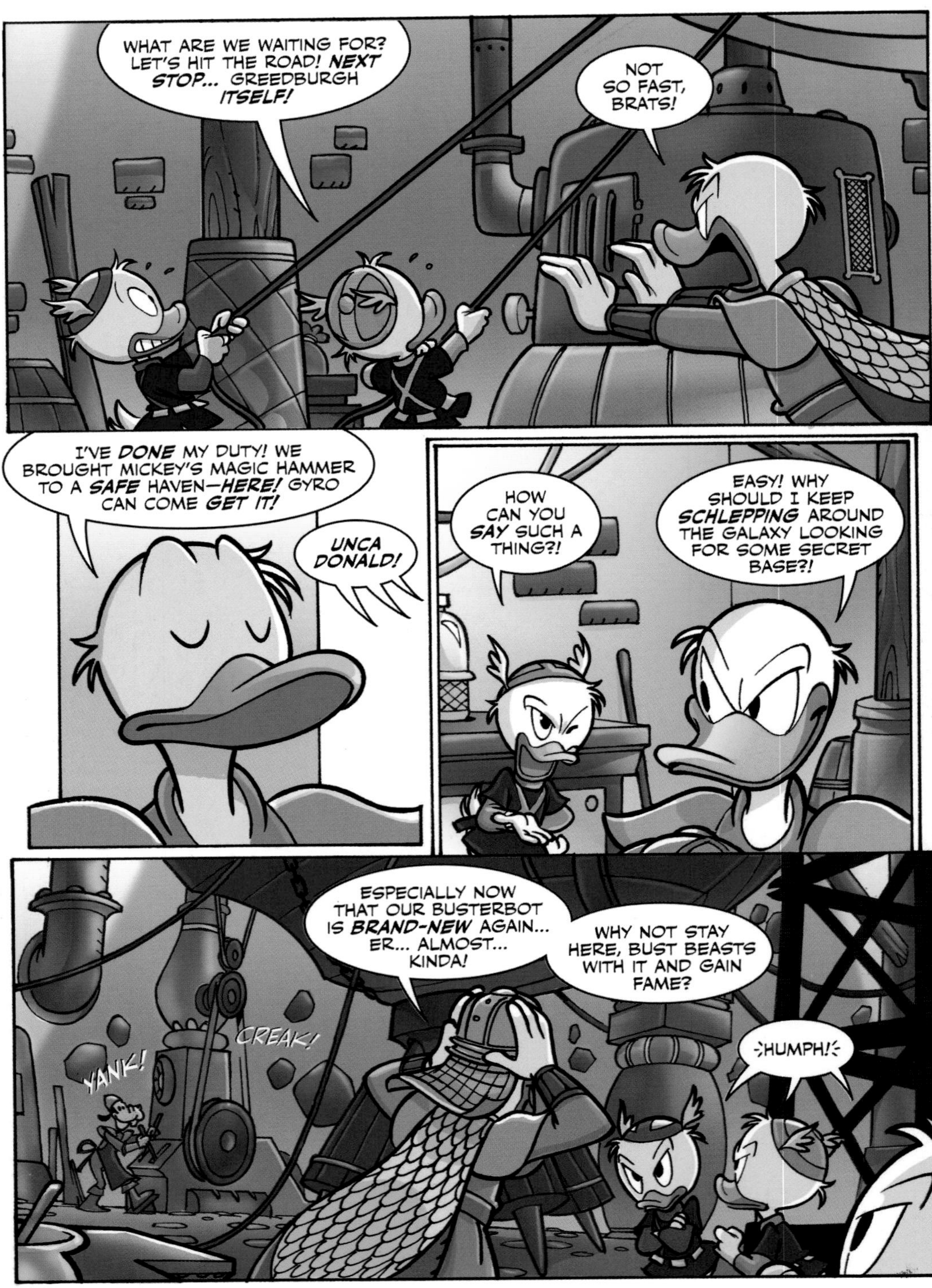
WHAT ARE WE WAITING FOR? LET'S HIT THE ROAD! NEXT STOP... GREEDBURGH ITSELF!
NOT SO FAST, BRATS!
I'VE DONE MY DUTY! WE BROUGHT MICKEY'S MAGIC HAMMER TO A SAFE HAVEN—HERE! GYRO CAN COME GET IT!
UNCA DONALD!
HOW CAN YOU SAY SUCH A THING?!
EASY! WHY SHOULD I KEEP SCHLEPPING AROUND THE GALAXY LOOKING FOR SOME SECRET BASE?!
ESPECIALLY NOW THAT OUR BUSTERBOT IS BRAND-NEW AGAIN... ER... ALMOST... KINDA!
WHY NOT STAY HERE, BUST BEASTS WITH IT AND GAIN FAME?
CREAK!
YANK!
HUMPH!

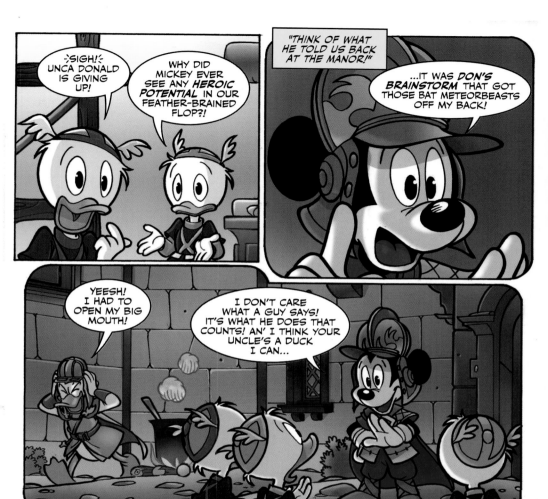

-:SIGH!:- UNCA DONALD IS GIVING UP!

WHY DID MICKEY EVER SEE ANY *HEROIC POTENTIAL* IN OUR FEATHER-BRAINED FLOP?!

"THINK OF WHAT HE TOLD US BACK AT THE MANOR!"

...IT WAS *DON'S BRAINSTORM* THAT GOT THOSE BAT METEORBEASTS OFF MY BACK!

YEESH! I HAD TO OPEN MY BIG MOUTH!

I DON'T CARE WHAT A GUY SAYS! IT'S WHAT HE DOES THAT COUNTS! AN' I THINK YOUR UNCLE'S A DUCK I CAN...

...TRUST!

OH, BROTHER! *I* DIDN'T TELL MICKEY TO *DECOY* THE BAD GUYS WITH A *FAKE* HAMMER—OR LEAVE *ME* TO SAVE THE REAL ONE!

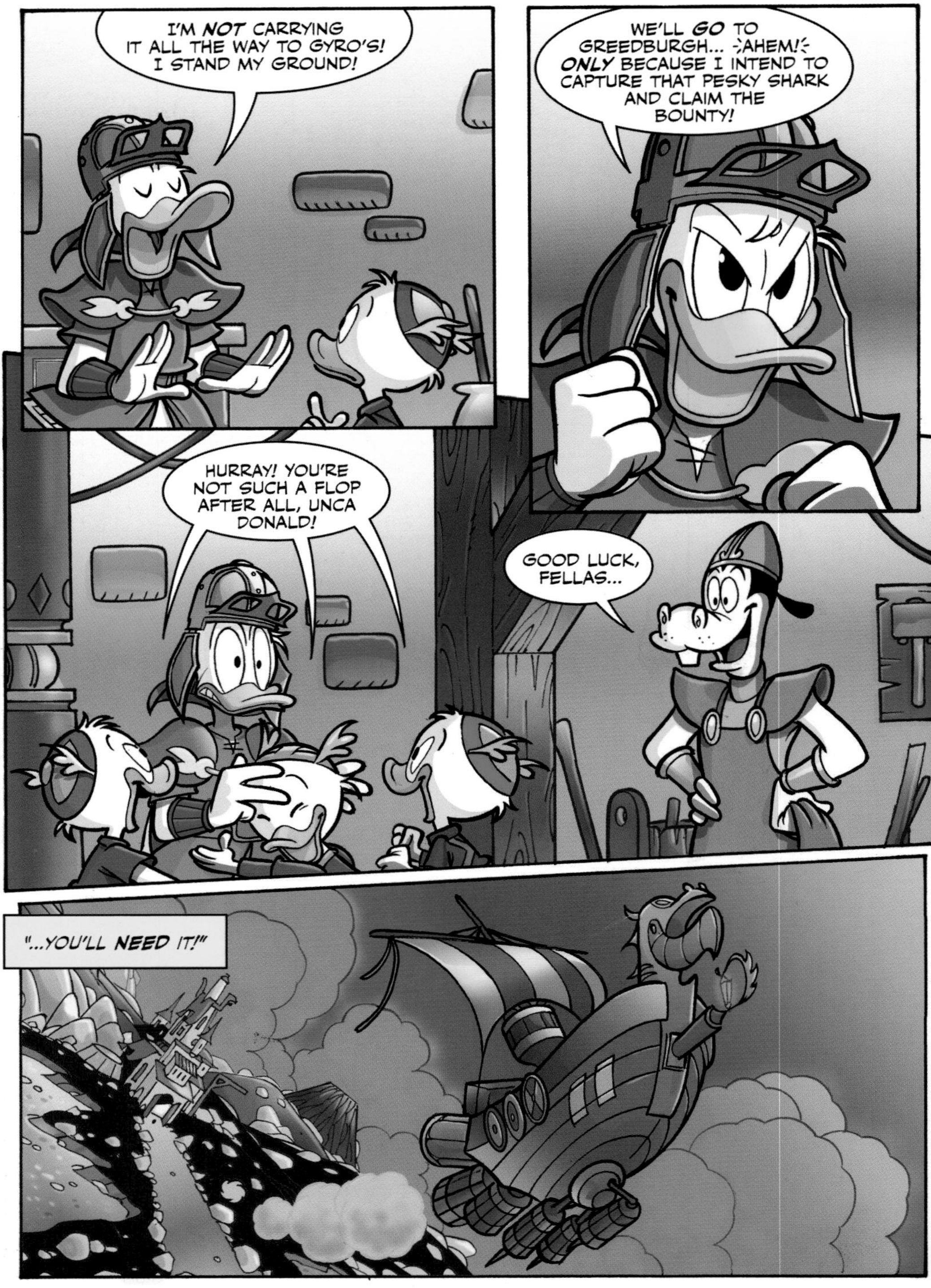
I'M NOT CARRYING IT ALL THE WAY TO GYRO'S! I STAND MY GROUND!
WE'LL GO TO GREEDBURGH... AHEM! ONLY BECAUSE I INTEND TO CAPTURE THAT PESKY SHARK AND CLAIM THE BOUNTY!
HURRAY! YOU'RE NOT SUCH A FLOP AFTER ALL, UNCA DONALD!
GOOD LUCK, FELLAS...
"...YOU'LL NEED IT!"

MEANTIME... BACK ON THE MOON OF THE DRAGON!

CLASS—COME TO ATTENTION! *PLEASE!* NO NOTE-PASSIN' OR GUM-CHEWIN'!

TODAY'S LESSON: *COMMERCE!* EACH OF FEUDARNIA'S TOWNSHIPS RUNS AN INDUSTRY OF ITS OWN!

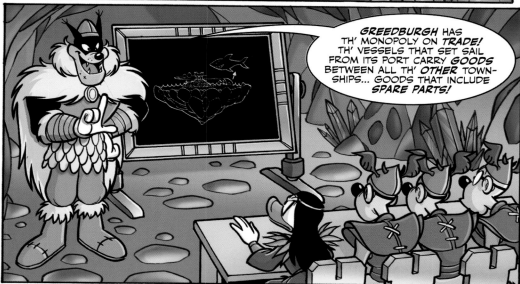

GREEDBURGH HAS TH' MONOPOLY ON *TRADE!* TH' VESSELS THAT SET SAIL FROM ITS PORT CARRY *GOODS* BETWEEN ALL TH' *OTHER* TOWNSHIPS... GOODS THAT INCLUDE *SPARE PARTS!*

QUESTION! IF MY FEROCIOUS SHARK METEORBEAST BLOCKADES GREEDBURGH HARBOR, WHAT IS THE RESULT?!

ANSWER! TH' VESSELS CAN'T *LEAVE!* AN' WITHOUT SPARE PARTS, *NO* BUSTERBOTS CAN BE REPAIRED! CONCLUSION?! VICTORY IS OURS! ⸫*HA! HAH! HAR!*⸫

Chapter 2
TEETH AND HAMMER

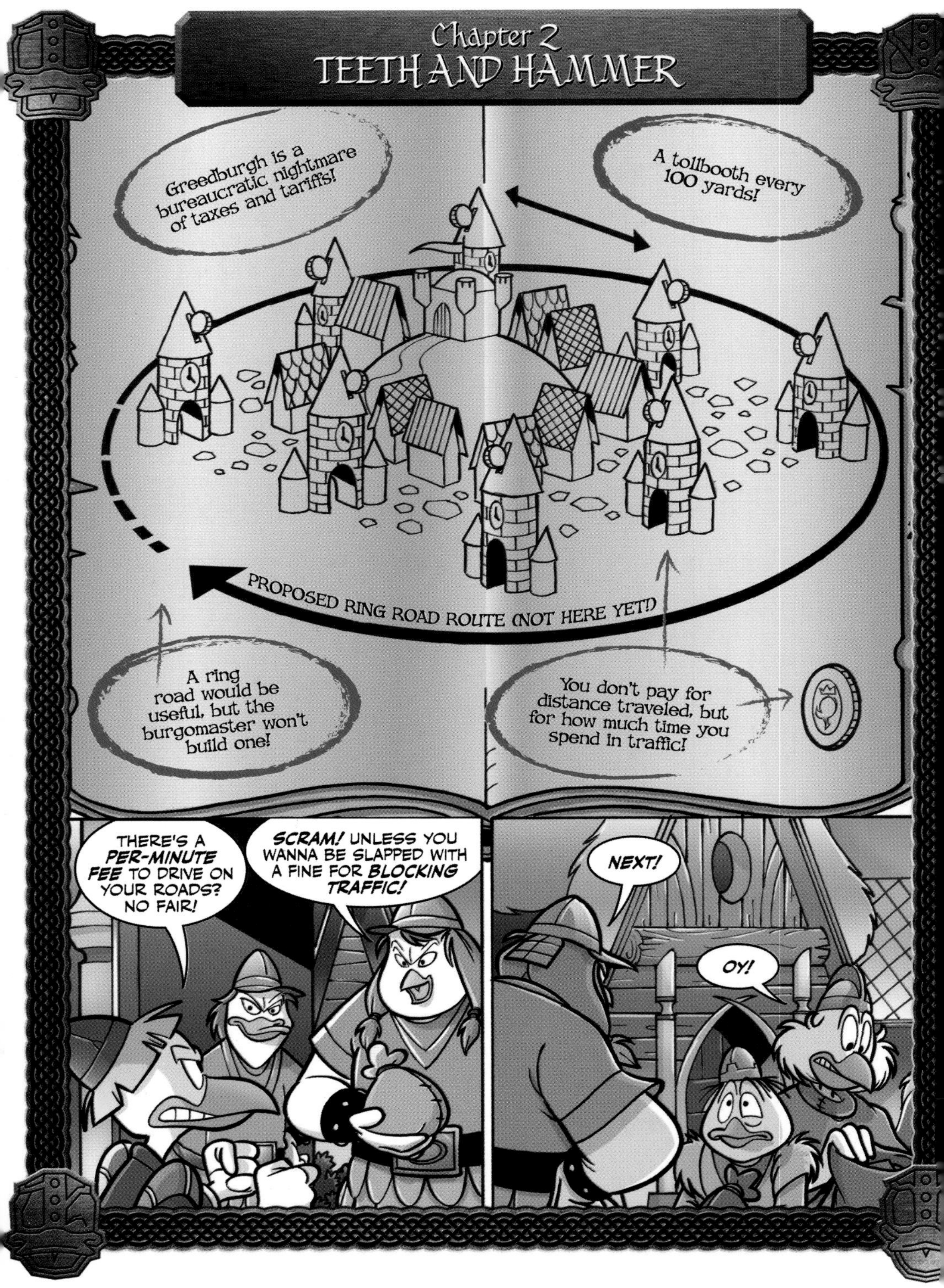

Greedburgh is a bureaucratic nightmare of taxes and tariffs!
A tollbooth every 100 yards!
PROPOSED RING ROAD ROUTE (NOT HERE YET!)
A ring road would be useful, but the burgomaster won't build one!
You don't pay for distance traveled, but for how much time you spend in traffic!
THERE'S A PER-MINUTE FEE TO DRIVE ON YOUR ROADS? NO FAIR!
SCRAM! UNLESS YOU WANNA BE SLAPPED WITH A FINE FOR BLOCKING TRAFFIC!
NEXT!
OY!

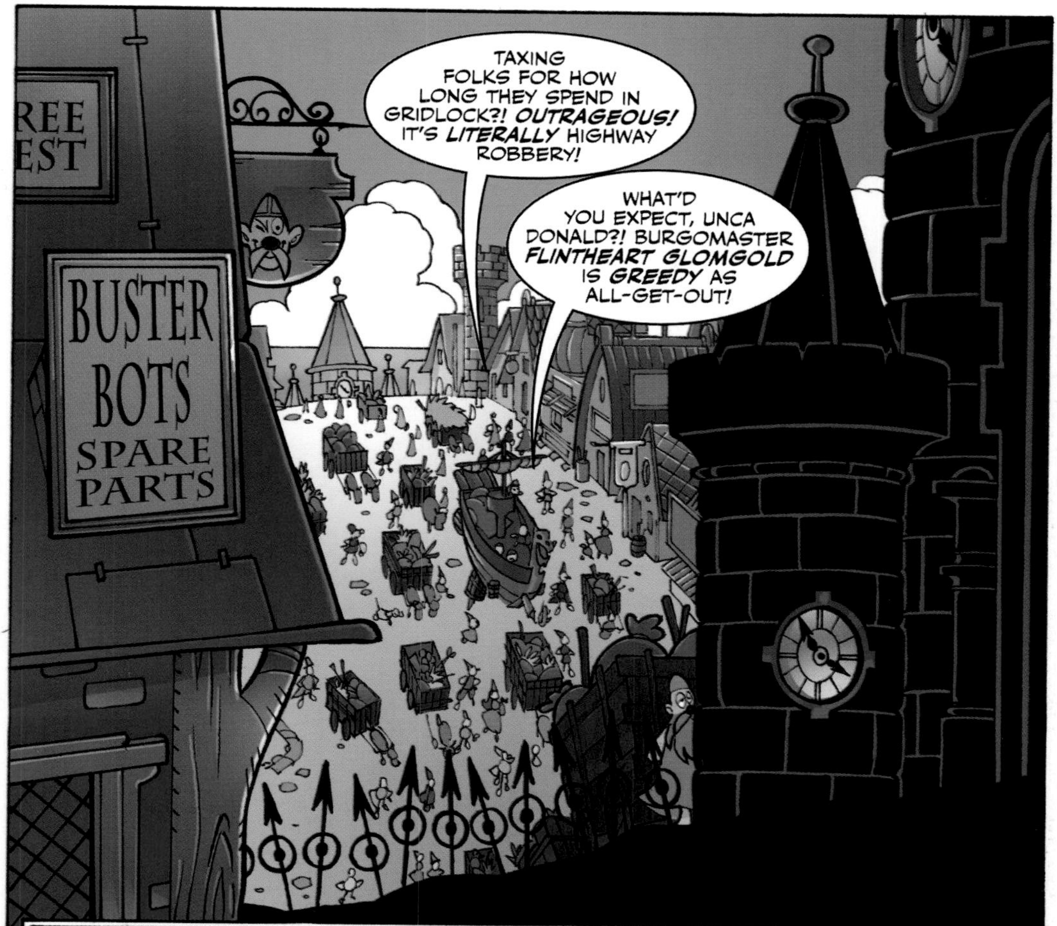
REE
EST
BUSTER BOTS SPARE PARTS
TAXING FOLKS FOR HOW LONG THEY SPEND IN GRIDLOCK?! OUTRAGEOUS! IT'S LITERALLY HIGHWAY ROBBERY!
WHAT'D YOU EXPECT, UNCA DONALD?! BURGOMASTER FLINTHEART GLOMGOLD IS GREEDY AS ALL-GET-OUT!

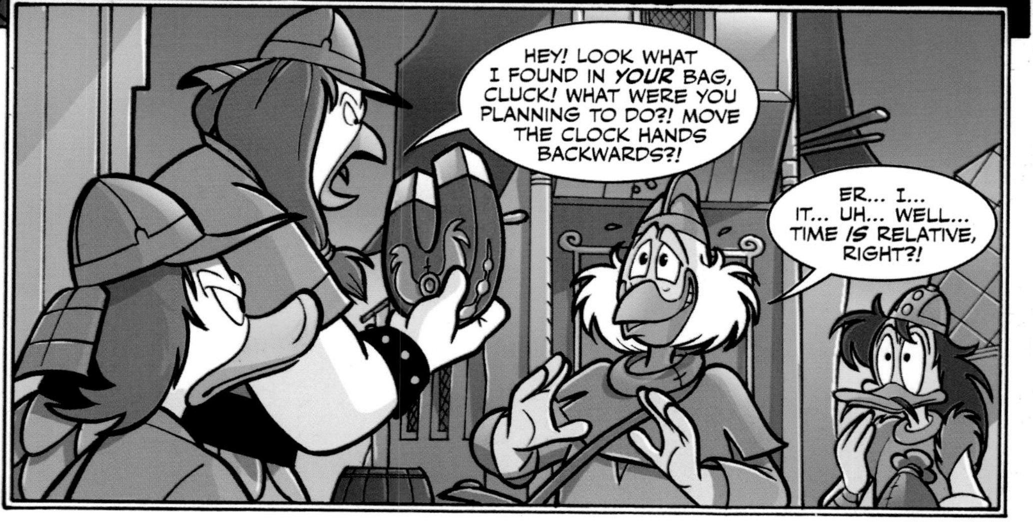
HEY! LOOK WHAT I FOUND IN YOUR BAG, CLUCK! WHAT WERE YOU PLANNING TO DO?! MOVE THE CLOCK HANDS BACKWARDS?!
ER... I... IT... UH... WELL... TIME IS RELATIVE, RIGHT?!

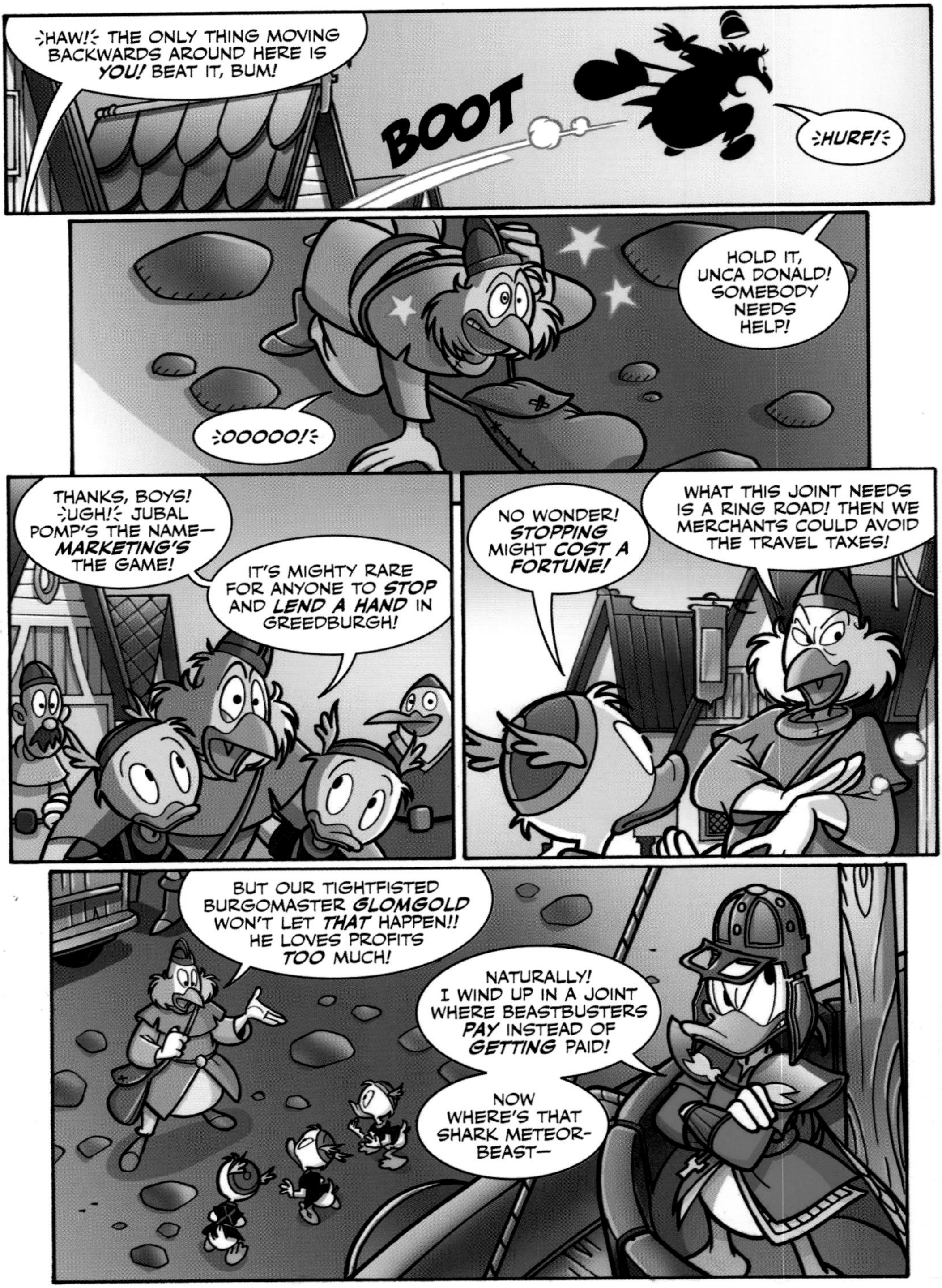

HAW! THE ONLY THING MOVING BACKWARDS AROUND HERE IS YOU! BEAT IT, BUM!
BOOT
HURF!
HOLD IT, UNCA DONALD! SOMEBODY NEEDS HELP!
OOOOO!
THANKS, BOYS! UGH! JUBAL POMP'S THE NAME— MARKETING'S THE GAME!
IT'S MIGHTY RARE FOR ANYONE TO STOP AND LEND A HAND IN GREEDBURGH!
NO WONDER! STOPPING MIGHT COST A FORTUNE!
WHAT THIS JOINT NEEDS IS A RING ROAD! THEN WE MERCHANTS COULD AVOID THE TRAVEL TAXES!
BUT OUR TIGHTFISTED BURGOMASTER GLOMGOLD WON'T LET THAT HAPPEN!! HE LOVES PROFITS TOO MUCH!
NATURALLY! I WIND UP IN A JOINT WHERE BEASTBUSTERS PAY INSTEAD OF GETTING PAID!
NOW WHERE'S THAT SHARK METEOR-BEAST—

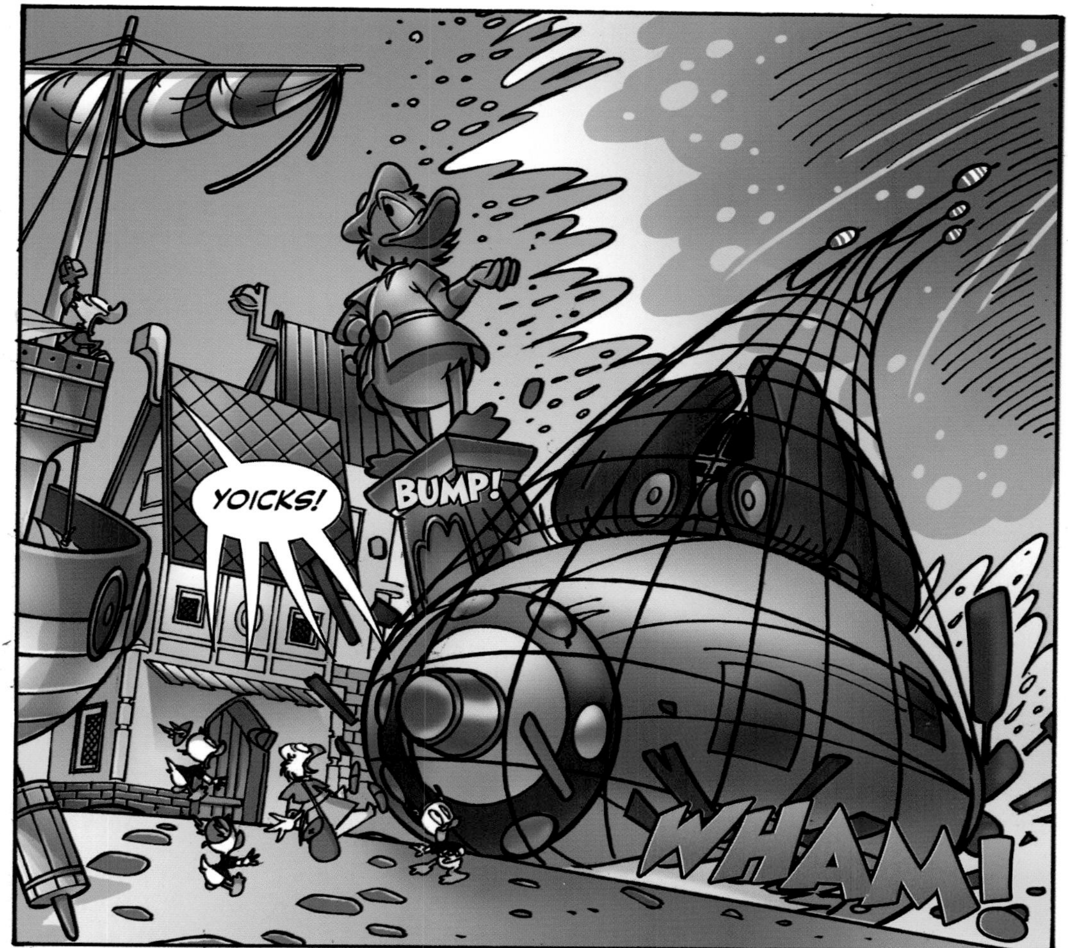

YOICKS!
BUMP!
WHAM!

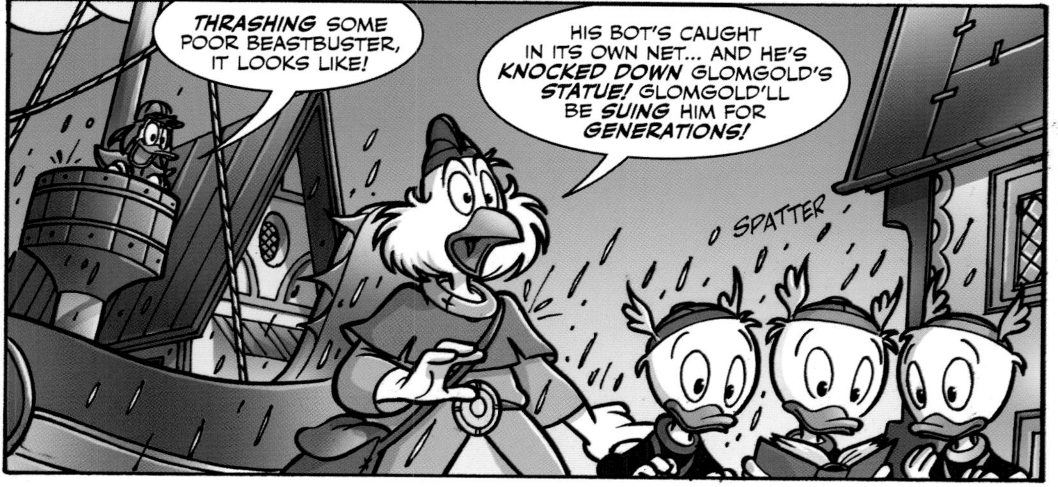

THRASHING SOME POOR BEASTBUSTER, IT LOOKS LIKE!
HIS BOT'S CAUGHT IN ITS OWN NET... AND HE'S KNOCKED DOWN GLOMGOLD'S STATUE! GLOMGOLD'LL BE SUING HIM FOR GENERATIONS!
SPATTER

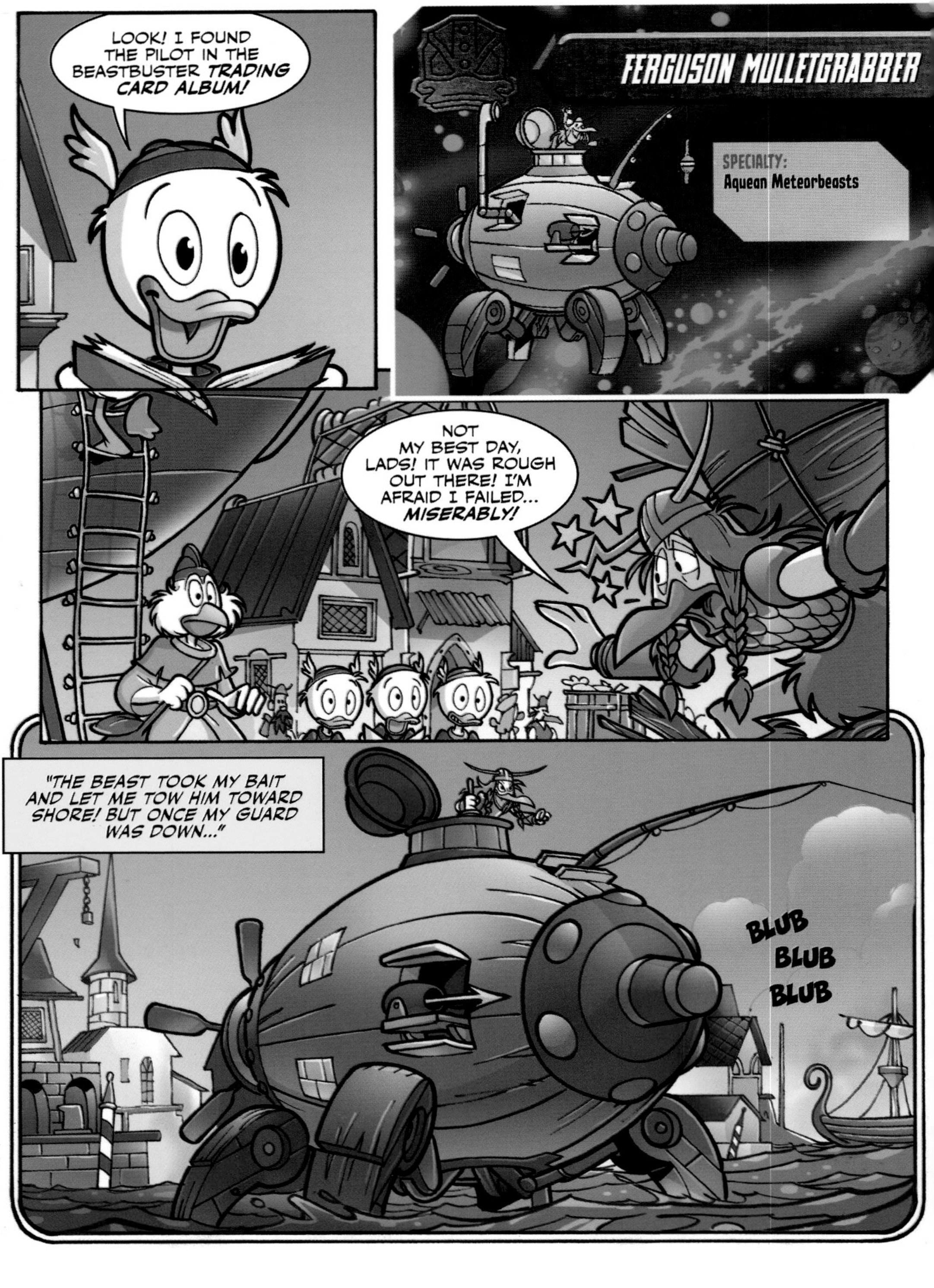
LOOK! I FOUND THE PILOT IN THE BEASTBUSTER TRADING CARD ALBUM!
FERGUSON MULLETGRABBER
SPECIALTY:
Aquean Meteorbeasts
NOT MY BEST DAY, LADS! IT WAS ROUGH OUT THERE! I'M AFRAID I FAILED... MISERABLY!
"THE BEAST TOOK MY BAIT AND LET ME TOW HIM TOWARD SHORE! BUT ONCE MY GUARD WAS DOWN..."
BLUB
BLUB
BLUB

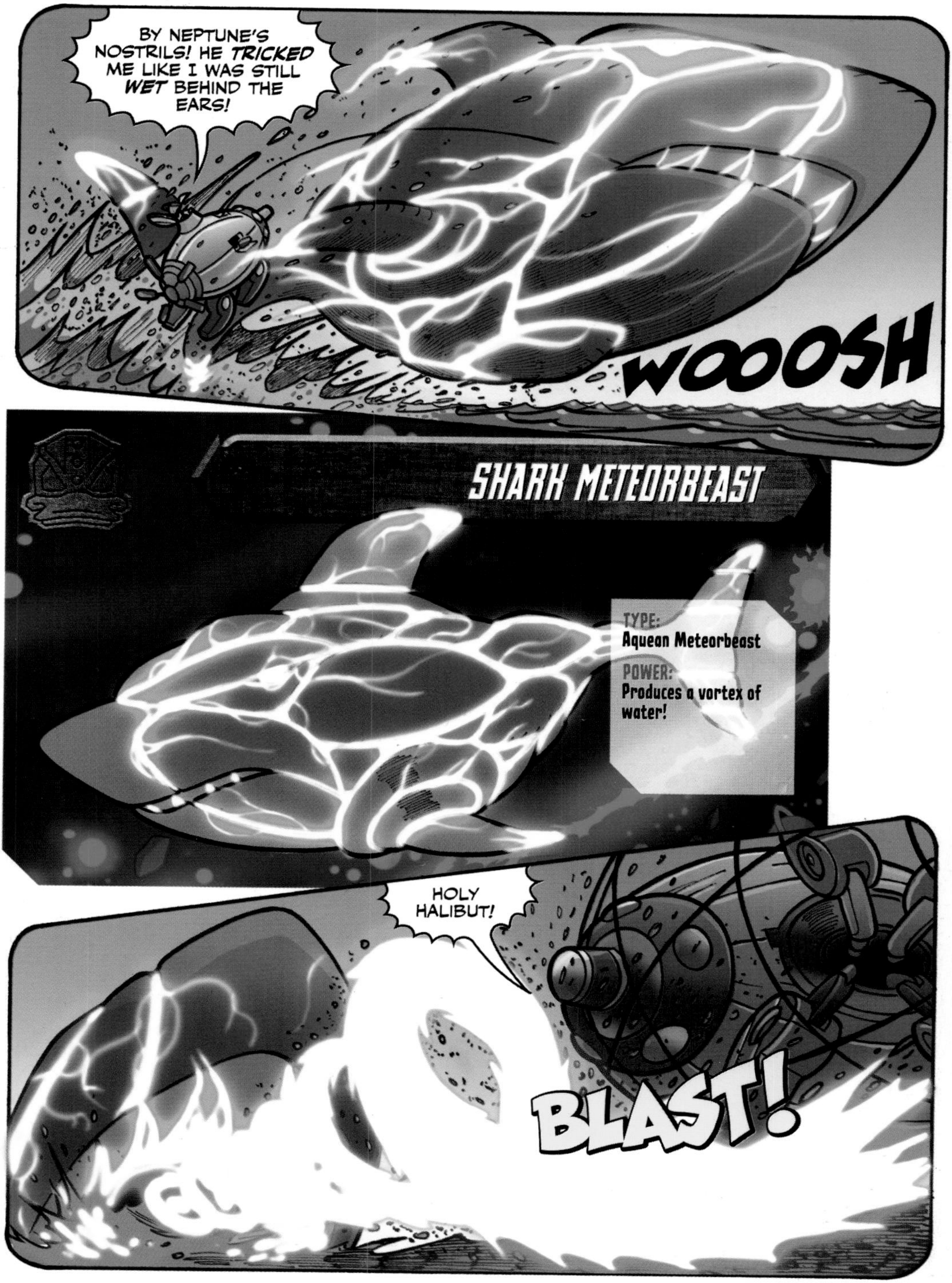

BY NEPTUNE'S NOSTRILS! HE TRICKED ME LIKE I WAS STILL WET BEHIND THE EARS!
WOOOSH
SHARK METEORBEAST
TYPE:
Aquean Meteorbeast
POWER:
Produces a vortex of water!
HOLY HALIBUT!
BLAST!

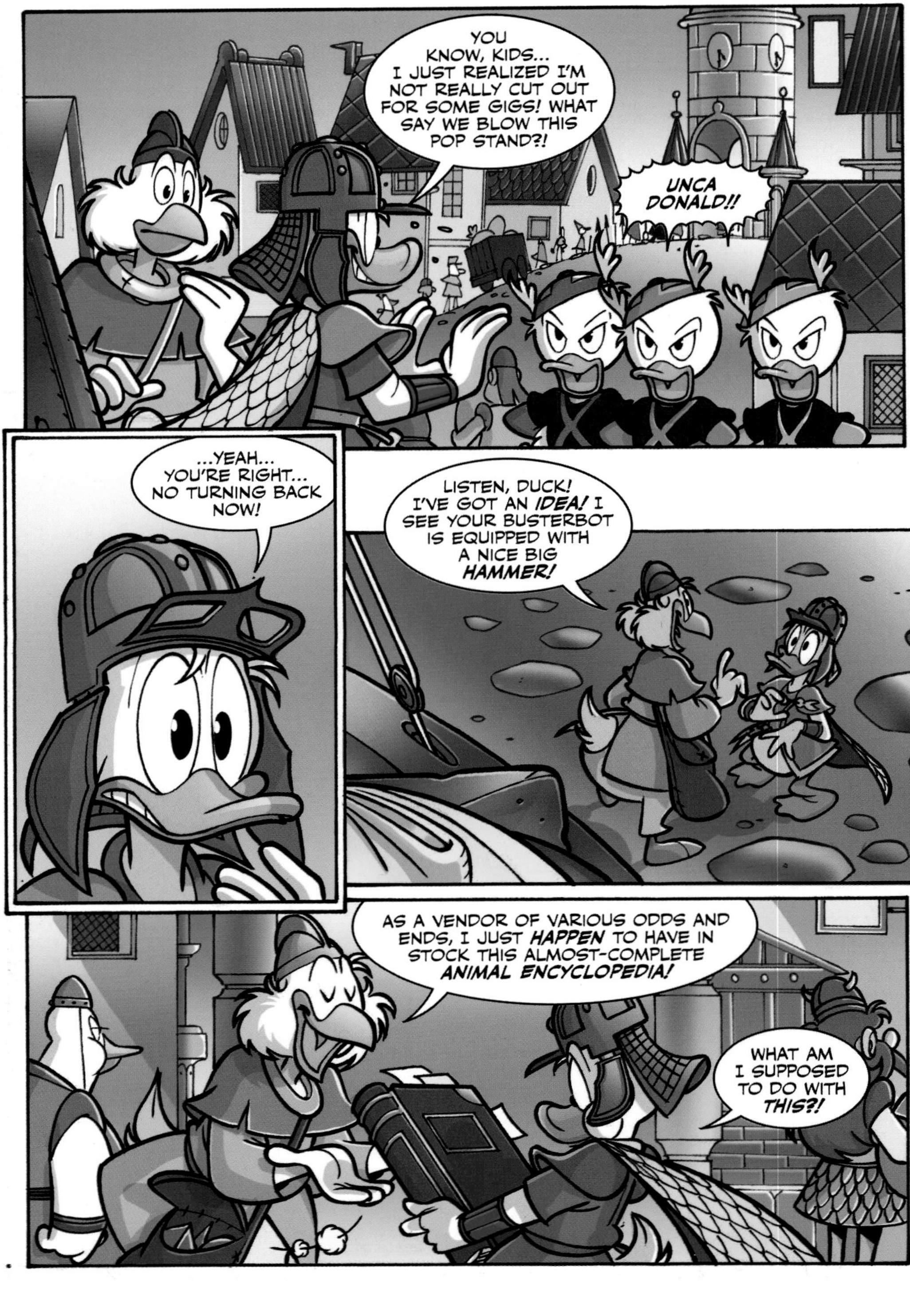
YOU KNOW, KIDS... I JUST REALIZED I'M NOT REALLY CUT OUT FOR SOME GIGS! WHAT SAY WE BLOW THIS POP STAND?!
UNCA DONALD!!
...YEAH... YOU'RE RIGHT... NO TURNING BACK NOW!
LISTEN, DUCK! I'VE GOT AN IDEA! I SEE YOUR BUSTERBOT IS EQUIPPED WITH A NICE BIG HAMMER!
AS A VENDOR OF VARIOUS ODDS AND ENDS, I JUST HAPPEN TO HAVE IN STOCK THIS ALMOST-COMPLETE ANIMAL ENCYCLOPEDIA!
WHAT AM I SUPPOSED TO DO WITH THIS?!

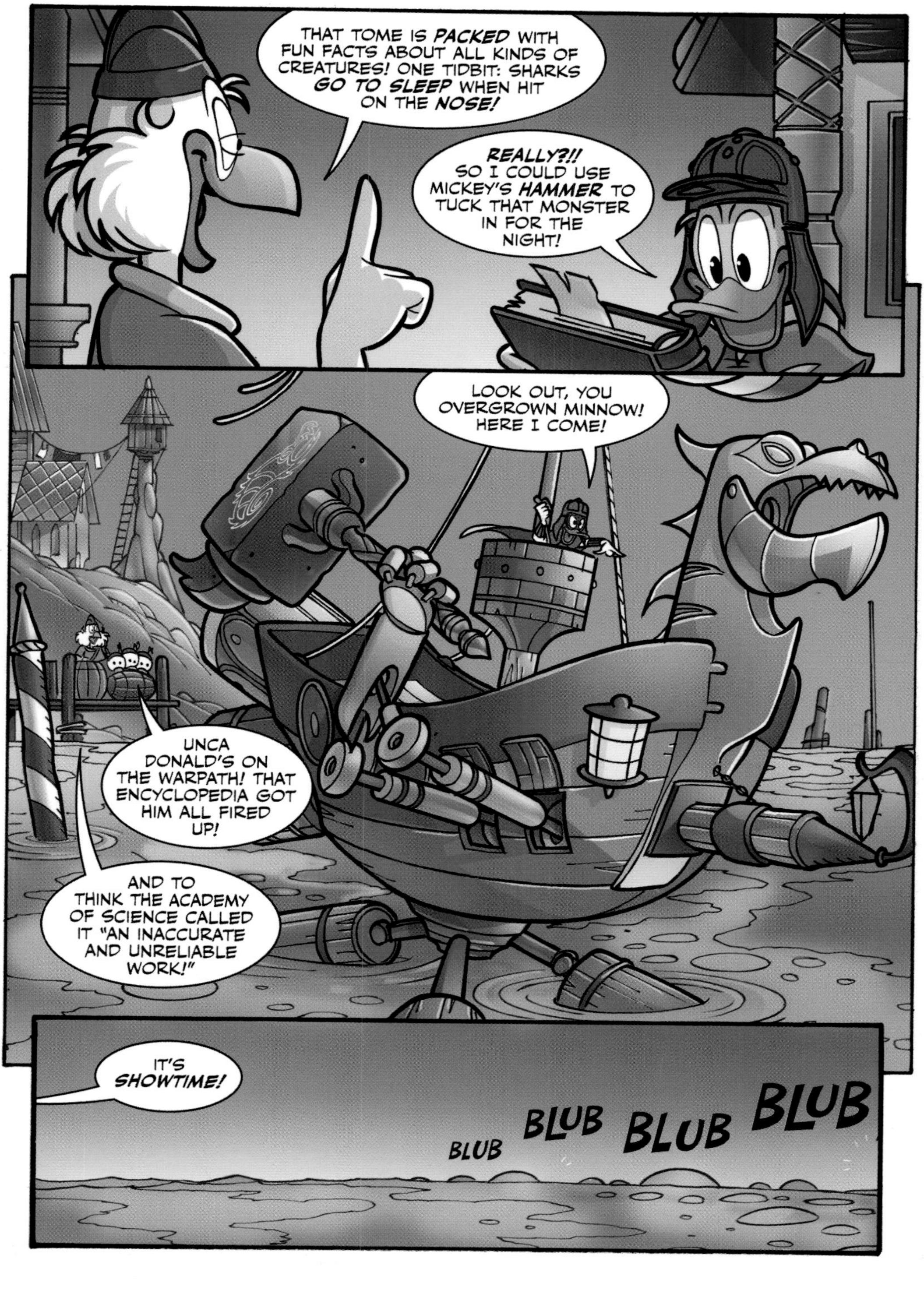
THAT TOME IS PACKED WITH FUN FACTS ABOUT ALL KINDS OF CREATURES! ONE TIDBIT: SHARKS GO TO SLEEP WHEN HIT ON THE NOSE!
REALLY?!! SO I COULD USE MICKEY'S HAMMER TO TUCK THAT MONSTER IN FOR THE NIGHT!
LOOK OUT, YOU OVERGROWN MINNOW! HERE I COME!
UNCA DONALD'S ON THE WARPATH! THAT ENCYCLOPEDIA GOT HIM ALL FIRED UP!
AND TO THINK THE ACADEMY OF SCIENCE CALLED IT "AN INACCURATE AND UNRELIABLE WORK!"
IT'S SHOWTIME!
BLUB BLUB BLUB BLUB

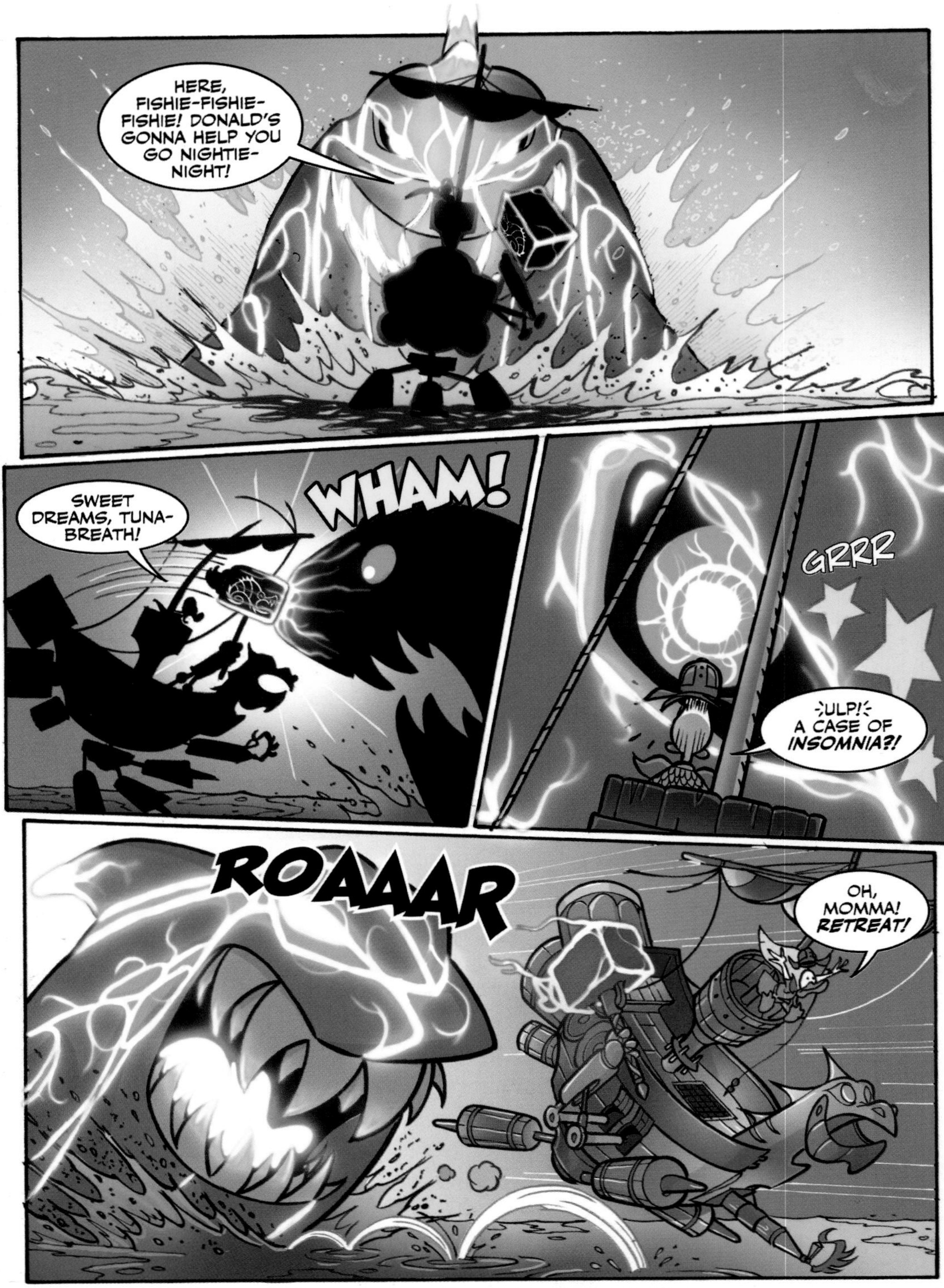

HERE, FISHIE-FISHIE-FISHIE! DONALD'S GONNA HELP YOU GO NIGHTIE-NIGHT!
WHAM!
SWEET DREAMS, TUNA-BREATH!
GRRR
ULP! A CASE OF *INSOMNIA?!*
ROAAAR
OH, MOMMA! *RETREAT!*

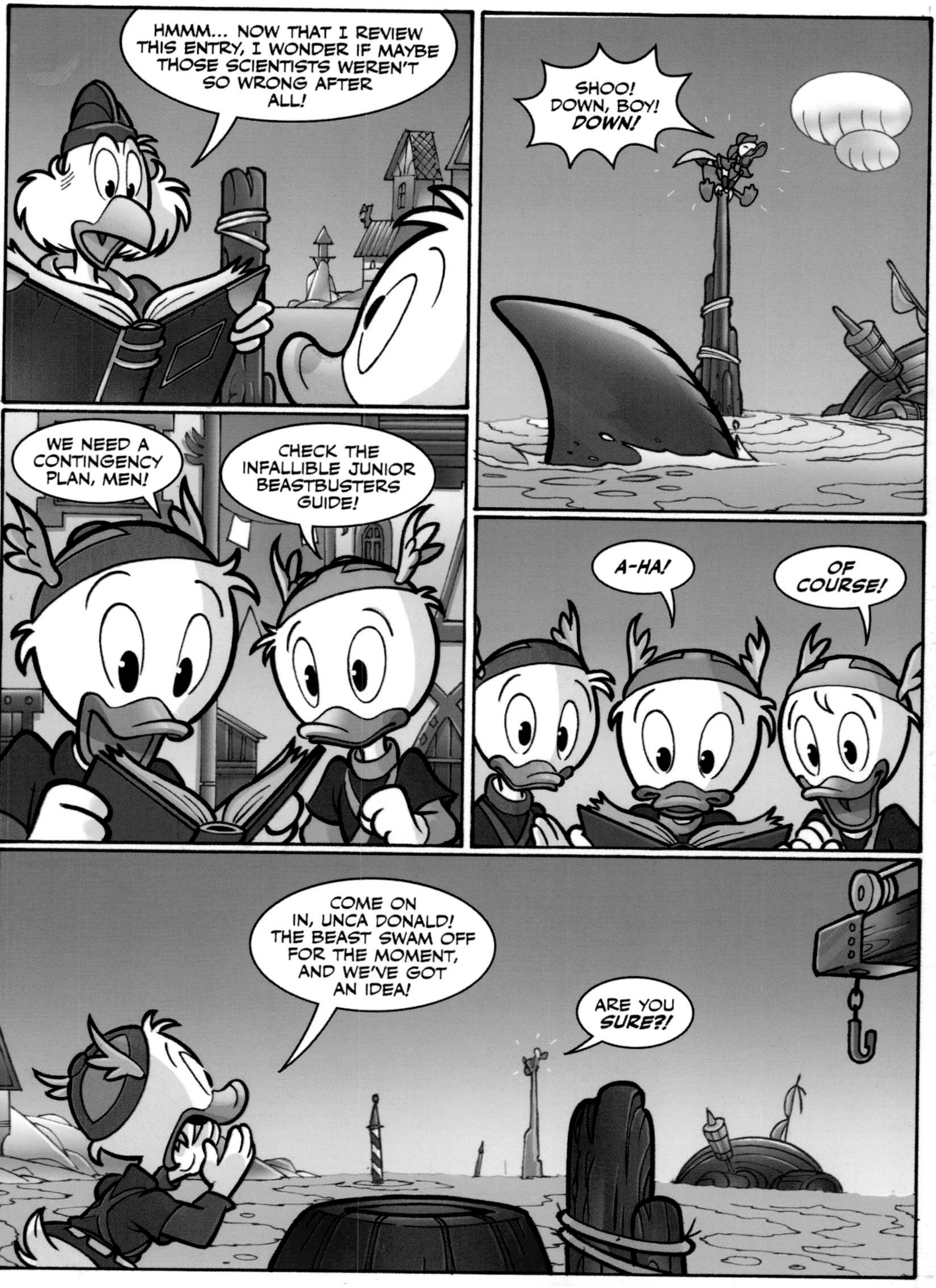
HMMM... NOW THAT I REVIEW THIS ENTRY, I WONDER IF MAYBE THOSE SCIENTISTS WEREN'T SO WRONG AFTER ALL!
SHOO! DOWN, BOY! DOWN!
WE NEED A CONTINGENCY PLAN, MEN!
CHECK THE INFALLIBLE JUNIOR BEASTBUSTERS GUIDE!
A-HA!
OF COURSE!
COME ON IN, UNCA DONALD! THE BEAST SWAM OFF FOR THE MOMENT, AND WE'VE GOT AN IDEA!
ARE YOU SURE?!

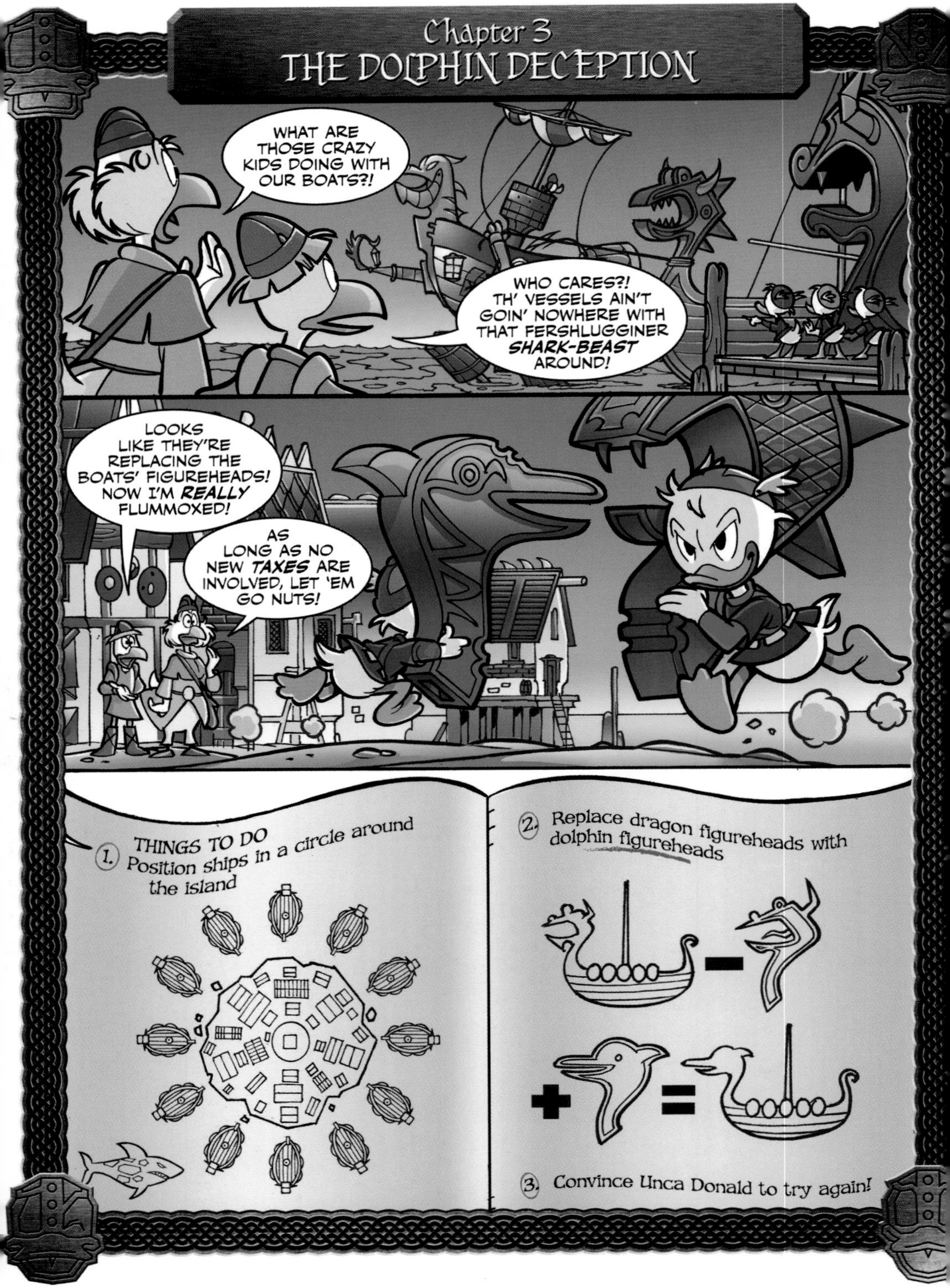
Chapter 3
THE DOLPHIN DECEPTION
WHAT ARE THOSE CRAZY KIDS DOING WITH OUR BOATS?!
WHO CARES?! TH' VESSELS AIN'T GOIN' NOWHERE WITH THAT FERSHLUGGINER SHARK-BEAST AROUND!
LOOKS LIKE THEY'RE REPLACING THE BOATS' FIGUREHEADS! NOW I'M REALLY FLUMMOXED!
AS LONG AS NO NEW TAXES ARE INVOLVED, LET 'EM GO NUTS!
THINGS TO DO
1. Position ships in a circle around the island
2. Replace dragon figureheads with dolphin figureheads
3. Convince Unca Donald to try again!

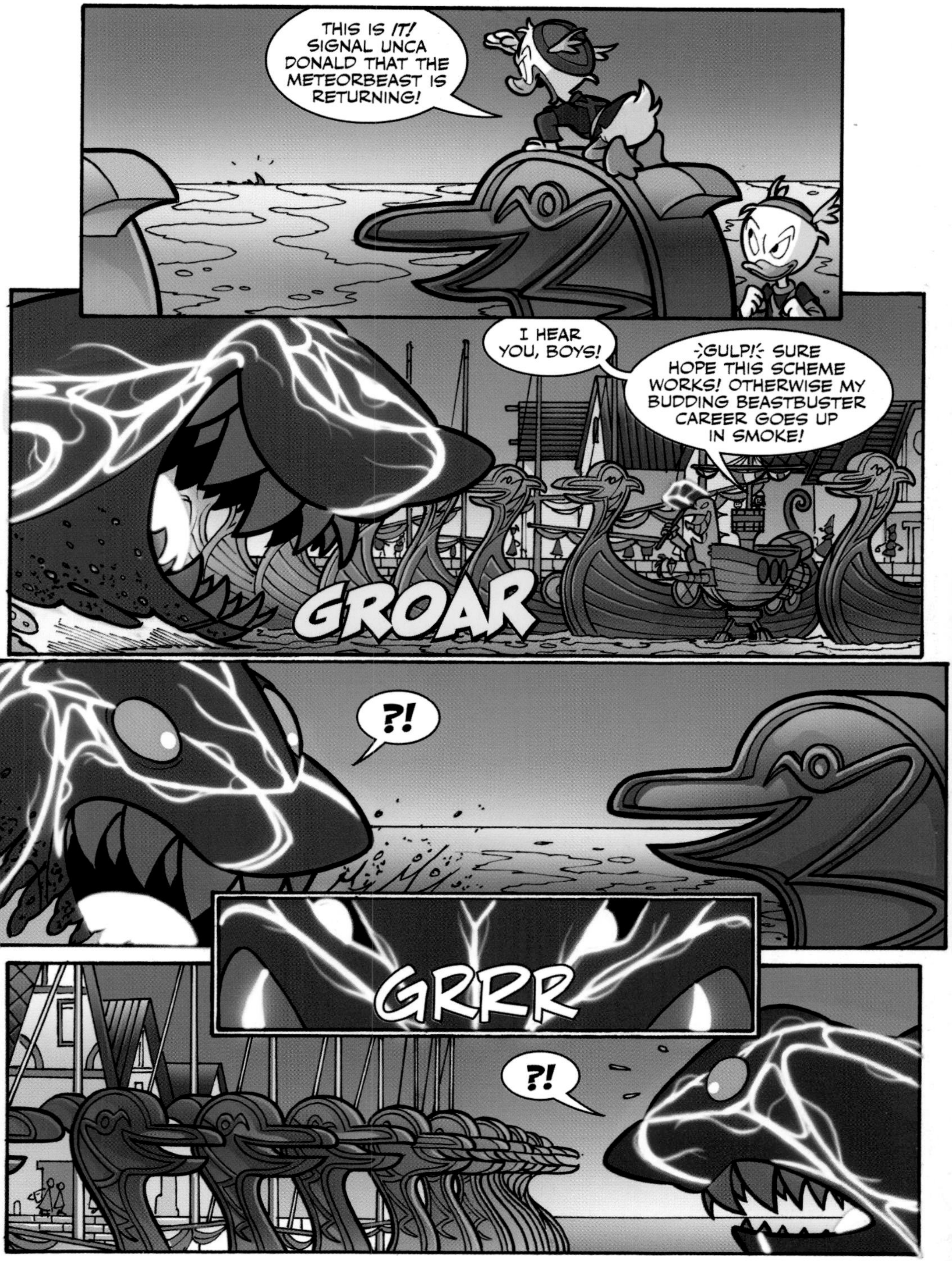
THIS IS IT! SIGNAL UNCA DONALD THAT THE METEORBEAST IS RETURNING!
I HEAR YOU, BOYS!
-GULP!- SURE HOPE THIS SCHEME WORKS! OTHERWISE MY BUDDING BEASTBUSTER CAREER GOES UP IN SMOKE!
GROAR
?!
GRRR
?!

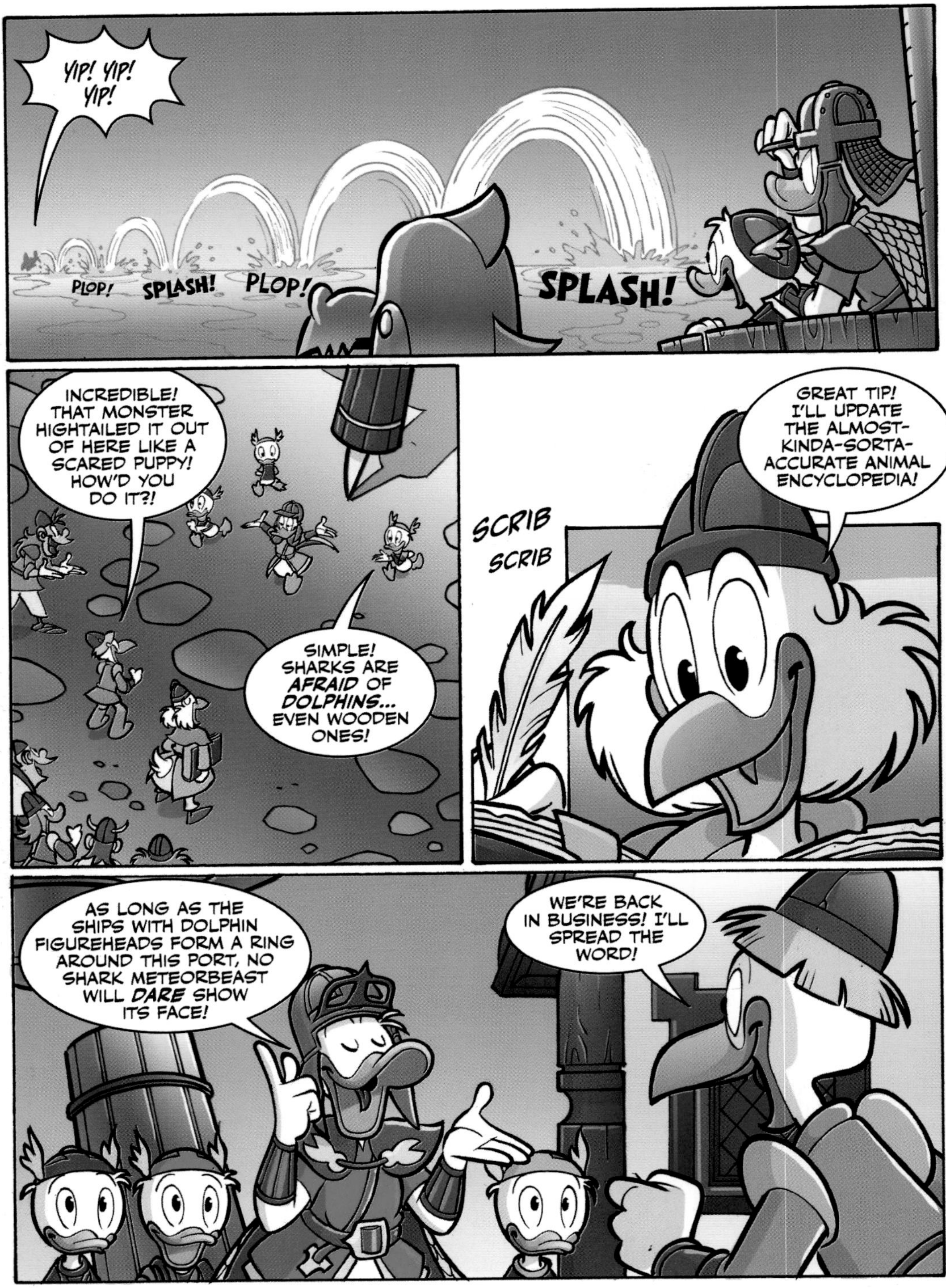
YIP! YIP! YIP!
PLOP!
SPLASH!
PLOP!
SPLASH!
INCREDIBLE! THAT MONSTER HIGHTAILED IT OUT OF HERE LIKE A SCARED PUPPY! HOW'D YOU DO IT?!
SIMPLE! SHARKS ARE AFRAID OF DOLPHINS... EVEN WOODEN ONES!
SCRIB SCRIB
GREAT TIP! I'LL UPDATE THE ALMOST-KINDA-SORTA-ACCURATE ANIMAL ENCYCLOPEDIA!
AS LONG AS THE SHIPS WITH DOLPHIN FIGUREHEADS FORM A RING AROUND THIS PORT, NO SHARK METEORBEAST WILL DARE SHOW ITS FACE!
WE'RE BACK IN BUSINESS! I'LL SPREAD THE WORD!

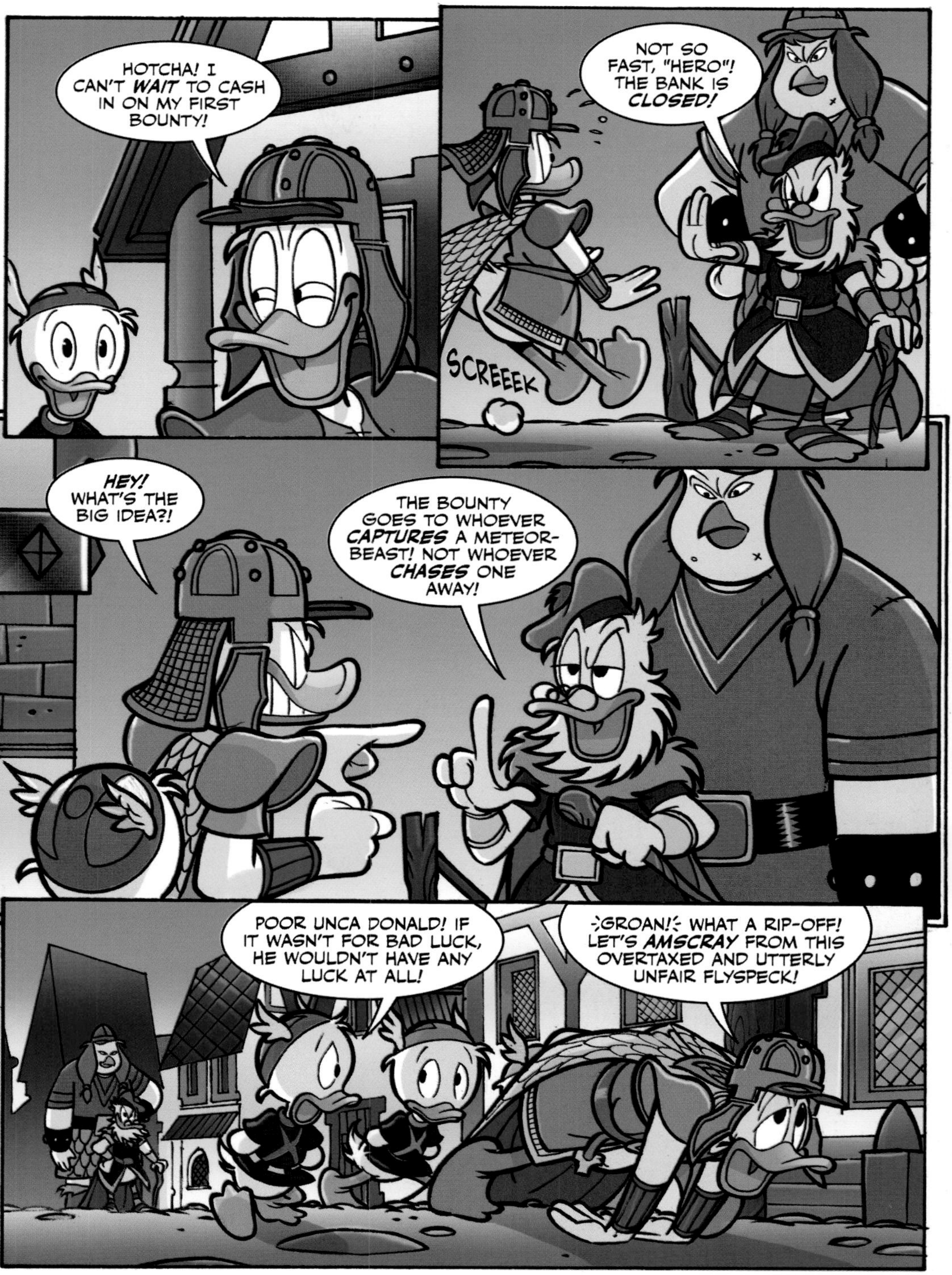
HOTCHA! I CAN'T *WAIT* TO CASH IN ON MY FIRST BOUNTY!
NOT SO FAST, "HERO"! THE BANK IS *CLOSED!*
SCREEEK
HEY! WHAT'S THE BIG IDEA?!
THE BOUNTY GOES TO WHOEVER *CAPTURES* A METEOR-BEAST! NOT WHOEVER *CHASES* ONE AWAY!
POOR UNCA DONALD! IF IT WASN'T FOR BAD LUCK, HE WOULDN'T HAVE ANY LUCK AT ALL!
GROAN! WHAT A RIP-OFF! LET'S *AMSCRAY* FROM THIS OVERTAXED AND UTTERLY UNFAIR FLYSPECK!

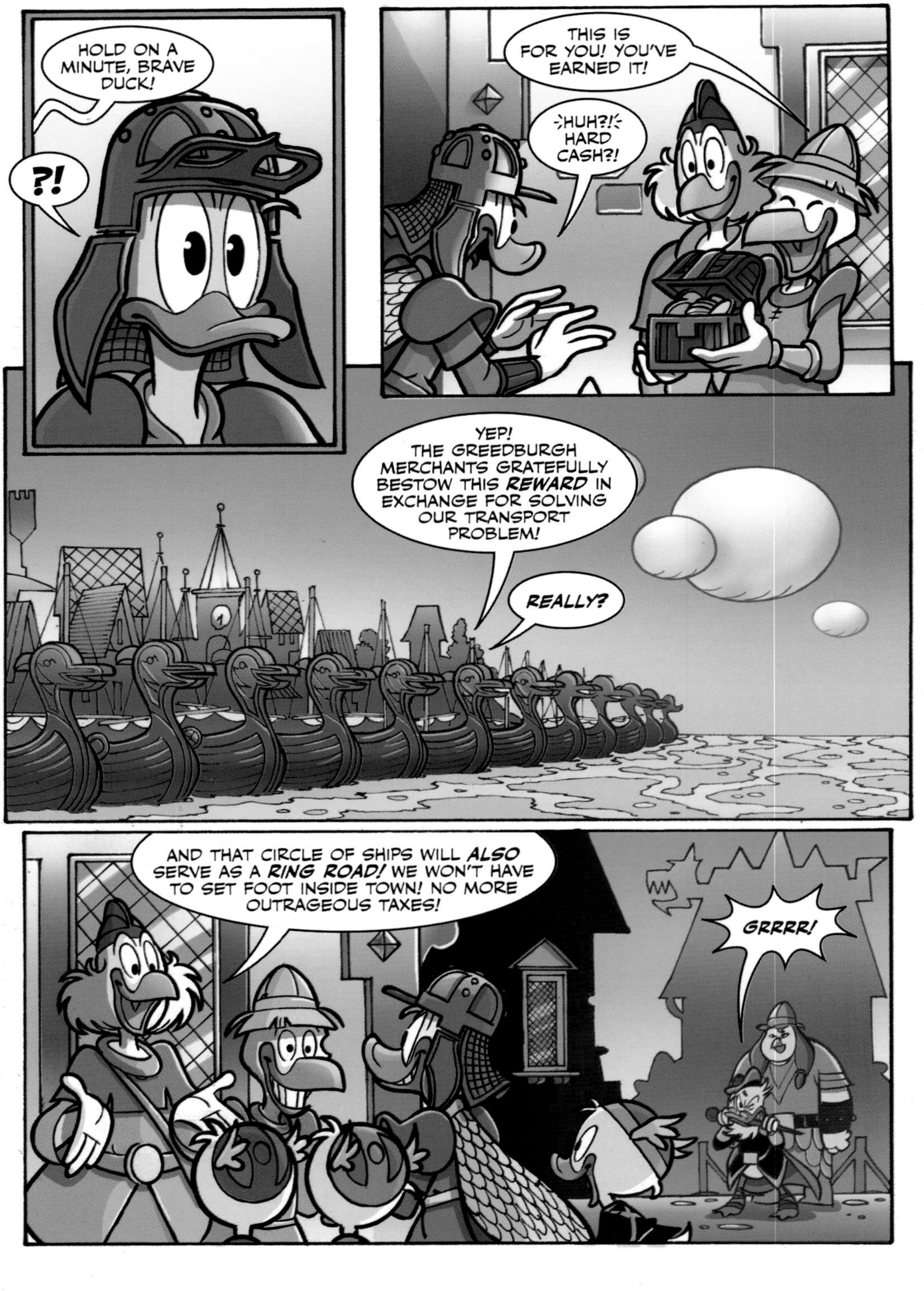
HOLD ON A MINUTE, BRAVE DUCK!
?!
THIS IS FOR YOU! YOU'VE EARNED IT!
HUH?! HARD CASH?!
YEP! THE GREEDBURGH MERCHANTS GRATEFULLY BESTOW THIS REWARD IN EXCHANGE FOR SOLVING OUR TRANSPORT PROBLEM!
REALLY?
AND THAT CIRCLE OF SHIPS WILL ALSO SERVE AS A RING ROAD! WE WON'T HAVE TO SET FOOT INSIDE TOWN! NO MORE OUTRAGEOUS TAXES!
GRRRR!

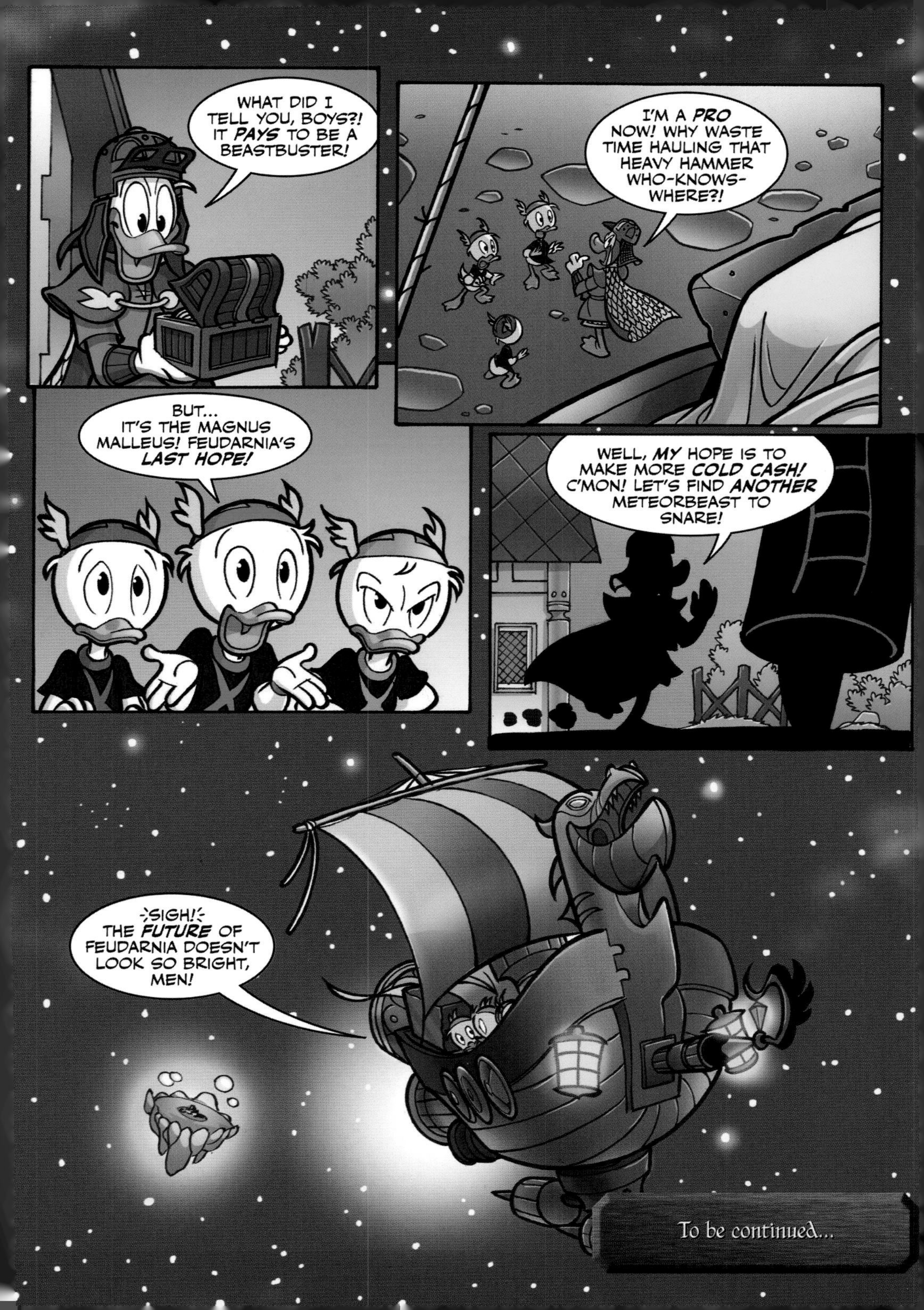
WHAT DID I TELL YOU, BOYS?! IT PAYS TO BE A BEASTBUSTER!
I'M A PRO NOW! WHY WASTE TIME HAULING THAT HEAVY HAMMER WHO-KNOWS-WHERE?!
BUT... IT'S THE MAGNUS MALLEUS! FEUDARNIA'S LAST HOPE!
WELL, MY HOPE IS TO MAKE MORE COLD CASH! C'MON! LET'S FIND ANOTHER METEORBEAST TO SNARE!
SIGH! THE FUTURE OF FEUDARNIA DOESN'T LOOK SO BRIGHT, MEN!
To be continued...

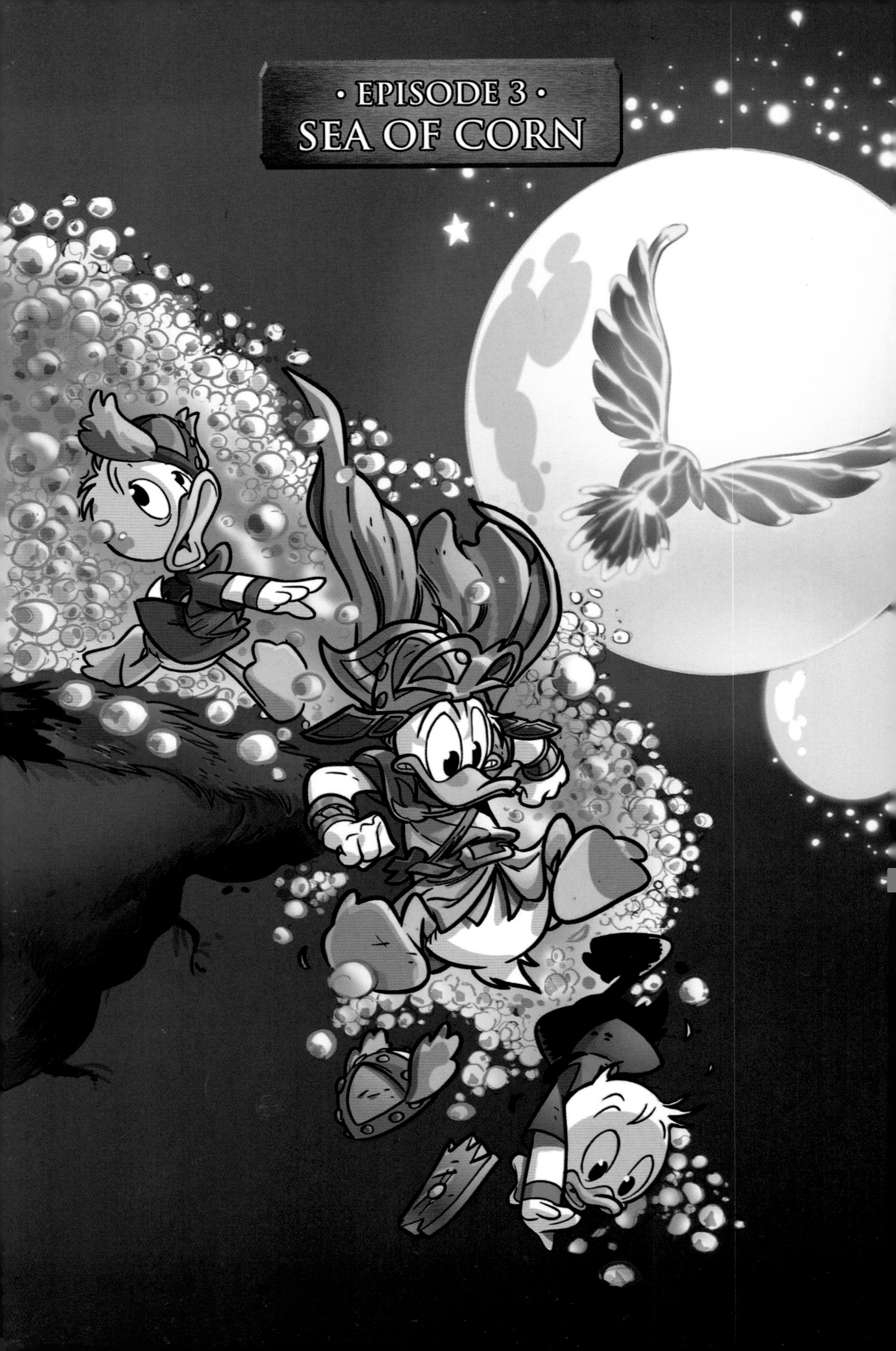
• EPISODE 3 •
SEA OF CORN

Chapter 1
I AM THE CHOSEN ONE!

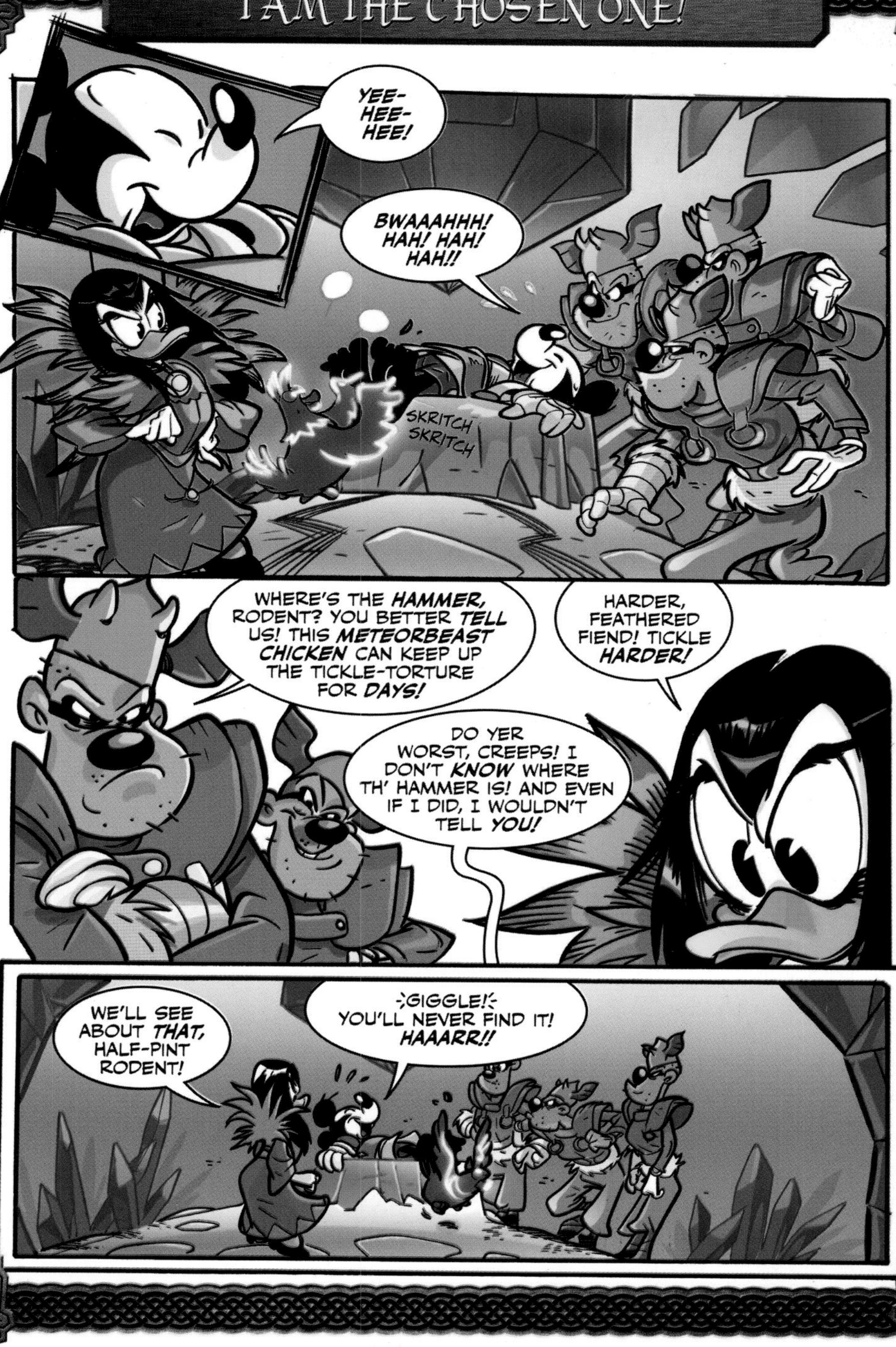
YEE-HEE-HEE!
BWAAAHHH! HAH! HAH! HAH!!
SKRITCH SKRITCH
WHERE'S THE HAMMER, RODENT? YOU BETTER TELL US! THIS METEORBEAST CHICKEN CAN KEEP UP THE TICKLE-TORTURE FOR DAYS!
HARDER, FEATHERED FIEND! TICKLE HARDER!
DO YER WORST, CREEPS! I DON'T KNOW WHERE TH' HAMMER IS! AND EVEN IF I DID, I WOULDN'T TELL YOU!
WE'LL SEE ABOUT THAT, HALF-PINT RODENT!
GIGGLE! YOU'LL NEVER FIND IT! HAAARR!!

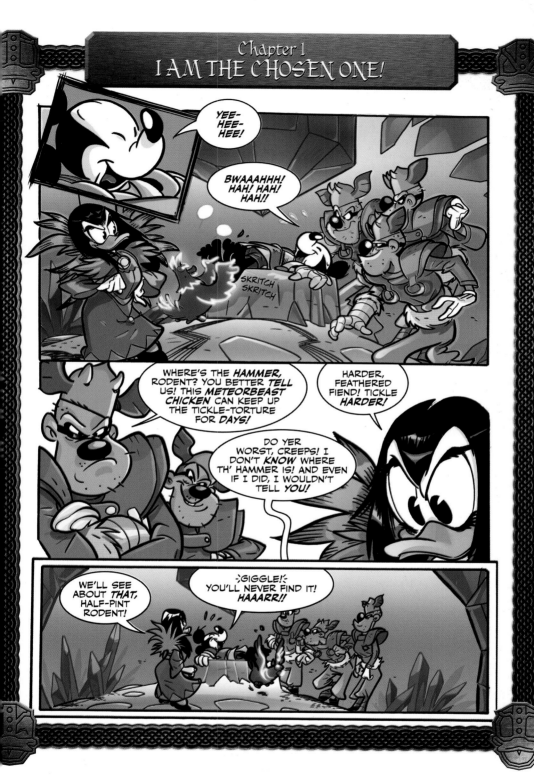

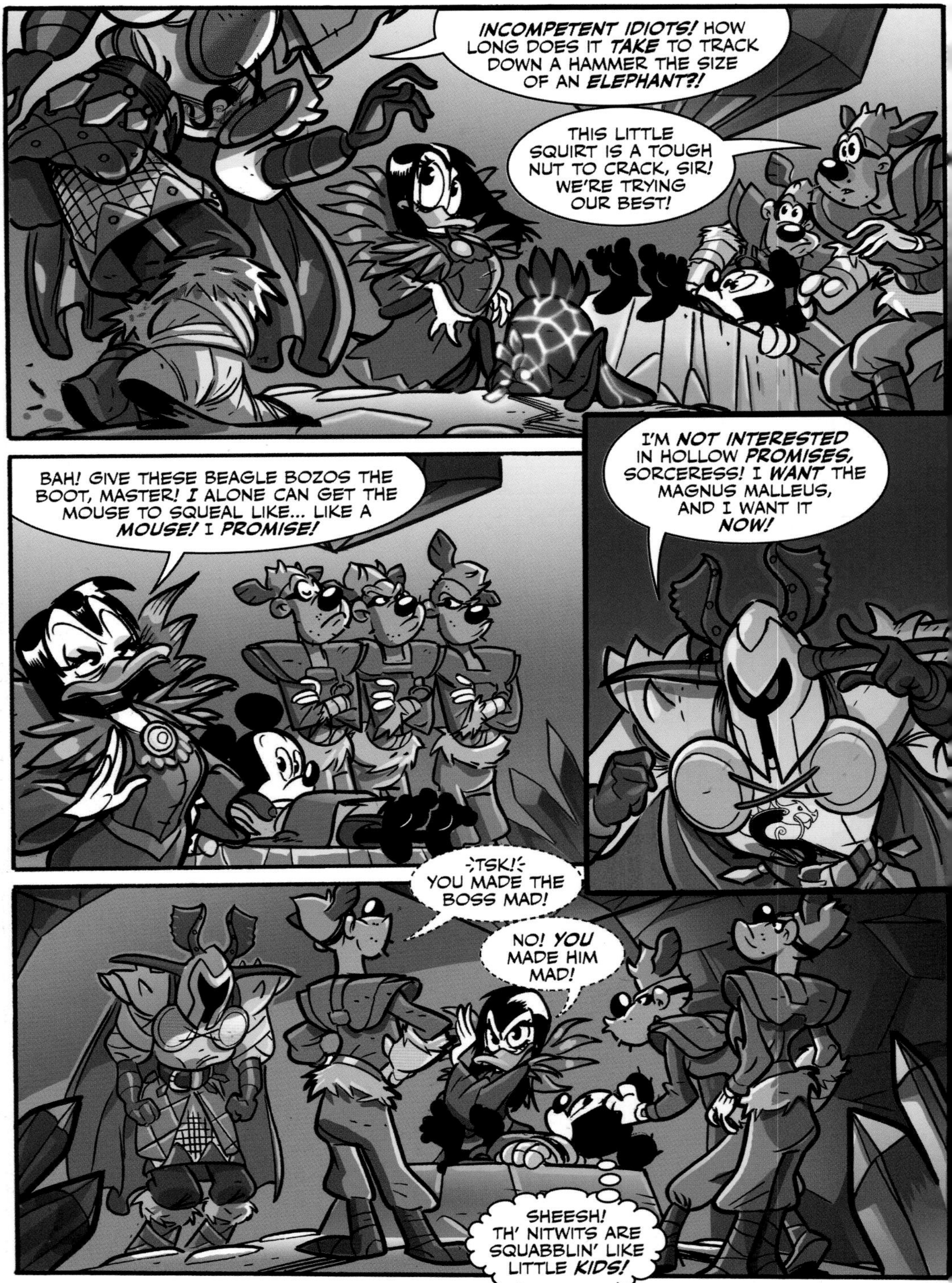
INCOMPETENT IDIOTS! HOW LONG DOES IT TAKE TO TRACK DOWN A HAMMER THE SIZE OF AN ELEPHANT?!
THIS LITTLE SQUIRT IS A TOUGH NUT TO CRACK, SIR! WE'RE TRYING OUR BEST!
BAH! GIVE THESE BEAGLE BOZOS THE BOOT, MASTER! I ALONE CAN GET THE MOUSE TO SQUEAL LIKE... LIKE A MOUSE! I PROMISE!
I'M NOT INTERESTED IN HOLLOW PROMISES, SORCERESS! I WANT THE MAGNUS MALLEUS, AND I WANT IT NOW!
TSK! YOU MADE THE BOSS MAD!
NO! YOU MADE HIM MAD!
SHEESH! TH' NITWITS ARE SQUABBLIN' LIKE LITTLE KIDS!

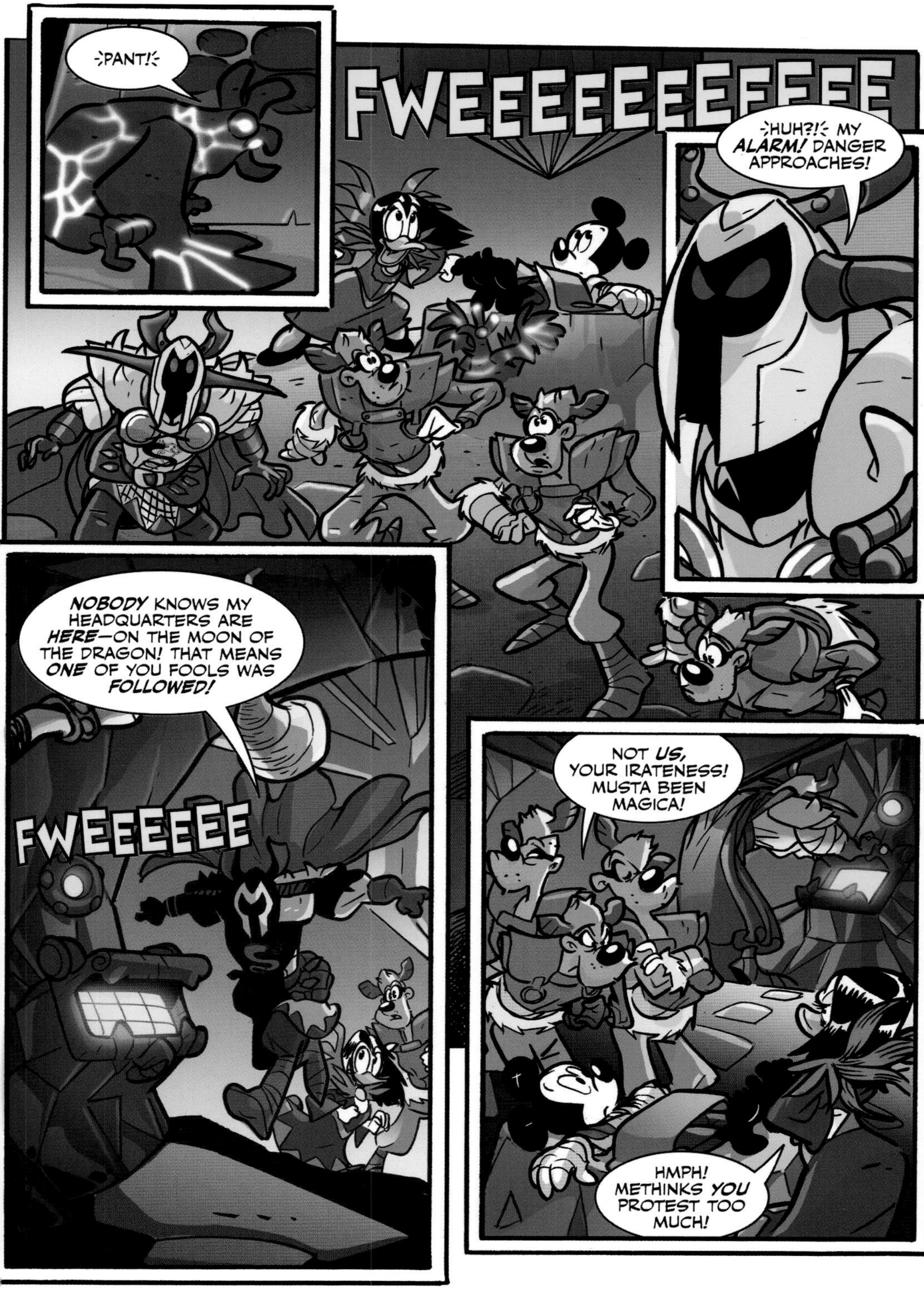

-PANT!-
FWEEEEEEEEEEEE
-HUH?!- MY ALARM! DANGER APPROACHES!
NOBODY KNOWS MY HEADQUARTERS ARE HERE—ON THE MOON OF THE DRAGON! THAT MEANS ONE OF YOU FOOLS WAS FOLLOWED!
FWEEEEEE
NOT US, YOUR IRATENESS! MUSTA BEEN MAGICA!
HMPH! METHINKS YOU PROTEST TOO MUCH!

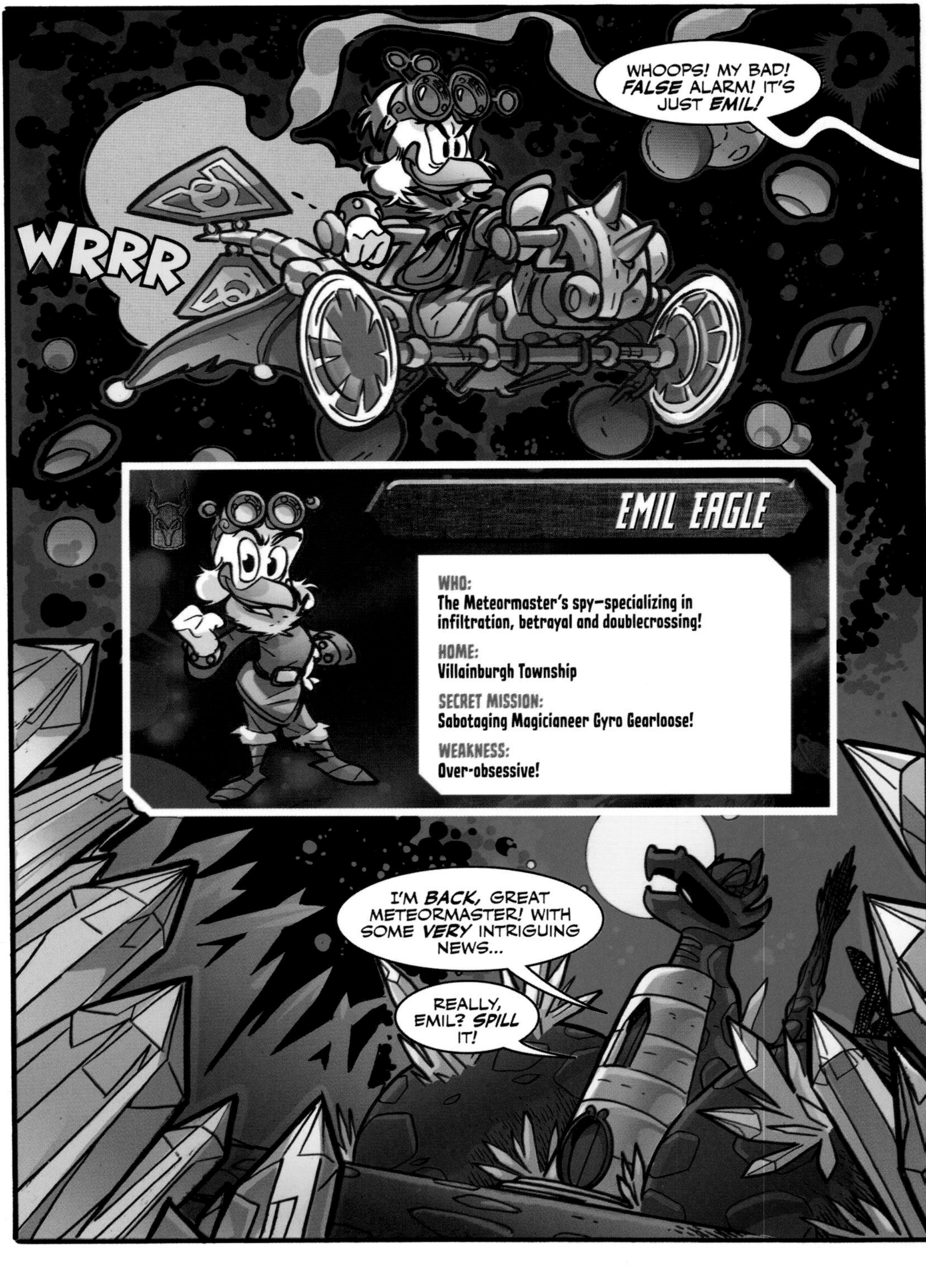

WHOOPS! MY BAD! FALSE ALARM! IT'S JUST EMIL!
WRRR
EMIL EAGLE
WHO:
The Meteormaster's spy—specializing in infiltration, betrayal and doublecrossing!
HOME:
Villainburgh Township
SECRET MISSION:
Sabotaging Magicianeer Gyro Gearloose!
WEAKNESS:
Over-obsessive!
I'M BACK, GREAT METEORMASTER! WITH SOME VERY INTRIGUING NEWS...
REALLY, EMIL? SPILL IT!

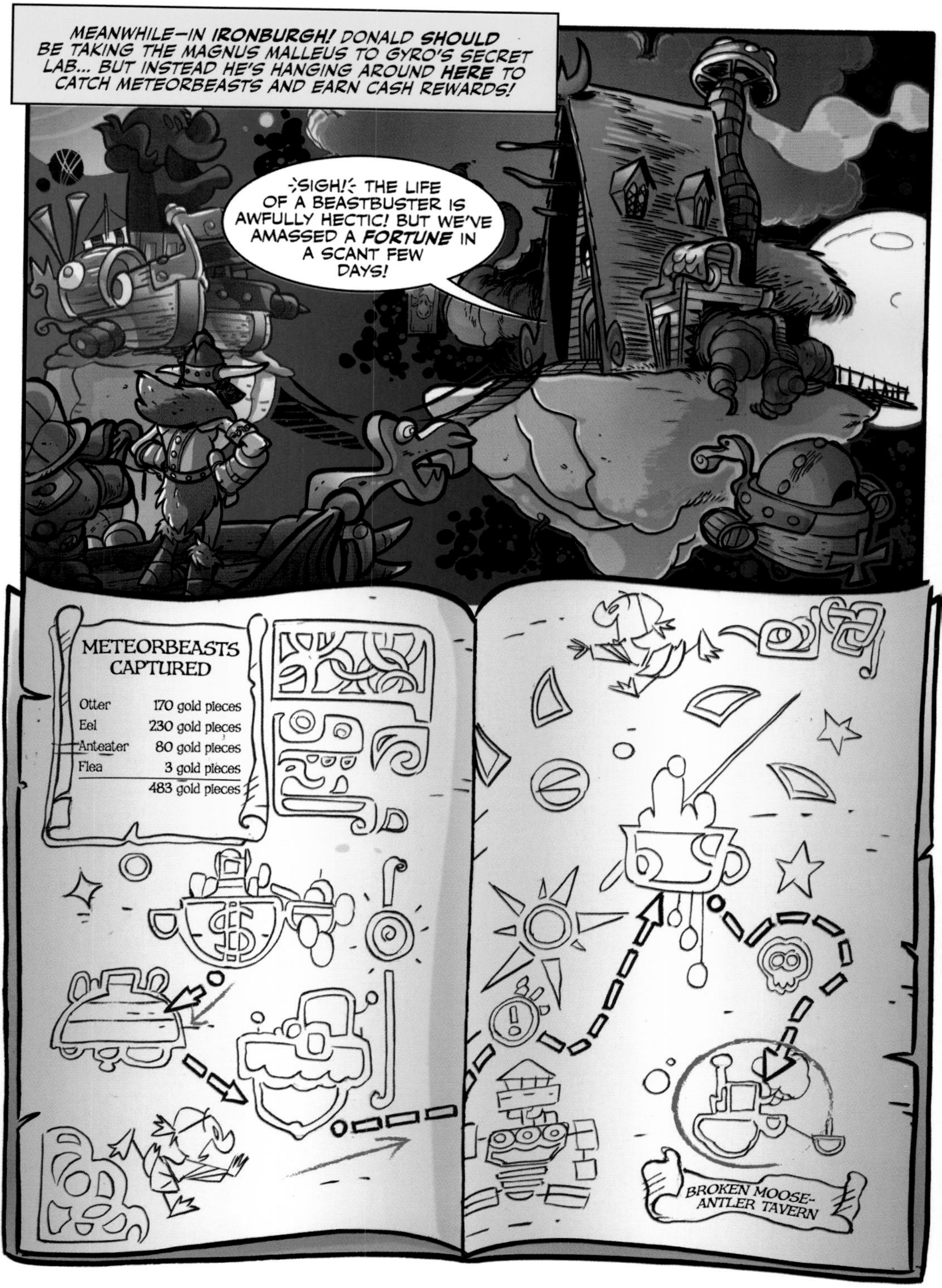
MEANWHILE—IN IRONBURGH! DONALD SHOULD BE TAKING THE MAGNUS MALLEUS TO GYRO'S SECRET LAB... BUT INSTEAD HE'S HANGING AROUND HERE TO CATCH METEORBEASTS AND EARN CASH REWARDS!
SIGH! THE LIFE OF A BEASTBUSTER IS AWFULLY HECTIC! BUT WE'VE AMASSED A FORTUNE IN A SCANT FEW DAYS!
METEORBEASTS CAPTURED
Otter 170 gold pieces
Eel 230 gold pieces
Anteater 80 gold pieces
Flea 3 gold pieces
483 gold pieces
BROKEN MOOSE-ANTLER TAVERN

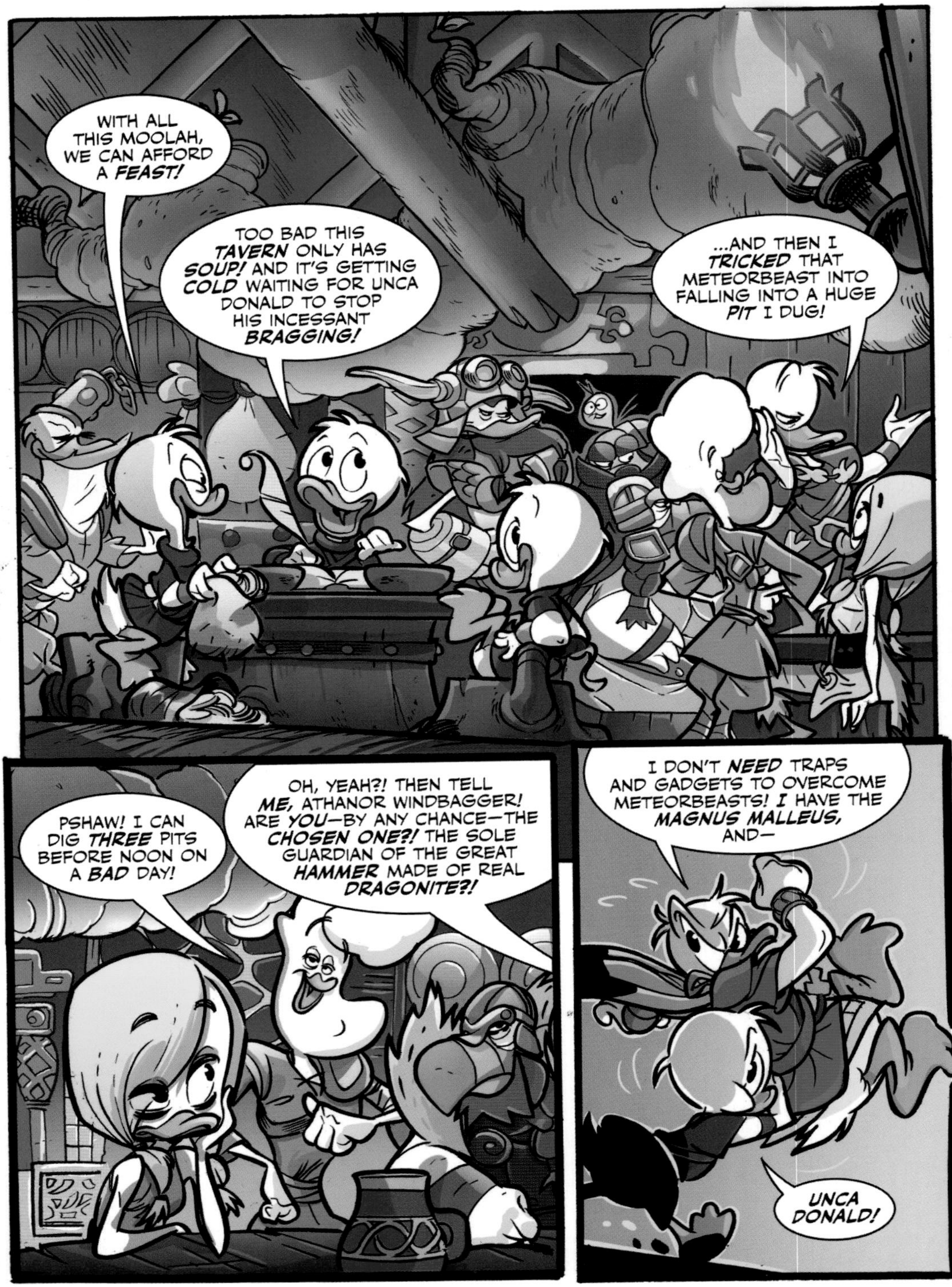
WITH ALL THIS MOOLAH, WE CAN AFFORD A FEAST!
TOO BAD THIS TAVERN ONLY HAS SOUP! AND IT'S GETTING COLD WAITING FOR UNCA DONALD TO STOP HIS INCESSANT BRAGGING!
...AND THEN I TRICKED THAT METEORBEAST INTO FALLING INTO A HUGE PIT I DUG!
PSHAW! I CAN DIG THREE PITS BEFORE NOON ON A BAD DAY!
OH, YEAH?! THEN TELL ME, ATHANOR WINDBAGGER! ARE YOU—BY ANY CHANCE—THE CHOSEN ONE?! THE SOLE GUARDIAN OF THE GREAT HAMMER MADE OF REAL DRAGONITE?!
I DON'T NEED TRAPS AND GADGETS TO OVERCOME METEORBEASTS! I HAVE THE MAGNUS MALLEUS, AND—
UNCA DONALD!

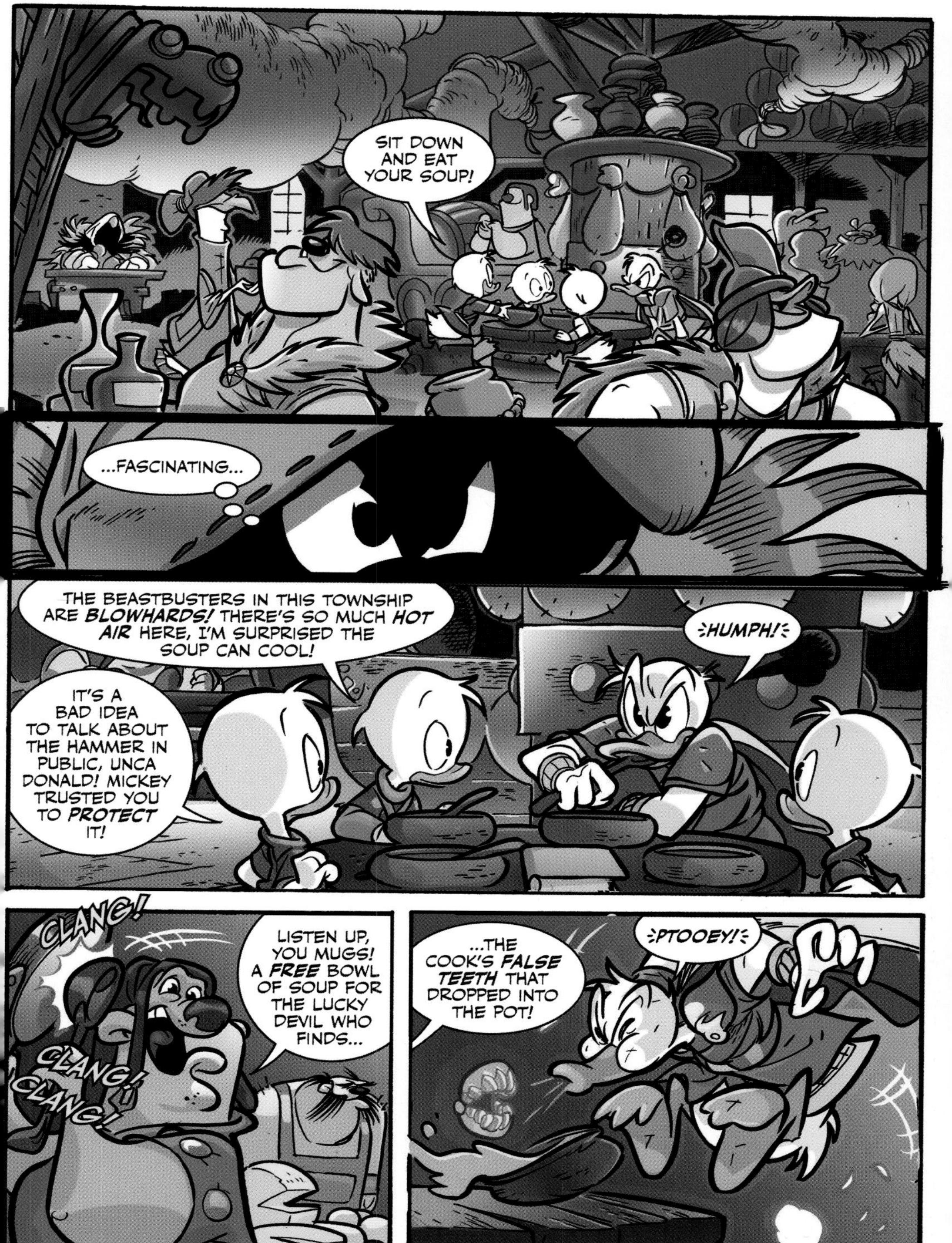
SIT DOWN AND EAT YOUR SOUP!
...FASCINATING...
THE BEASTBUSTERS IN THIS TOWNSHIP ARE BLOWHARDS! THERE'S SO MUCH HOT AIR HERE, I'M SURPRISED THE SOUP CAN COOL!
HUMPH!
IT'S A BAD IDEA TO TALK ABOUT THE HAMMER IN PUBLIC, UNCA DONALD! MICKEY TRUSTED YOU TO PROTECT IT!
CLANG!
CLANG! CLANG!
LISTEN UP, YOU MUGS! A FREE BOWL OF SOUP FOR THE LUCKY DEVIL WHO FINDS...
...THE COOK'S FALSE TEETH THAT DROPPED INTO THE POT!
PTOOEY!

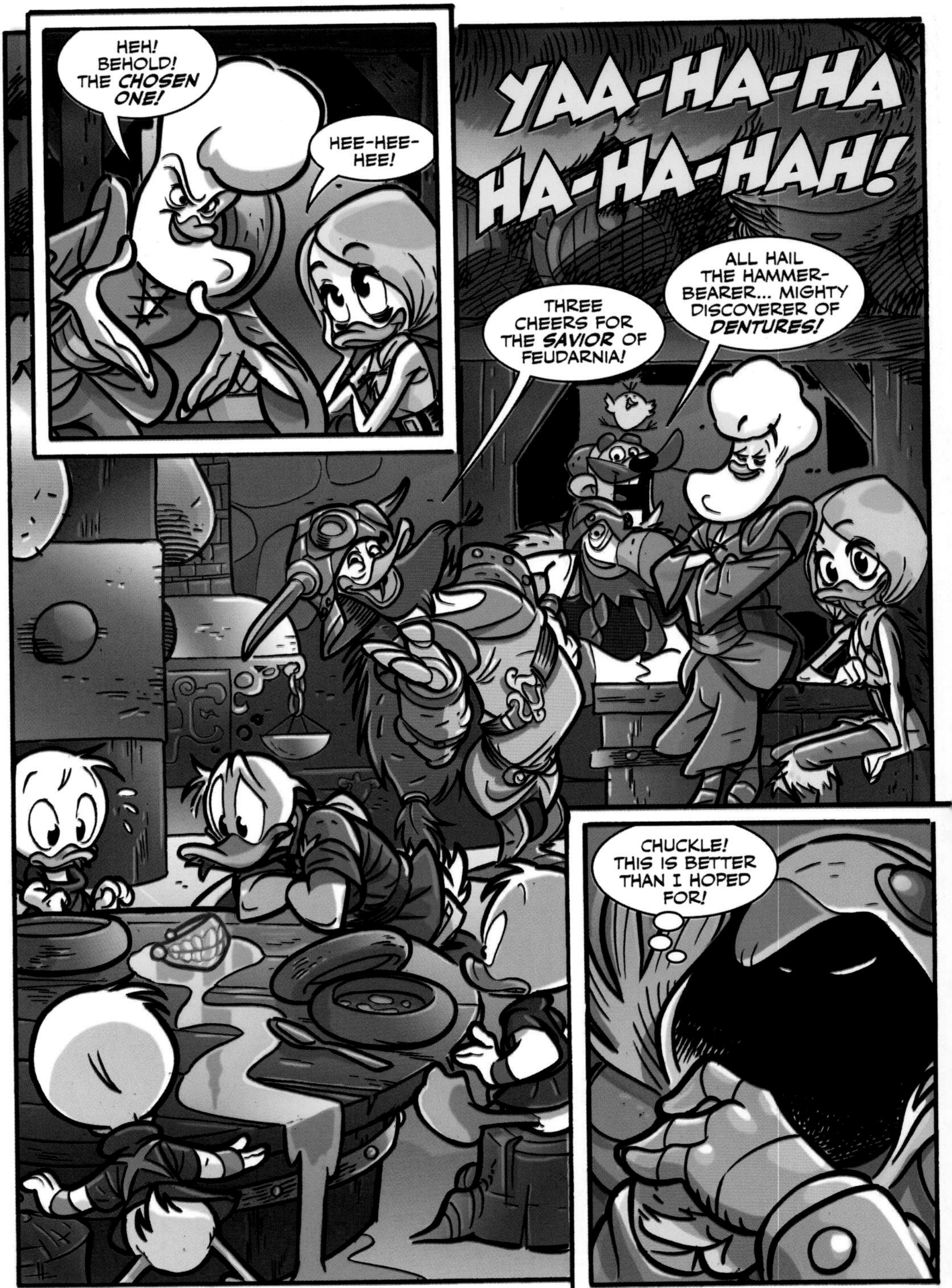
HEH! BEHOLD! THE *CHOSEN ONE!*
HEE-HEE-HEE!
YAA-HA-HA HA-HA-HAH!
THREE CHEERS FOR THE *SAVIOR* OF FEUDARNIA!
ALL HAIL THE HAMMER-BEARER... MIGHTY DISCOVERER OF *DENTURES!*
CHUCKLE! THIS IS BETTER THAN I HOPED FOR!

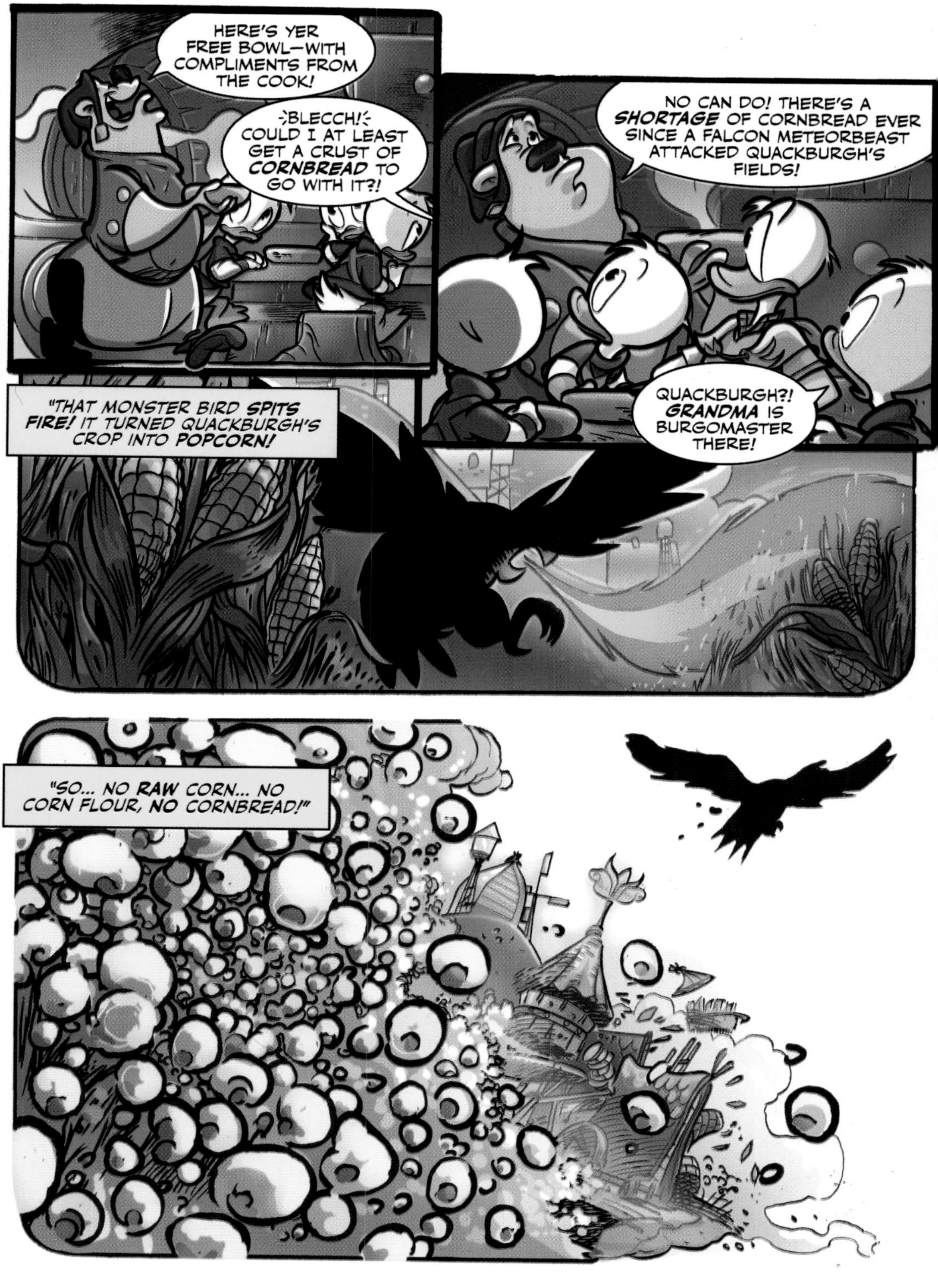
HERE'S YER FREE BOWL—WITH COMPLIMENTS FROM THE COOK!
BLECCH! COULD I AT LEAST GET A CRUST OF CORNBREAD TO GO WITH IT?!
NO CAN DO! THERE'S A SHORTAGE OF CORNBREAD EVER SINCE A FALCON METEORBEAST ATTACKED QUACKBURGH'S FIELDS!
QUACKBURGH?! GRANDMA IS BURGOMASTER THERE!
"THAT MONSTER BIRD SPITS FIRE! IT TURNED QUACKBURGH'S CROP INTO POPCORN!
"SO... NO RAW CORN... NO CORN FLOUR, NO CORNBREAD!"

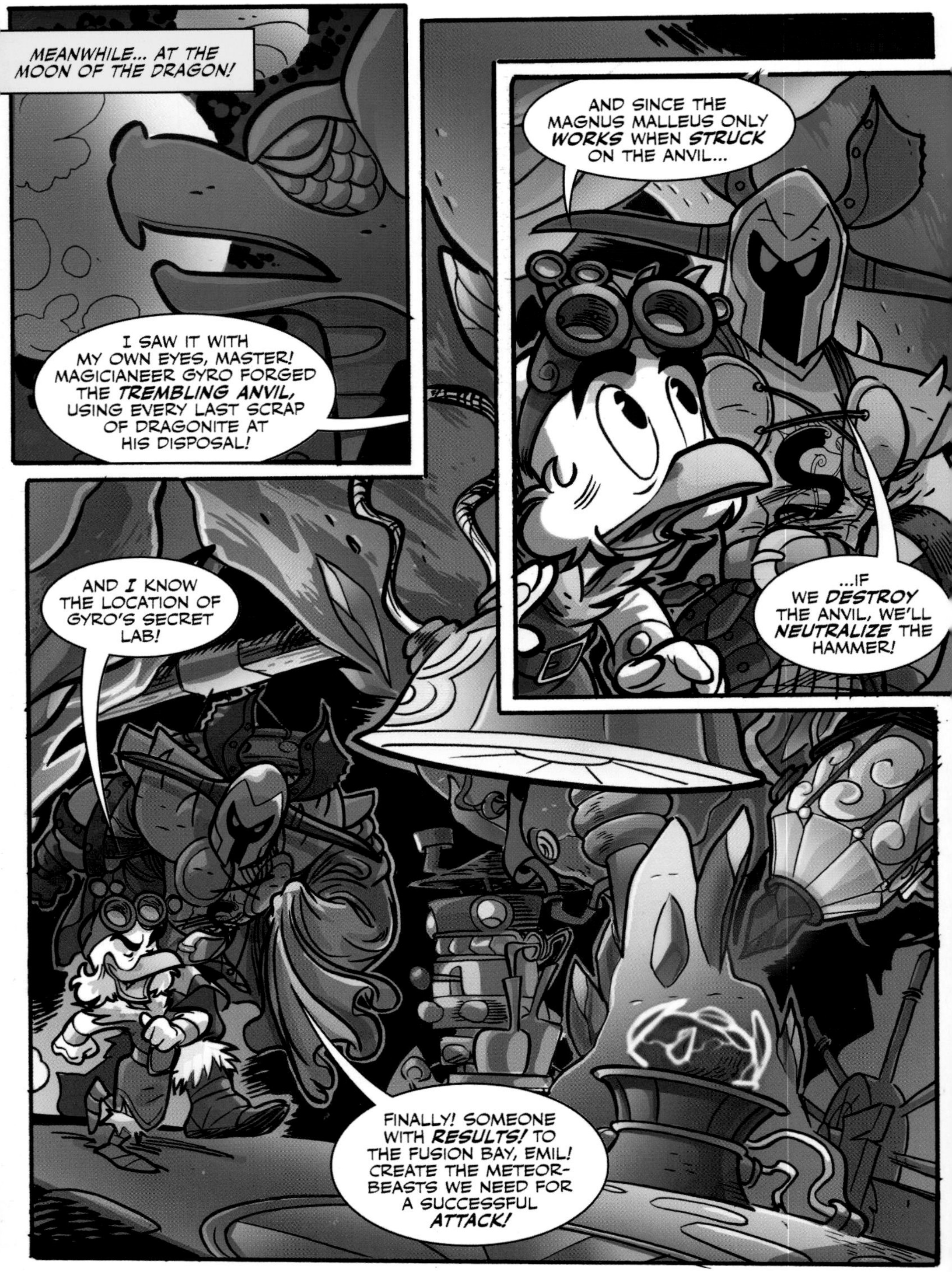

MEANWHILE... AT THE MOON OF THE DRAGON!
I SAW IT WITH MY OWN EYES, MASTER! MAGICIANEER GYRO FORGED THE TREMBLING ANVIL, USING EVERY LAST SCRAP OF DRAGONITE AT HIS DISPOSAL!
AND SINCE THE MAGNUS MALLEUS ONLY WORKS WHEN STRUCK ON THE ANVIL...
...IF WE DESTROY THE ANVIL, WE'LL NEUTRALIZE THE HAMMER!
AND I KNOW THE LOCATION OF GYRO'S SECRET LAB!
FINALLY! SOMEONE WITH RESULTS! TO THE FUSION BAY, EMIL! CREATE THE METEOR-BEASTS WE NEED FOR A SUCCESSFUL ATTACK!

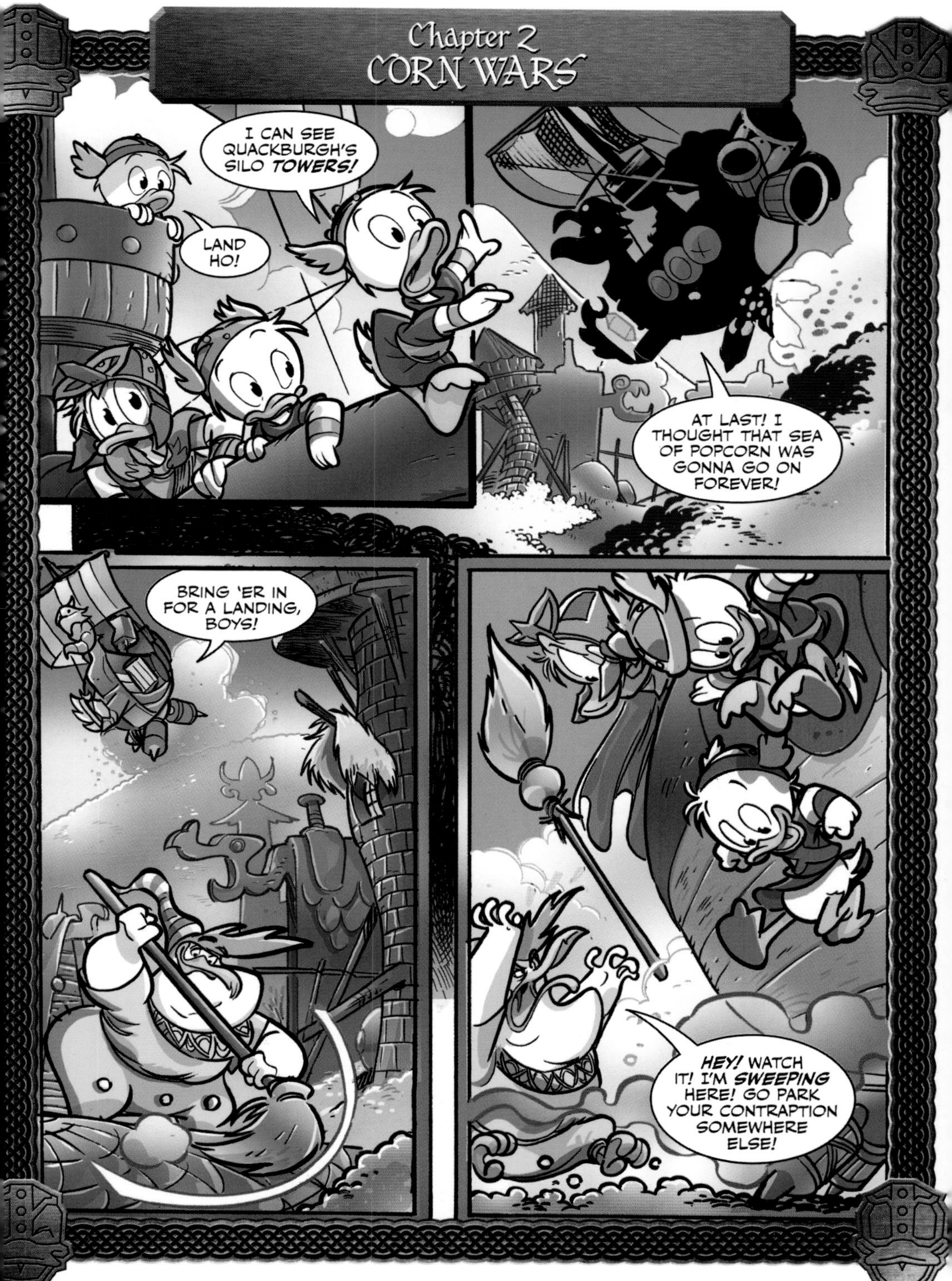
Chapter 2
CORN WARS
I CAN SEE QUACKBURGH'S SILO TOWERS!
LAND HO!
AT LAST! I THOUGHT THAT SEA OF POPCORN WAS GONNA GO ON FOREVER!
BRING 'ER IN FOR A LANDING, BOYS!
HEY! WATCH IT! I'M SWEEPING HERE! GO PARK YOUR CONTRAPTION SOMEWHERE ELSE!

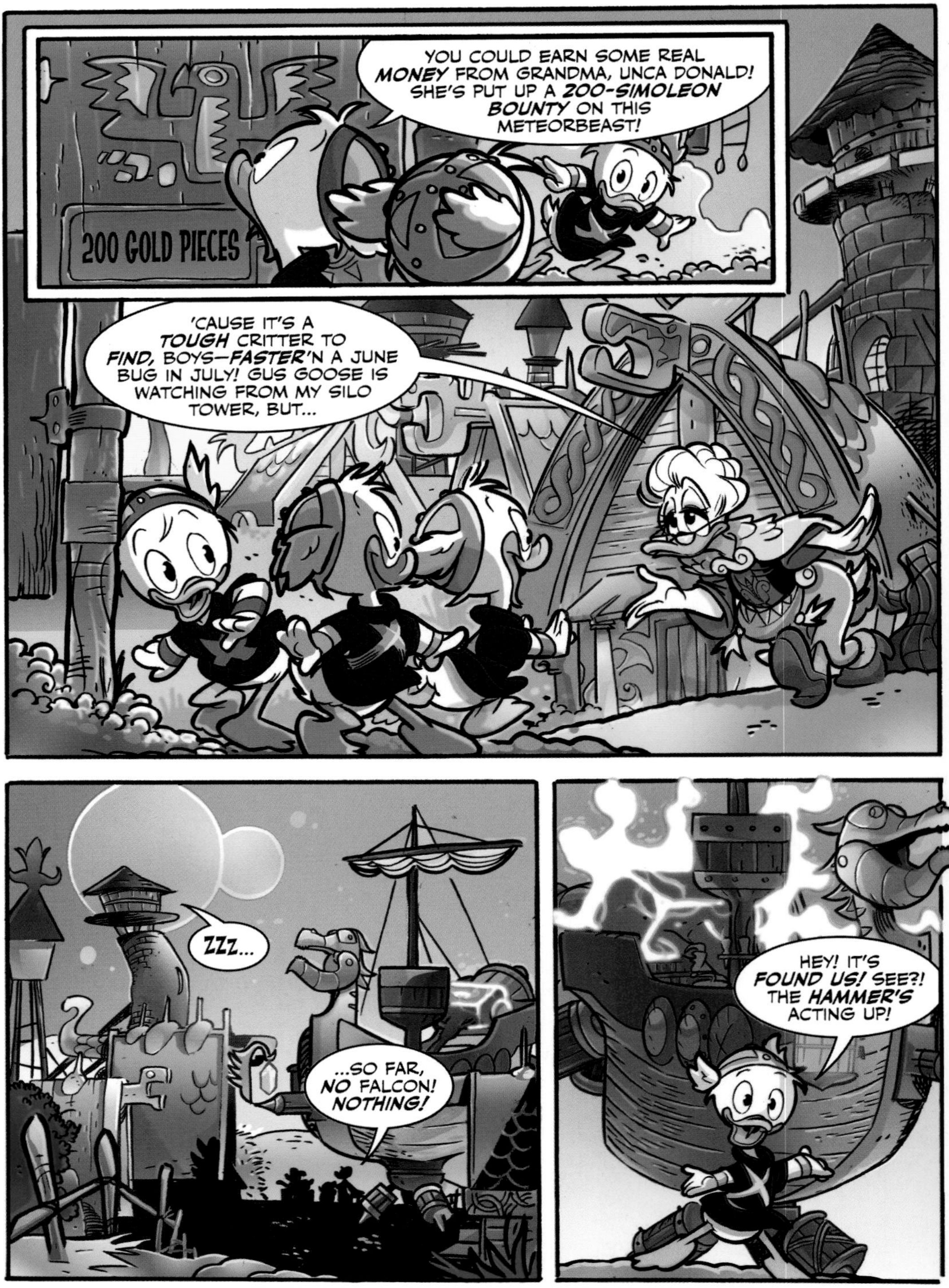
200 GOLD PIECES
YOU COULD EARN SOME REAL MONEY FROM GRANDMA, UNCA DONALD! SHE'S PUT UP A 200-SIMOLEON BOUNTY ON THIS METEORBEAST!
'CAUSE IT'S A TOUGH CRITTER TO FIND, BOYS—FASTER'N A JUNE BUG IN JULY! GUS GOOSE IS WATCHING FROM MY SILO TOWER, BUT...
ZZZ...
...SO FAR, NO FALCON! NOTHING!
HEY! IT'S FOUND US! SEE?! THE HAMMER'S ACTING UP!

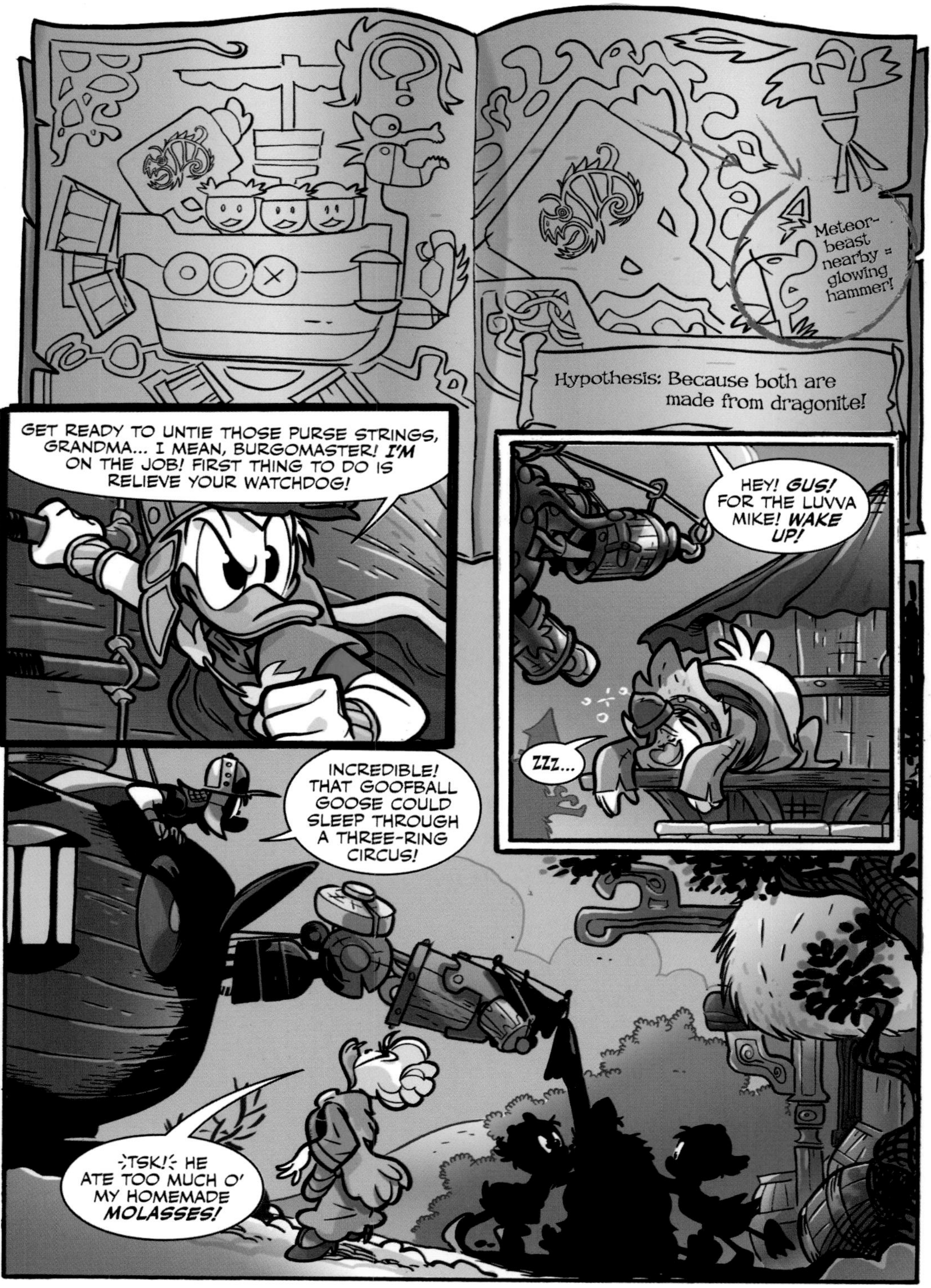
Meteor-beast nearby = glowing hammer!
Hypothesis: Because both are made from dragonite!
GET READY TO UNTIE THOSE PURSE STRINGS, GRANDMA... I MEAN, BURGOMASTER! I'M ON THE JOB! FIRST THING TO DO IS RELIEVE YOUR WATCHDOG!
HEY! GUS! FOR THE LUVVA MIKE! WAKE UP!
ZZZ...
INCREDIBLE! THAT GOOFBALL GOOSE COULD SLEEP THROUGH A THREE-RING CIRCUS!
TSK! HE ATE TOO MUCH O' MY HOMEMADE MOLASSES!

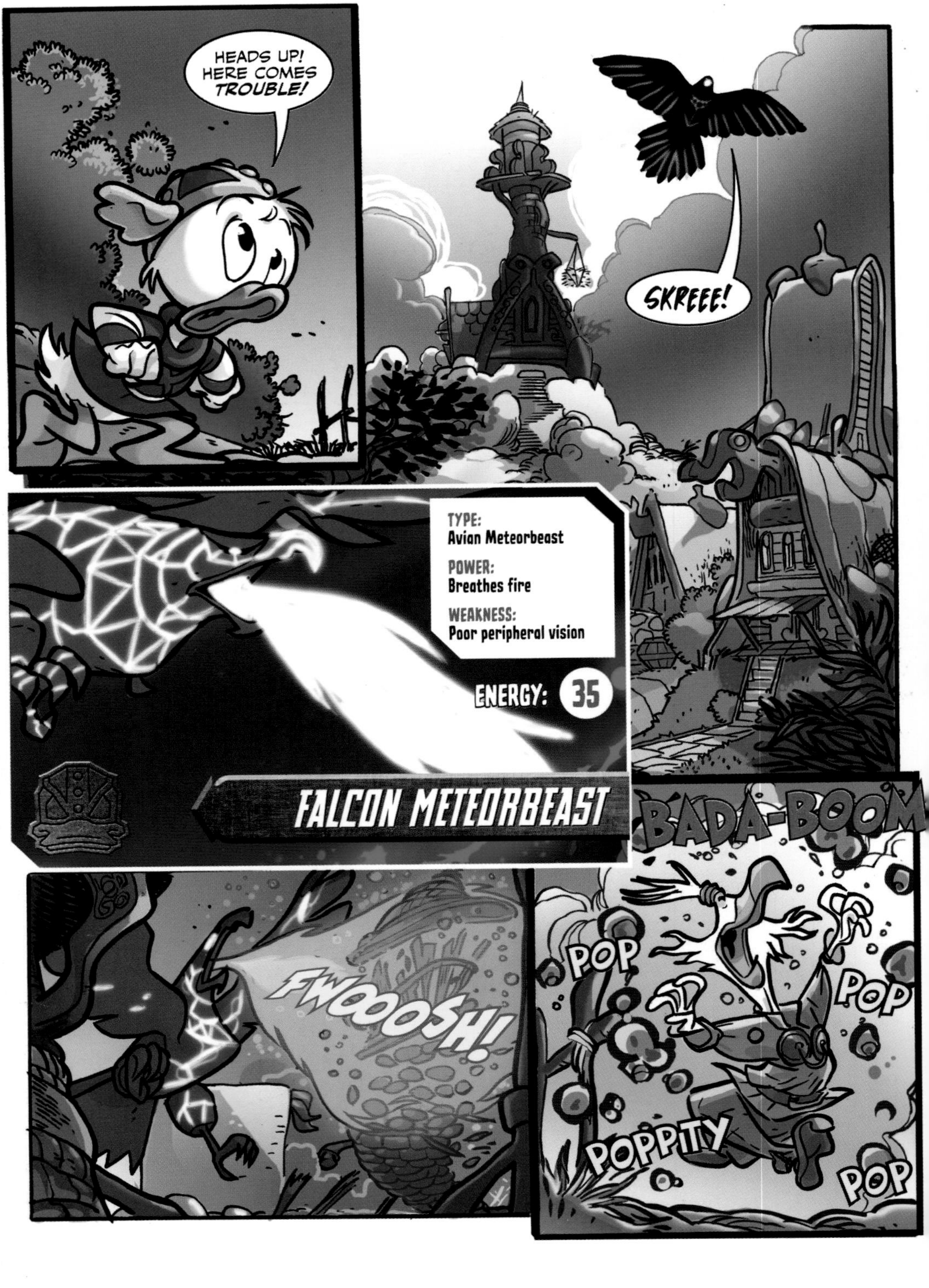
HEADS UP! HERE COMES TROUBLE!
SKREEE!
TYPE:
Avian Meteorbeast
POWER:
Breathes fire
WEAKNESS:
Poor peripheral vision
ENERGY: 35
FALCON METEORBEAST
BADA-BOOM
FWOOOSH!
POP
POP
POPPTY
POP

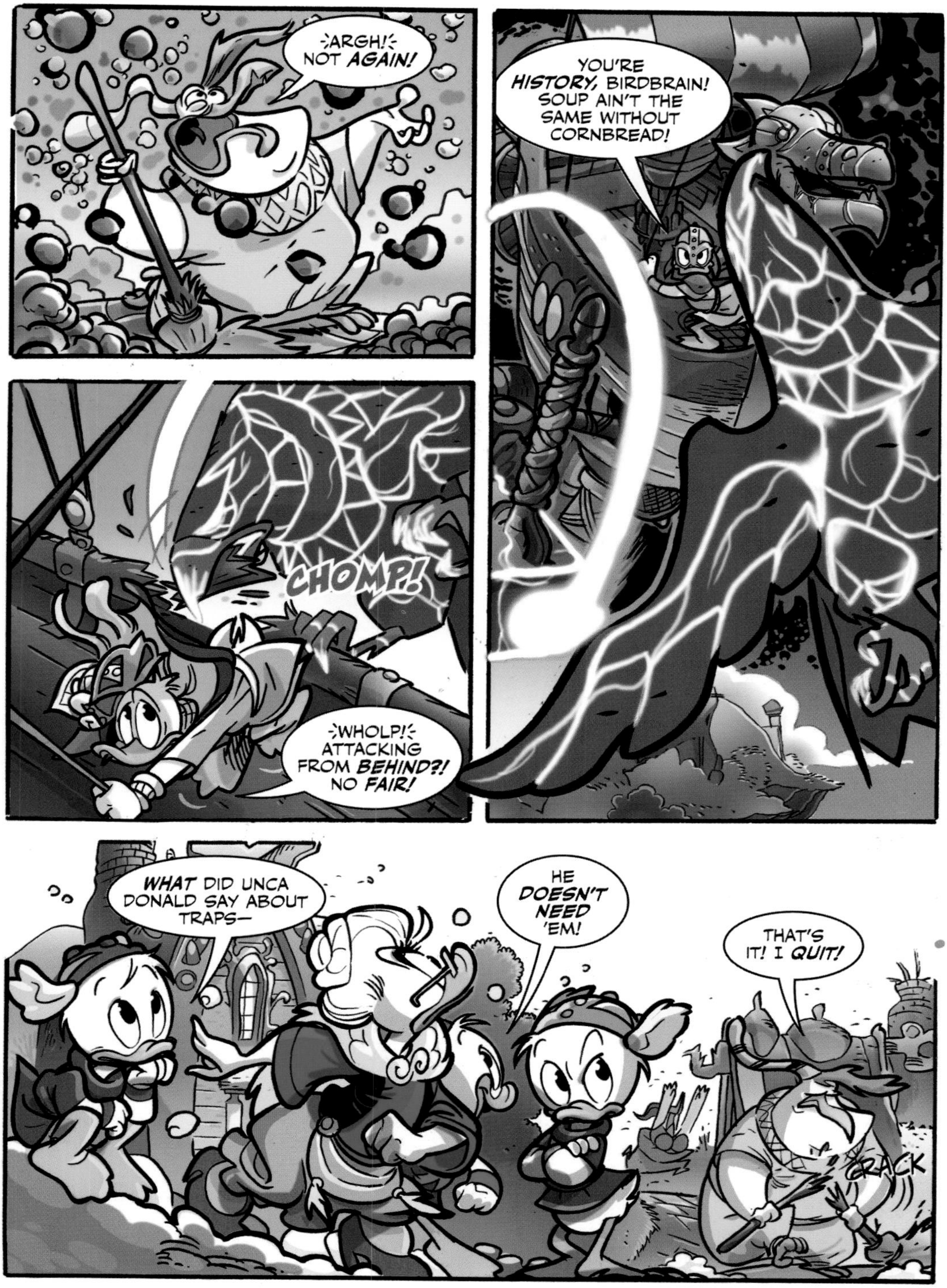

ARGH! NOT AGAIN!
YOU'RE HISTORY, BIRDBRAIN! SOUP AIN'T THE SAME WITHOUT CORNBREAD!
CHOMP!
WHOLP! ATTACKING FROM BEHIND?! NO FAIR!
WHAT DID UNCA DONALD SAY ABOUT TRAPS—
HE DOESN'T NEED 'EM!
THAT'S IT! I QUIT!
CRACK

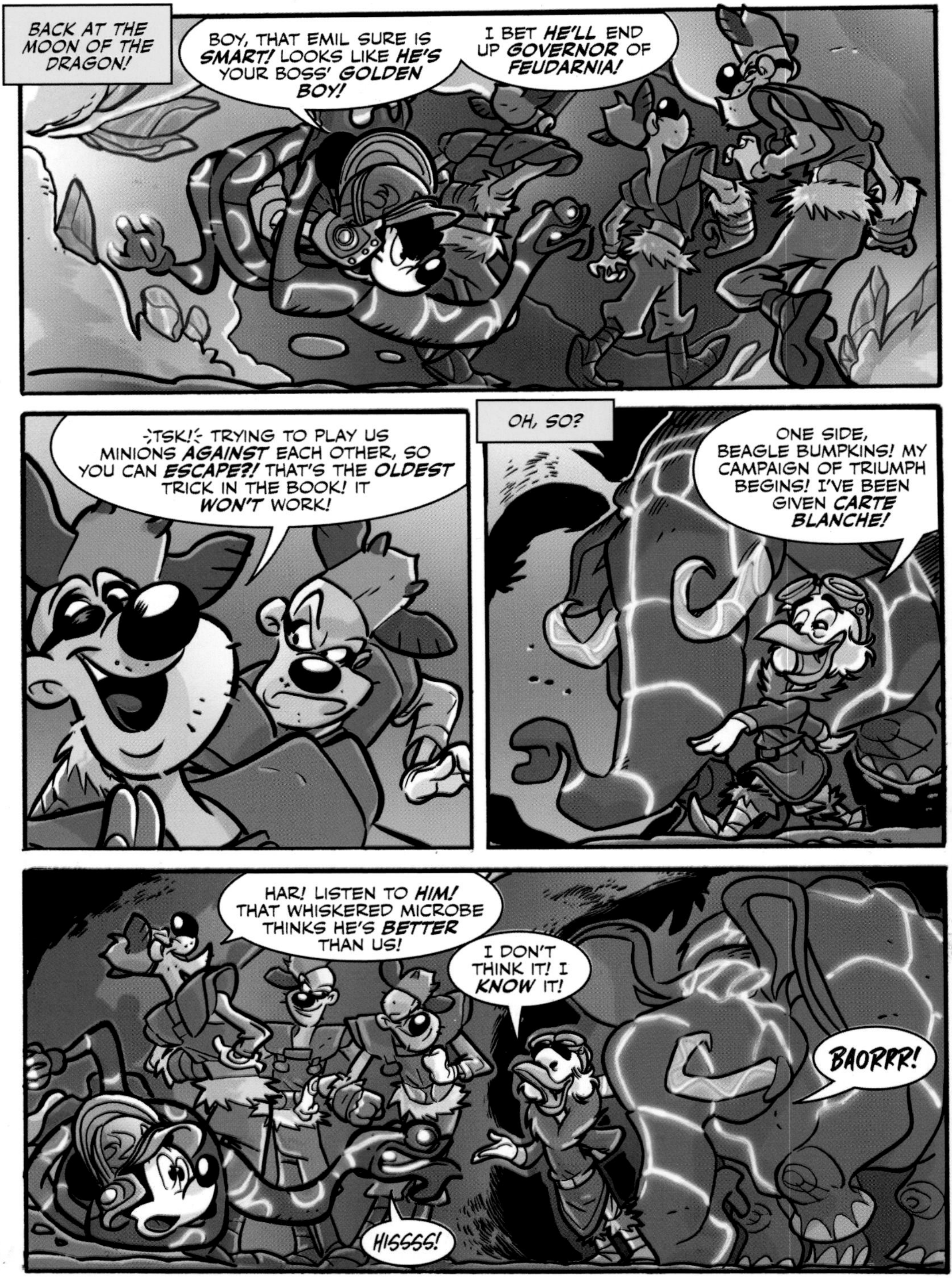
BACK AT THE MOON OF THE DRAGON!
BOY, THAT EMIL SURE IS SMART! LOOKS LIKE HE'S YOUR BOSS' GOLDEN BOY!
I BET HE'LL END UP GOVERNOR OF FEUDARNIA!
TSK! TRYING TO PLAY US MINIONS AGAINST EACH OTHER, SO YOU CAN ESCAPE?! THAT'S THE OLDEST TRICK IN THE BOOK! IT WON'T WORK!
OH, SO?
ONE SIDE, BEAGLE BUMPKINS! MY CAMPAIGN OF TRIUMPH BEGINS! I'VE BEEN GIVEN CARTE BLANCHE!
HAR! LISTEN TO HIM! THAT WHISKERED MICROBE THINKS HE'S BETTER THAN US!
I DON'T THINK IT! I KNOW IT!
BAORRR!
HISSSS!

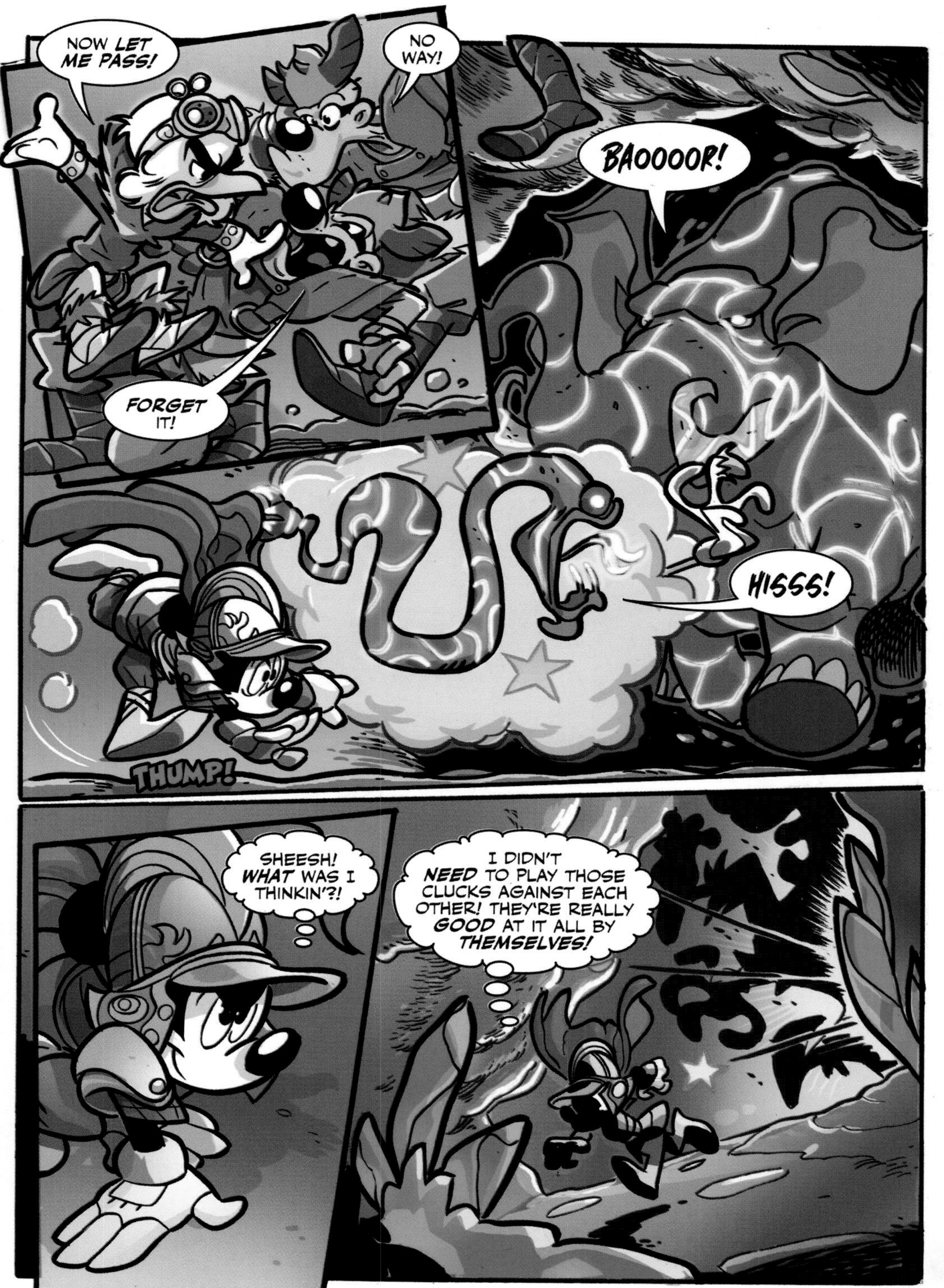
NOW LET ME PASS!
NO WAY!
FORGET IT!
BAOOOOR!
HISSS!
THUMP!
SHEESH! WHAT WAS I THINKIN'?!
I DIDN'T NEED TO PLAY THOSE CLUCKS AGAINST EACH OTHER! THEY'RE REALLY GOOD AT IT ALL BY THEMSELVES!

Chapter 3
A STICKY PLAN

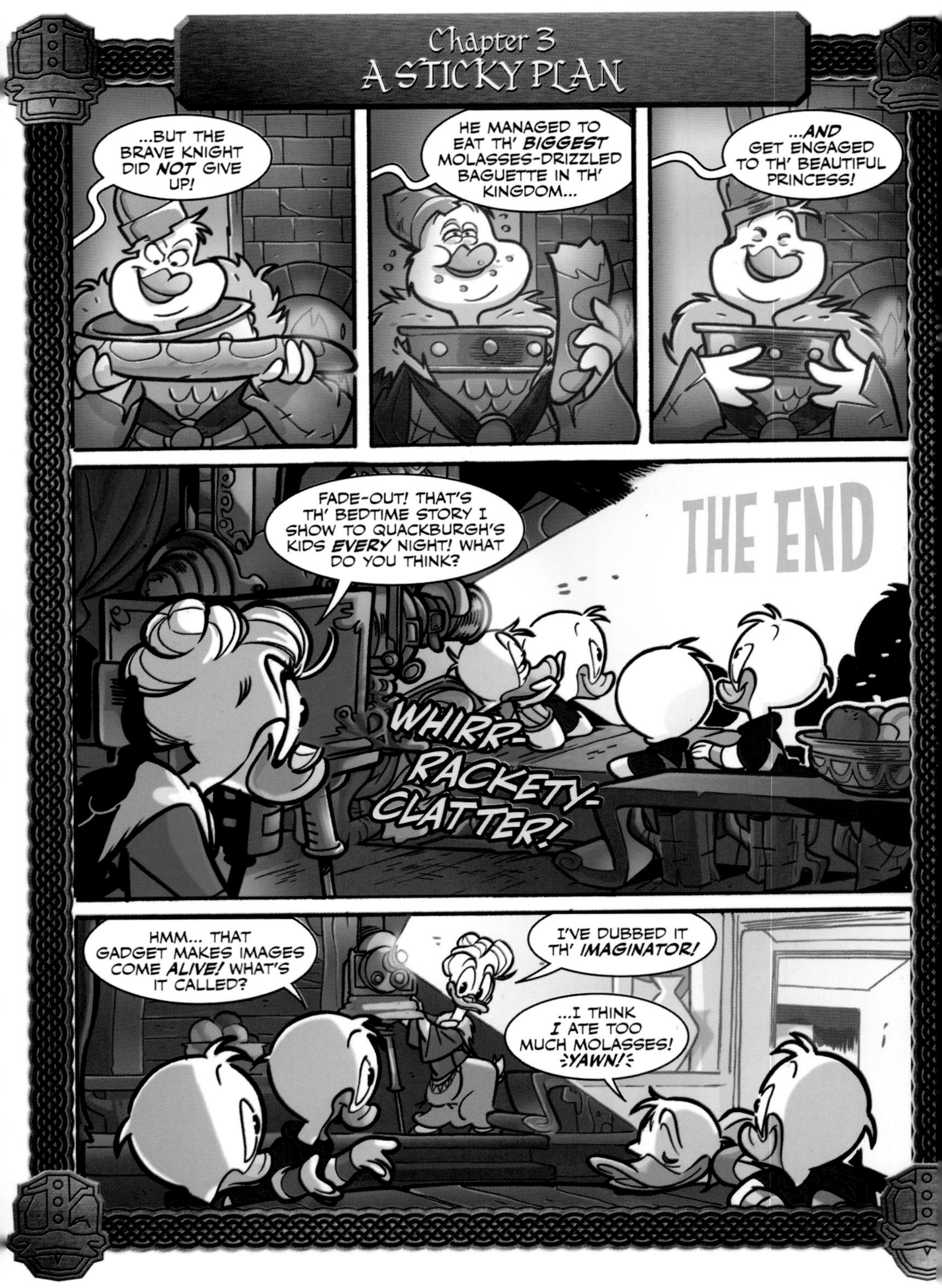

...BUT THE BRAVE KNIGHT DID NOT GIVE UP!
HE MANAGED TO EAT TH' BIGGEST MOLASSES-DRIZZLED BAGUETTE IN TH' KINGDOM...
...AND GET ENGAGED TO TH' BEAUTIFUL PRINCESS!
FADE-OUT! THAT'S TH' BEDTIME STORY I SHOW TO QUACKBURGH'S KIDS EVERY NIGHT! WHAT DO YOU THINK?
THE END
WHIRR-RACKETY-CLATTER!
HMM... THAT GADGET MAKES IMAGES COME ALIVE! WHAT'S IT CALLED?
I'VE DUBBED IT TH' IMAGINATOR!
...I THINK I ATE TOO MUCH MOLASSES! YAWN!

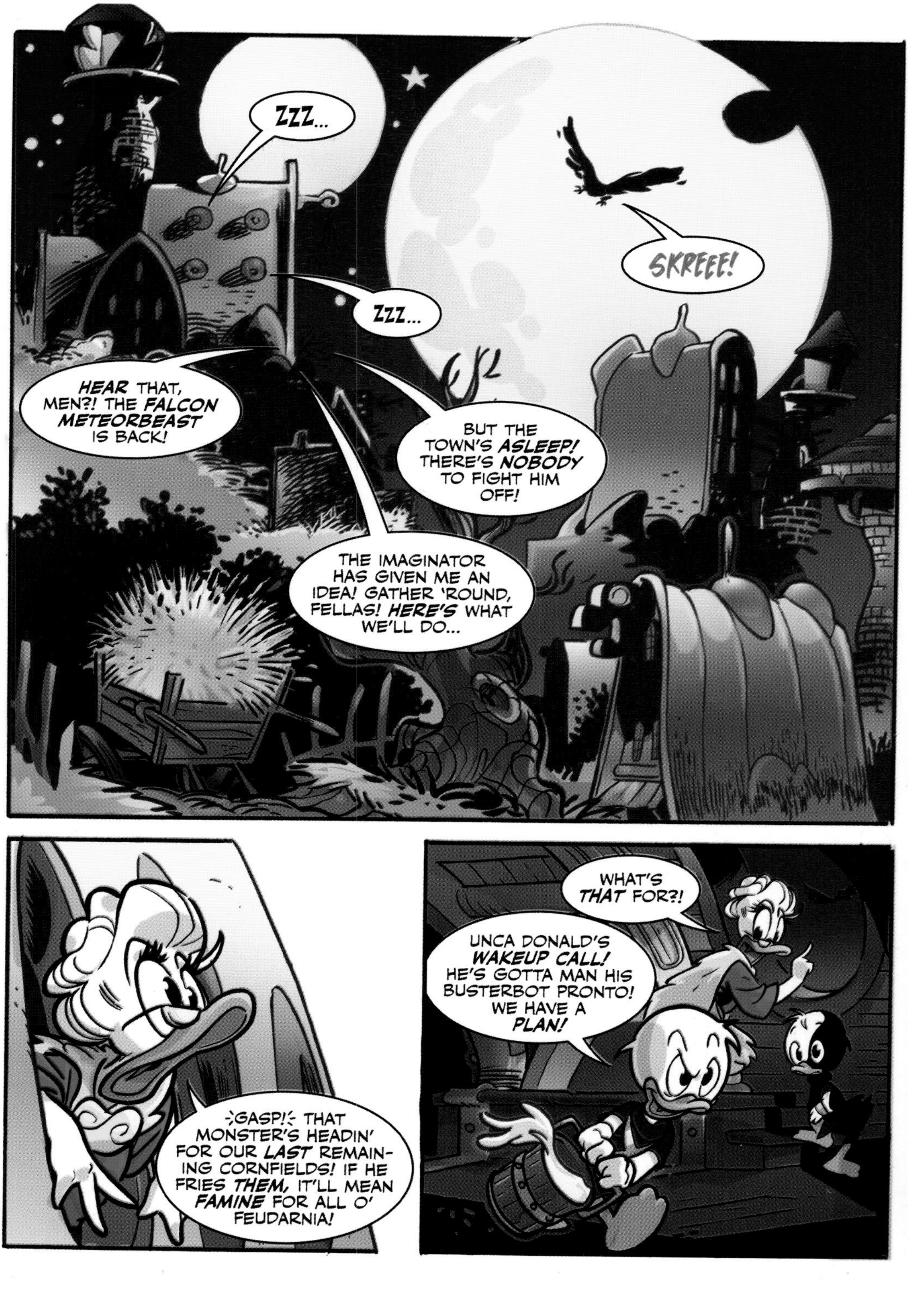

ZZZ...
ZZZ...
SKREEE!
HEAR THAT, MEN?! THE FALCON METEORBEAST IS BACK!
BUT THE TOWN'S ASLEEP! THERE'S NOBODY TO FIGHT HIM OFF!
THE IMAGINATOR HAS GIVEN ME AN IDEA! GATHER 'ROUND, FELLAS! HERE'S WHAT WE'LL DO...
-GASP!- THAT MONSTER'S HEADIN' FOR OUR LAST REMAINING CORNFIELDS! IF HE FRIES THEM, IT'LL MEAN FAMINE FOR ALL O' FEUDARNIA!
WHAT'S THAT FOR?!
UNCA DONALD'S WAKEUP CALL! HE'S GOTTA MAN HIS BUSTERBOT PRONTO! WE HAVE A PLAN!

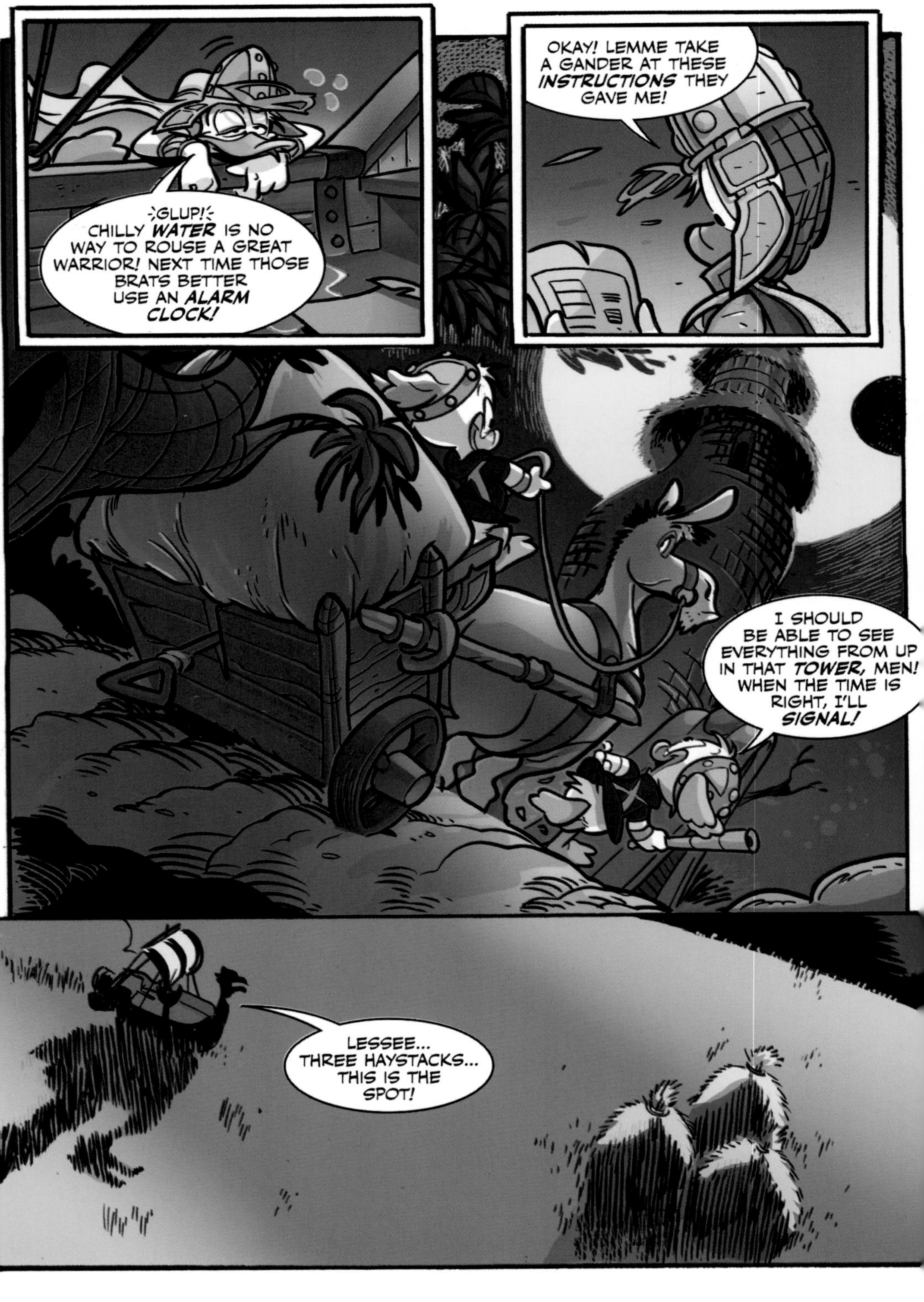

¡GLUP!¡ CHILLY WATER IS NO WAY TO ROUSE A GREAT WARRIOR! NEXT TIME THOSE BRATS BETTER USE AN ALARM CLOCK!
OKAY! LEMME TAKE A GANDER AT THESE INSTRUCTIONS THEY GAVE ME!
I SHOULD BE ABLE TO SEE EVERYTHING FROM UP IN THAT TOWER, MEN! WHEN THE TIME IS RIGHT, I'LL SIGNAL!
LESSEE... THREE HAYSTACKS... THIS IS THE SPOT!

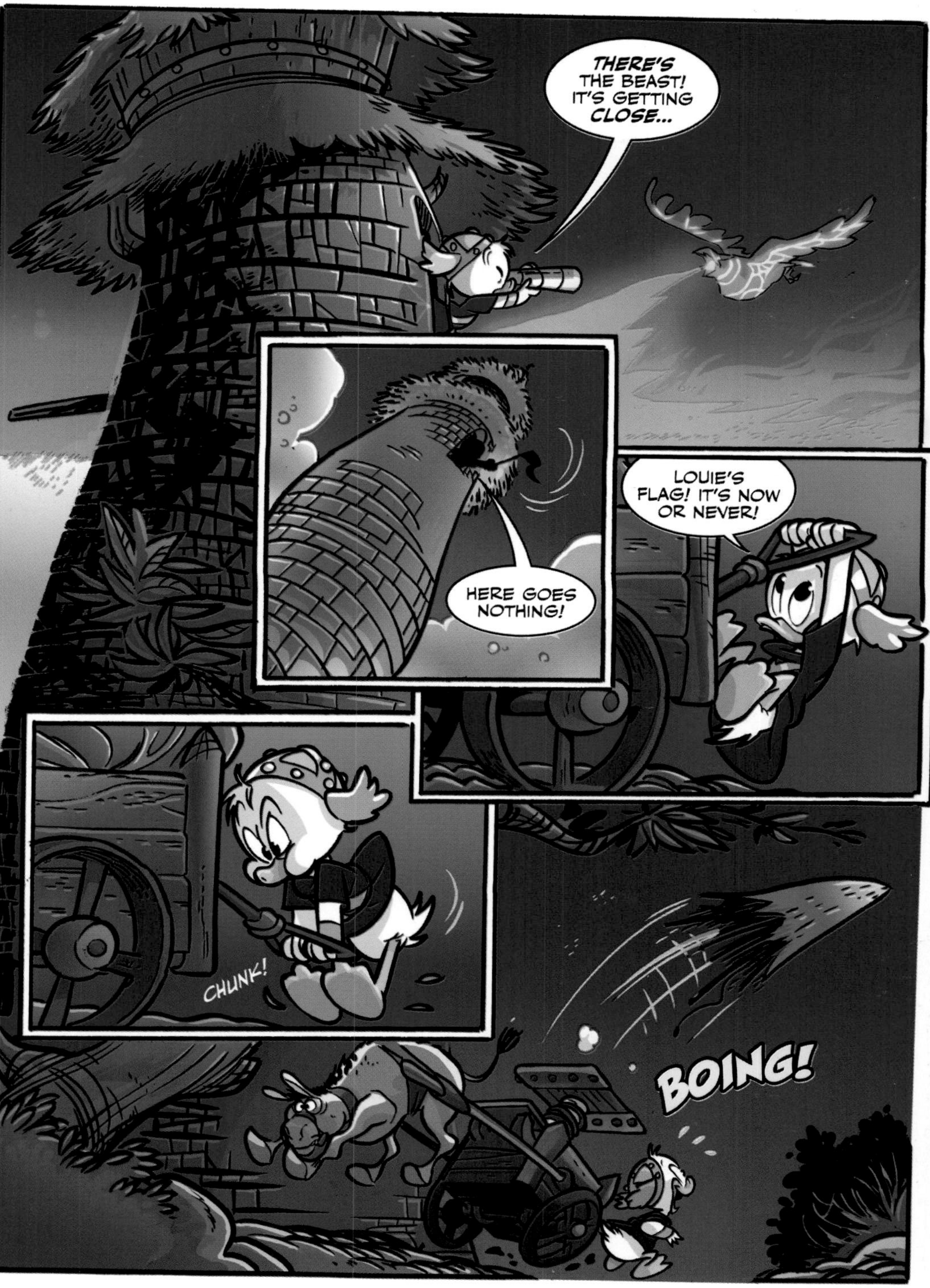
THERE'S THE BEAST! IT'S GETTING CLOSE...
HERE GOES NOTHING!
LOUIE'S FLAG! IT'S NOW OR NEVER!
CHUNK!
BOING!

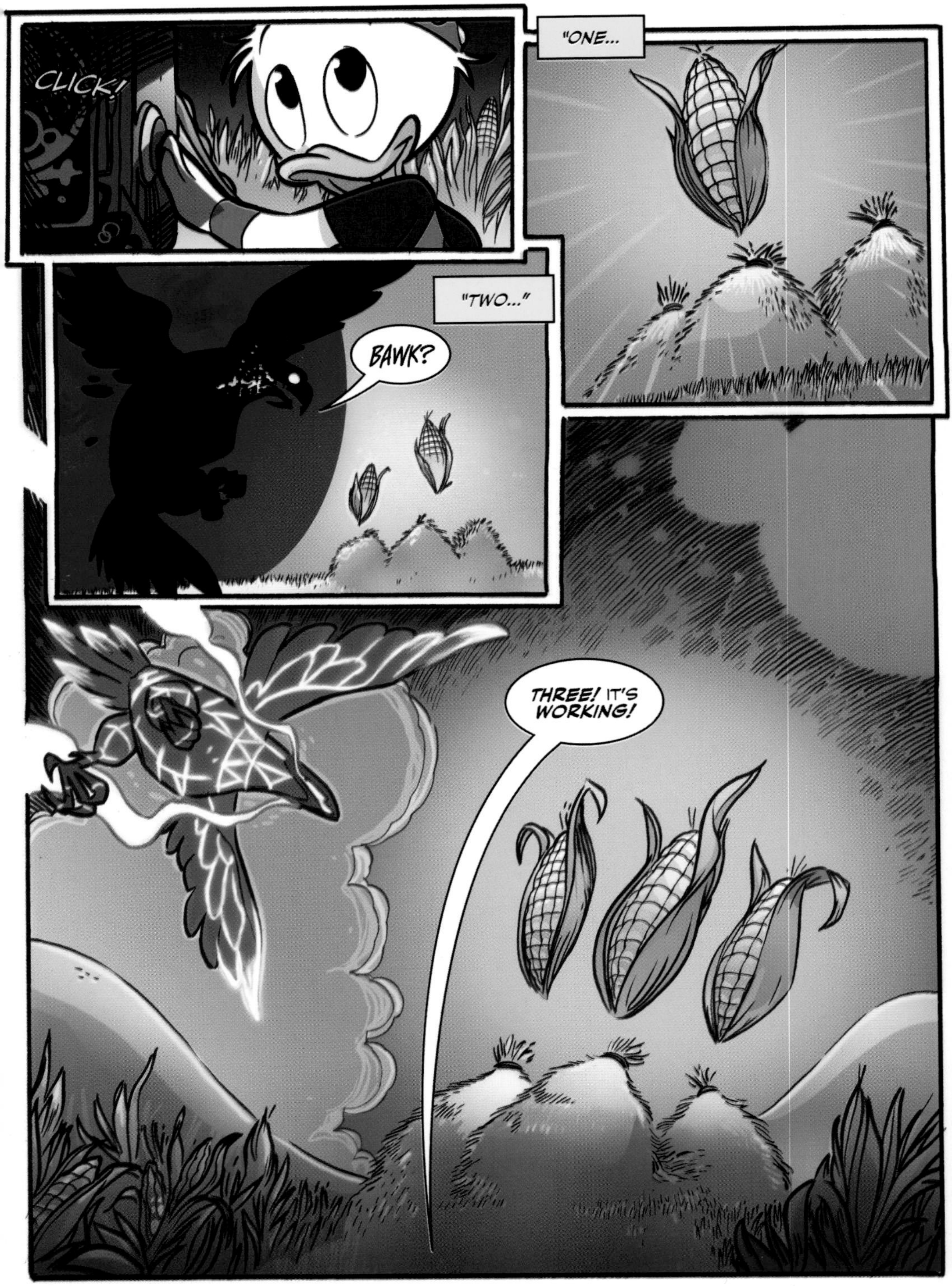
CLICK!
"ONE...
"TWO..."
BAWK?
THREE! IT'S WORKING!

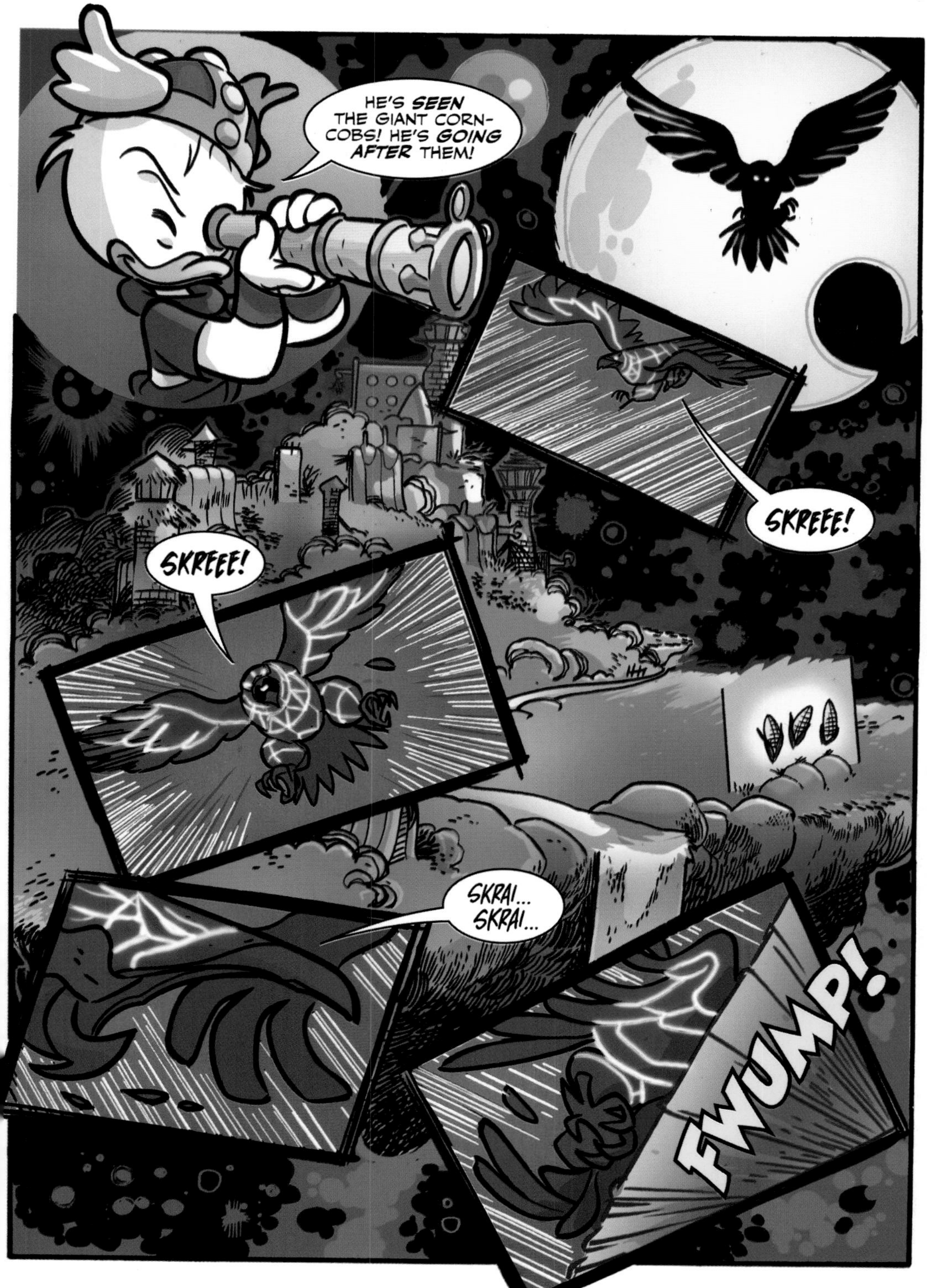
HE'S *SEEN* THE GIANT CORN-COBS! HE'S *GOING AFTER* THEM!
SKREEE!
SKREEE!
SKRAI... SKRAI...
FWUMP!

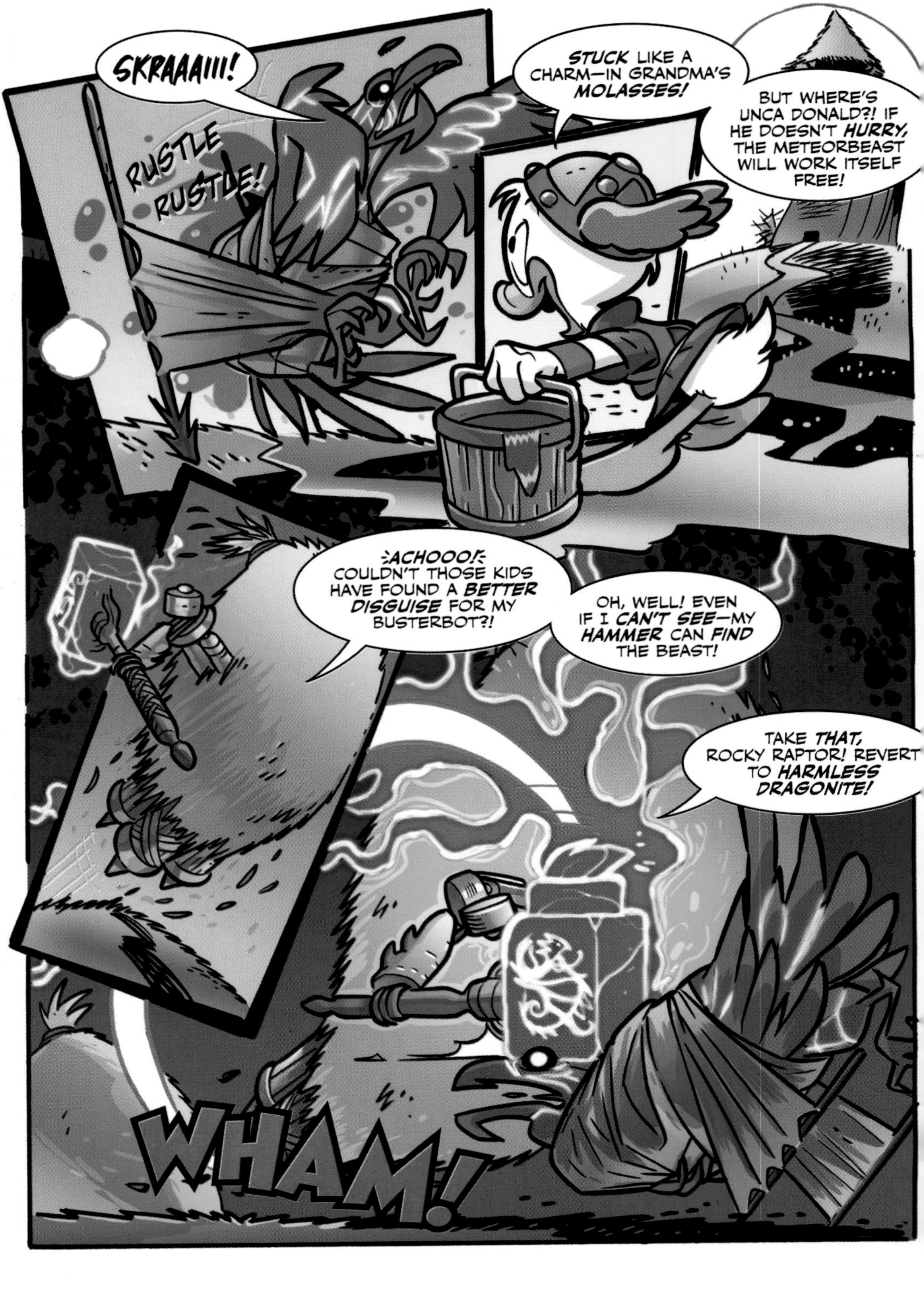
SKRAAAIII!
RUSTLE RUSTLE!
STUCK LIKE A CHARM—IN GRANDMA'S MOLASSES!
BUT WHERE'S UNCA DONALD?! IF HE DOESN'T HURRY, THE METEORBEAST WILL WORK ITSELF FREE!
ACHOOO! COULDN'T THOSE KIDS HAVE FOUND A BETTER DISGUISE FOR MY BUSTERBOT?!
OH, WELL! EVEN IF I CAN'T SEE—MY HAMMER CAN FIND THE BEAST!
TAKE THAT, ROCKY RAPTOR! REVERT TO HARMLESS DRAGONITE!
WHAM!

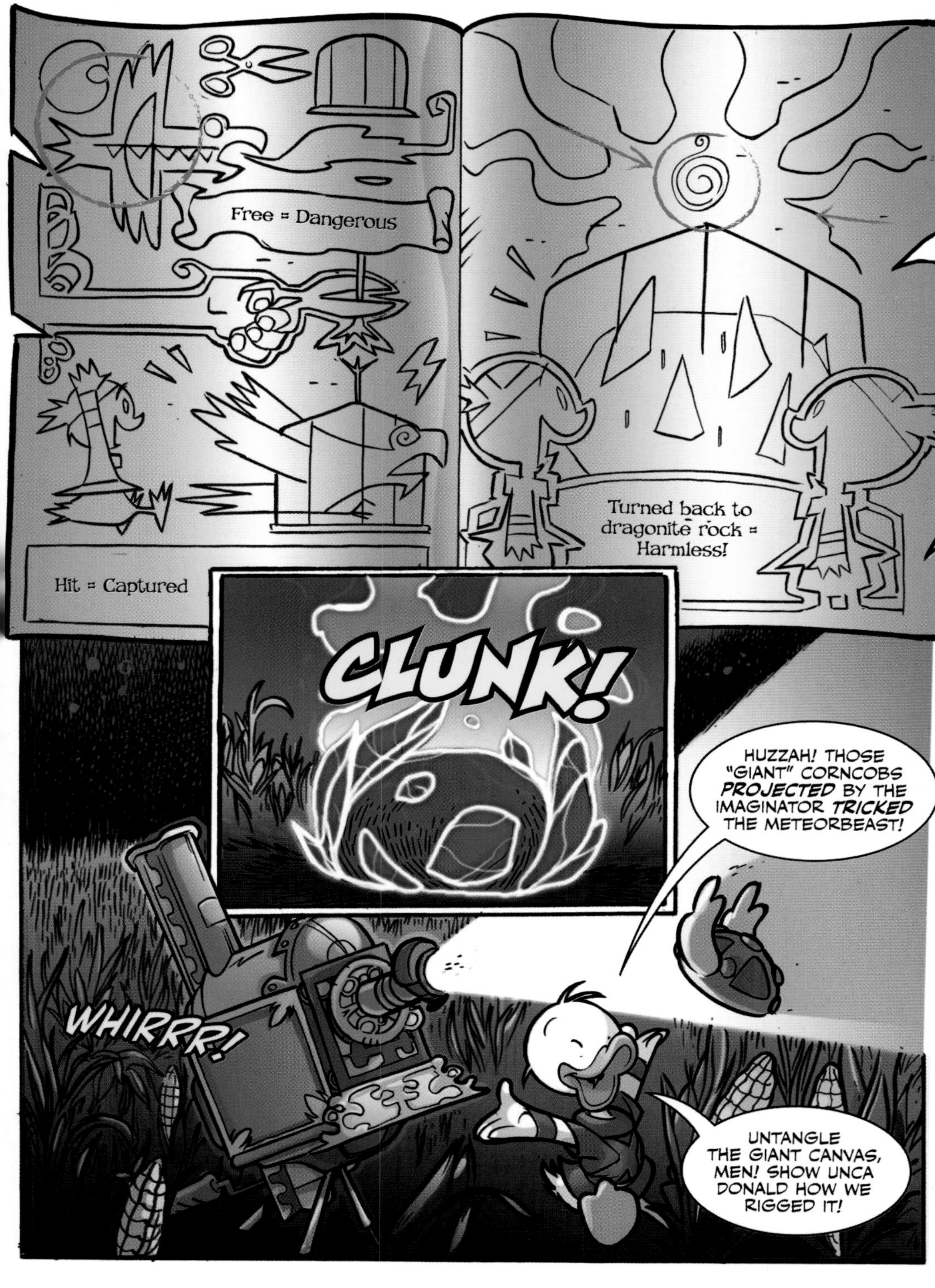

Free = Dangerous
Hit = Captured
Turned back to dragonite rock = Harmless!
CLUNK!
HUZZAH! THOSE "GIANT" CORNCOBS PROJECTED BY THE IMAGINATOR TRICKED THE METEORBEAST!
WHIRRR!
UNTANGLE THE GIANT CANVAS, MEN! SHOW UNCA DONALD HOW WE RIGGED IT!

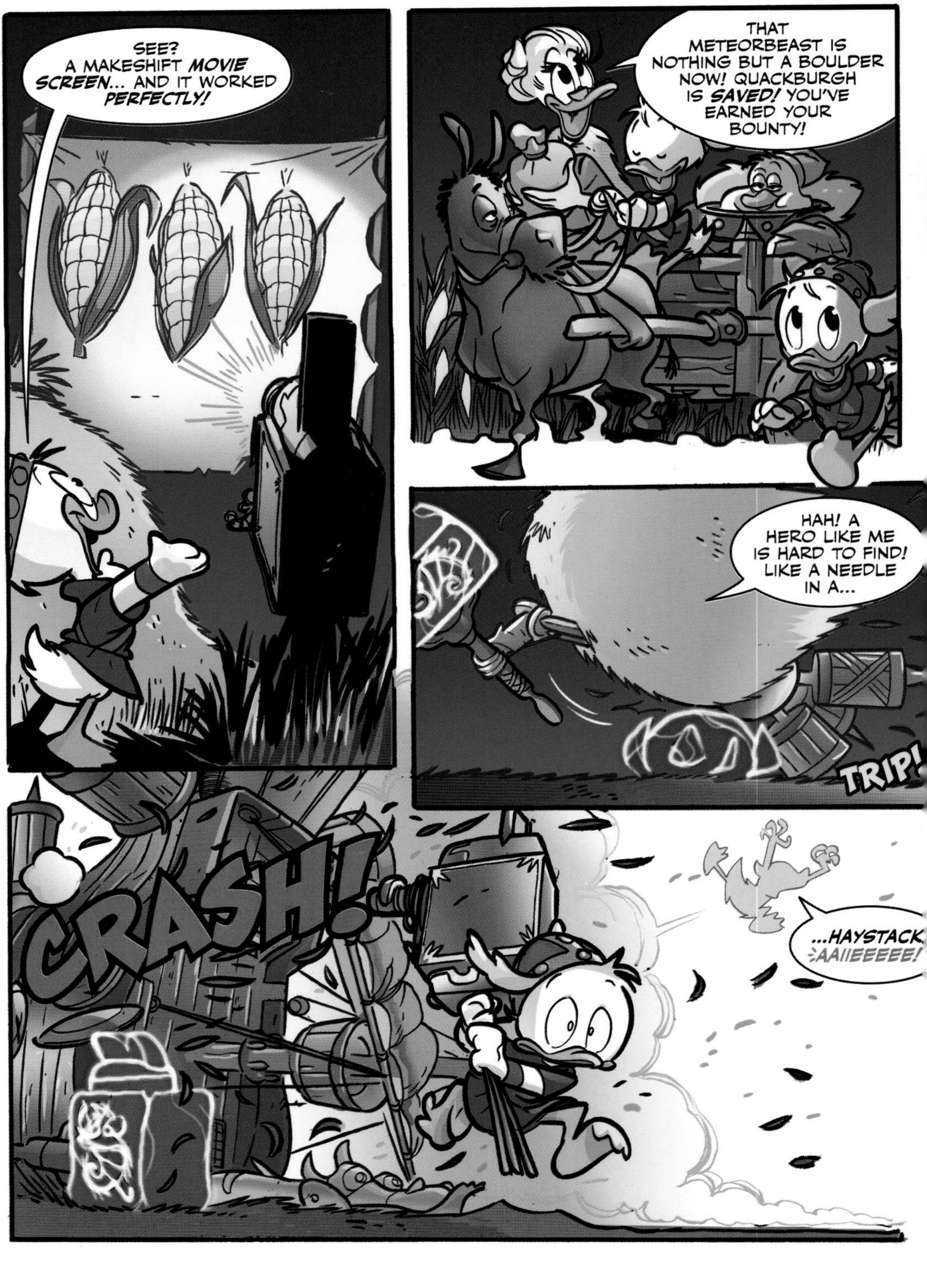

SEE? A MAKESHIFT MOVIE SCREEN... AND IT WORKED PERFECTLY!
THAT METEORBEAST IS NOTHING BUT A BOULDER NOW! QUACKBURGH IS SAVED! YOU'VE EARNED YOUR BOUNTY!
HAH! A HERO LIKE ME IS HARD TO FIND! LIKE A NEEDLE IN A...
TRIP!
CRASH!
...HAYSTACK AAIIEEEEE!

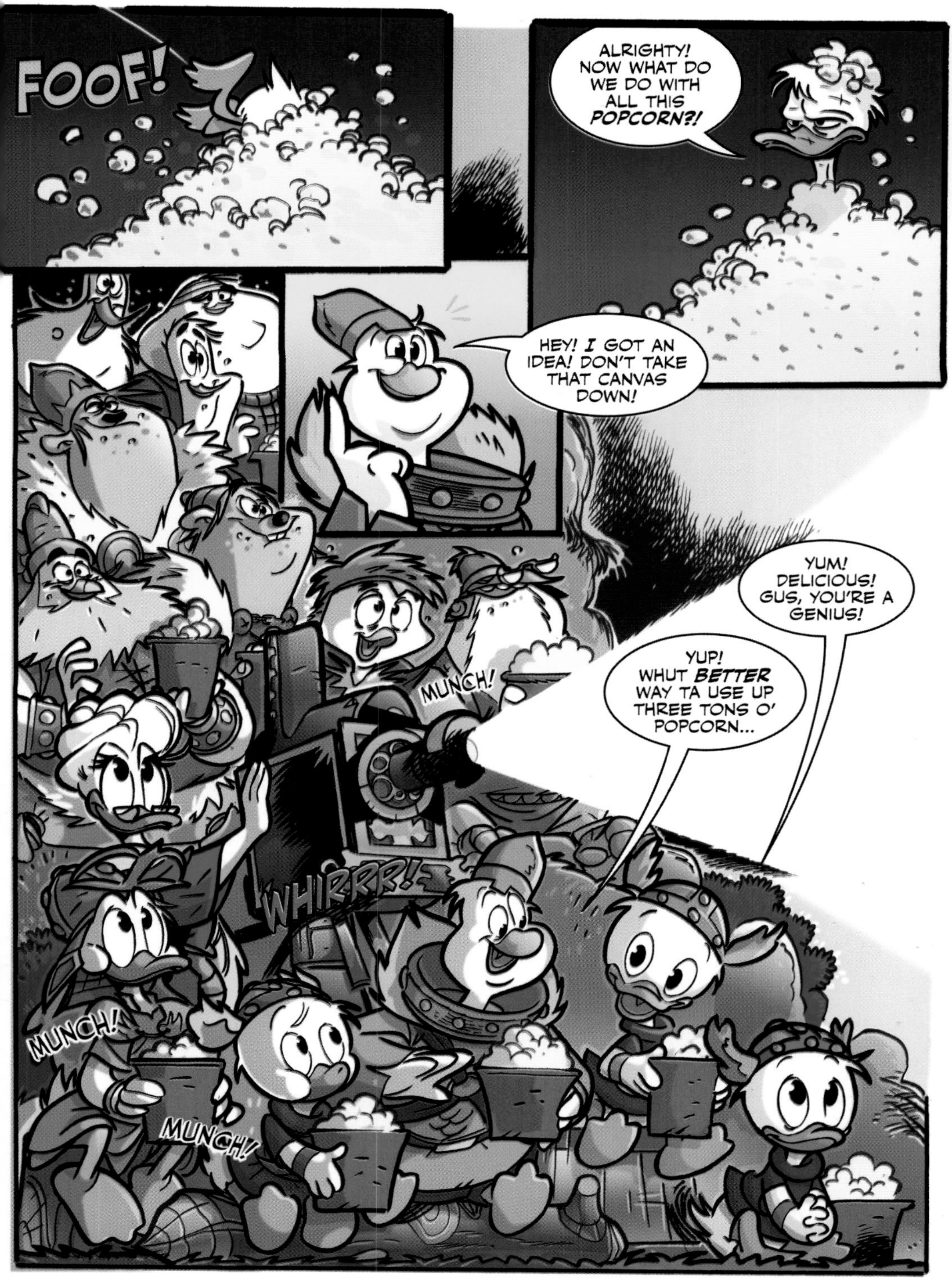
FOOF!
ALRIGHTY! NOW WHAT DO WE DO WITH ALL THIS POPCORN?!
HEY! I GOT AN IDEA! DON'T TAKE THAT CANVAS DOWN!
MUNCH!
WHIRRR!
YUM! DELICIOUS! GUS, YOU'RE A GENIUS!
YUP! WHUT BETTER WAY TA USE UP THREE TONS O' POPCORN...
MUNCH!
MUNCH!

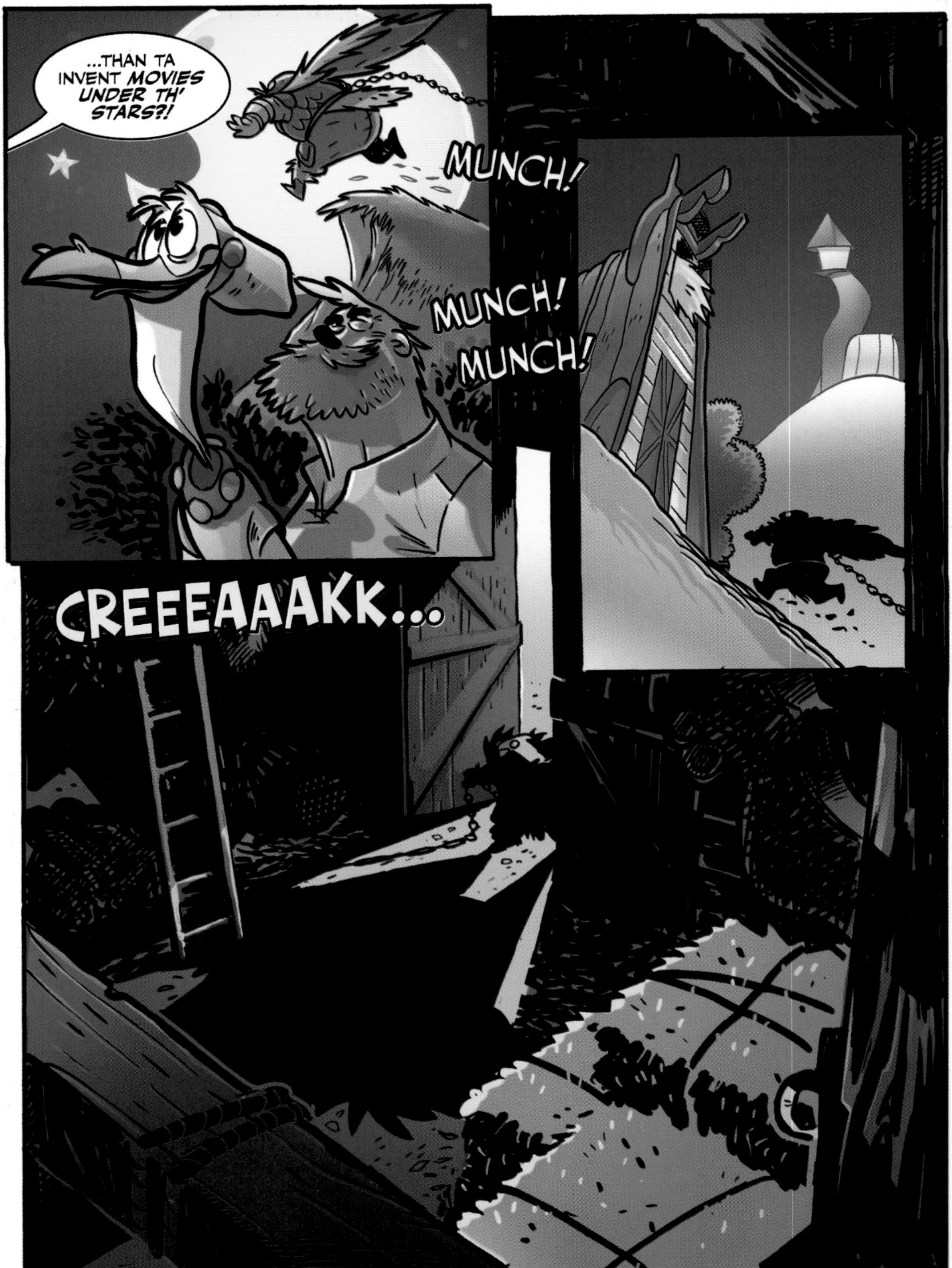
...THAN TA INVENT MOVIES UNDER TH' STARS?!
MUNCH!
MUNCH!
MUNCH!
CREEEAAAKK...

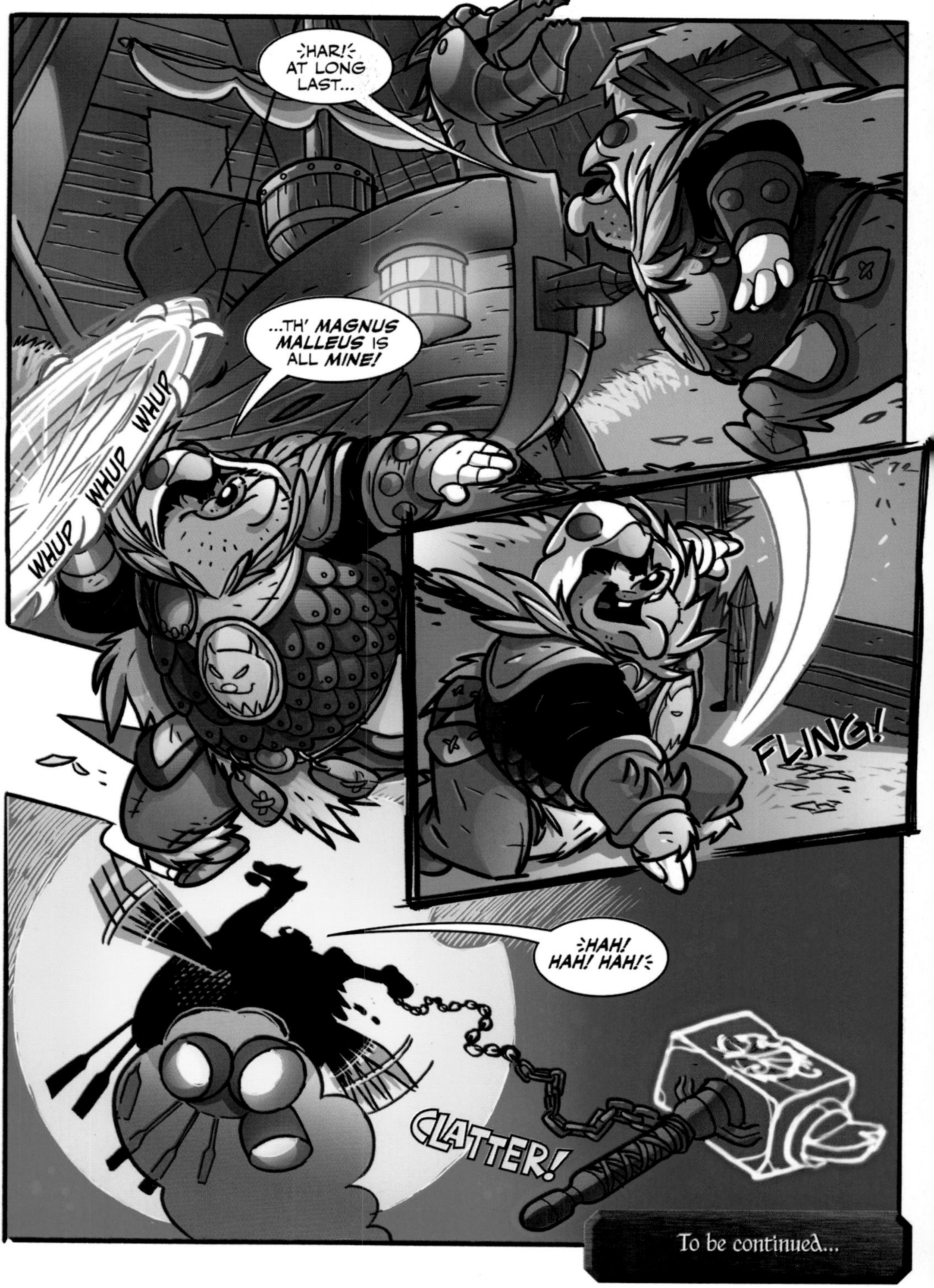
HAR! AT LONG LAST...
...TH' MAGNUS MALLEUS IS ALL MINE!
WHUP WHUP WHUP WHUP
FLING!
HAH! HAH! HAH!
CLATTER!
To be continued...

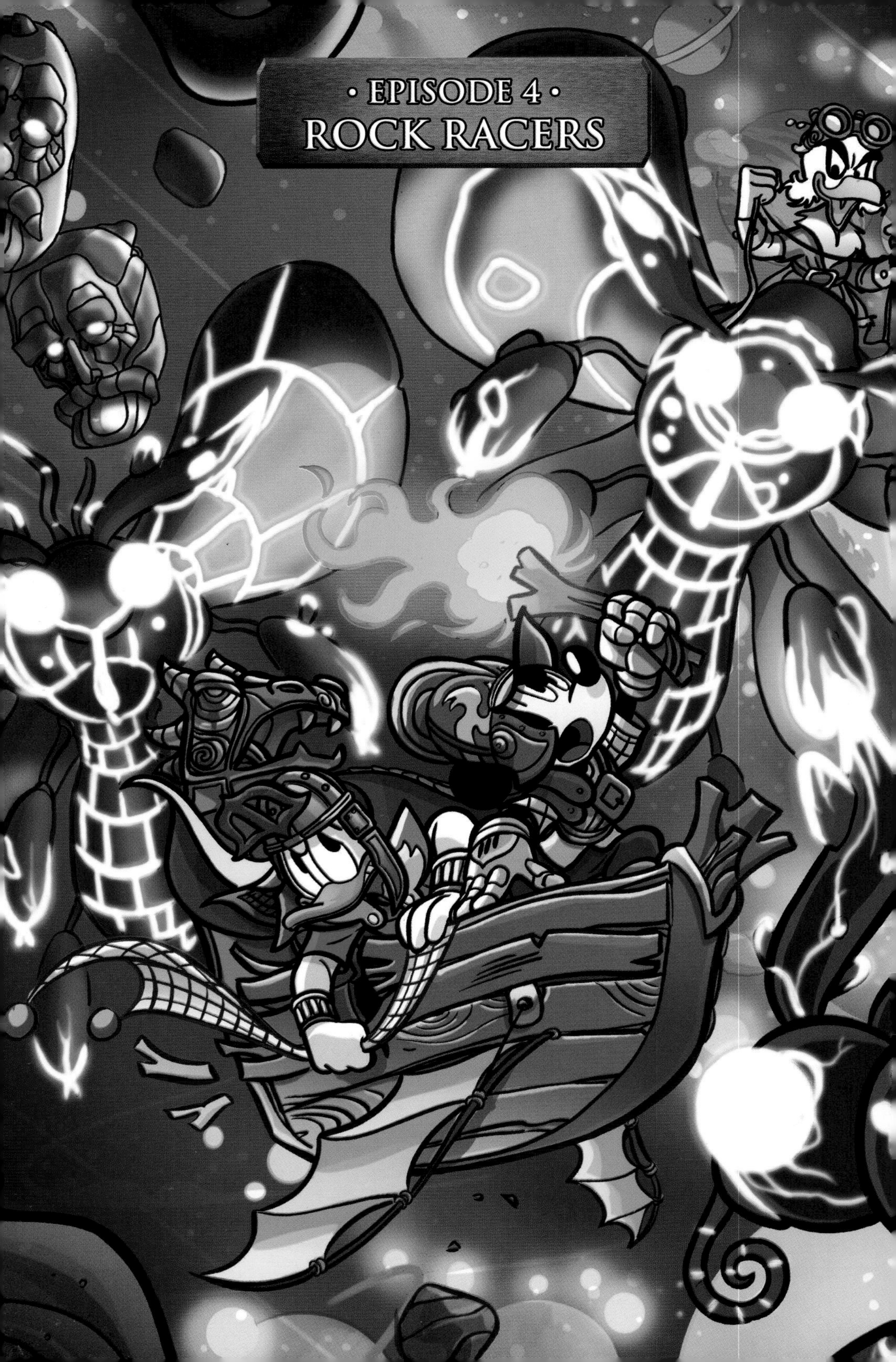

• EPISODE 4 •
ROCK RACERS

Chapter 1
BETWEEN AN ANVIL AND A HARD PLACE

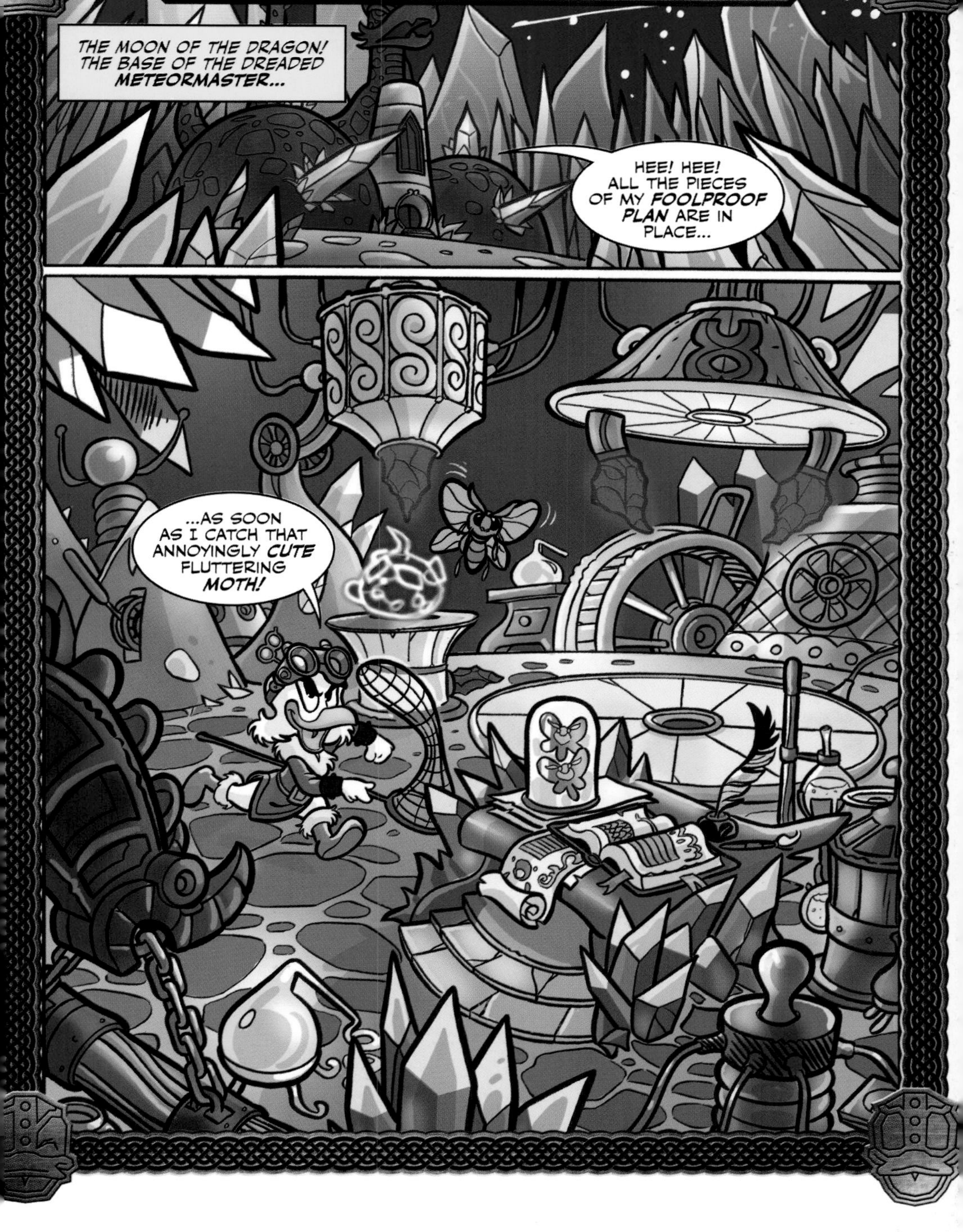
THE MOON OF THE DRAGON! THE BASE OF THE DREADED METEORMASTER...
HEE! HEE! ALL THE PIECES OF MY FOOLPROOF PLAN ARE IN PLACE...
...AS SOON AS I CATCH THAT ANNOYINGLY CUTE FLUTTERING MOTH!

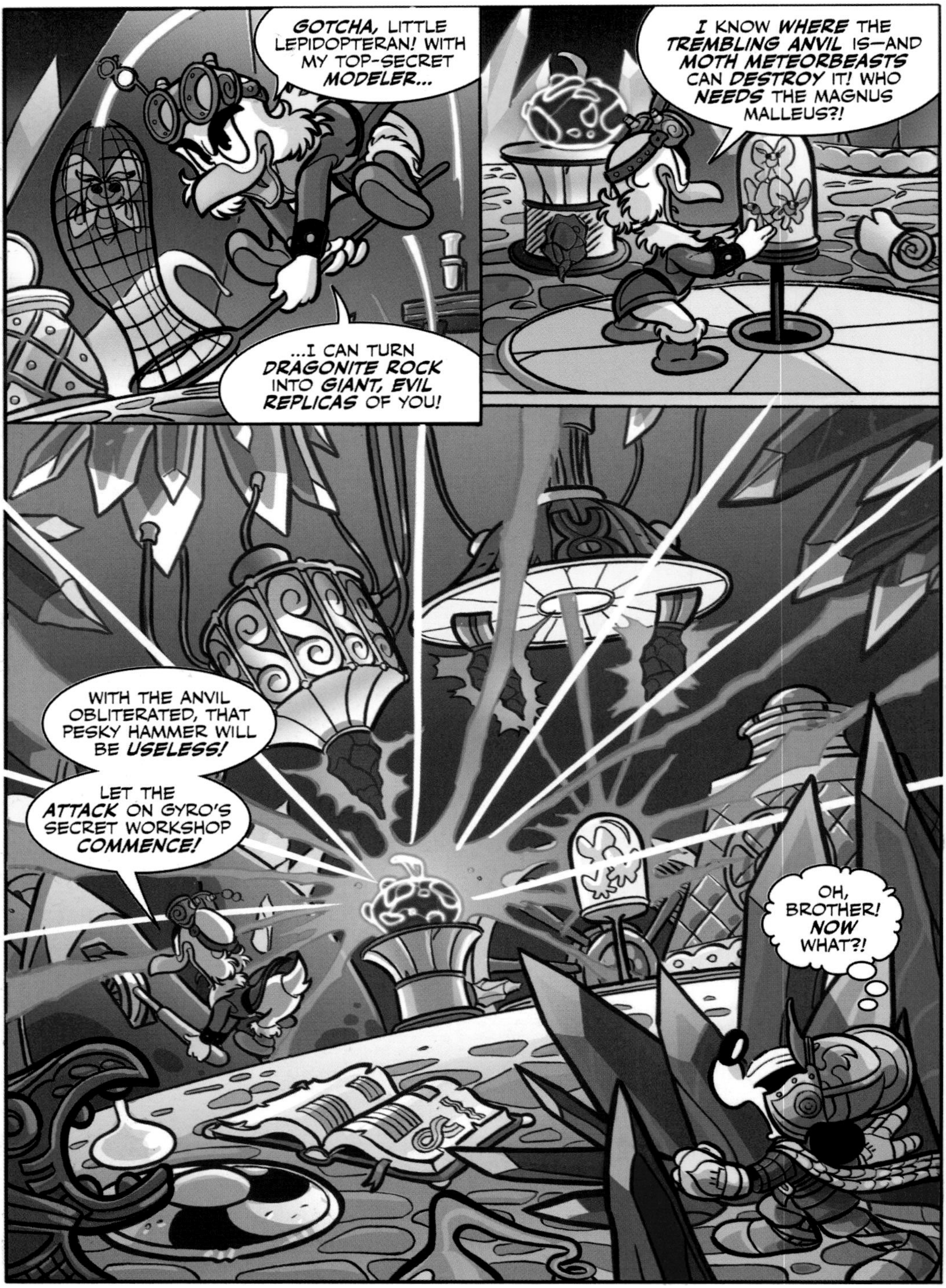

GOTCHA, LITTLE LEPIDOPTERAN! WITH MY TOP-SECRET MODELER...
...I CAN TURN DRAGONITE ROCK INTO GIANT, EVIL REPLICAS OF YOU!
I KNOW WHERE THE TREMBLING ANVIL IS—AND MOTH METEORBEASTS CAN DESTROY IT! WHO NEEDS THE MAGNUS MALLEUS?!
WITH THE ANVIL OBLITERATED, THAT PESKY HAMMER WILL BE USELESS!
LET THE ATTACK ON GYRO'S SECRET WORKSHOP COMMENCE!
OH, BROTHER! NOW WHAT?!

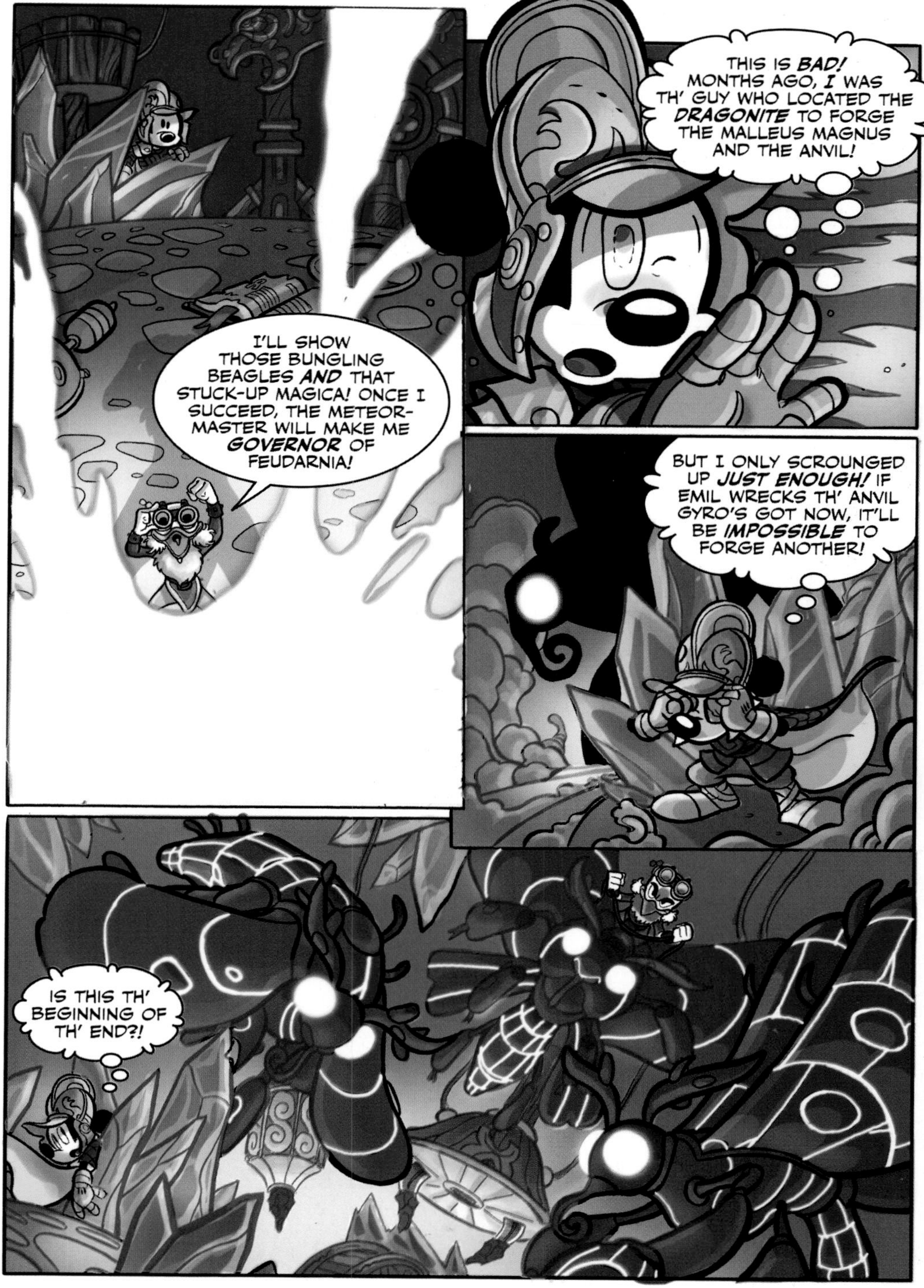
THIS IS BAD! MONTHS AGO, I WAS TH' GUY WHO LOCATED THE DRAGONITE TO FORGE THE MALLEUS MAGNUS AND THE ANVIL!
I'LL SHOW THOSE BUNGLING BEAGLES AND THAT STUCK-UP MAGICA! ONCE I SUCCEED, THE METEOR-MASTER WILL MAKE ME GOVERNOR OF FEUDARNIA!
BUT I ONLY SCROUNGED UP JUST ENOUGH! IF EMIL WRECKS TH' ANVIL GYRO'S GOT NOW, IT'LL BE IMPOSSIBLE TO FORGE ANOTHER!
IS THIS TH' BEGINNING OF TH' END?!

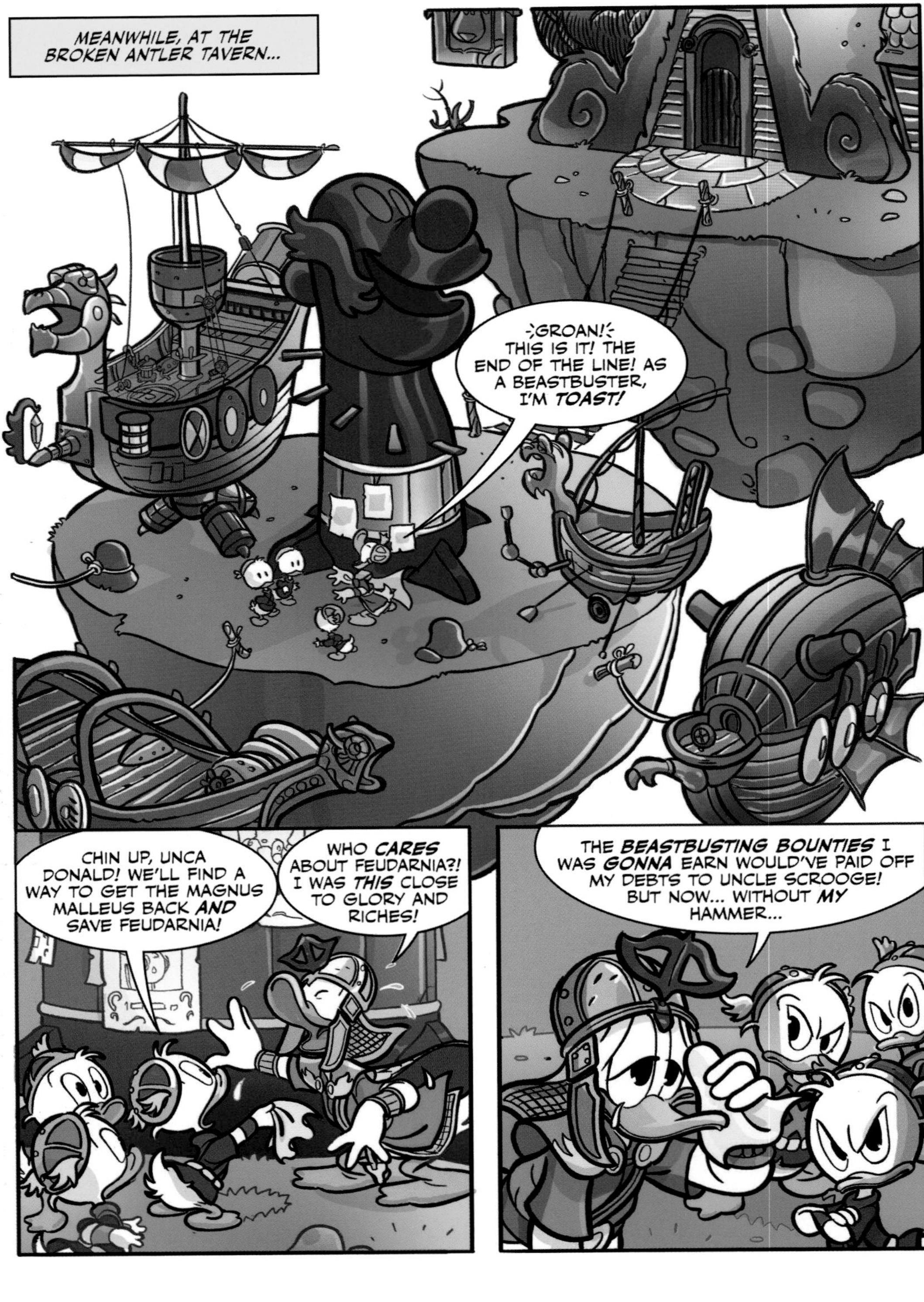
MEANWHILE, AT THE BROKEN ANTLER TAVERN...
-GROAN!- THIS IS IT! THE END OF THE LINE! AS A BEASTBUSTER, I'M *TOAST!*
CHIN UP, UNCA DONALD! WE'LL FIND A WAY TO GET THE MAGNUS MALLEUS BACK *AND* SAVE FEUDARNIA!
WHO *CARES* ABOUT FEUDARNIA?! I WAS *THIS* CLOSE TO GLORY AND RICHES!
THE *BEASTBUSTING BOUNTIES* I WAS *GONNA* EARN WOULD'VE PAID OFF MY DEBTS TO UNCLE SCROOGE! BUT NOW... WITHOUT *MY* HAMMER...

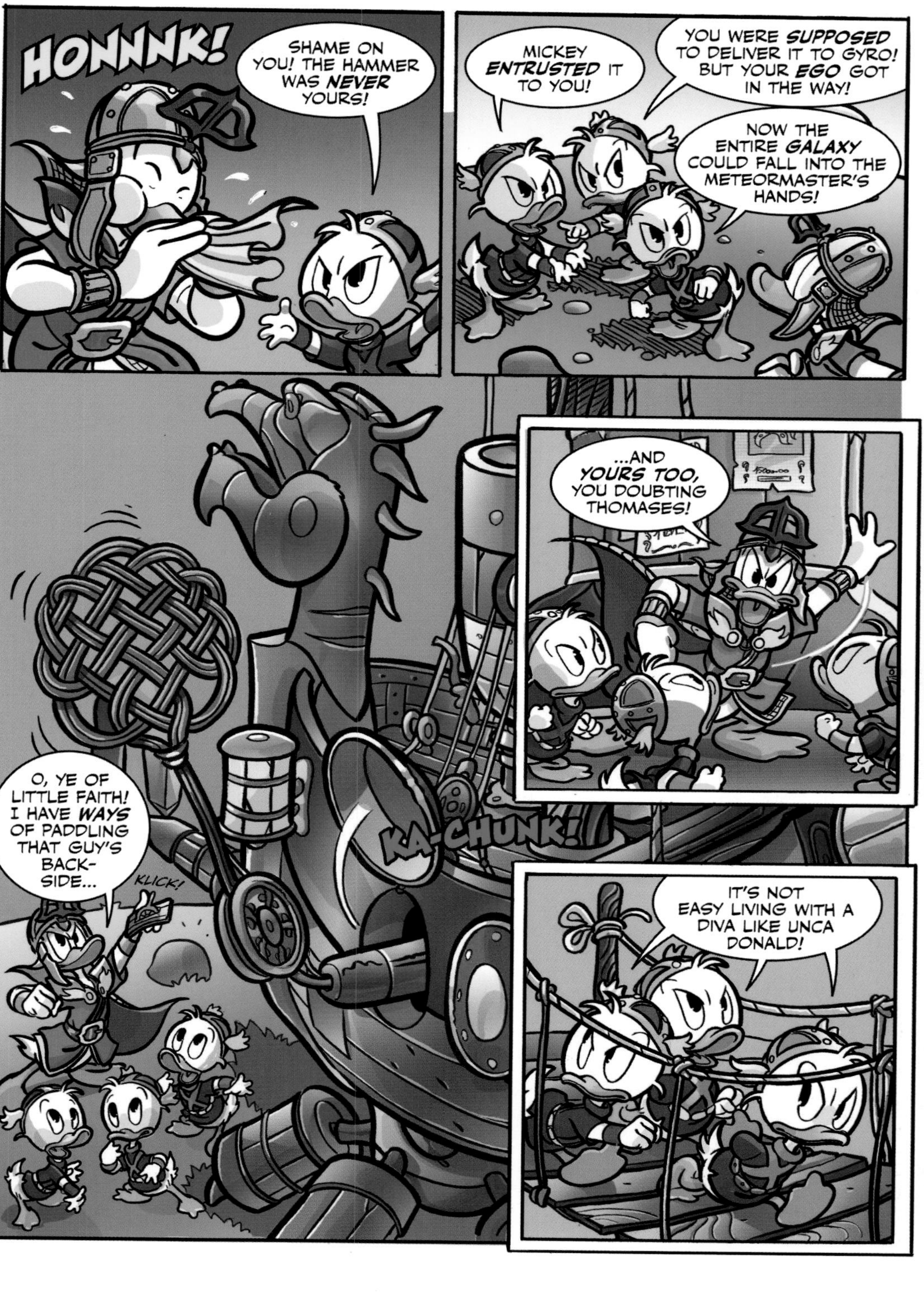
HONNNK!
SHAME ON YOU! THE HAMMER WAS NEVER YOURS!
MICKEY ENTRUSTED IT TO YOU!
YOU WERE SUPPOSED TO DELIVER IT TO GYRO! BUT YOUR EGO GOT IN THE WAY!
NOW THE ENTIRE GALAXY COULD FALL INTO THE METEORMASTER'S HANDS!
...AND YOURS TOO, YOU DOUBTING THOMASES!
O, YE OF LITTLE FAITH! I HAVE WAYS OF PADDLING THAT GUY'S BACK-SIDE...
KLICK!
KA-CHUNK!
IT'S NOT EASY LIVING WITH A DIVA LIKE UNCA DONALD!

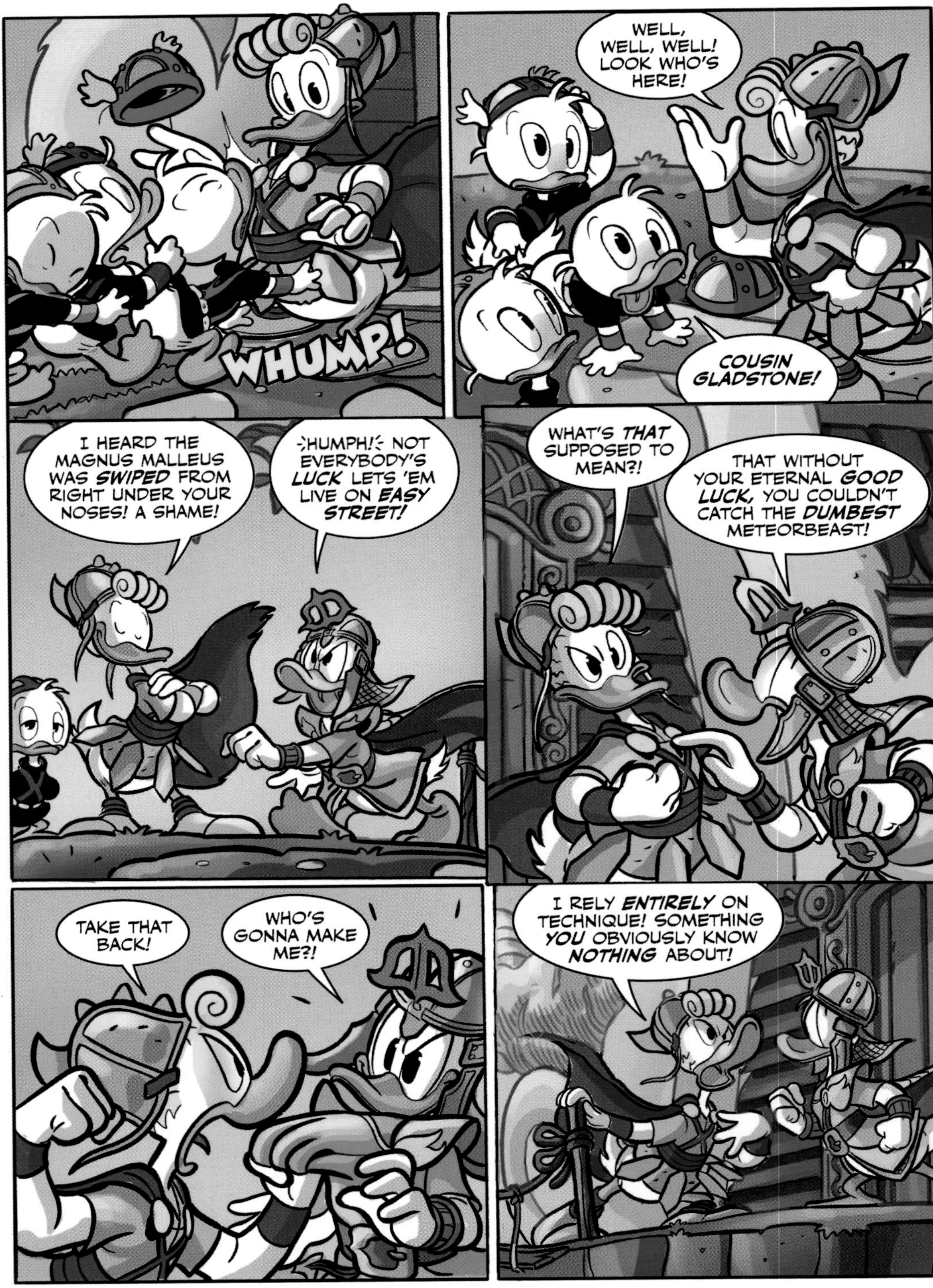
WHUMP!
WELL, WELL, WELL! LOOK WHO'S HERE!
COUSIN GLADSTONE!
I HEARD THE MAGNUS MALLEUS WAS SWIPED FROM RIGHT UNDER YOUR NOSES! A SHAME!
HUMPH! NOT EVERYBODY'S LUCK LETS 'EM LIVE ON EASY STREET!
WHAT'S THAT SUPPOSED TO MEAN?!
THAT WITHOUT YOUR ETERNAL GOOD LUCK, YOU COULDN'T CATCH THE DUMBEST METEORBEAST!
TAKE THAT BACK!
WHO'S GONNA MAKE ME?!
I RELY ENTIRELY ON TECHNIQUE! SOMETHING YOU OBVIOUSLY KNOW NOTHING ABOUT!

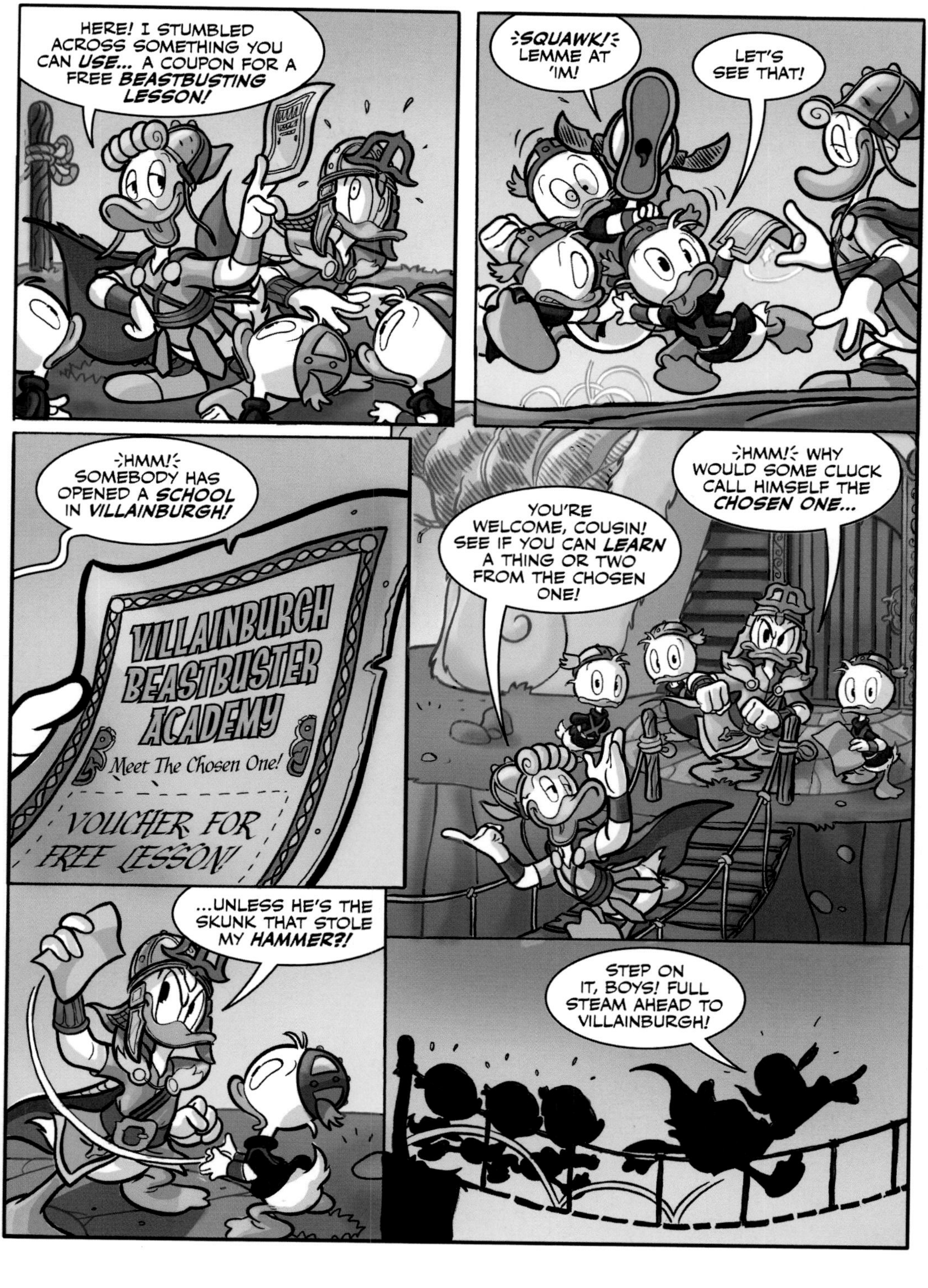
HERE! I STUMBLED ACROSS SOMETHING YOU CAN USE... A COUPON FOR A FREE BEASTBUSTING LESSON!
SQUAWK! LEMME AT 'IM!
LET'S SEE THAT!
HMM! SOMEBODY HAS OPENED A SCHOOL IN VILLAINBURGH!
VILLAINBURGH BEASTBUSTER ACADEMY
Meet The Chosen One!
VOUCHER FOR FREE LESSON!
YOU'RE WELCOME, COUSIN! SEE IF YOU CAN LEARN A THING OR TWO FROM THE CHOSEN ONE!
HMM! WHY WOULD SOME CLUCK CALL HIMSELF THE CHOSEN ONE...
...UNLESS HE'S THE SKUNK THAT STOLE MY HAMMER?!
STEP ON IT, BOYS! FULL STEAM AHEAD TO VILLAINBURGH!

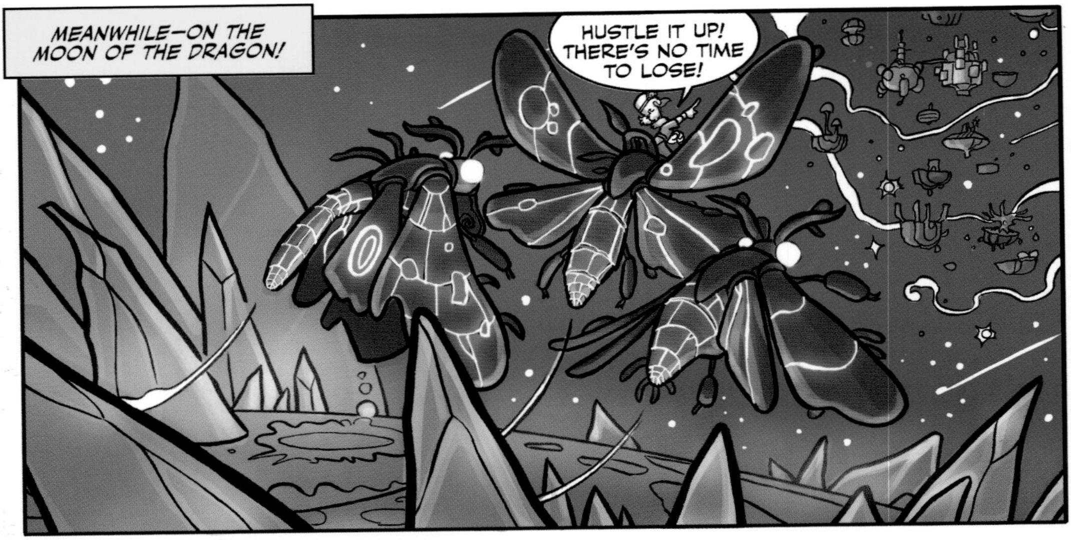
MEANWHILE—ON THE MOON OF THE DRAGON!
HUSTLE IT UP! THERE'S NO TIME TO LOSE!

MOTH METEORBEAST

TYPE:
Terrean Meteorbeast

POWER:
Shoots granite missiles

WEAKNESS:
Cracks around the joints in its rocky skin

ENERGY: 35

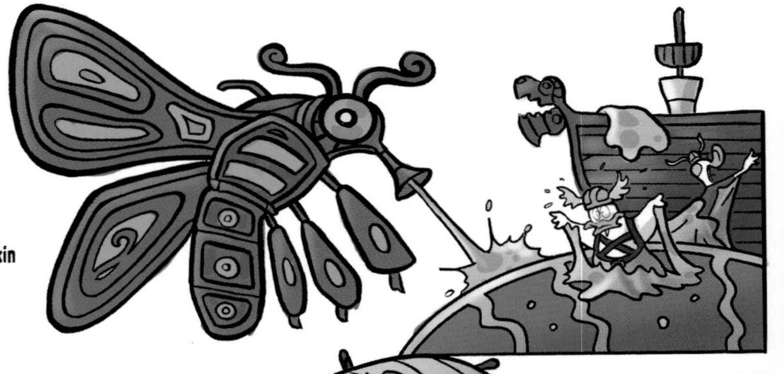

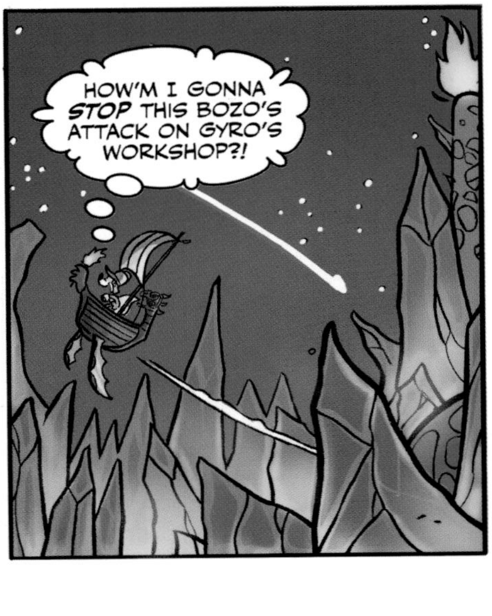
HOW'M I GONNA *STOP* THIS BOZO'S ATTACK ON GYRO'S WORKSHOP?!

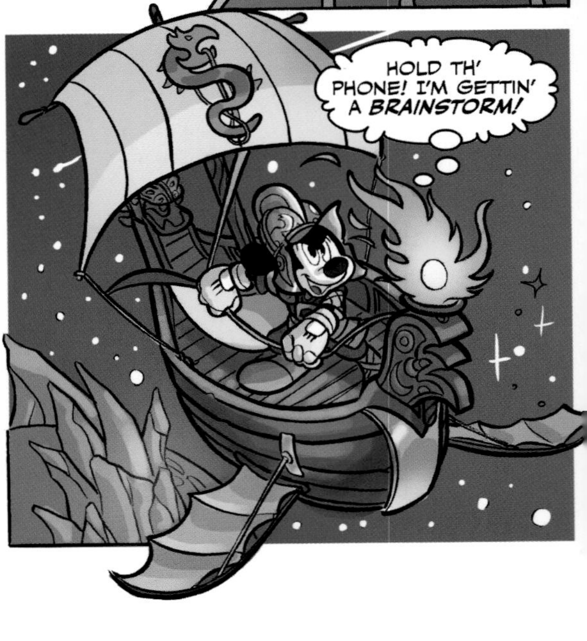
HOLD TH' PHONE! I'M GETTIN' A *BRAINSTORM!*

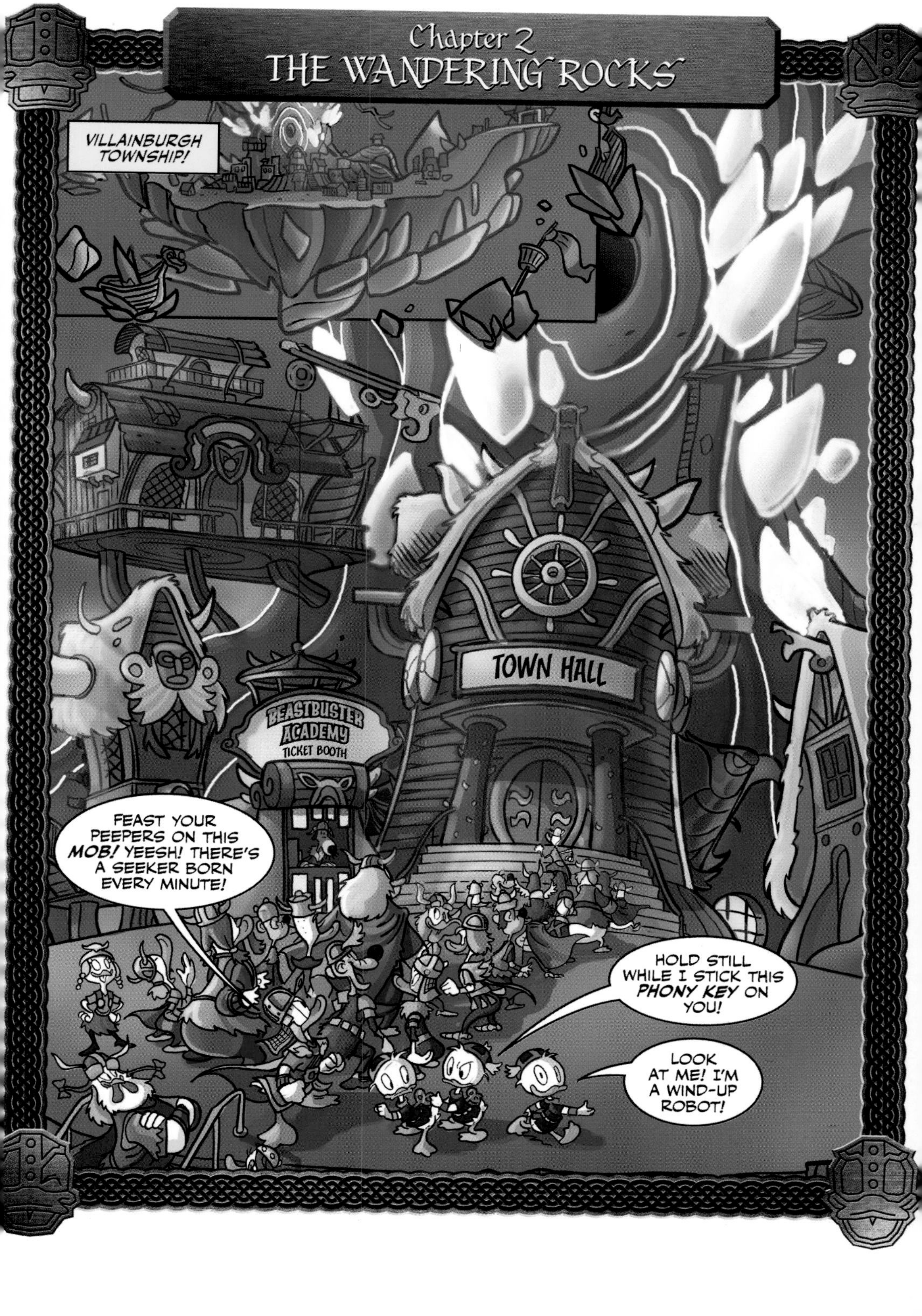
Chapter 2
THE WANDERING ROCKS
VILLAINBURGH TOWNSHIP!
TOWN HALL
BEASTBUSTER ACADEMY TICKET BOOTH
FEAST YOUR PEEPERS ON THIS MOB! YEESH! THERE'S A SEEKER BORN EVERY MINUTE!
HOLD STILL WHILE I STICK THIS PHONY KEY ON YOU!
LOOK AT ME! I'M A WIND-UP ROBOT!

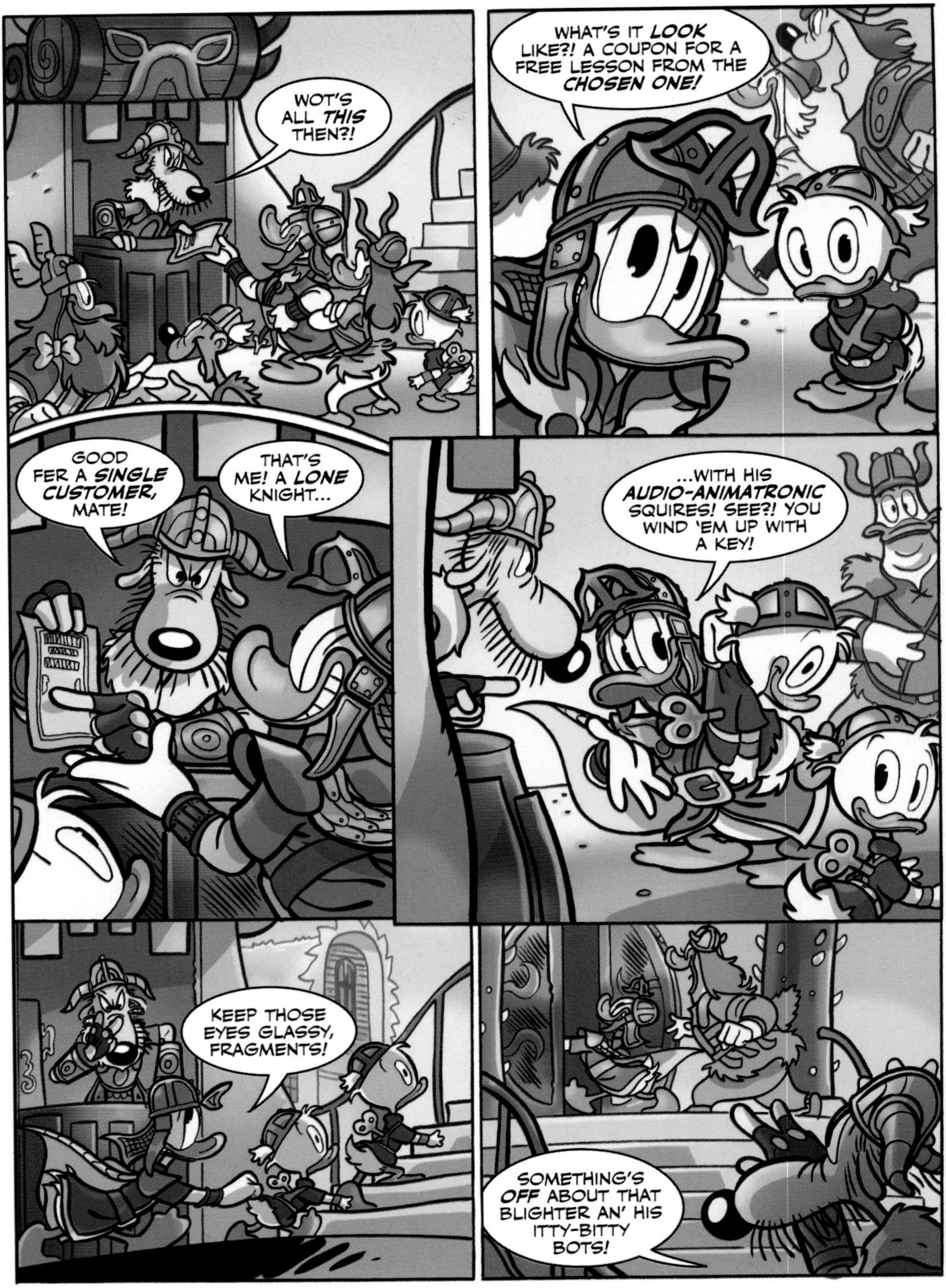
WOT'S ALL *THIS* THEN?!
WHAT'S IT *LOOK* LIKE?! A COUPON FOR A FREE LESSON FROM THE *CHOSEN ONE!*
GOOD FER A *SINGLE CUSTOMER,* MATE!
THAT'S ME! A *LONE* KNIGHT...
...WITH HIS *AUDIO-ANIMATRONIC* SQUIRES! SEE?! YOU WIND 'EM UP WITH A KEY!
KEEP THOSE EYES GLASSY, FRAGMENTS!
SOMETHING'S *OFF* ABOUT THAT BLIGHTER AN' HIS ITTY-BITTY BOTS!

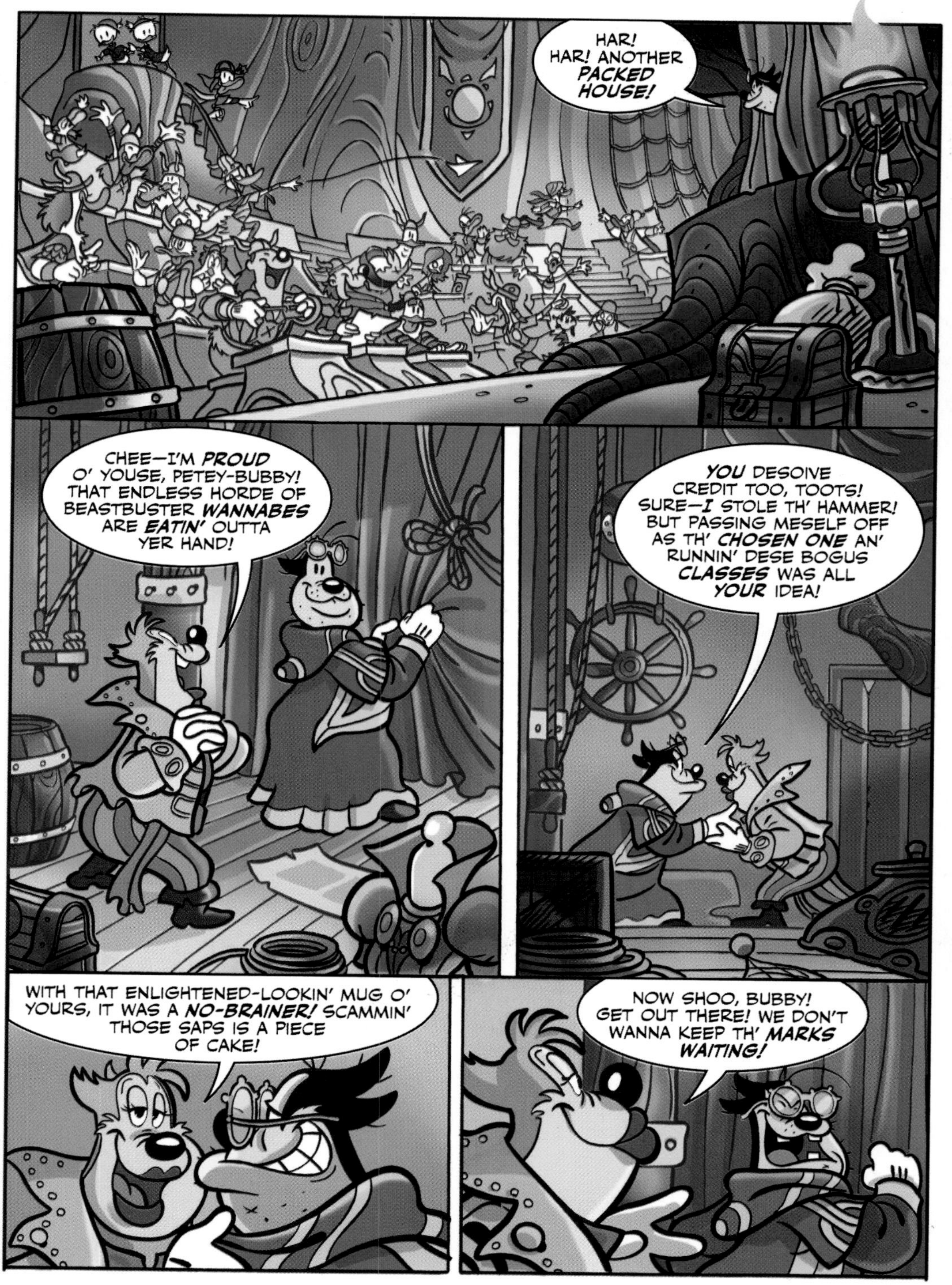

HAR! HAR! ANOTHER PACKED HOUSE!
CHEE—I'M PROUD O' YOUSE, PETEY-BUBBY! THAT ENDLESS HORDE OF BEASTBUSTER WANNABES ARE EATIN' OUTTA YER HAND!
YOU DESOIVE CREDIT TOO, TOOTS! SURE—I STOLE TH' HAMMER! BUT PASSING MESELF OFF AS TH' CHOSEN ONE AN' RUNNIN' DESE BOGUS CLASSES WAS ALL YOUR IDEA!
WITH THAT ENLIGHTENED-LOOKIN' MUG O' YOURS, IT WAS A NO-BRAINER! SCAMMIN' THOSE SAPS IS A PIECE OF CAKE!
NOW SHOO, BUBBY! GET OUT THERE! WE DON'T WANNA KEEP TH' MARKS WAITING!

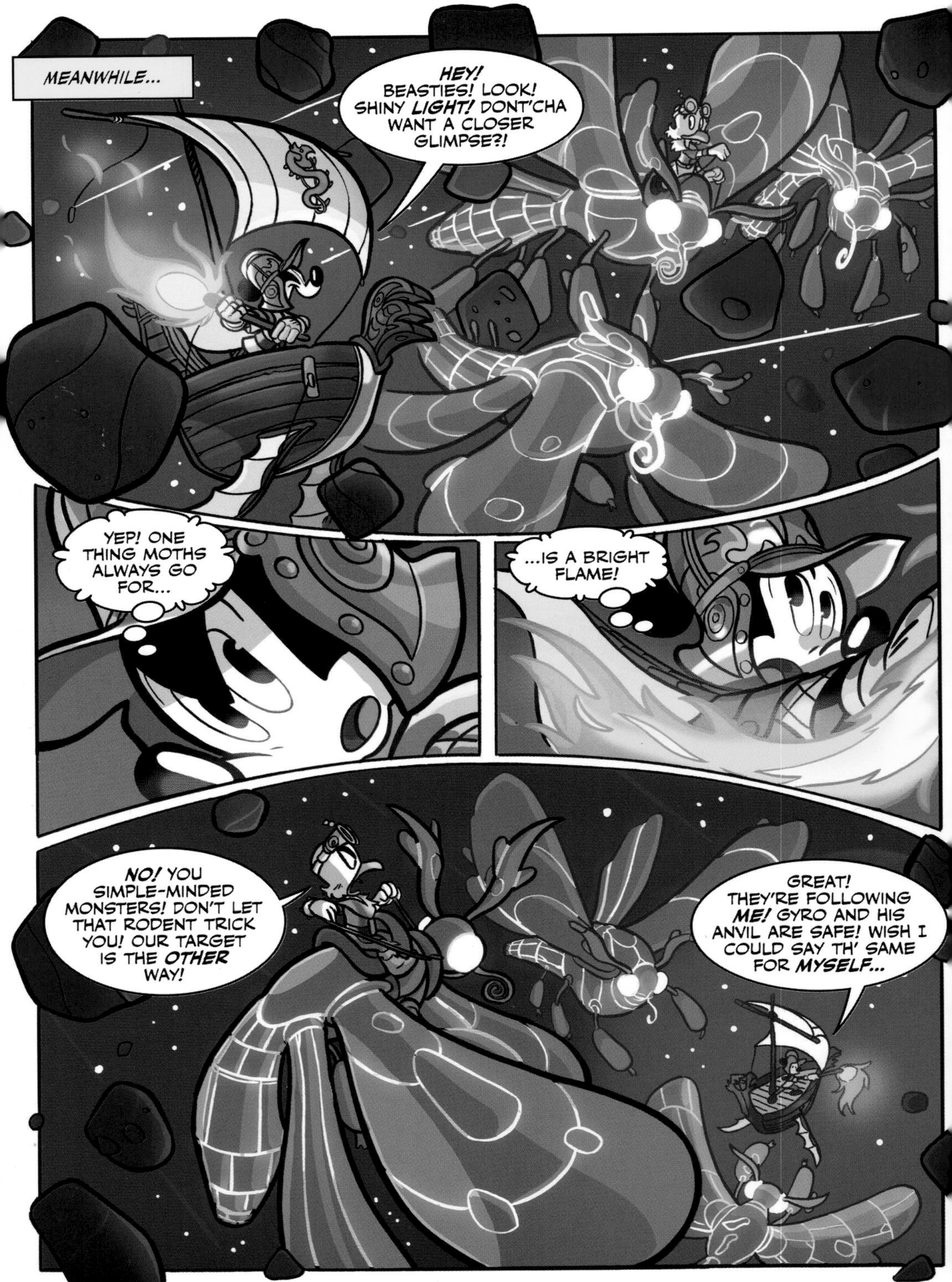
MEANWHILE...
HEY! BEASTIES! LOOK! SHINY LIGHT! DONT'CHA WANT A CLOSER GLIMPSE?!
YEP! ONE THING MOTHS ALWAYS GO FOR...
...IS A BRIGHT FLAME!
NO! YOU SIMPLE-MINDED MONSTERS! DON'T LET THAT RODENT TRICK YOU! OUR TARGET IS THE OTHER WAY!
GREAT! THEY'RE FOLLOWING ME! GYRO AND HIS ANVIL ARE SAFE! WISH I COULD SAY TH' SAME FOR MYSELF...

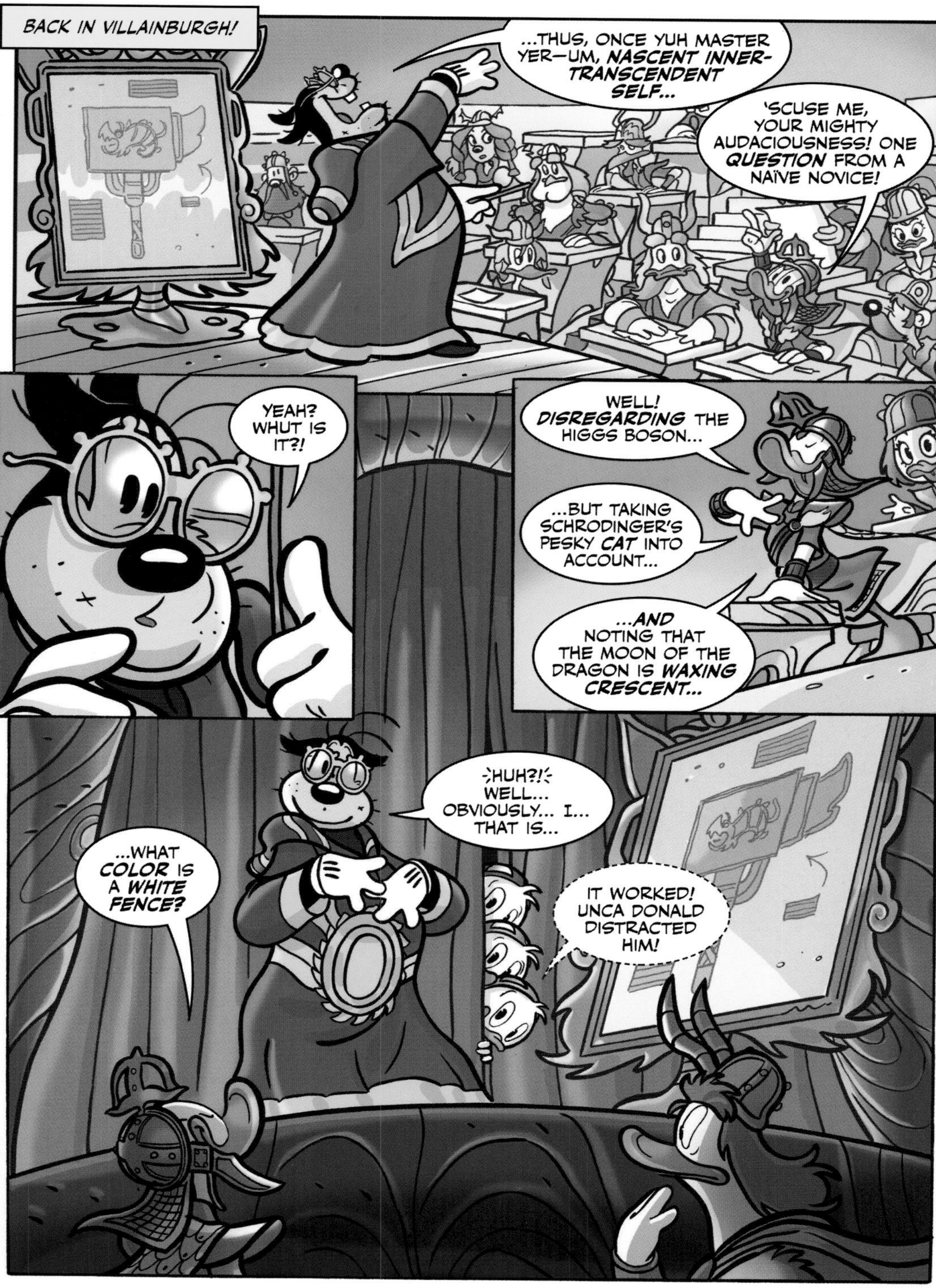
BACK IN VILLAINBURGH!
...THUS, ONCE YUH MASTER YER—UM, NASCENT INNER-TRANSCENDENT SELF...
'SCUSE ME, YOUR MIGHTY AUDACIOUSNESS! ONE QUESTION FROM A NAÏVE NOVICE!
YEAH? WHUT IS IT?!
WELL! DISREGARDING THE HIGGS BOSON...
...BUT TAKING SCHRODINGER'S PESKY CAT INTO ACCOUNT...
...AND NOTING THAT THE MOON OF THE DRAGON IS WAXING CRESCENT...
HUH?! WELL... OBVIOUSLY... I... THAT IS...
...WHAT COLOR IS A WHITE FENCE?
IT WORKED! UNCA DONALD DISTRACTED HIM!

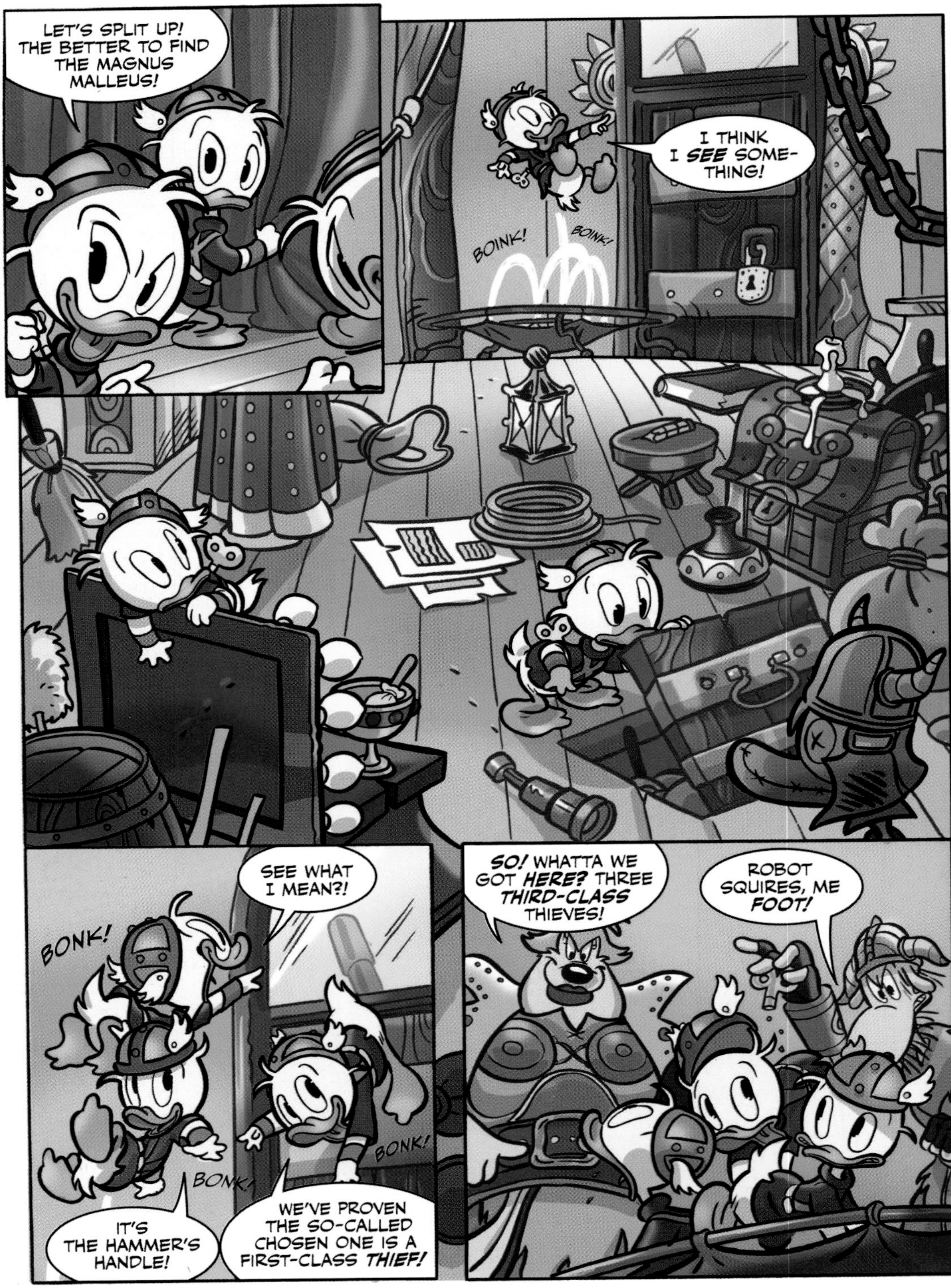
LET'S SPLIT UP! THE BETTER TO FIND THE MAGNUS MALLEUS!
I THINK I *SEE* SOME-THING!
BOINK!
BOINK!
SEE WHAT I MEAN?!
BONK!
BONK!
BONK!
IT'S THE HAMMER'S HANDLE!
WE'VE PROVEN THE SO-CALLED CHOSEN ONE IS A FIRST-CLASS *THIEF!*
SO! WHATTA WE GOT *HERE?* THREE *THIRD-CLASS* THIEVES!
ROBOT SQUIRES, ME *FOOT!*

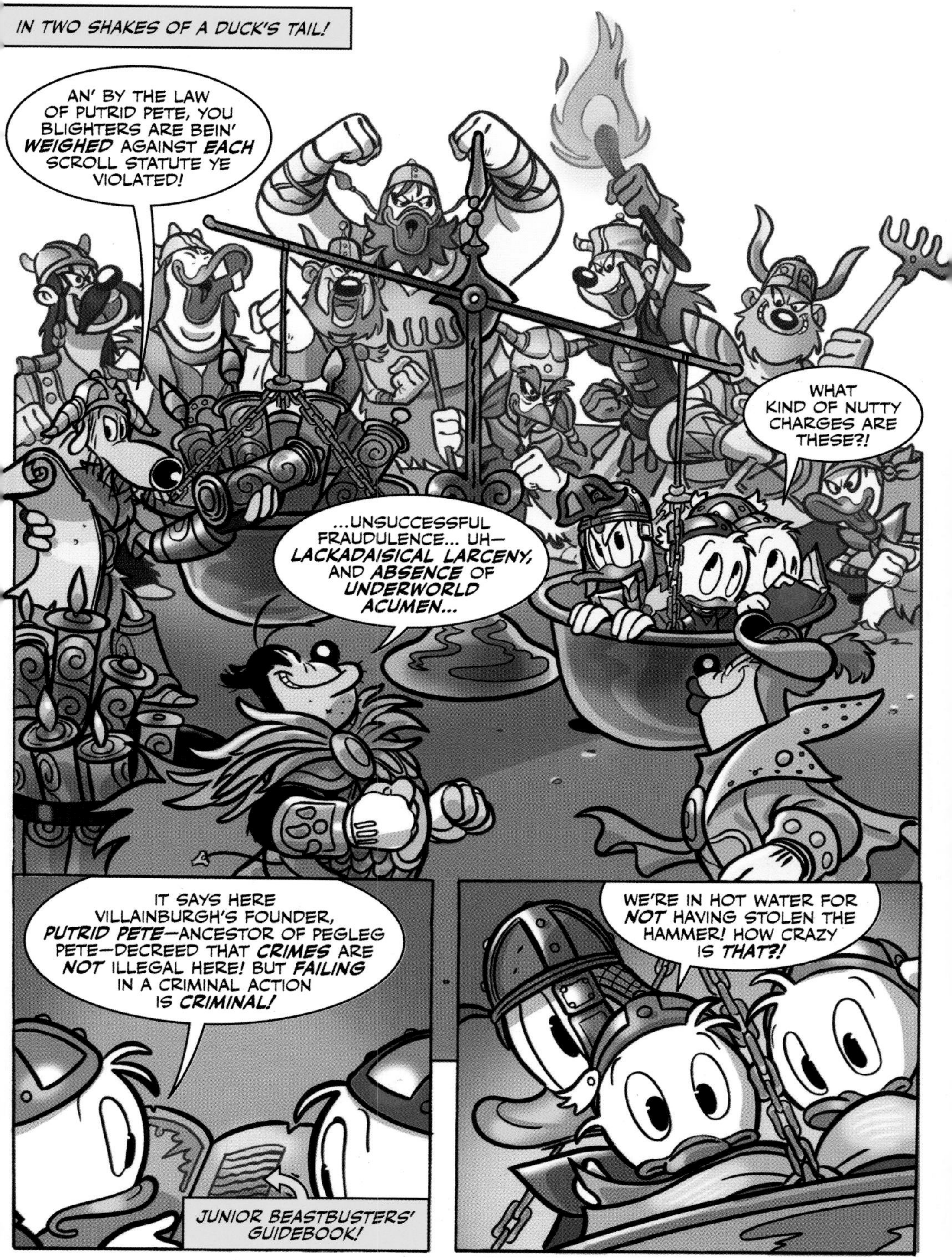
IN TWO SHAKES OF A DUCK'S TAIL!
AN' BY THE LAW OF PUTRID PETE, YOU BLIGHTERS ARE BEIN' WEIGHED AGAINST EACH SCROLL STATUTE YE VIOLATED!
WHAT KIND OF NUTTY CHARGES ARE THESE?!
...UNSUCCESSFUL FRAUDULENCE... UH— LACKADAISICAL LARCENY, AND ABSENCE OF UNDERWORLD ACUMEN...
IT SAYS HERE VILLAINBURGH'S FOUNDER, PUTRID PETE—ANCESTOR OF PEGLEG PETE—DECREED THAT CRIMES ARE NOT ILLEGAL HERE! BUT FAILING IN A CRIMINAL ACTION IS CRIMINAL!
JUNIOR BEASTBUSTERS' GUIDEBOOK!
WE'RE IN HOT WATER FOR NOT HAVING STOLEN THE HAMMER! HOW CRAZY IS THAT?!

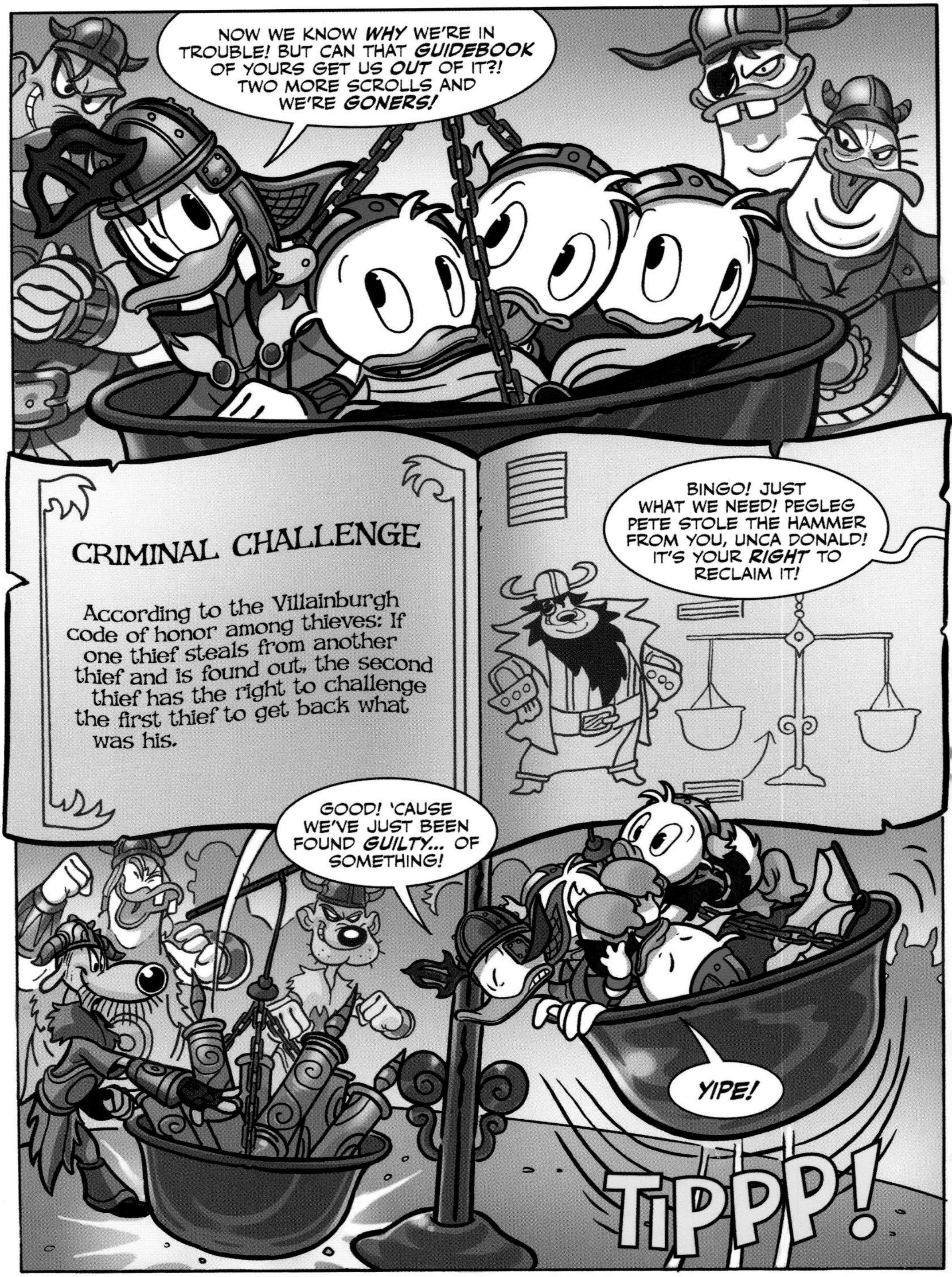
NOW WE KNOW WHY WE'RE IN TROUBLE! BUT CAN THAT GUIDEBOOK OF YOURS GET US OUT OF IT?! TWO MORE SCROLLS AND WE'RE GONERS!
CRIMINAL CHALLENGE
According to the Villainburgh code of honor among thieves: If one thief steals from another thief and is found out, the second thief has the right to challenge the first thief to get back what was his.
BINGO! JUST WHAT WE NEED! PEGLEG PETE STOLE THE HAMMER FROM YOU, UNCA DONALD! IT'S YOUR RIGHT TO RECLAIM IT!
GOOD! 'CAUSE WE'VE JUST BEEN FOUND GUILTY... OF SOMETHING!
YIPE!
TIPPP!

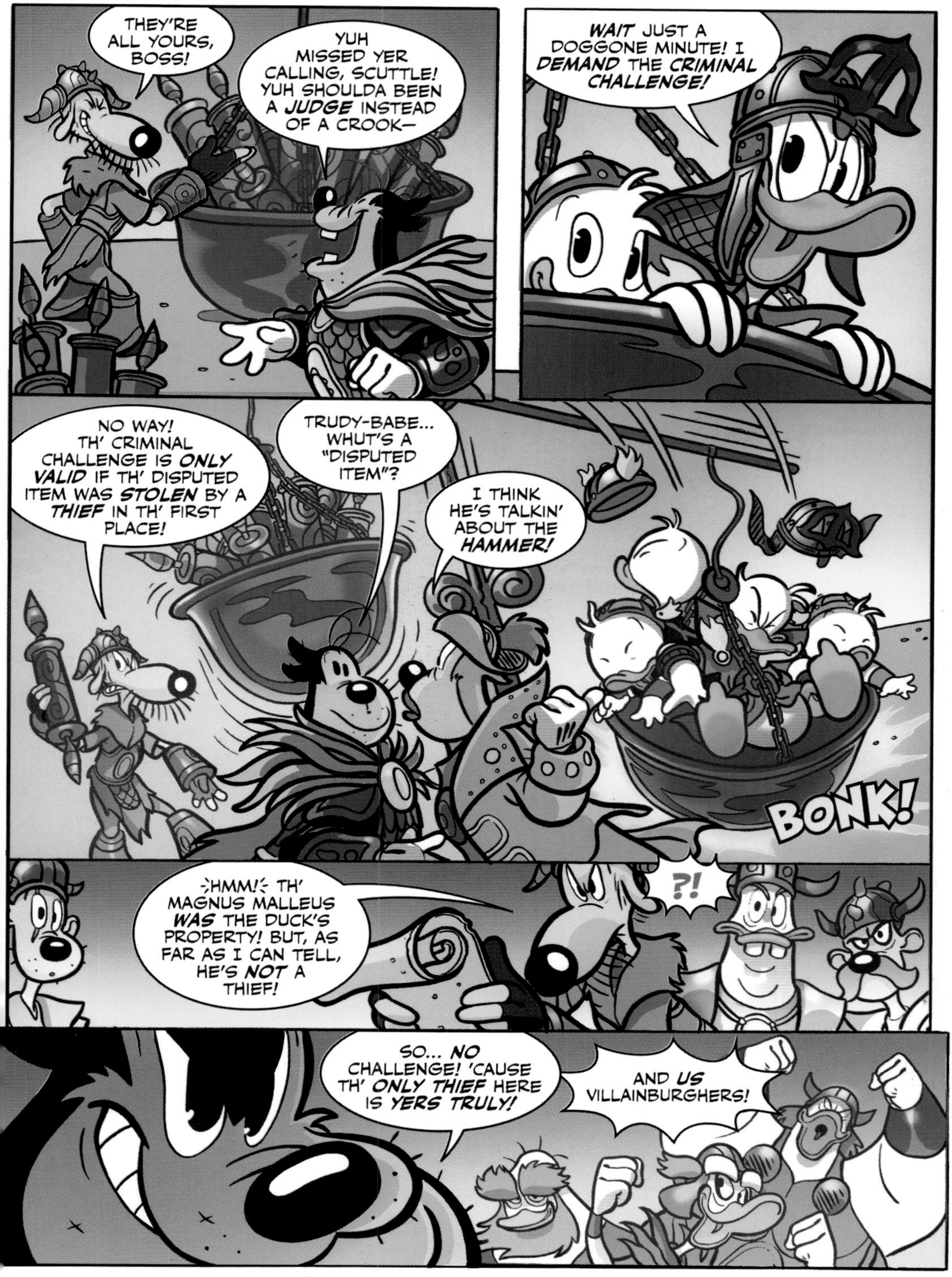
THEY'RE ALL YOURS, BOSS!
YUH MISSED YER CALLING, SCUTTLE! YUH SHOULDA BEEN A JUDGE INSTEAD OF A CROOK—
WAIT JUST A DOGGONE MINUTE! I DEMAND THE CRIMINAL CHALLENGE!
NO WAY! TH' CRIMINAL CHALLENGE IS ONLY VALID IF TH' DISPUTED ITEM WAS STOLEN BY A THIEF IN TH' FIRST PLACE!
TRUDY-BABE... WHUT'S A "DISPUTED ITEM"?
I THINK HE'S TALKIN' ABOUT THE HAMMER!
BONK!
HMM! TH' MAGNUS MALLEUS WAS THE DUCK'S PROPERTY! BUT, AS FAR AS I CAN TELL, HE'S NOT A THIEF!
?!
SO... NO CHALLENGE! 'CAUSE TH' ONLY THIEF HERE IS YERS TRULY!
AND US VILLAINBURGHERS!

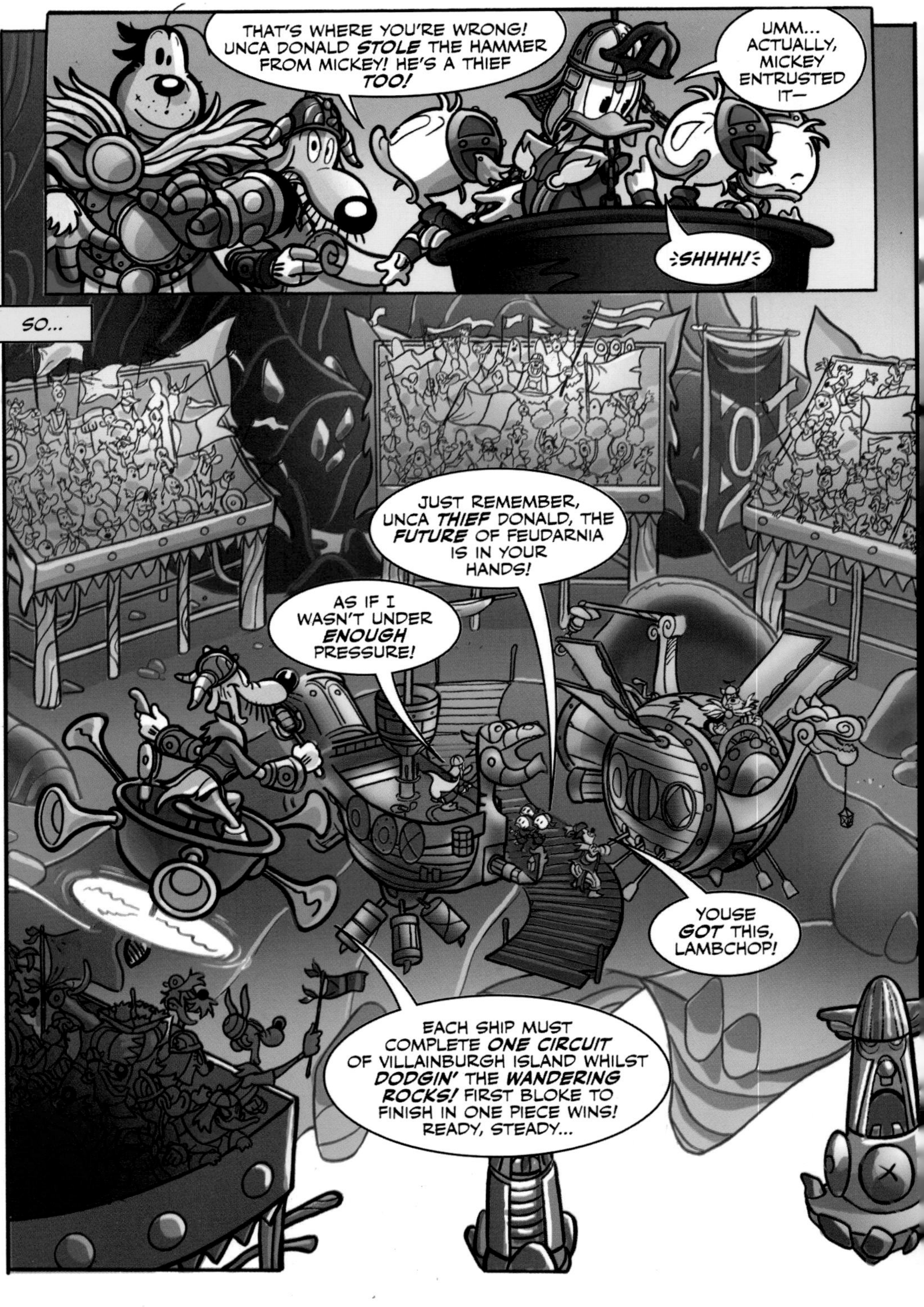
THAT'S WHERE YOU'RE WRONG! UNCA DONALD STOLE THE HAMMER FROM MICKEY! HE'S A THIEF TOO!
UMM... ACTUALLY, MICKEY ENTRUSTED IT—
SHHHH!
SO...
JUST REMEMBER, UNCA THIEF DONALD, THE FUTURE OF FEUDARNIA IS IN YOUR HANDS!
AS IF I WASN'T UNDER ENOUGH PRESSURE!
YOUSE GOT THIS, LAMBCHOP!
EACH SHIP MUST COMPLETE ONE CIRCUIT OF VILLAINBURGH ISLAND WHILST DODGIN' THE WANDERING ROCKS! FIRST BLOKE TO FINISH IN ONE PIECE WINS! READY, STEADY...

Chapter 3
RUN, RODENT, RUN

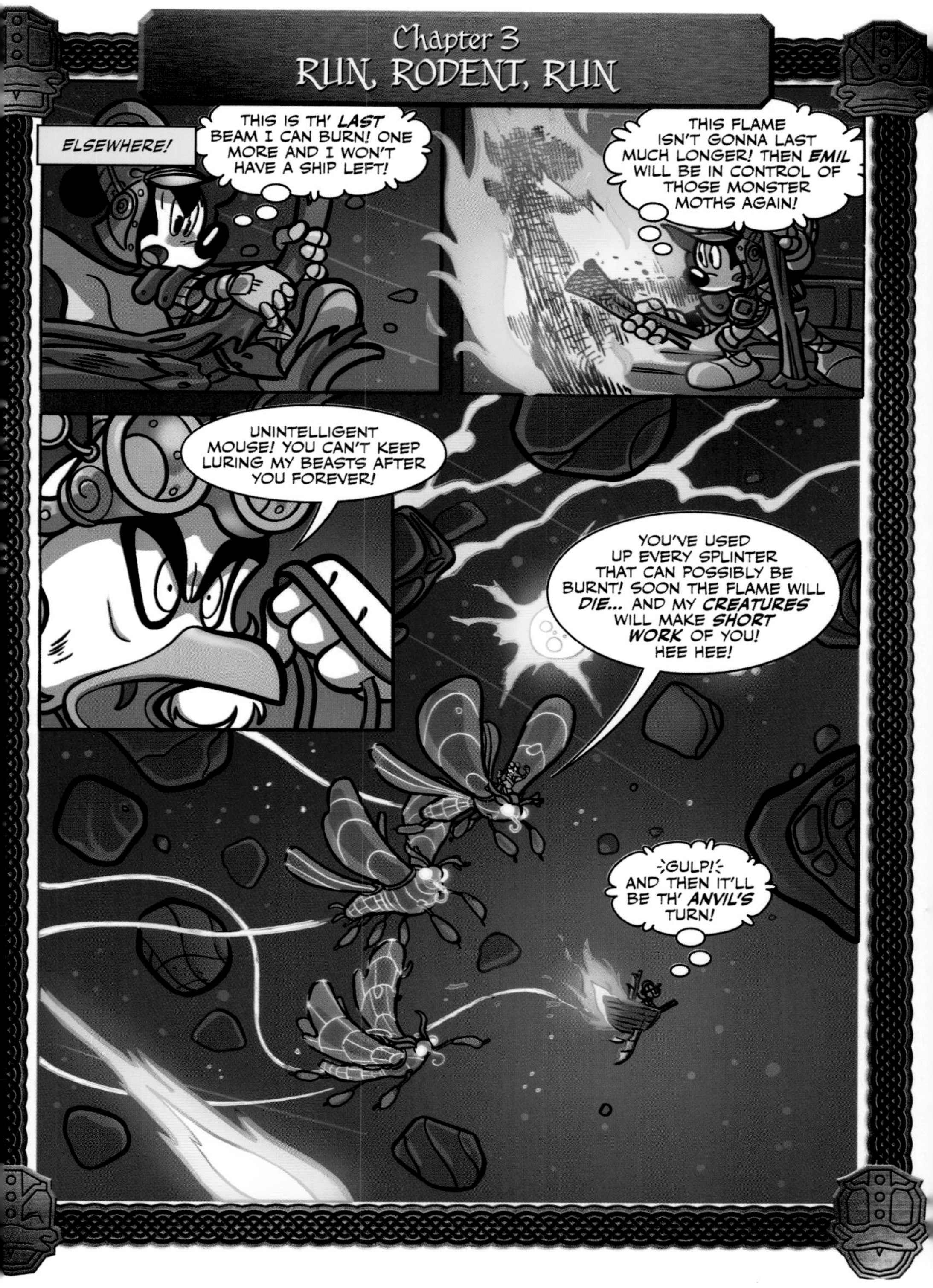

ELSEWHERE!
THIS IS TH' LAST BEAM I CAN BURN! ONE MORE AND I WON'T HAVE A SHIP LEFT!
THIS FLAME ISN'T GONNA LAST MUCH LONGER! THEN EMIL WILL BE IN CONTROL OF THOSE MONSTER MOTHS AGAIN!
UNINTELLIGENT MOUSE! YOU CAN'T KEEP LURING MY BEASTS AFTER YOU FOREVER!
YOU'VE USED UP EVERY SPLINTER THAT CAN POSSIBLY BE BURNT! SOON THE FLAME WILL DIE... AND MY CREATURES WILL MAKE SHORT WORK OF YOU! HEE HEE!
GULP! AND THEN IT'LL BE TH' ANVIL'S TURN!

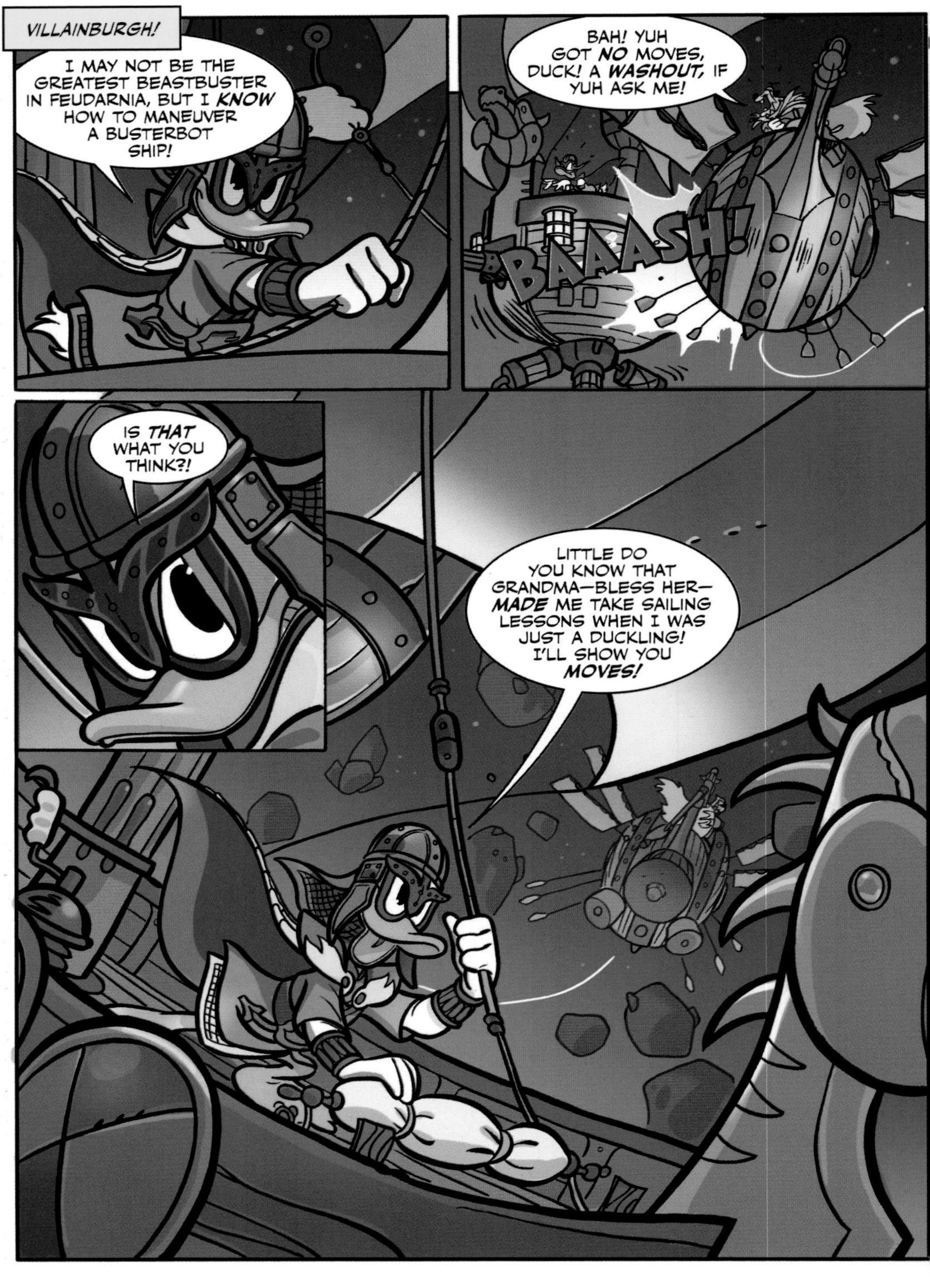
VILLAINBURGH!
I MAY NOT BE THE GREATEST BEASTBUSTER IN FEUDARNIA, BUT I KNOW HOW TO MANEUVER A BUSTERBOT SHIP!
BAH! YUH GOT NO MOVES, DUCK! A WASHOUT, IF YUH ASK ME!
BAAASH!
IS THAT WHAT YOU THINK?!
LITTLE DO YOU KNOW THAT GRANDMA—BLESS HER—MADE ME TAKE SAILING LESSONS WHEN I WAS JUST A DUCKLING! I'LL SHOW YOU MOVES!

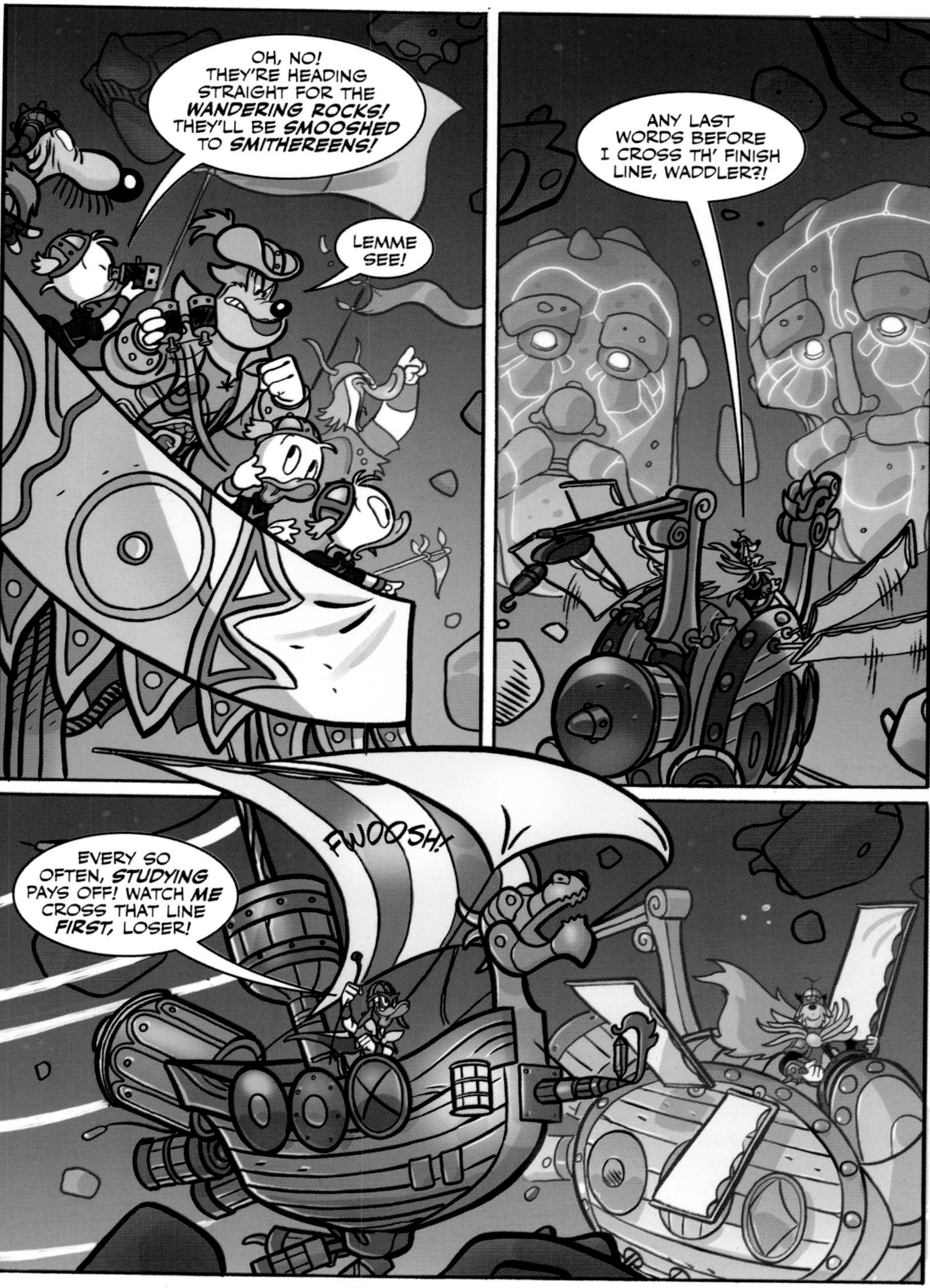
OH, NO! THEY'RE HEADING STRAIGHT FOR THE WANDERING ROCKS! THEY'LL BE SMOOSHED TO SMITHEREENS!
LEMME SEE!
ANY LAST WORDS BEFORE I CROSS TH' FINISH LINE, WADDLER?!
EVERY SO OFTEN, STUDYING PAYS OFF! WATCH ME CROSS THAT LINE FIRST, LOSER!
FWOOSH!

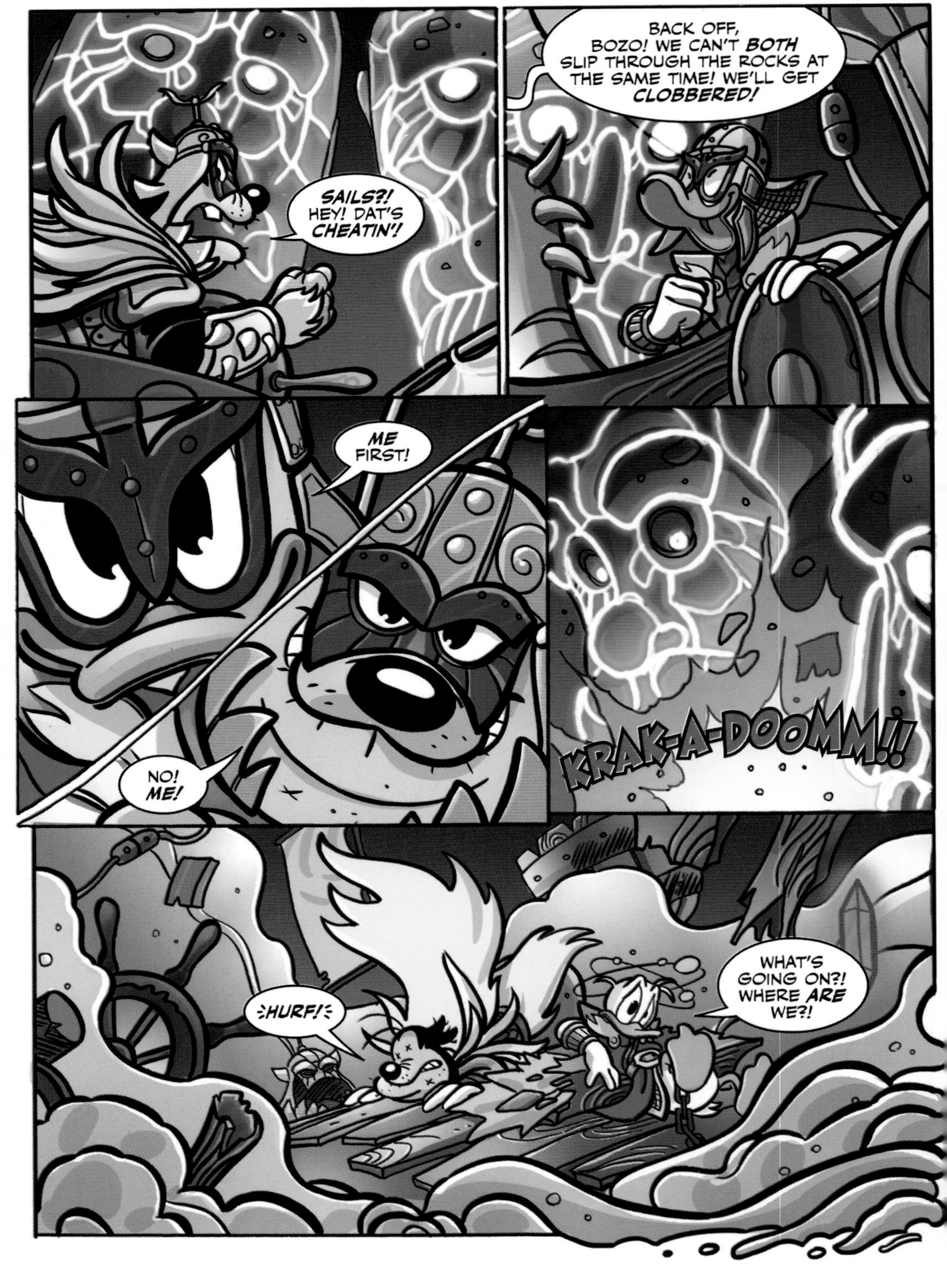
SAILS?! HEY! DAT'S CHEATIN'!
BACK OFF, BOZO! WE CAN'T BOTH SLIP THROUGH THE ROCKS AT THE SAME TIME! WE'LL GET CLOBBERED!
ME FIRST!
NO! ME!
KRAK-A-DOOMM!!
HURF!
WHAT'S GOING ON?! WHERE ARE WE?!

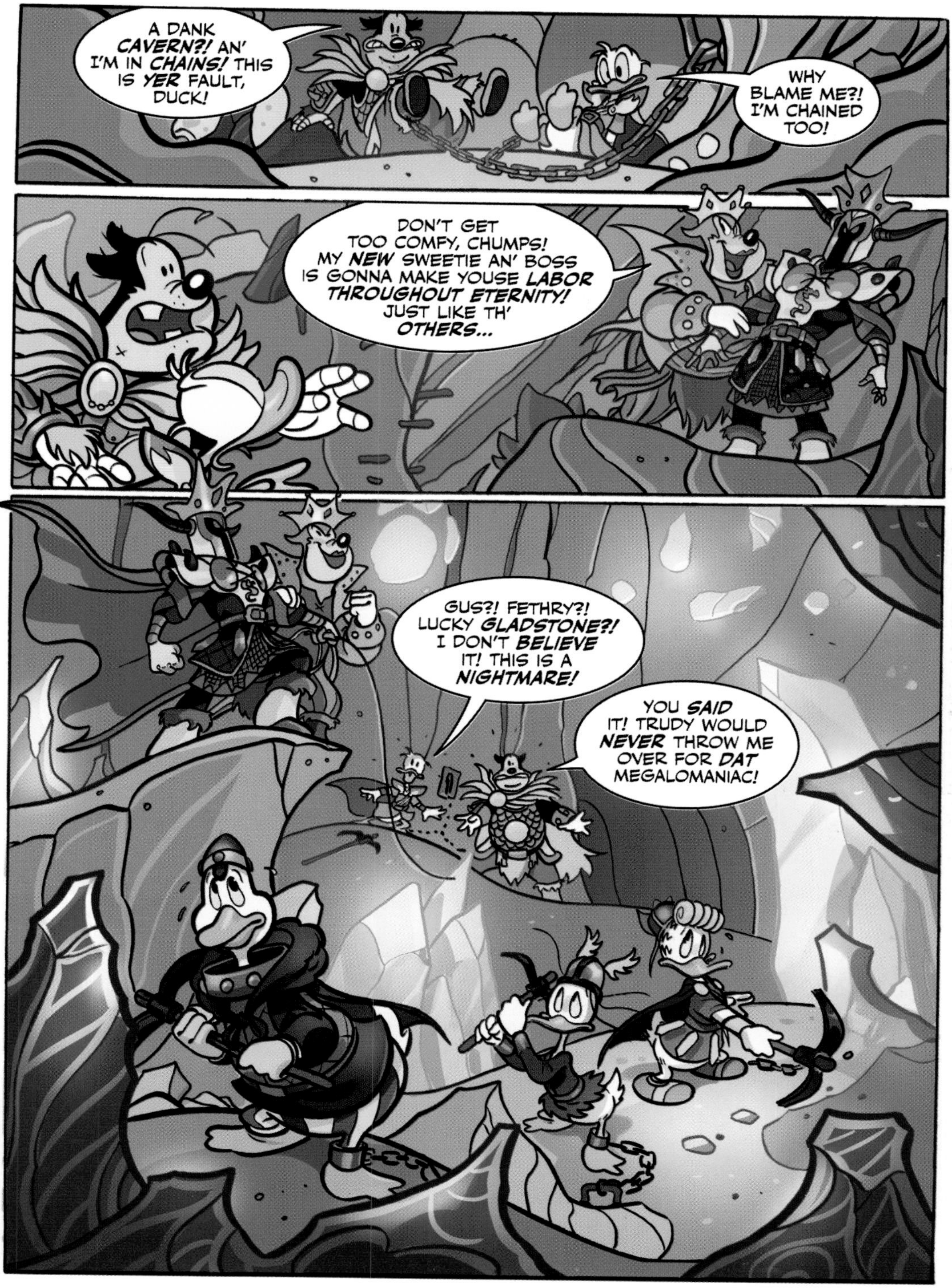
A DANK CAVERN?! AN' I'M IN CHAINS! THIS IS YER FAULT, DUCK!
WHY BLAME ME?! I'M CHAINED TOO!
DON'T GET TOO COMFY, CHUMPS! MY NEW SWEETIE AN' BOSS IS GONNA MAKE YOUSE LABOR THROUGHOUT ETERNITY! JUST LIKE TH' OTHERS...
GUS?! FETHRY?! LUCKY GLADSTONE?! I DON'T BELIEVE IT! THIS IS A NIGHTMARE!
YOU SAID IT! TRUDY WOULD NEVER THROW ME OVER FOR DAT MEGALOMANIAC!

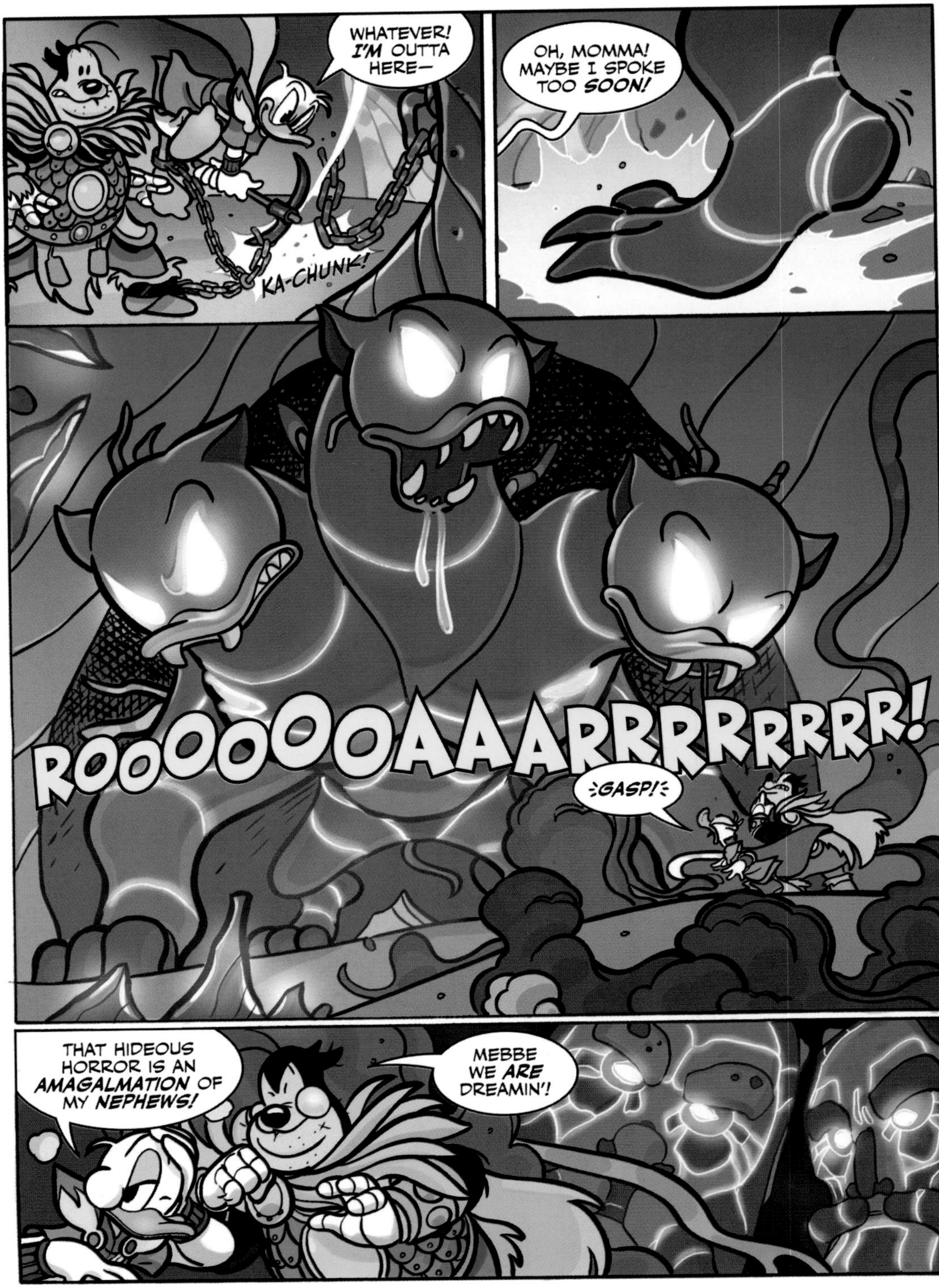
WHATEVER! I'M OUTTA HERE—
KA-CHUNK!
OH, MOMMA! MAYBE I SPOKE TOO SOON!
ROOOOOOOAAARRRRRRRR!
GASP!
THAT HIDEOUS HORROR IS AN AMAGALMATION OF MY NEPHEWS!
MEBBE WE ARE DREAMIN'!

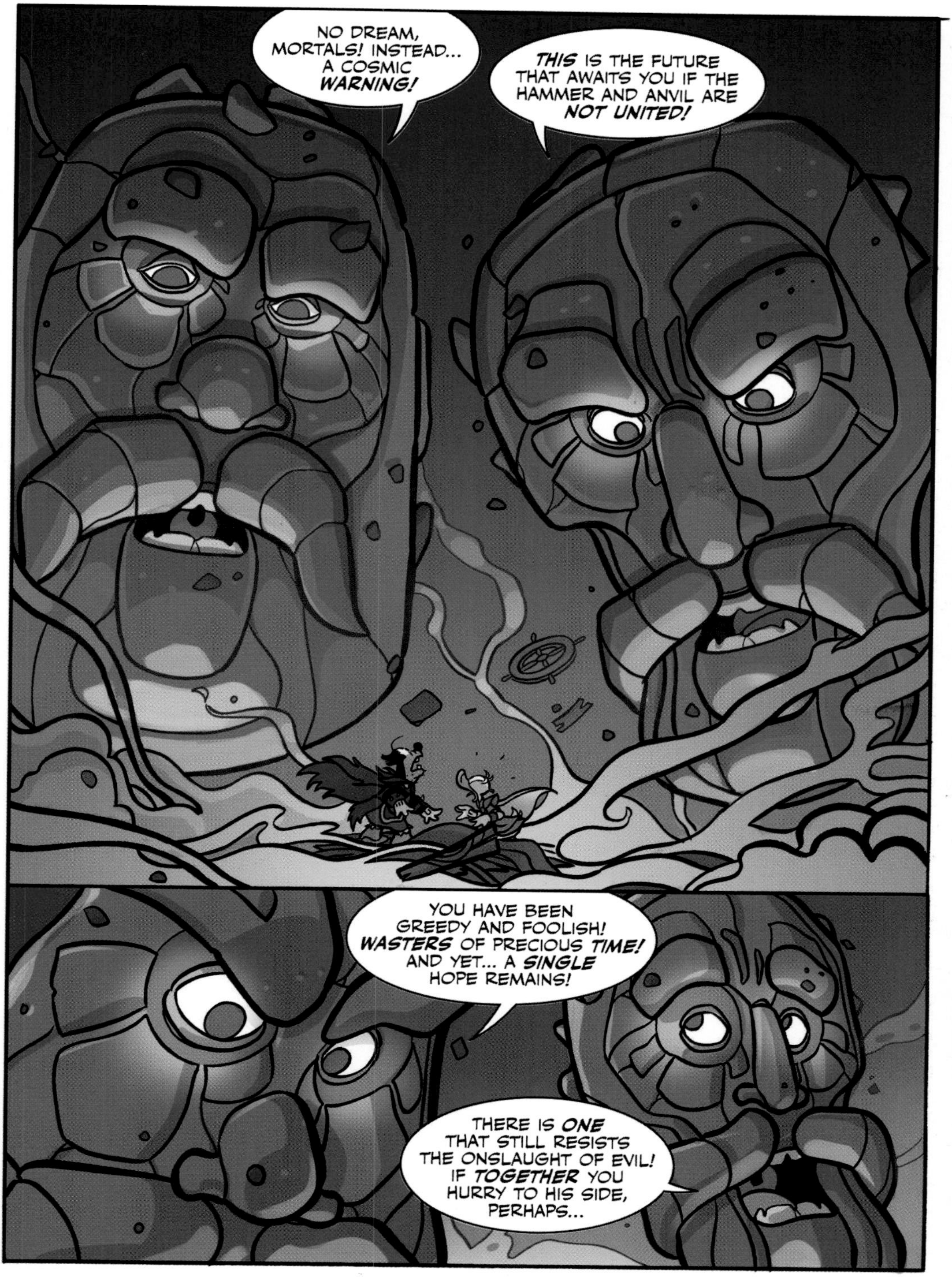
NO DREAM, MORTALS! INSTEAD... A COSMIC WARNING!
THIS IS THE FUTURE THAT AWAITS YOU IF THE HAMMER AND ANVIL ARE NOT UNITED!
YOU HAVE BEEN GREEDY AND FOOLISH! WASTERS OF PRECIOUS TIME! AND YET... A SINGLE HOPE REMAINS!
THERE IS ONE THAT STILL RESISTS THE ONSLAUGHT OF EVIL! IF TOGETHER YOU HURRY TO HIS SIDE, PERHAPS...

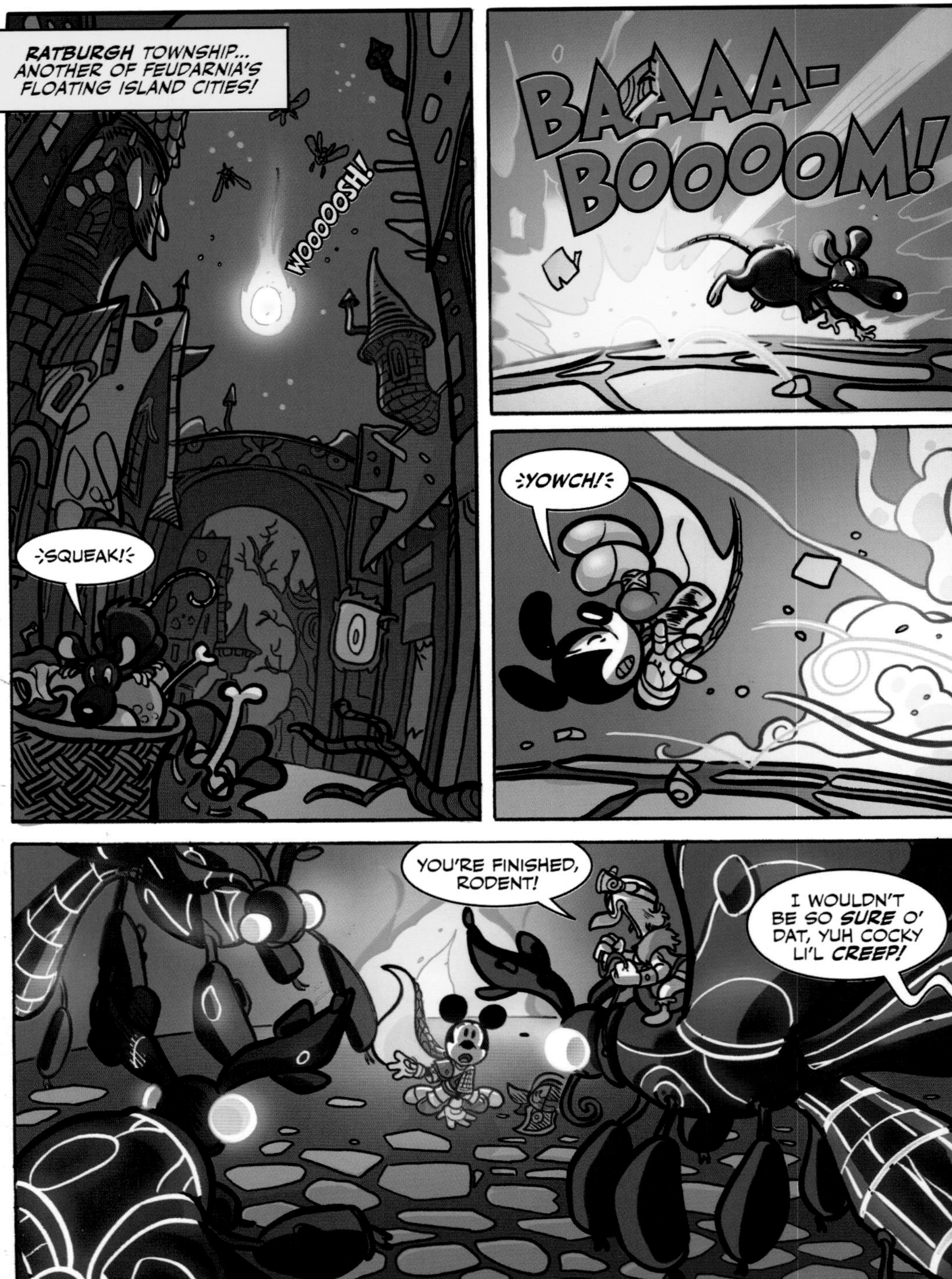
RATBURGH TOWNSHIP... ANOTHER OF FEUDARNIA'S FLOATING ISLAND CITIES!
WOOOOOSH!
SQUEAK!
BAAAA-BOOOOOM!
YOWCH!
YOU'RE FINISHED, RODENT!
I WOULDN'T BE SO SURE O' DAT, YUH COCKY LI'L CREEP!

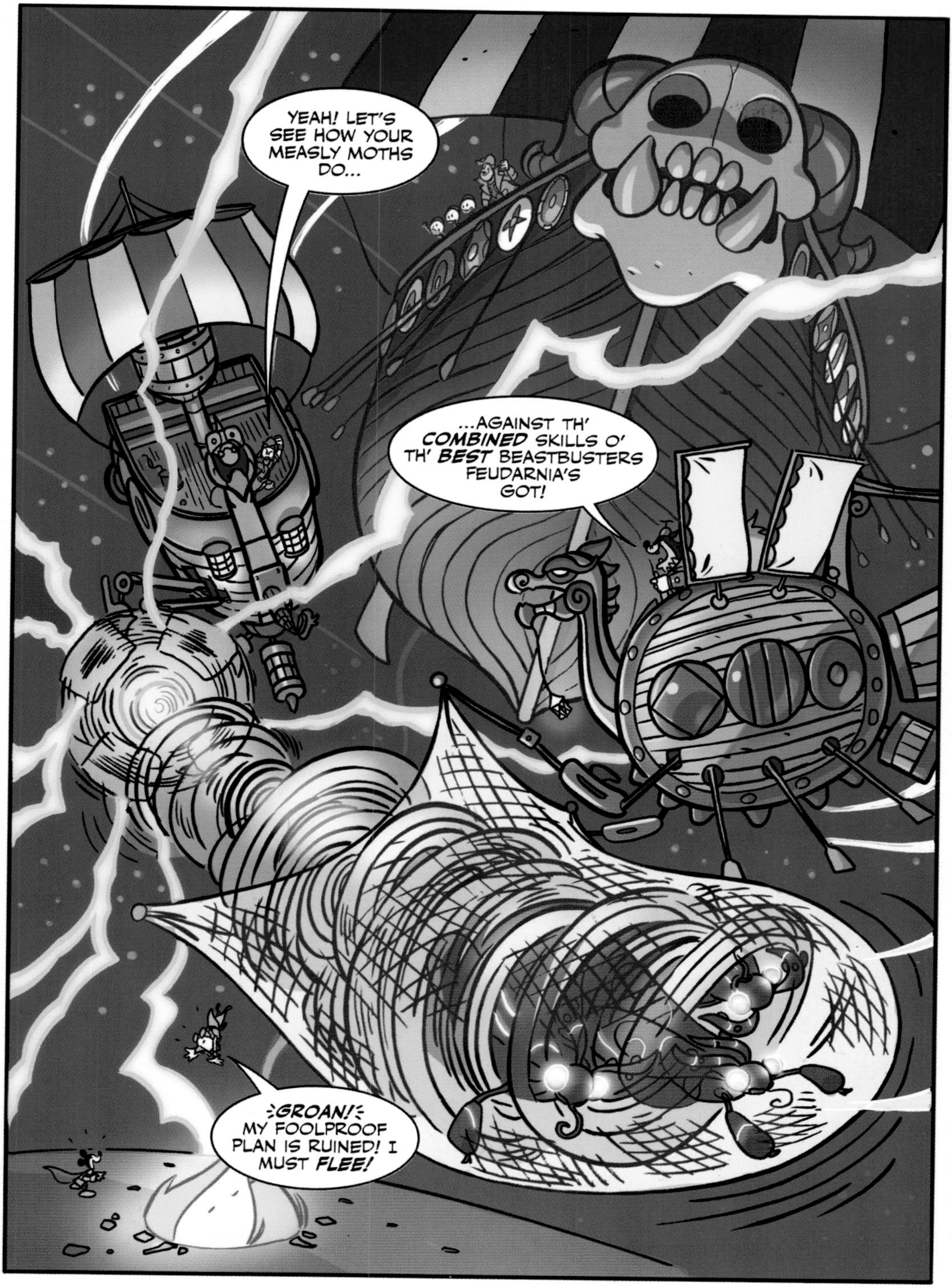
YEAH! LET'S SEE HOW YOUR MEASLY MOTHS DO...
...AGAINST TH' COMBINED SKILLS O' TH' BEST BEASTBUSTERS FEUDARNIA'S GOT!
GROAN! MY FOOLPROOF PLAN IS RUINED! I MUST FLEE!

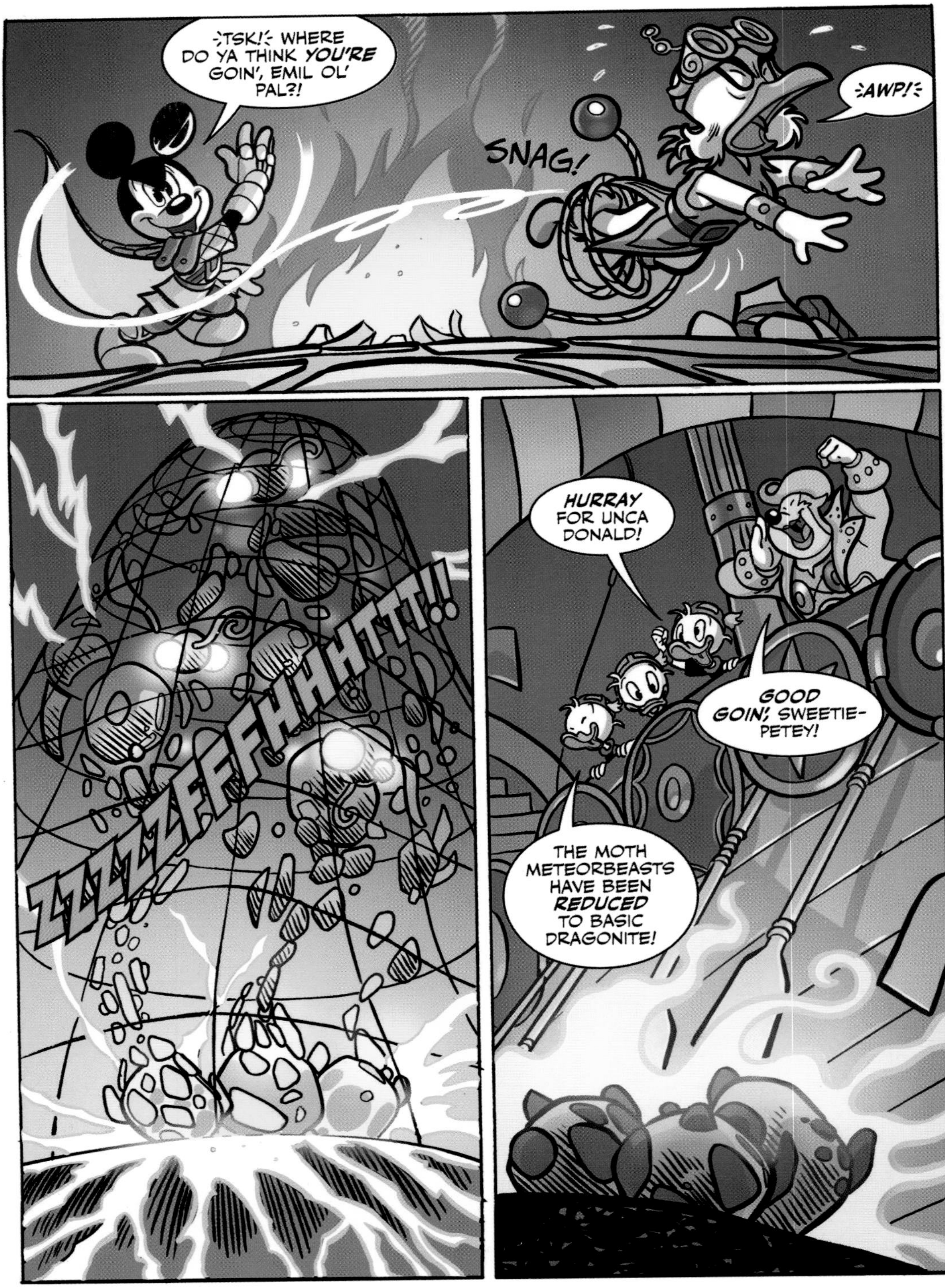

TSK! WHERE DO YA THINK YOU'RE GOIN', EMIL OL' PAL?!
AWP!
SNAG!
ZZZZZZFFFFHHHTTT!!
HURRAY FOR UNCA DONALD!
GOOD GOIN', SWEETIE-PETEY!
THE MOTH METEORBEASTS HAVE BEEN REDUCED TO BASIC DRAGONITE!

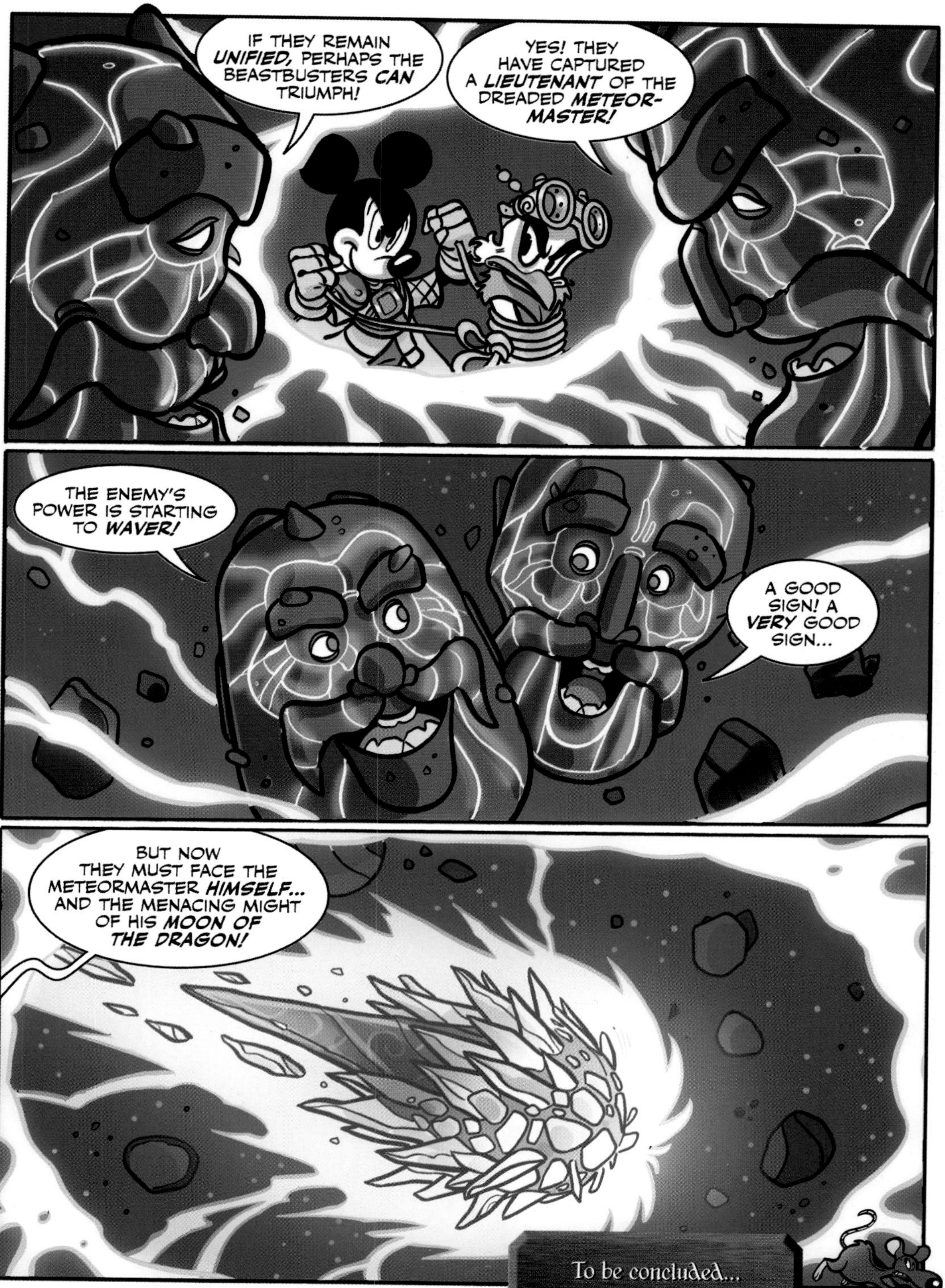
IF THEY REMAIN UNIFIED, PERHAPS THE BEASTBUSTERS CAN TRIUMPH!
YES! THEY HAVE CAPTURED A LIEUTENANT OF THE DREADED METEOR-MASTER!
THE ENEMY'S POWER IS STARTING TO WAVER!
A GOOD SIGN! A VERY GOOD SIGN...
BUT NOW THEY MUST FACE THE METEORMASTER HIMSELF... AND THE MENACING MIGHT OF HIS MOON OF THE DRAGON!
To be concluded...

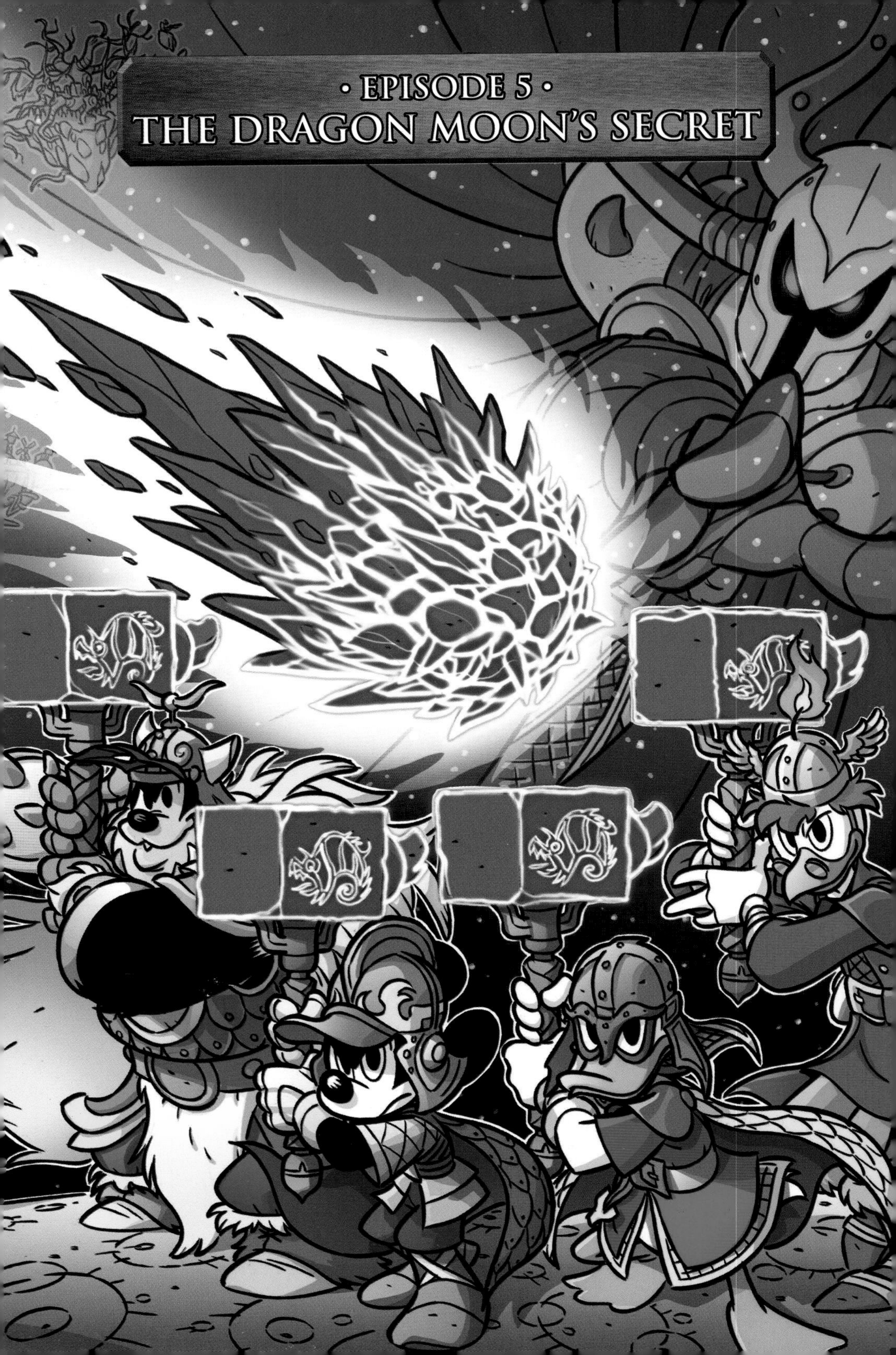

• EPISODE 5 •
THE DRAGON MOON'S SECRET

Chapter 1
IN SEARCH OF A ROUTE

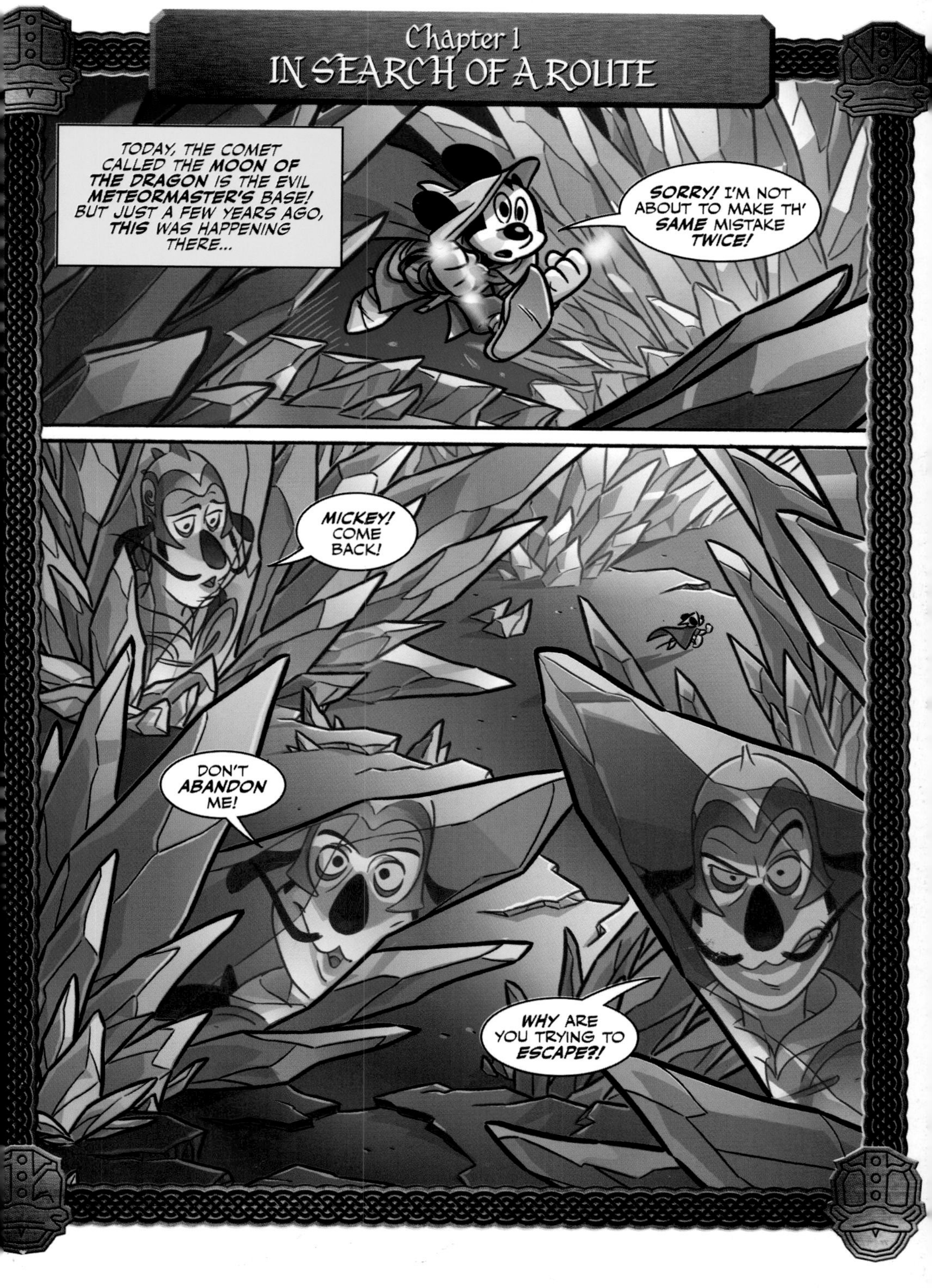
TODAY, THE COMET CALLED THE MOON OF THE DRAGON IS THE EVIL METEORMASTER'S BASE! BUT JUST A FEW YEARS AGO, THIS WAS HAPPENING THERE...
SORRY! I'M NOT ABOUT TO MAKE TH' SAME MISTAKE TWICE!
MICKEY! COME BACK!
DON'T ABANDON ME!
WHY ARE YOU TRYING TO ESCAPE?!

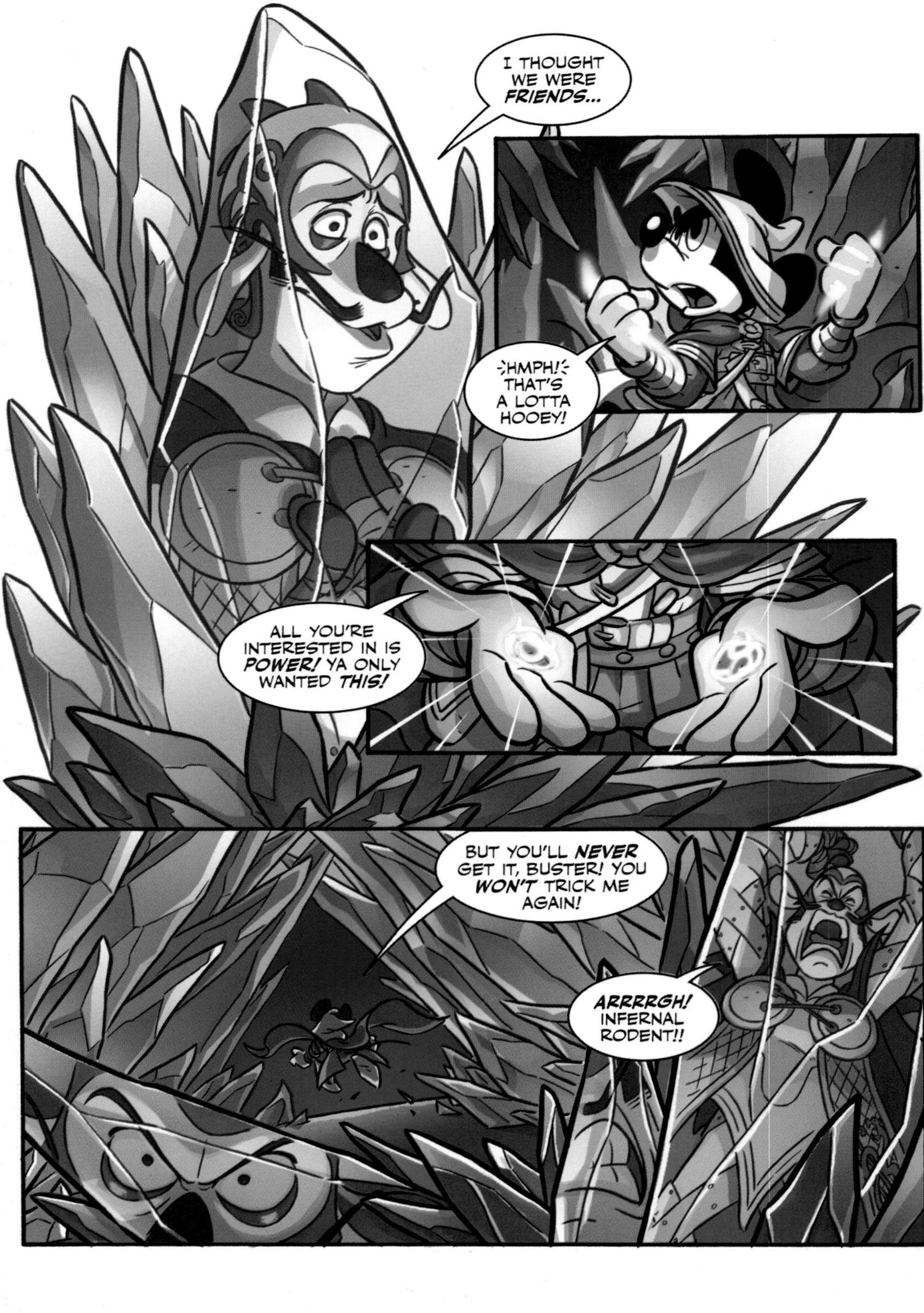
I THOUGHT WE WERE FRIENDS...
HMPH! THAT'S A LOTTA HOOEY!
ALL YOU'RE INTERESTED IN IS POWER! YA ONLY WANTED THIS!
BUT YOU'LL NEVER GET IT, BUSTER! YOU WON'T TRICK ME AGAIN!
ARRRRGH! INFERNAL RODENT!!

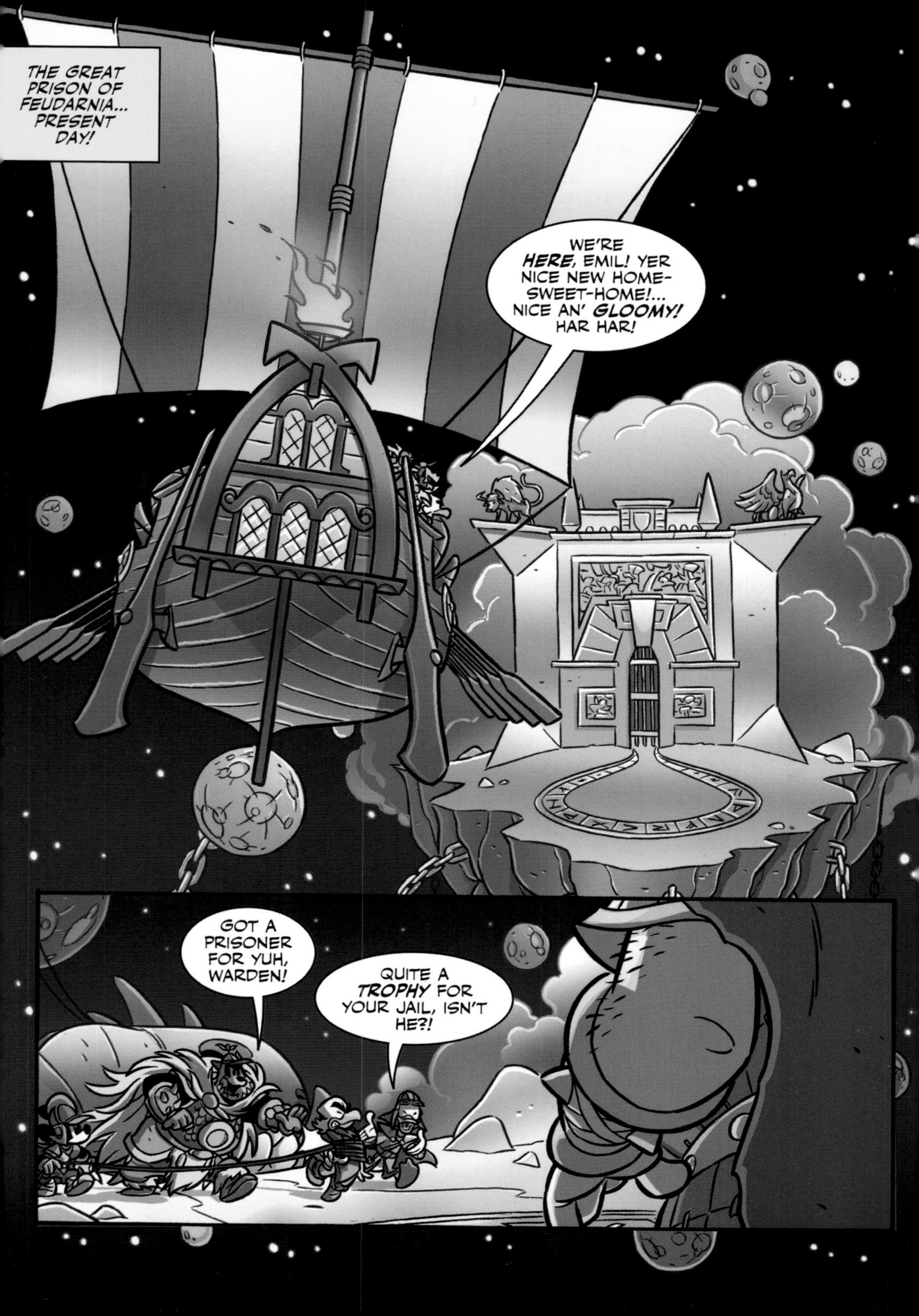
THE GREAT PRISON OF FEUDARNIA... PRESENT DAY!
WE'RE *HERE*, EMIL! YER NICE NEW HOME-SWEET-HOME!... NICE AN' *GLOOMY!* HAR HAR!
GOT A PRISONER FOR YUH, WARDEN!
QUITE A *TROPHY* FOR YOUR JAIL, ISN'T HE?!

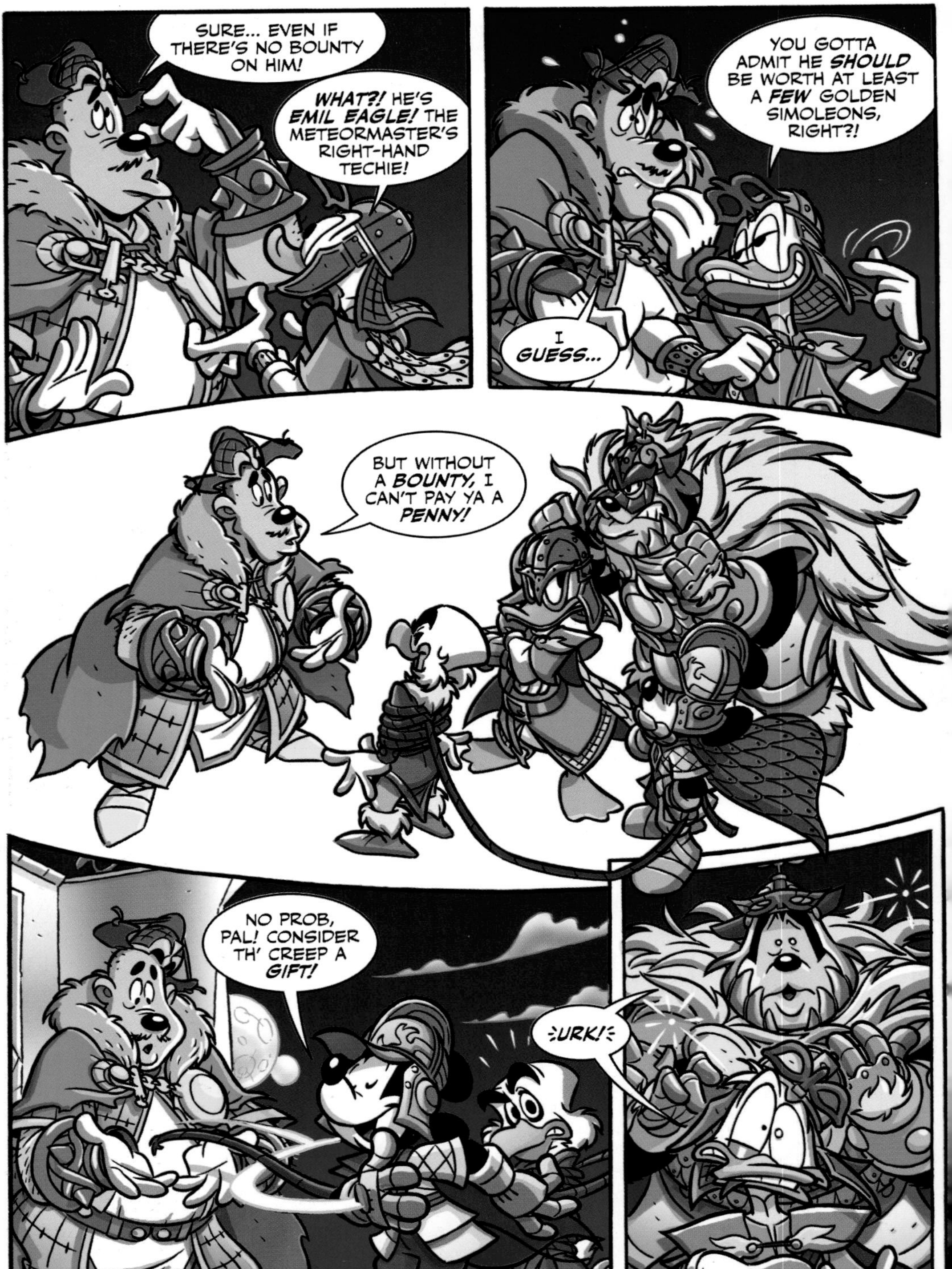
SURE... EVEN IF THERE'S NO BOUNTY ON HIM!
WHAT?! HE'S EMIL EAGLE! THE METEORMASTER'S RIGHT-HAND TECHIE!
YOU GOTTA ADMIT HE SHOULD BE WORTH AT LEAST A FEW GOLDEN SIMOLEONS, RIGHT?!
I GUESS...
BUT WITHOUT A BOUNTY, I CAN'T PAY YA A PENNY!
NO PROB, PAL! CONSIDER TH' CREEP A GIFT!
URK!

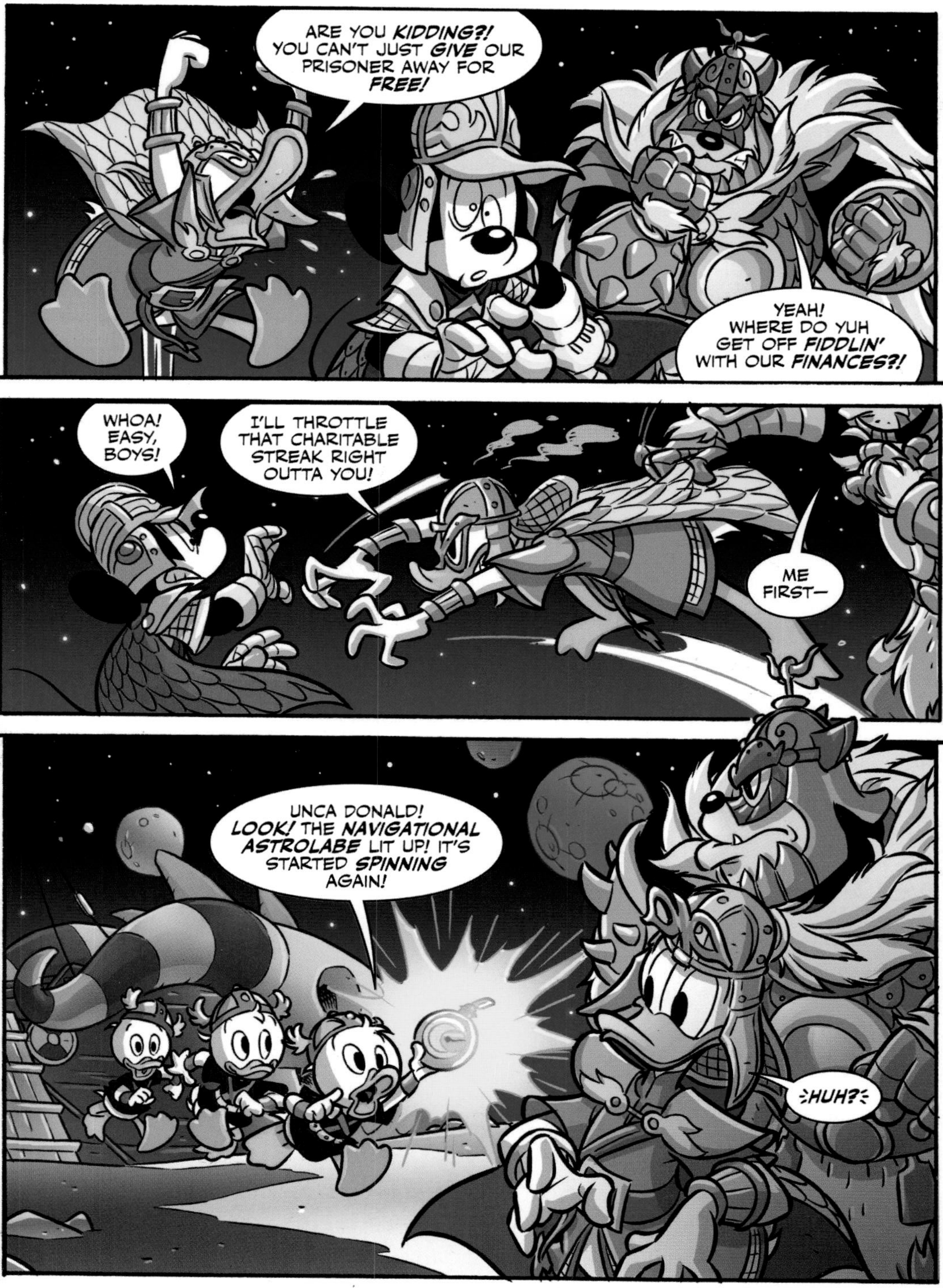
ARE YOU KIDDING?! YOU CAN'T JUST GIVE OUR PRISONER AWAY FOR FREE!
YEAH! WHERE DO YUH GET OFF FIDDLIN' WITH OUR FINANCES?!
WHOA! EASY, BOYS!
I'LL THROTTLE THAT CHARITABLE STREAK RIGHT OUTTA YOU!
ME FIRST—
UNCA DONALD! LOOK! THE NAVIGATIONAL ASTROLABE LIT UP! IT'S STARTED SPINNING AGAIN!
HUH?

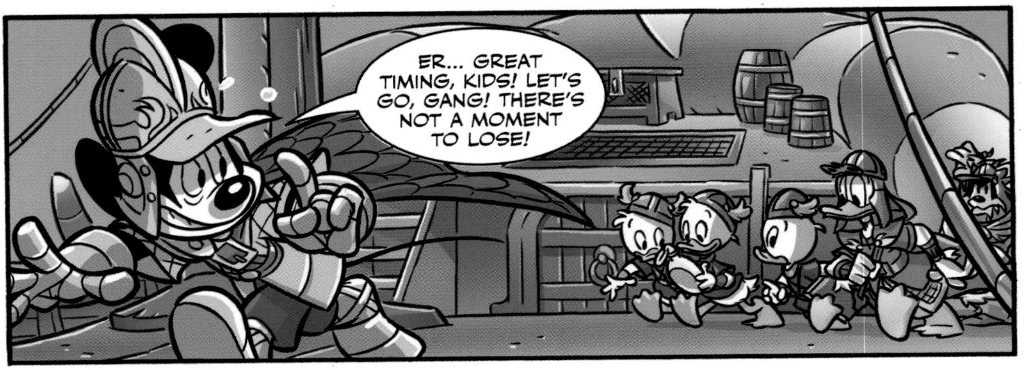
ER... GREAT TIMING, KIDS! LET'S GO, GANG! THERE'S NOT A MOMENT TO LOSE!

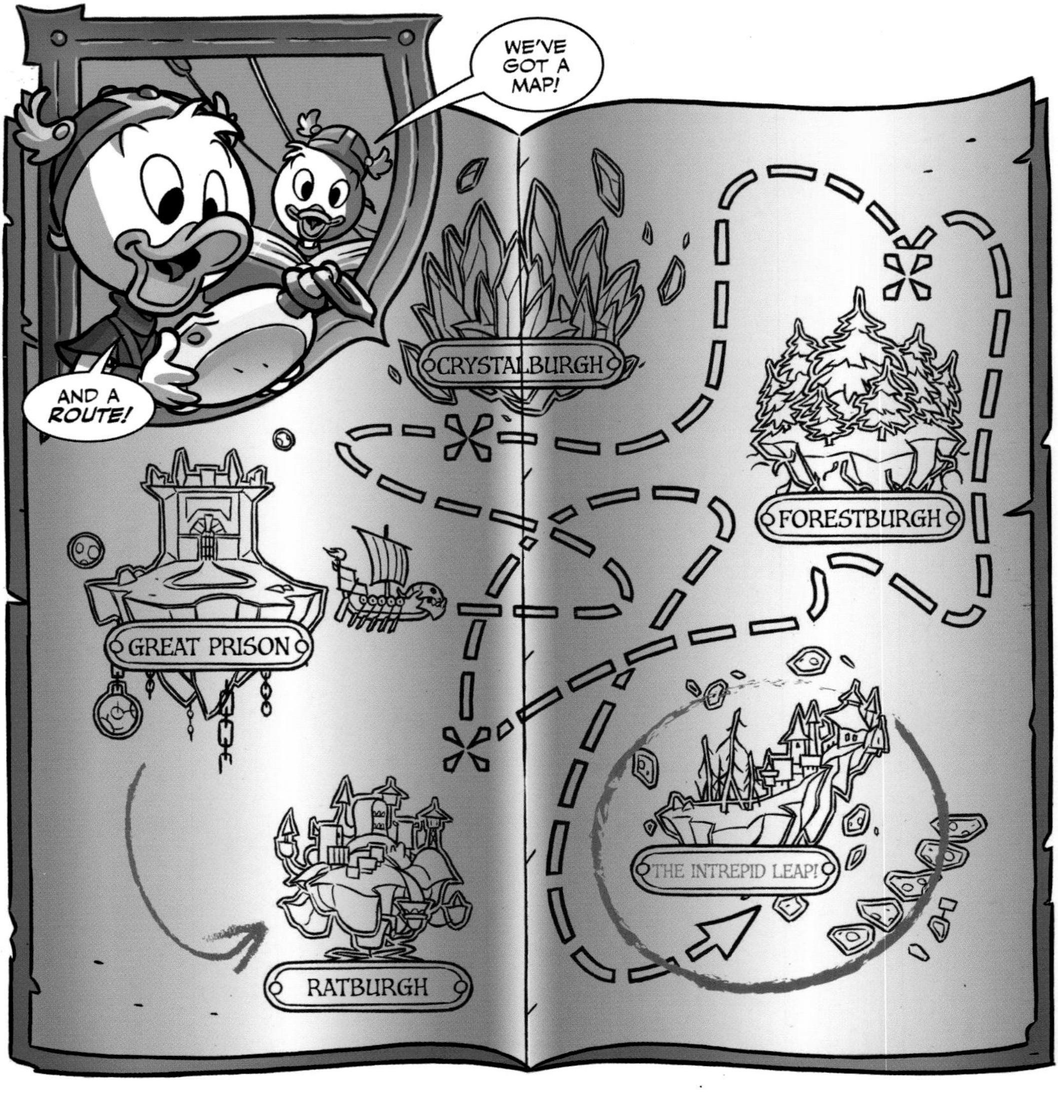
WE'VE GOT A MAP!
AND A ROUTE!
CRYSTALBURGH
FORESTBURGH
GREAT PRISON
THE INTREPID LEAP!
RATBURGH

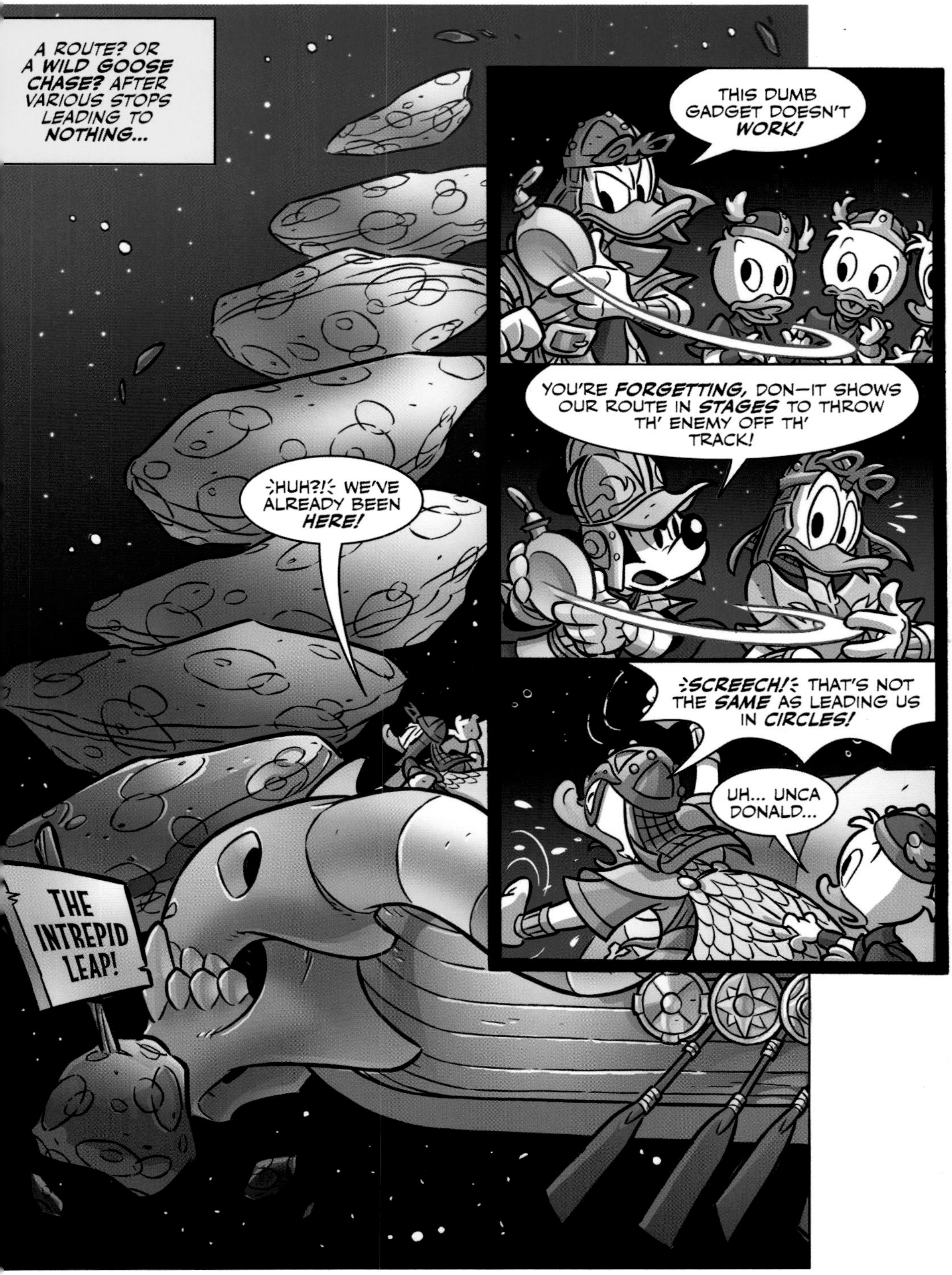
A ROUTE? OR A WILD GOOSE CHASE? AFTER VARIOUS STOPS LEADING TO NOTHING...
THIS DUMB GADGET DOESN'T WORK!
YOU'RE FORGETTING, DON—IT SHOWS OUR ROUTE IN STAGES TO THROW TH' ENEMY OFF TH' TRACK!
HUH?! WE'VE ALREADY BEEN HERE!
SCREECH! THAT'S NOT THE SAME AS LEADING US IN CIRCLES!
UH... UNCA DONALD...
THE INTREPID LEAP!

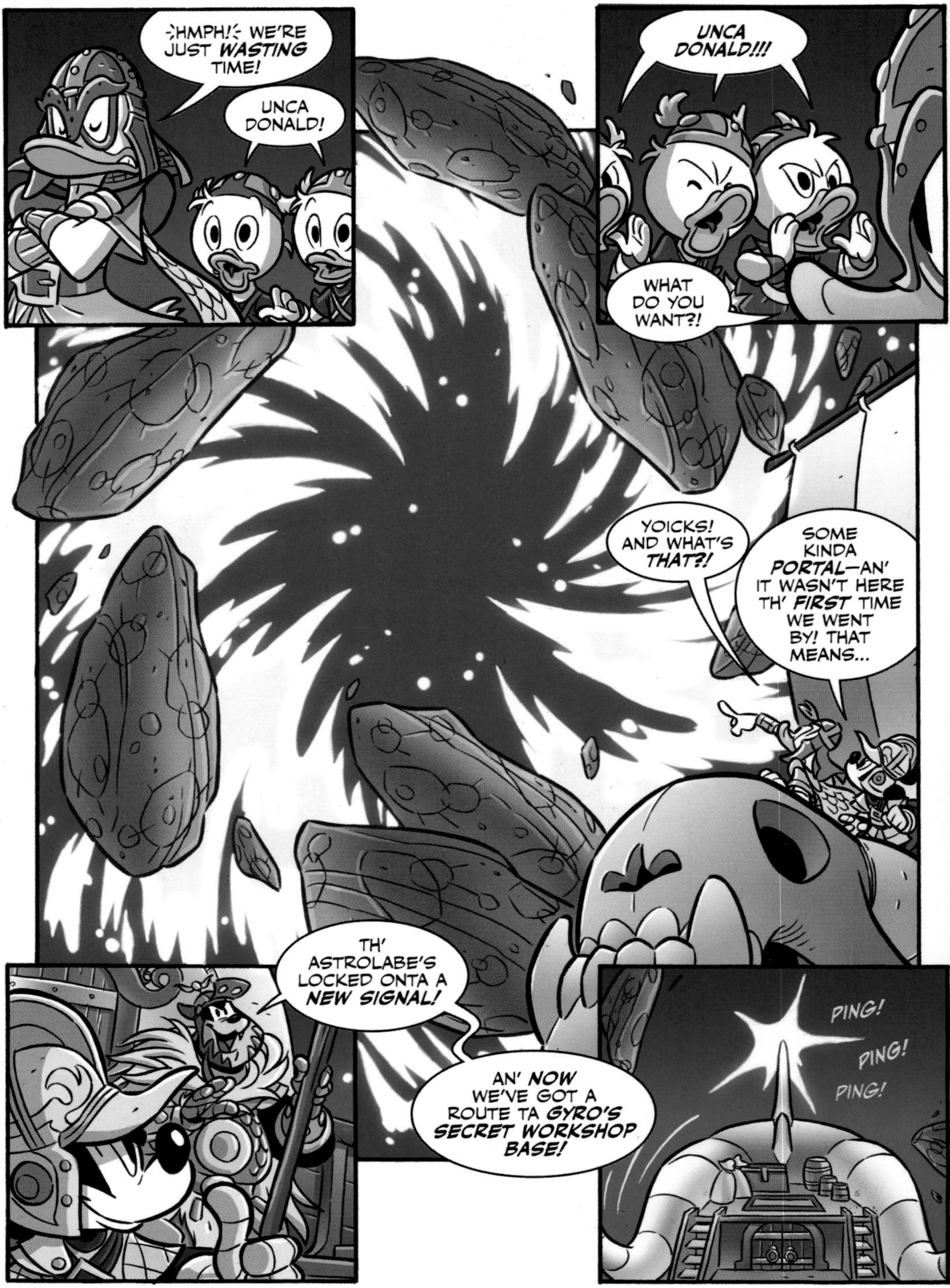

-HMPH!- WE'RE JUST WASTING TIME!
UNCA DONALD!
UNCA DONALD!!!
WHAT DO YOU WANT?!
YOICKS! AND WHAT'S THAT?!
SOME KINDA PORTAL—AN' IT WASN'T HERE TH' FIRST TIME WE WENT BY! THAT MEANS...
TH' ASTROLABE'S LOCKED ONTA A NEW SIGNAL!
AN' NOW WE'VE GOT A ROUTE TA GYRO'S SECRET WORKSHOP BASE!
PING!
PING!
PING!

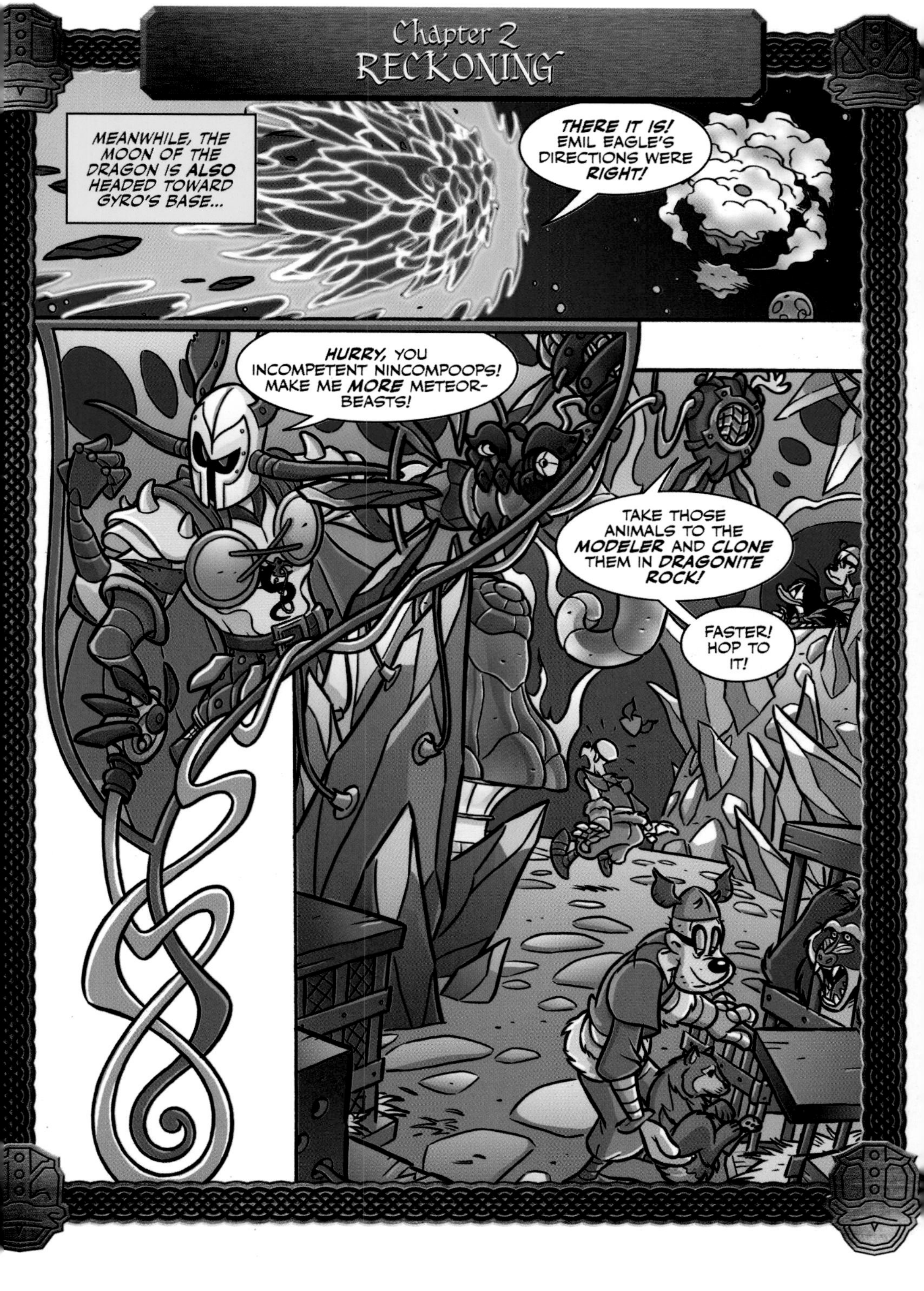
Chapter 2
RECKONING
MEANWHILE, THE MOON OF THE DRAGON IS ALSO HEADED TOWARD GYRO'S BASE...
THERE IT IS! EMIL EAGLE'S DIRECTIONS WERE RIGHT!
HURRY, YOU INCOMPETENT NINCOMPOOPS! MAKE ME MORE METEOR-BEASTS!
TAKE THOSE ANIMALS TO THE MODELER AND CLONE THEM IN DRAGONITE ROCK!
FASTER! HOP TO IT!

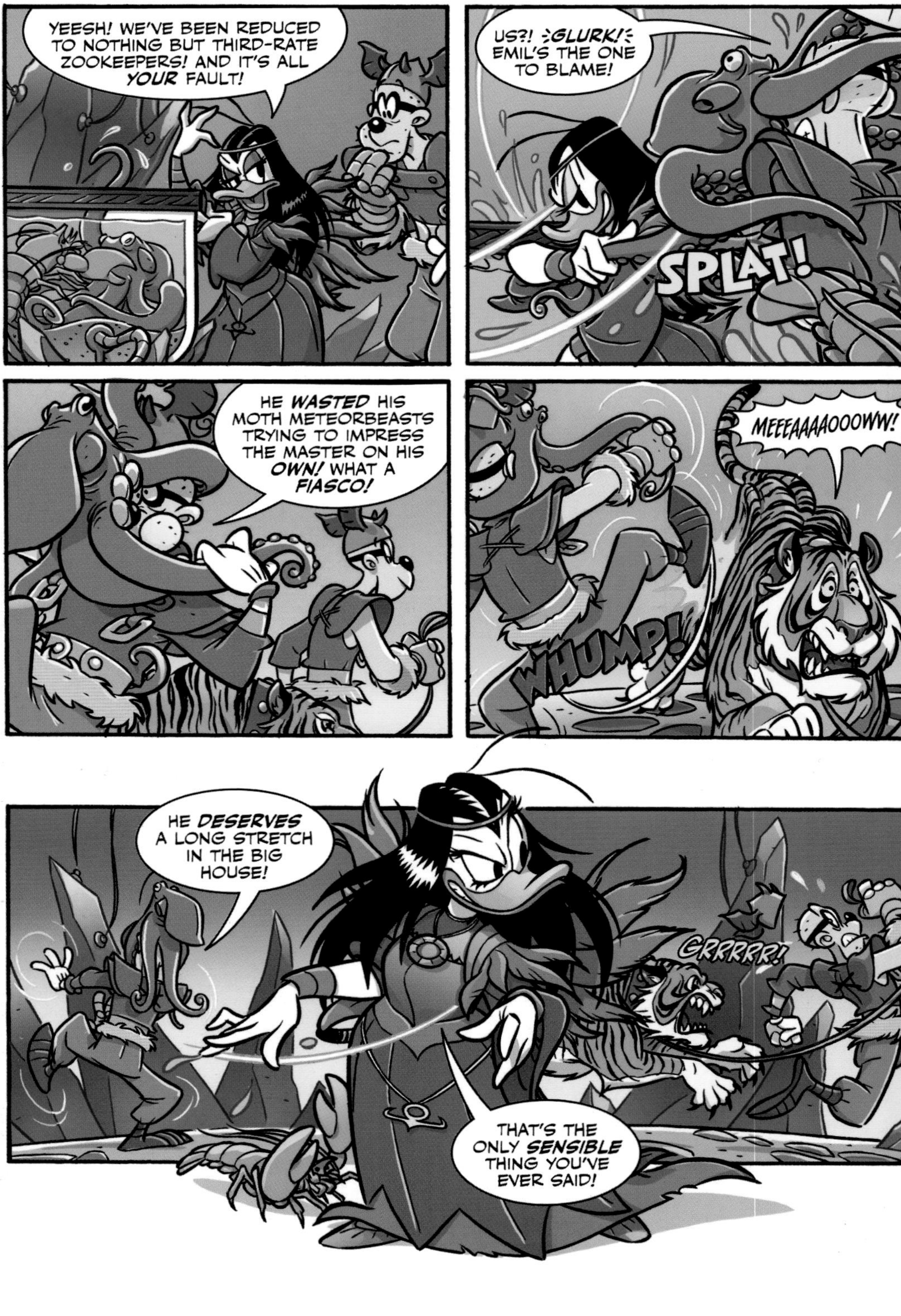
YEESH! WE'VE BEEN REDUCED TO NOTHING BUT THIRD-RATE ZOOKEEPERS! AND IT'S ALL YOUR FAULT!
US?! -GLURK!- EMIL'S THE ONE TO BLAME!
SPLAT!
HE WASTED HIS MOTH METEORBEASTS TRYING TO IMPRESS THE MASTER ON HIS OWN! WHAT A FIASCO!
MEEEAAAAOOOWW!
WHUMP!
HE DESERVES A LONG STRETCH IN THE BIG HOUSE!
GRRRRR!
THAT'S THE ONLY SENSIBLE THING YOU'VE EVER SAID!

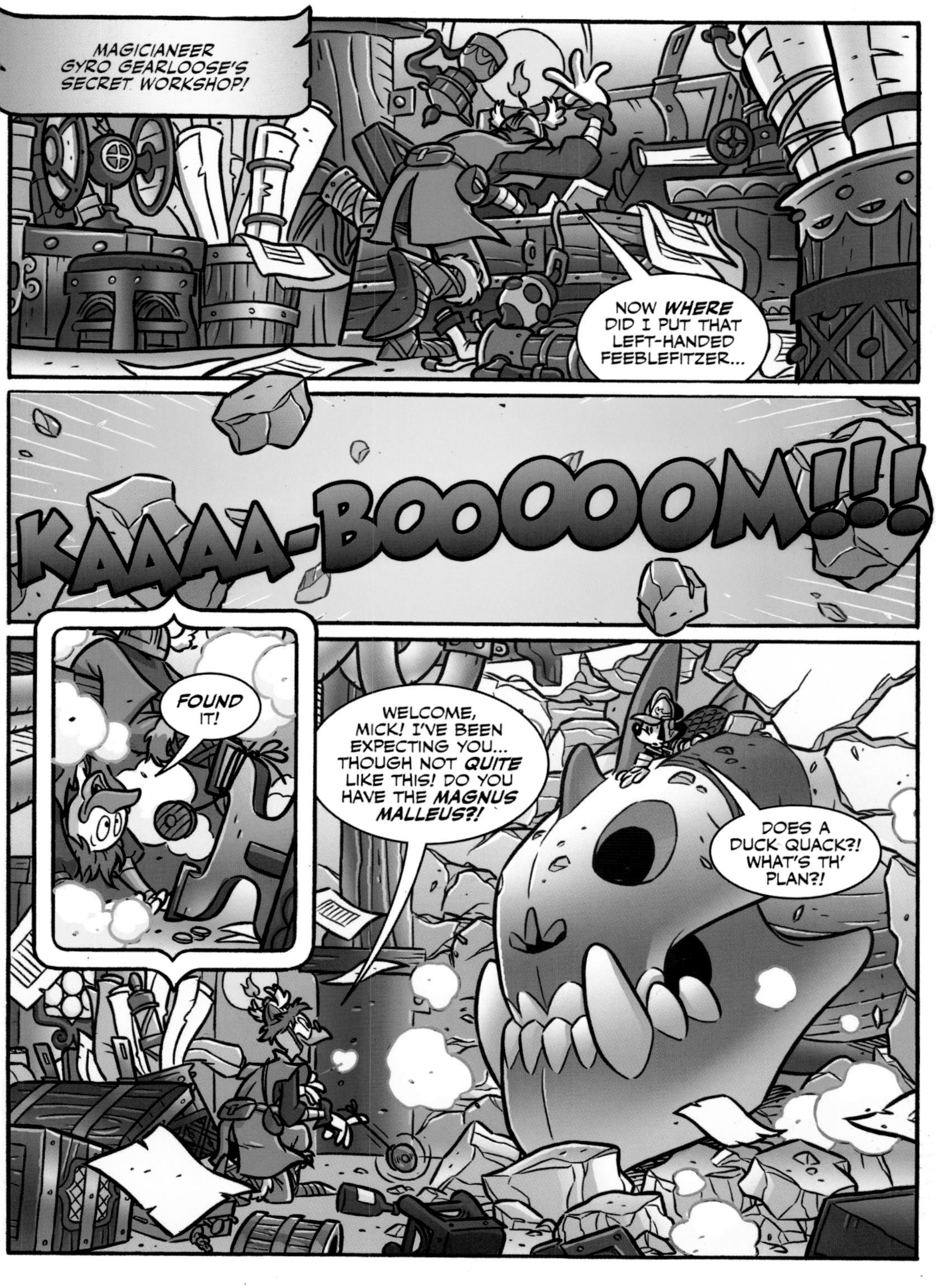
MAGICIANEER GYRO GEARLOOSE'S SECRET WORKSHOP!
NOW WHERE DID I PUT THAT LEFT-HANDED FEEBLEFITZER...
KAAAA-BOOOOOOM!!!
FOUND IT!
WELCOME, MICK! I'VE BEEN EXPECTING YOU... THOUGH NOT QUITE LIKE THIS! DO YOU HAVE THE MAGNUS MALLEUS?!
DOES A DUCK QUACK?! WHAT'S TH' PLAN?!

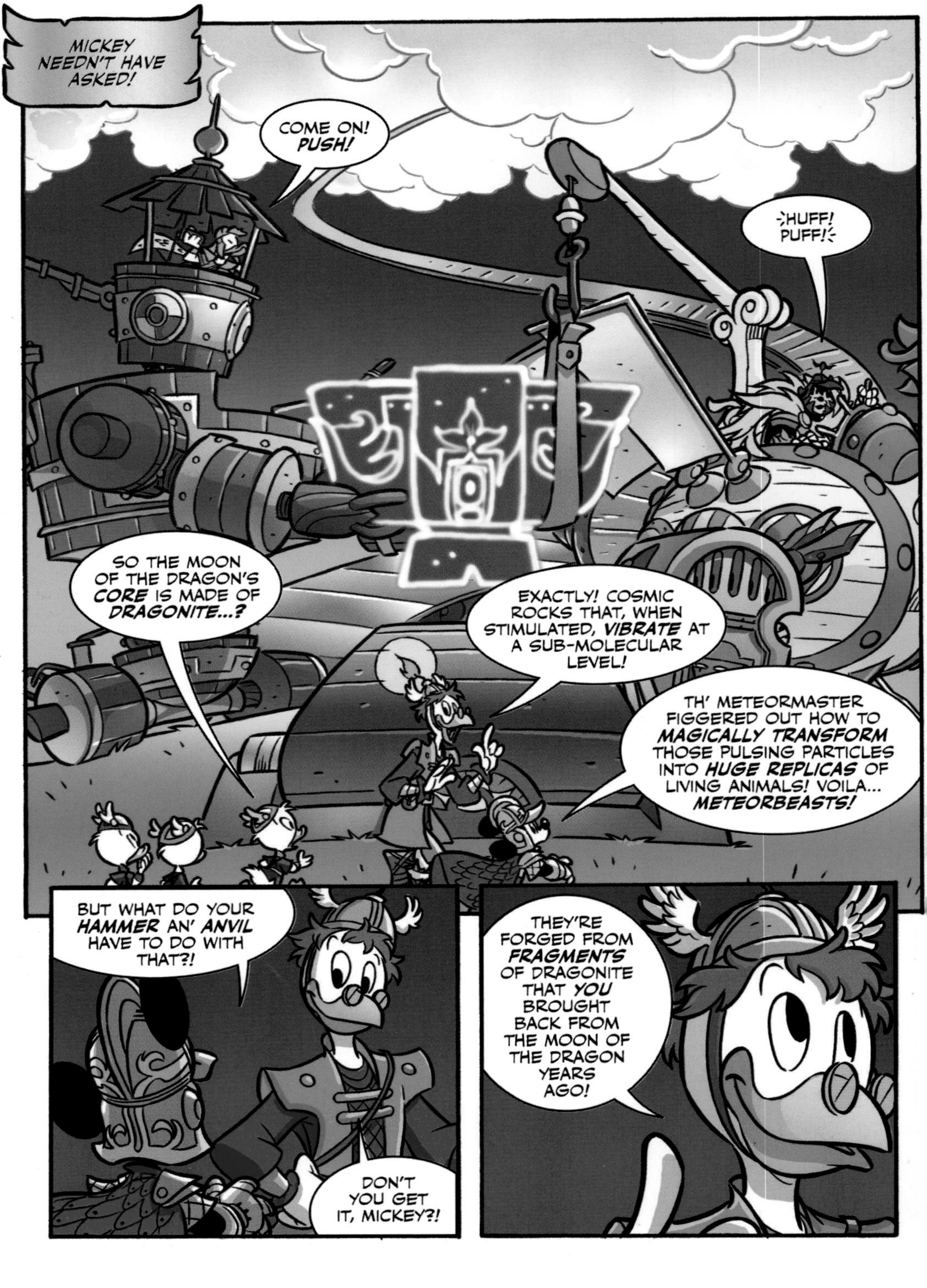
MICKEY NEEDN'T HAVE ASKED!
COME ON! PUSH!
HUFF! PUFF!
SO THE MOON OF THE DRAGON'S CORE IS MADE OF DRAGONITE...?
EXACTLY! COSMIC ROCKS THAT, WHEN STIMULATED, VIBRATE AT A SUB-MOLECULAR LEVEL!
TH' METEORMASTER FIGGERED OUT HOW TO MAGICALLY TRANSFORM THOSE PULSING PARTICLES INTO HUGE REPLICAS OF LIVING ANIMALS! VOILA... METEORBEASTS!
BUT WHAT DO YOUR HAMMER AN' ANVIL HAVE TO DO WITH THAT?!
DON'T YOU GET IT, MICKEY?!
THEY'RE FORGED FROM FRAGMENTS OF DRAGONITE THAT YOU BROUGHT BACK FROM THE MOON OF THE DRAGON YEARS AGO!

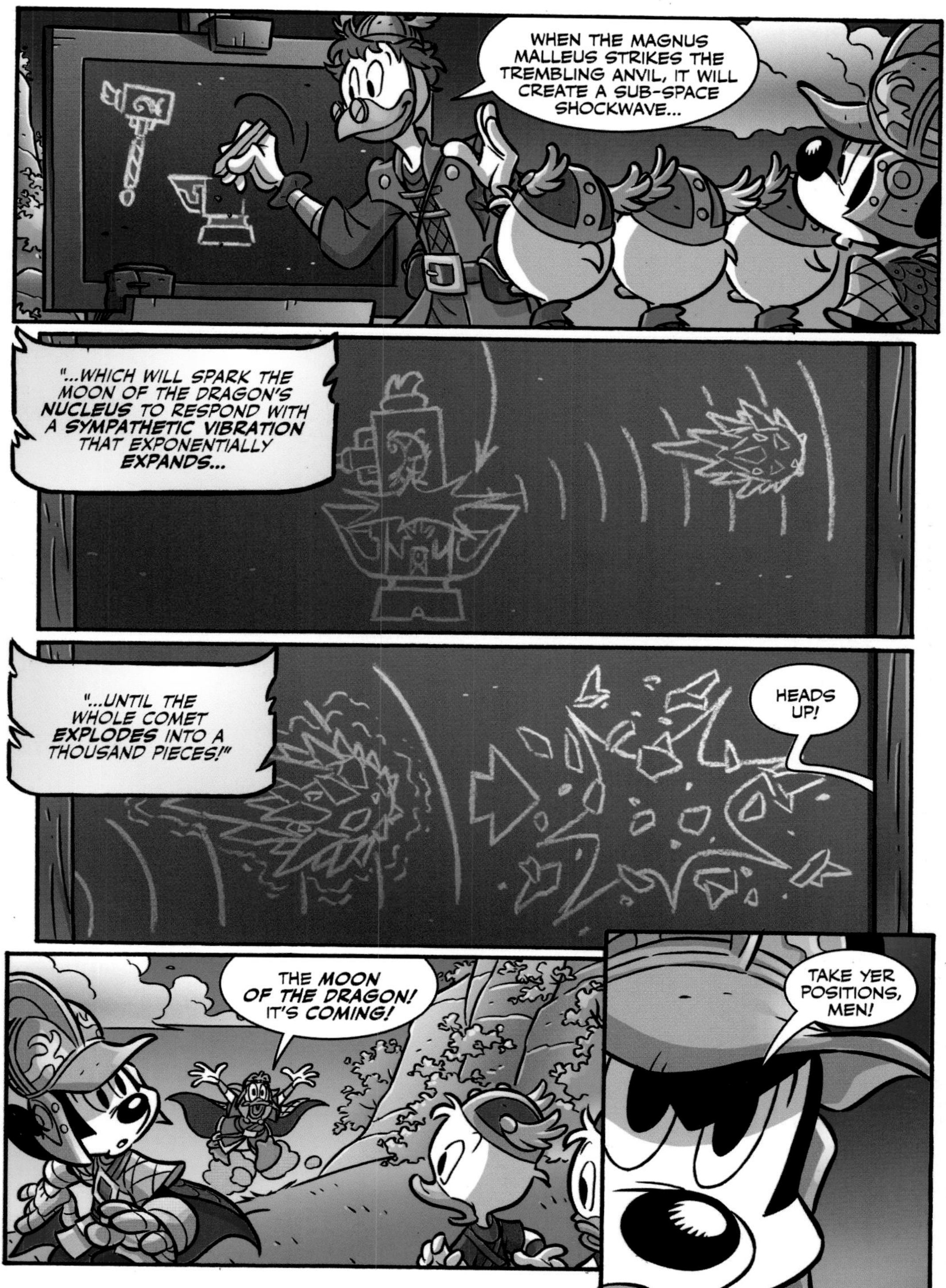
WHEN THE MAGNUS MALLEUS STRIKES THE TREMBLING ANVIL, IT WILL CREATE A SUB-SPACE SHOCKWAVE...
"...WHICH WILL SPARK THE MOON OF THE DRAGON'S NUCLEUS TO RESPOND WITH A SYMPATHETIC VIBRATION THAT EXPONENTIALLY EXPANDS...
"...UNTIL THE WHOLE COMET EXPLODES INTO A THOUSAND PIECES!"
HEADS UP!
THE MOON OF THE DRAGON! IT'S COMING!
TAKE YER POSITIONS, MEN!

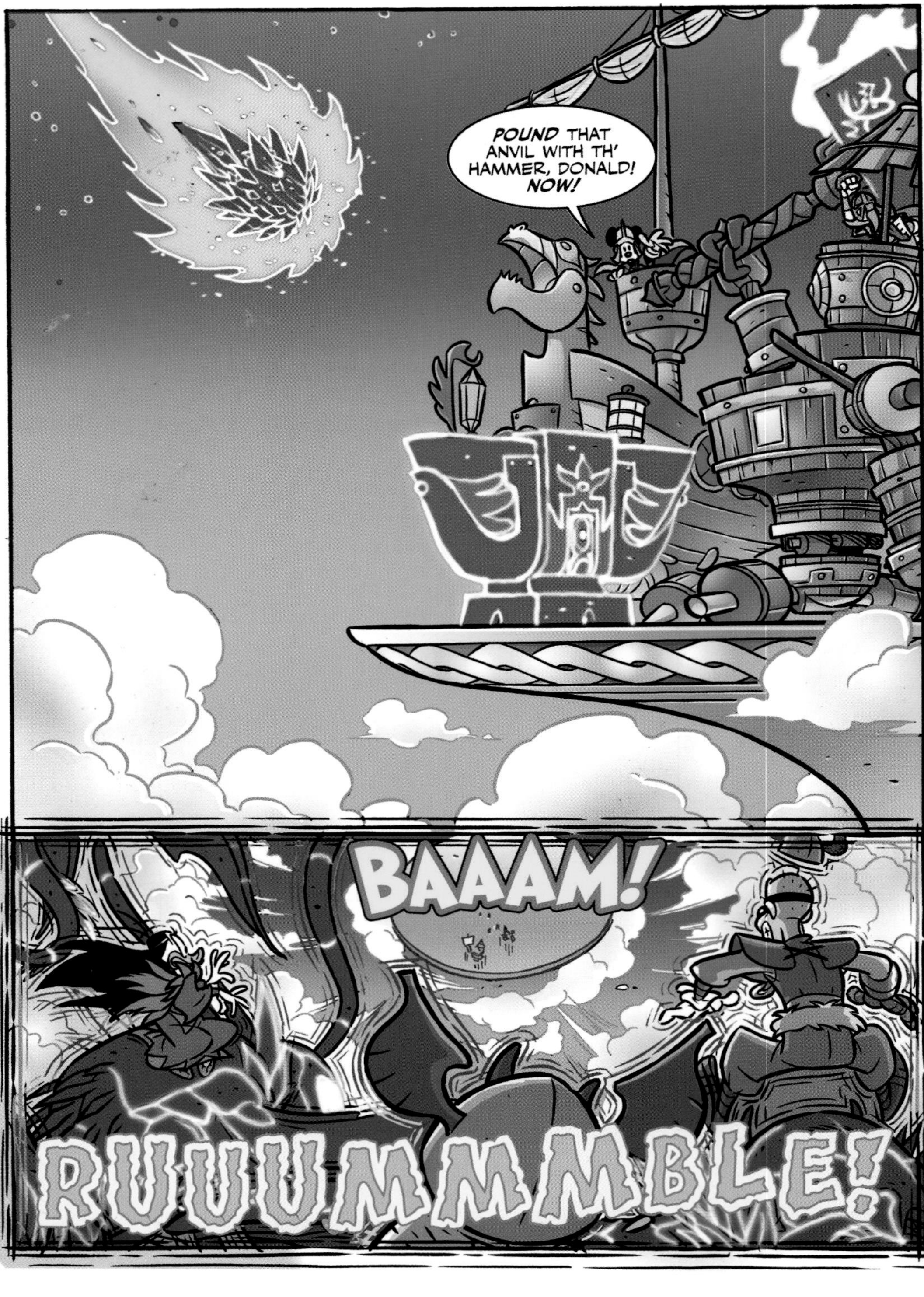
POUND THAT ANVIL WITH TH' HAMMER, DONALD! NOW!
BAAAM!
RUUUMMMBLE!

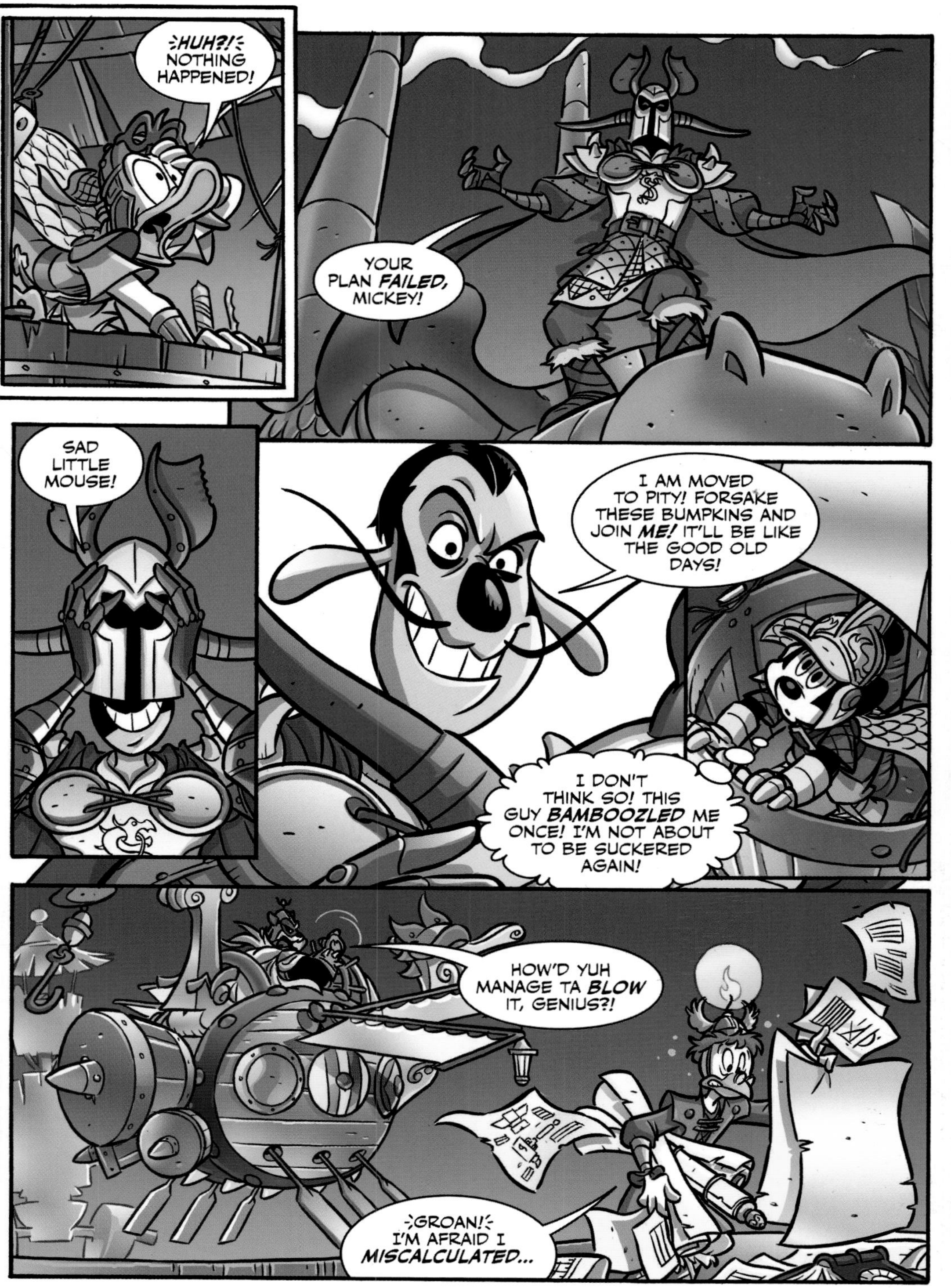

HUH?! NOTHING HAPPENED!
YOUR PLAN FAILED, MICKEY!
SAD LITTLE MOUSE!
I AM MOVED TO PITY! FORSAKE THESE BUMPKINS AND JOIN ME! IT'LL BE LIKE THE GOOD OLD DAYS!
I DON'T THINK SO! THIS GUY BAMBOOZLED ME ONCE! I'M NOT ABOUT TO BE SUCKERED AGAIN!
HOW'D YUH MANAGE TA BLOW IT, GENIUS?!
GROAN! I'M AFRAID I MISCALCULATED...

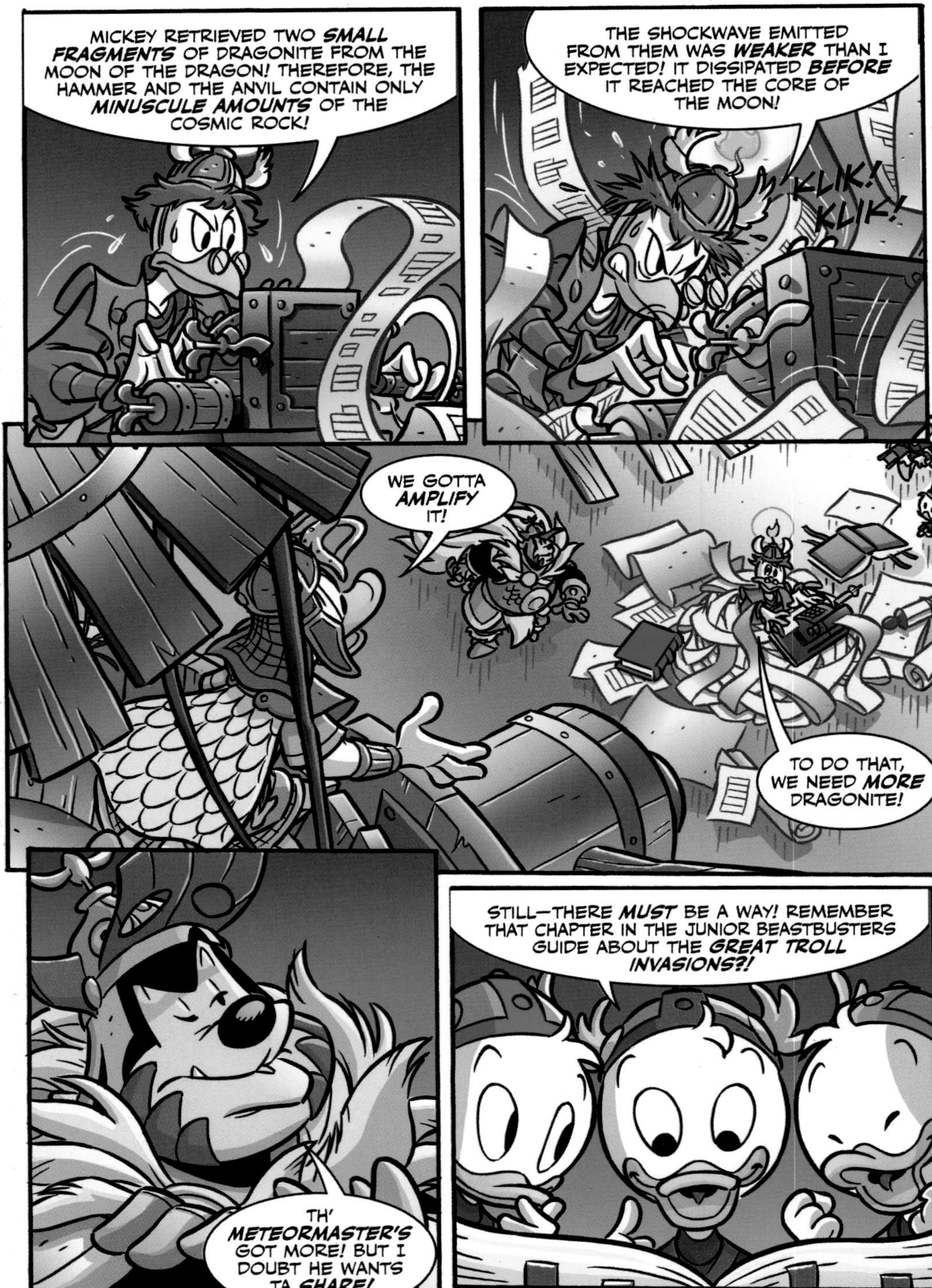
MICKEY RETRIEVED TWO SMALL FRAGMENTS OF DRAGONITE FROM THE MOON OF THE DRAGON! THEREFORE, THE HAMMER AND THE ANVIL CONTAIN ONLY MINUSCULE AMOUNTS OF THE COSMIC ROCK!
THE SHOCKWAVE EMITTED FROM THEM WAS WEAKER THAN I EXPECTED! IT DISSIPATED BEFORE IT REACHED THE CORE OF THE MOON!
KLIK! KLIK!
WE GOTTA AMPLIFY IT!
TO DO THAT, WE NEED MORE DRAGONITE!
TH' METEORMASTER'S GOT MORE! BUT I DOUBT HE WANTS TA SHARE!
STILL—THERE MUST BE A WAY! REMEMBER THAT CHAPTER IN THE JUNIOR BEASTBUSTERS GUIDE ABOUT THE GREAT TROLL INVASIONS?!

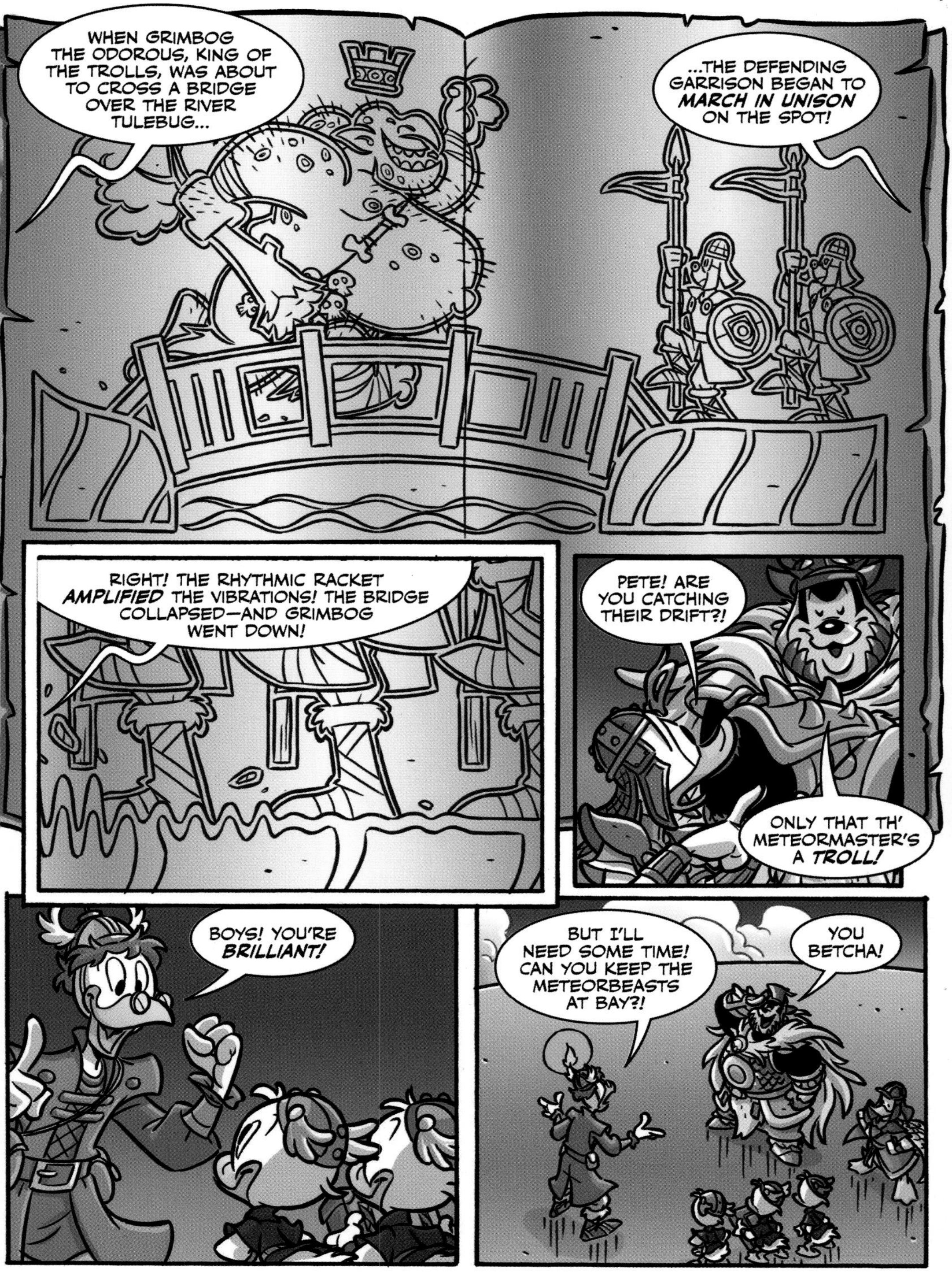
WHEN GRIMBOG THE ODOROUS, KING OF THE TROLLS, WAS ABOUT TO CROSS A BRIDGE OVER THE RIVER TULEBUG...
...THE DEFENDING GARRISON BEGAN TO *MARCH IN UNISON* ON THE SPOT!
RIGHT! THE RHYTHMIC RACKET *AMPLIFIED* THE VIBRATIONS! THE BRIDGE COLLAPSED—AND GRIMBOG WENT DOWN!
PETE! ARE YOU CATCHING THEIR DRIFT?!
ONLY THAT TH' METEORMASTER'S A *TROLL!*
BOYS! YOU'RE *BRILLIANT!*
BUT I'LL NEED SOME TIME! CAN YOU KEEP THE METEORBEASTS AT BAY?!
YOU BETCHA!

Chapter 3
UNITED WE WIN

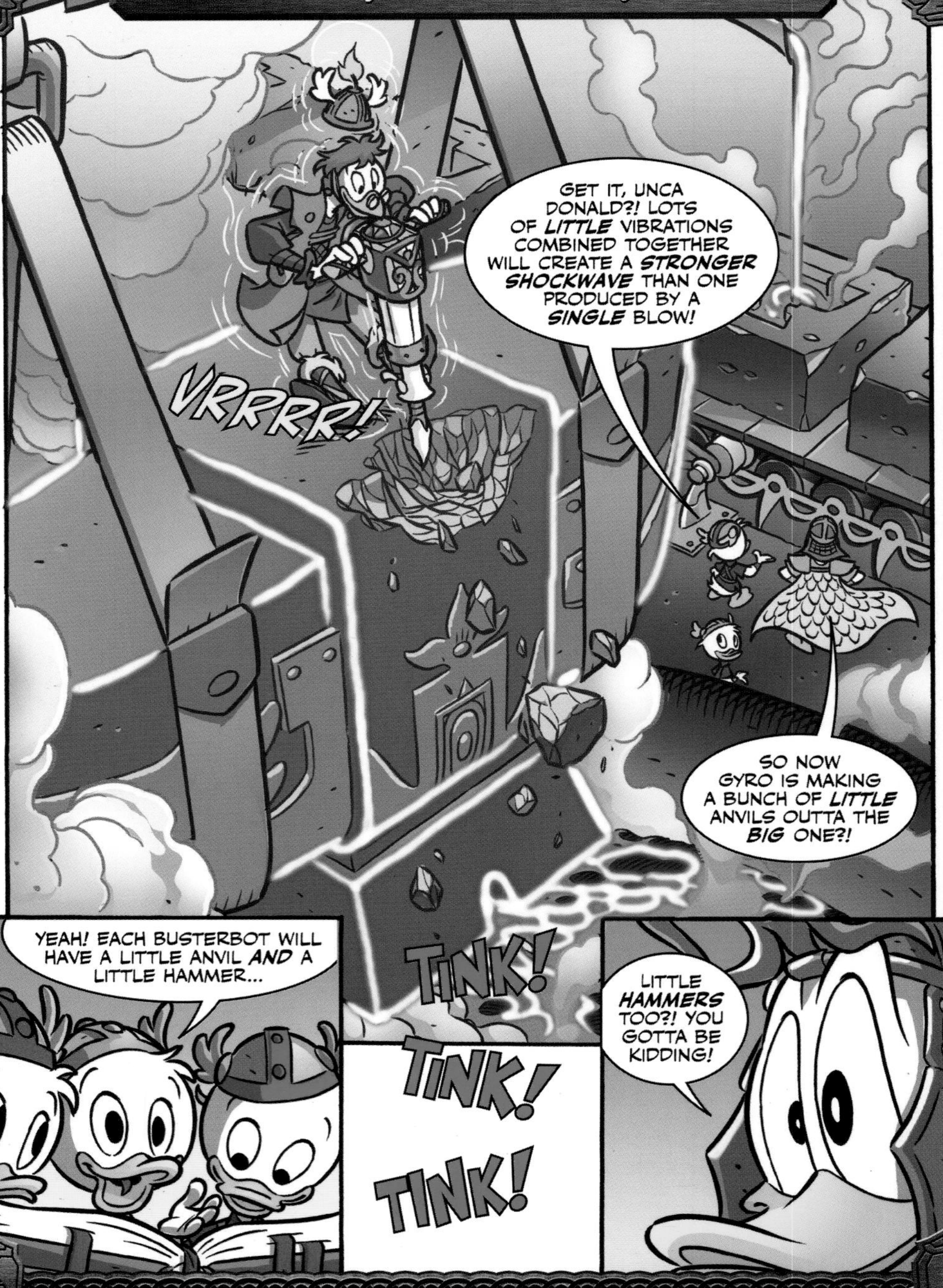

GET IT, UNCA DONALD?! LOTS OF LITTLE VIBRATIONS COMBINED TOGETHER WILL CREATE A STRONGER SHOCKWAVE THAN ONE PRODUCED BY A SINGLE BLOW!
VRRRRR!
SO NOW GYRO IS MAKING A BUNCH OF LITTLE ANVILS OUTTA THE BIG ONE?!
YEAH! EACH BUSTERBOT WILL HAVE A LITTLE ANVIL AND A LITTLE HAMMER...
TINK!
TINK!
TINK!
LITTLE HAMMERS TOO?! YOU GOTTA BE KIDDING!

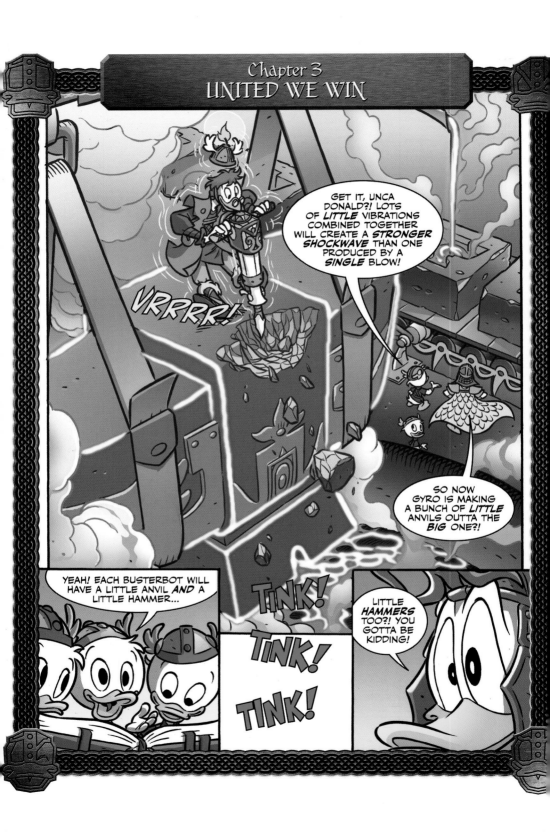

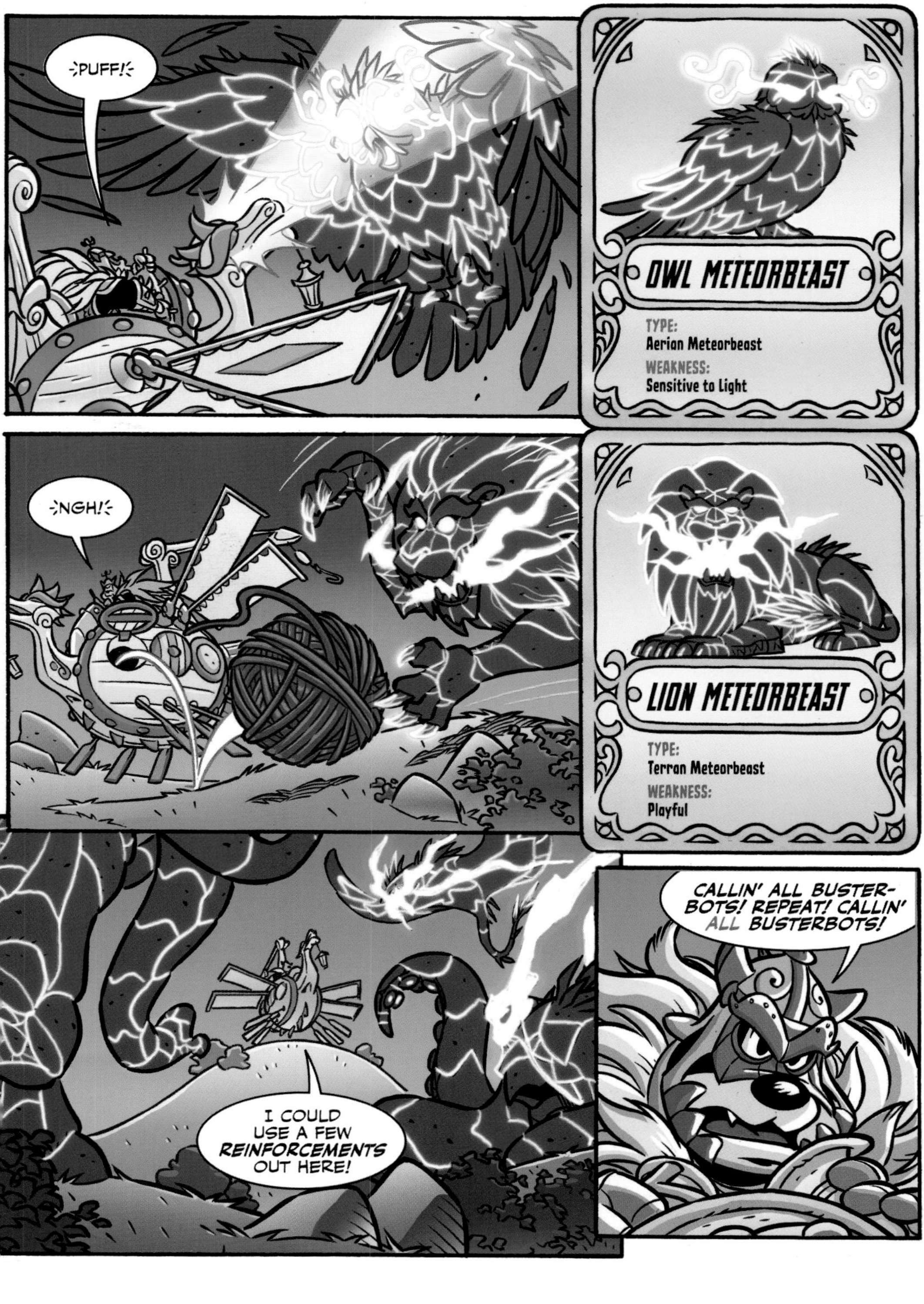
PUFF!
OWL METEORBEAST
TYPE:
Aerian Meteorbeast
WEAKNESS:
Sensitive to Light
NGH!
LION METEORBEAST
TYPE:
Terran Meteorbeast
WEAKNESS:
Playful
I COULD USE A FEW REINFORCEMENTS OUT HERE!
CALLIN' ALL BUSTER-BOTS! REPEAT! CALLIN' ALL BUSTERBOTS!

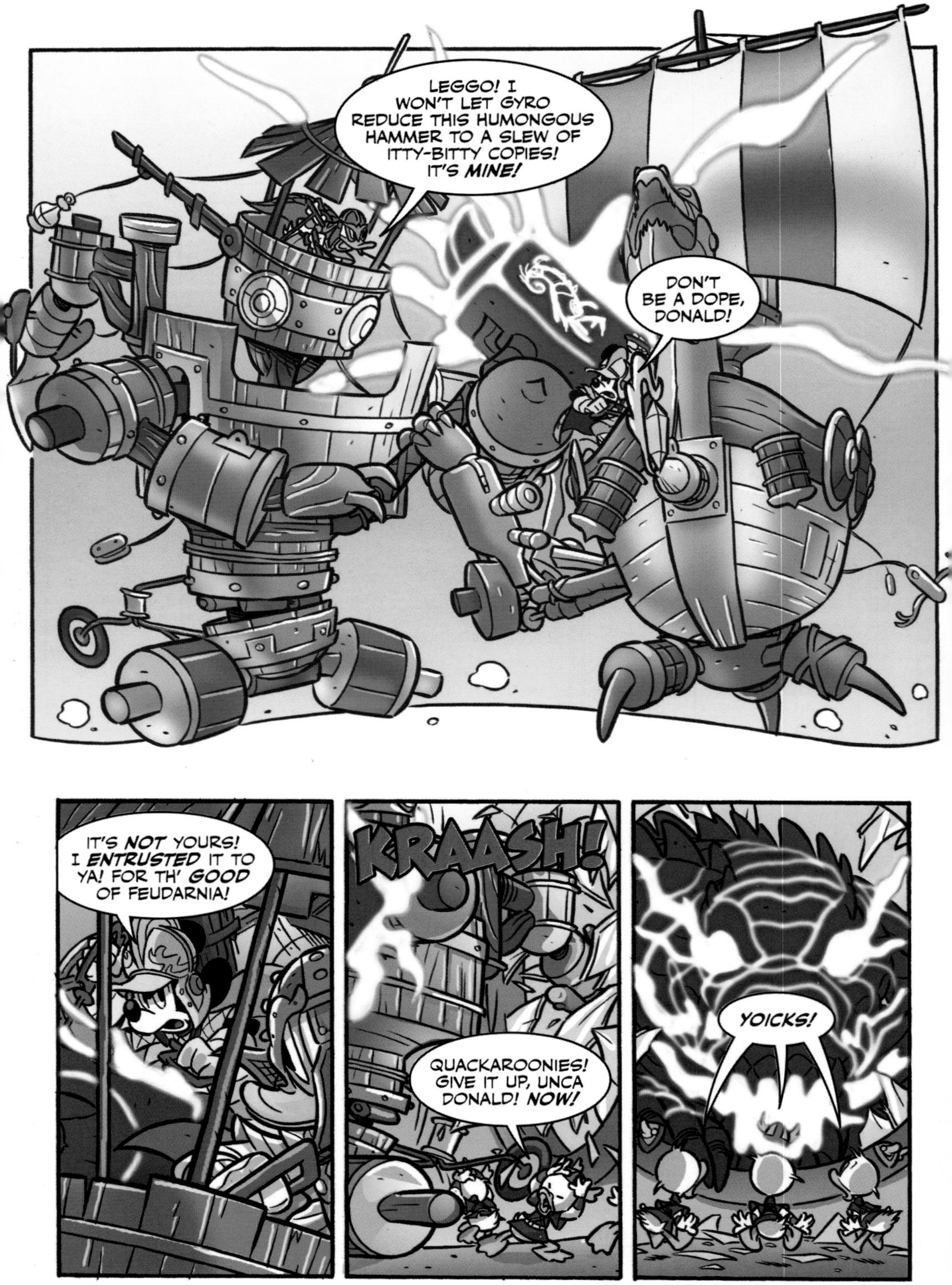

LEGGO! I WON'T LET GYRO REDUCE THIS HUMONGOUS HAMMER TO A SLEW OF ITTY-BITTY COPIES! IT'S ***MINE!***
DON'T BE A DOPE, DONALD!
IT'S ***NOT*** YOURS! I ***ENTRUSTED*** IT TO YA! FOR TH' ***GOOD*** OF FEUDARNIA!
KRAASH!
QUACKAROONIES! GIVE IT UP, UNCA DONALD! ***NOW!***
YOICKS!

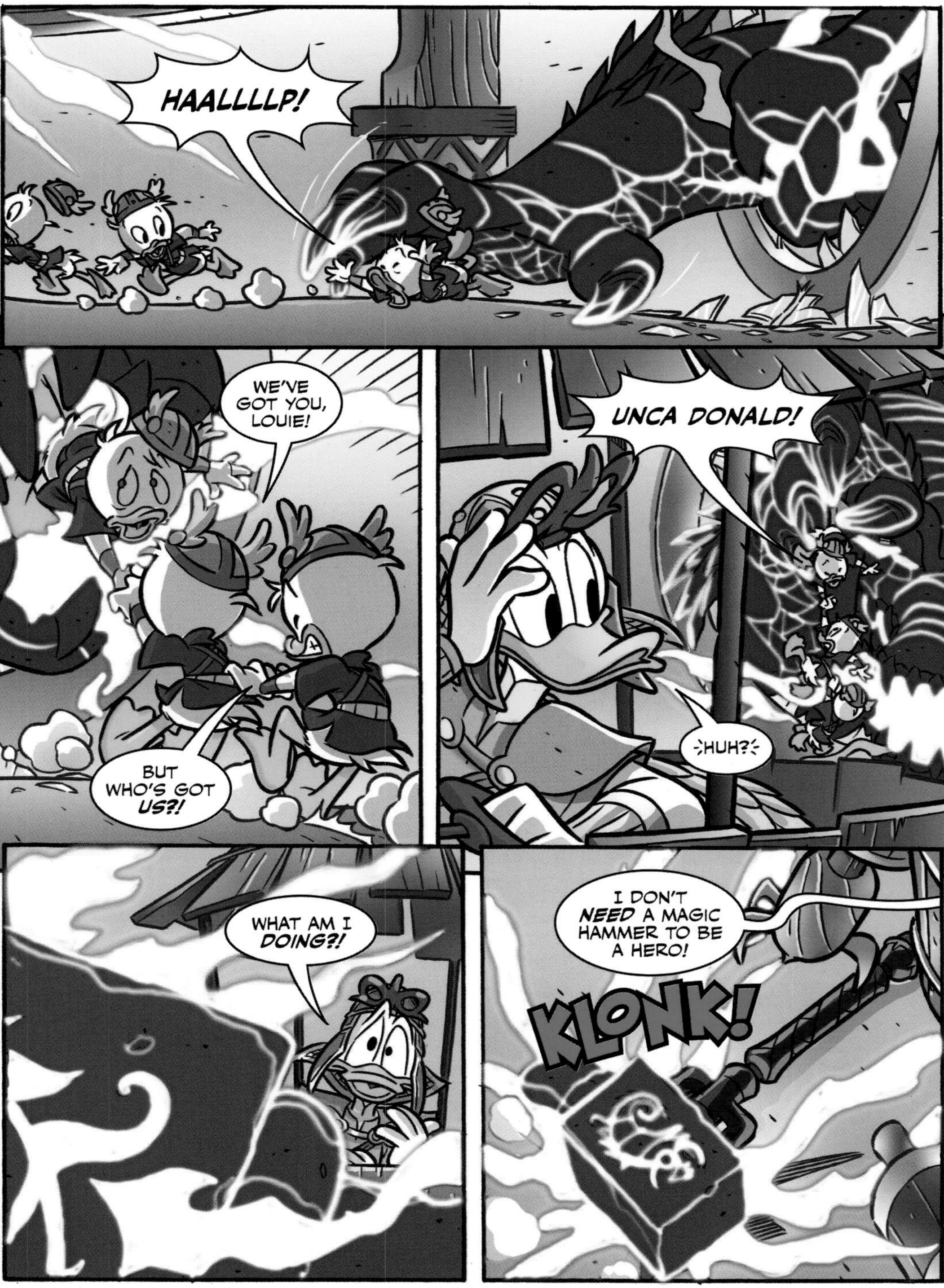
HAALLLLP!
WE'VE GOT YOU, LOUIE!
BUT WHO'S GOT US?!
UNCA DONALD!
HUH?
WHAT AM I DOING?!
I DON'T NEED A MAGIC HAMMER TO BE A HERO!
KLONK!

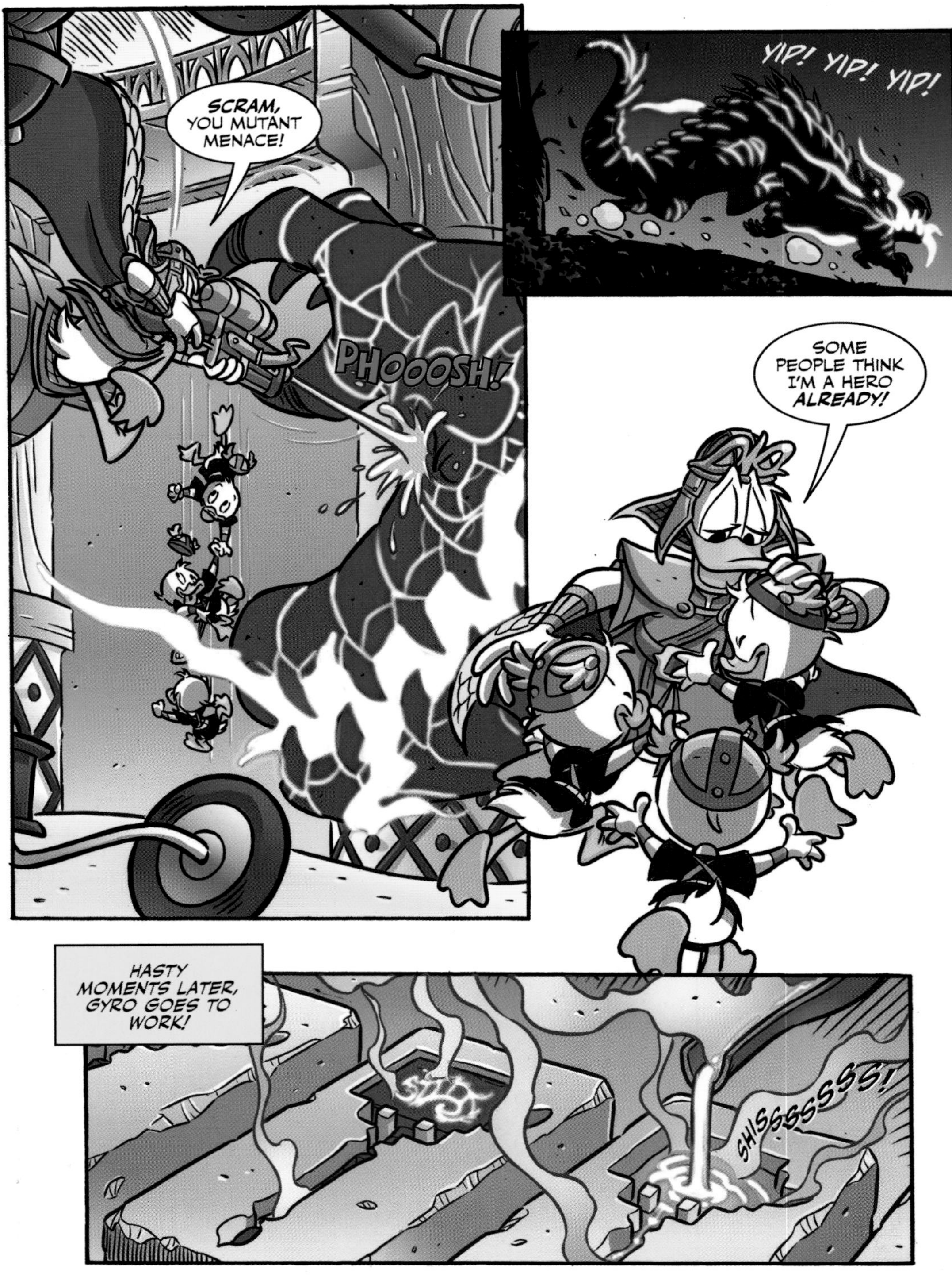
SCRAM, YOU MUTANT MENACE!
PHOOOSH!
YIP! YIP! YIP!
SOME PEOPLE THINK I'M A HERO ALREADY!
HASTY MOMENTS LATER, GYRO GOES TO WORK!
SHISSSSSSS!

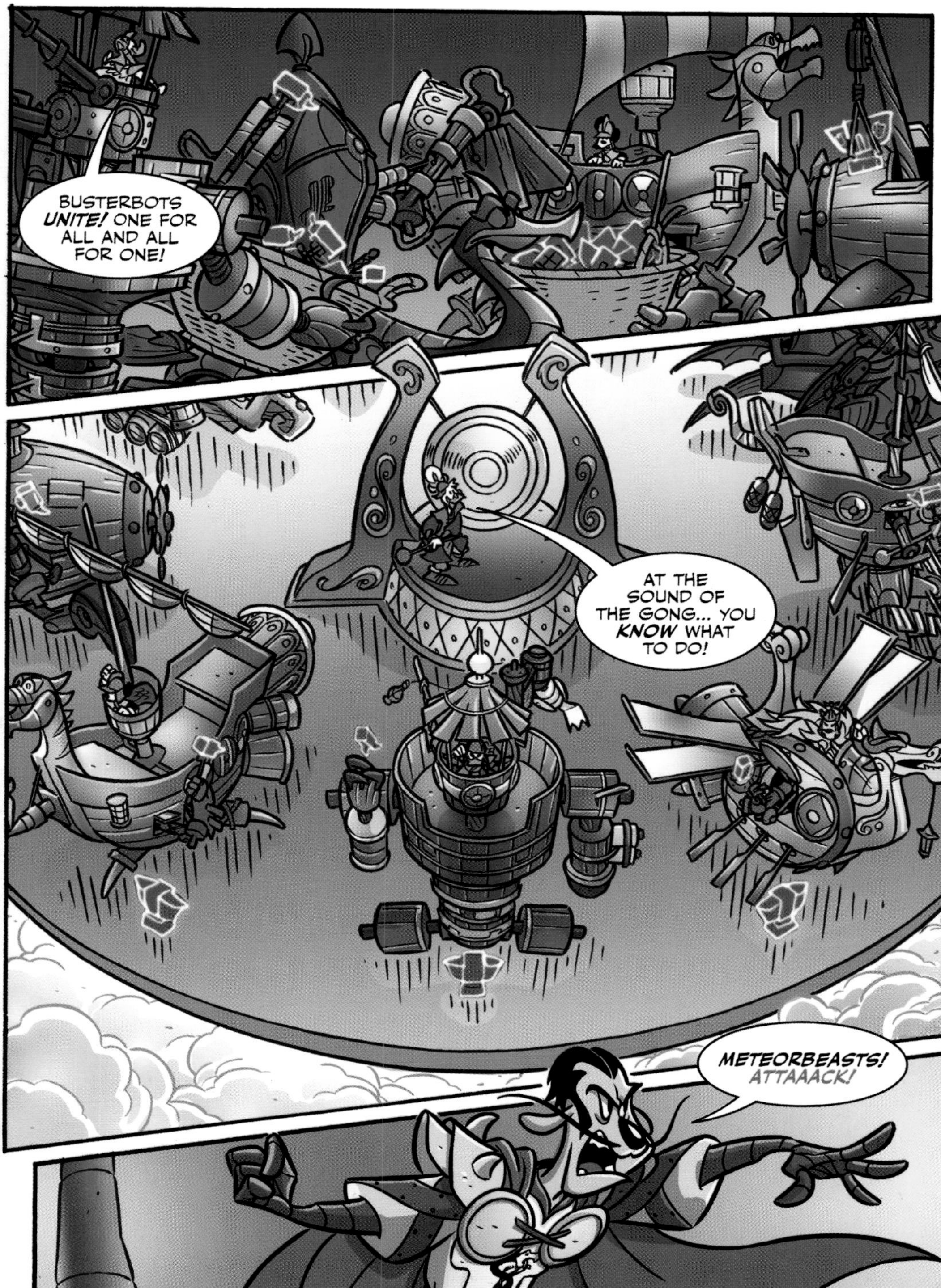
BUSTERBOTS UNITE! ONE FOR ALL AND ALL FOR ONE!
AT THE SOUND OF THE GONG... YOU KNOW WHAT TO DO!
METEORBEASTS! ATTAAACK!

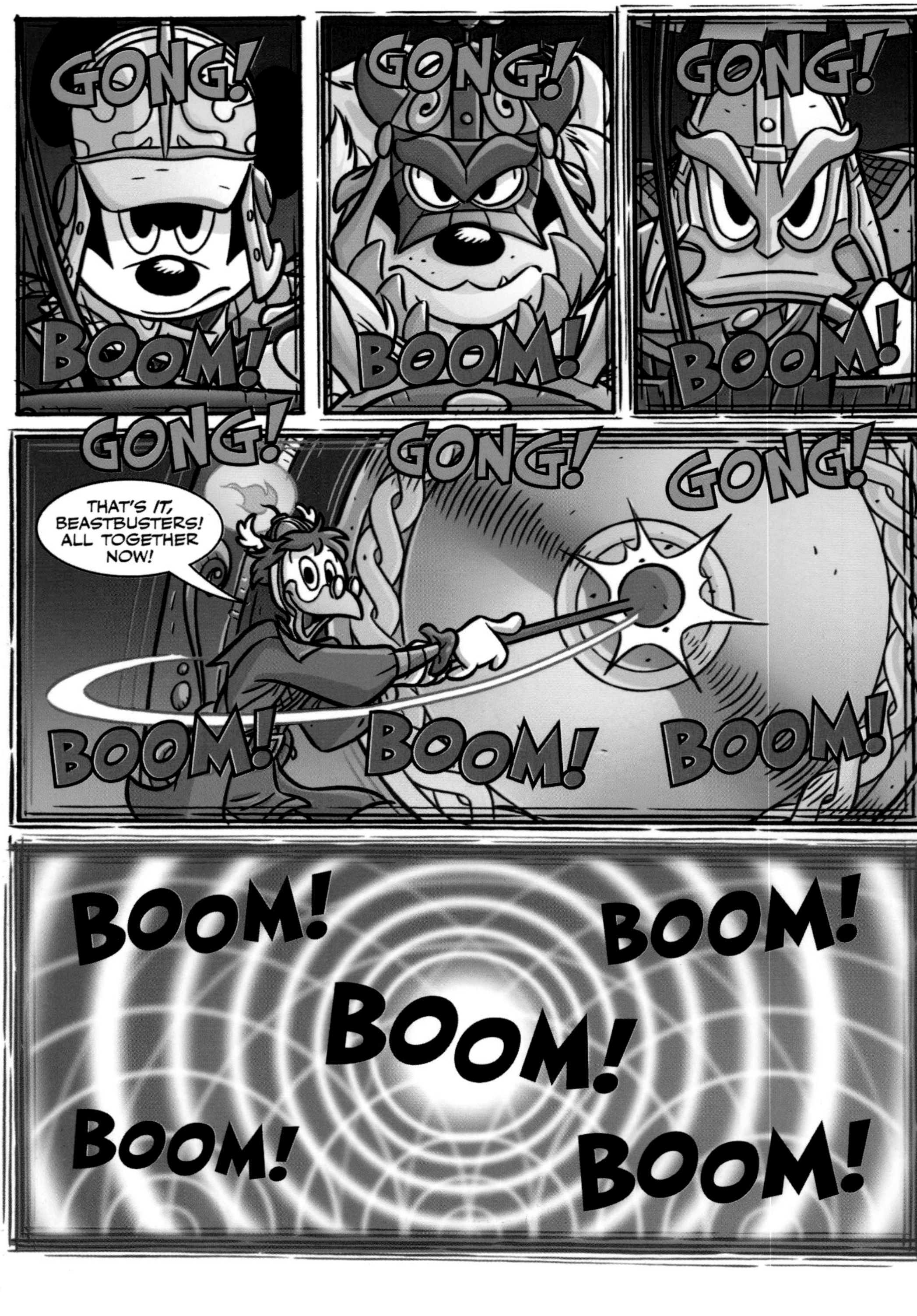
GONG!
BOOM!
GONG!
BOOM!
GONG!
BOOM!
GONG!
GONG!
GONG!
THAT'S *IT*, BEASTBUSTERS! ALL TOGETHER NOW!
BOOM!
BOOM!
BOOM!
BOOM!
BOOM!
BOOM!
BOOM!
BOOM!

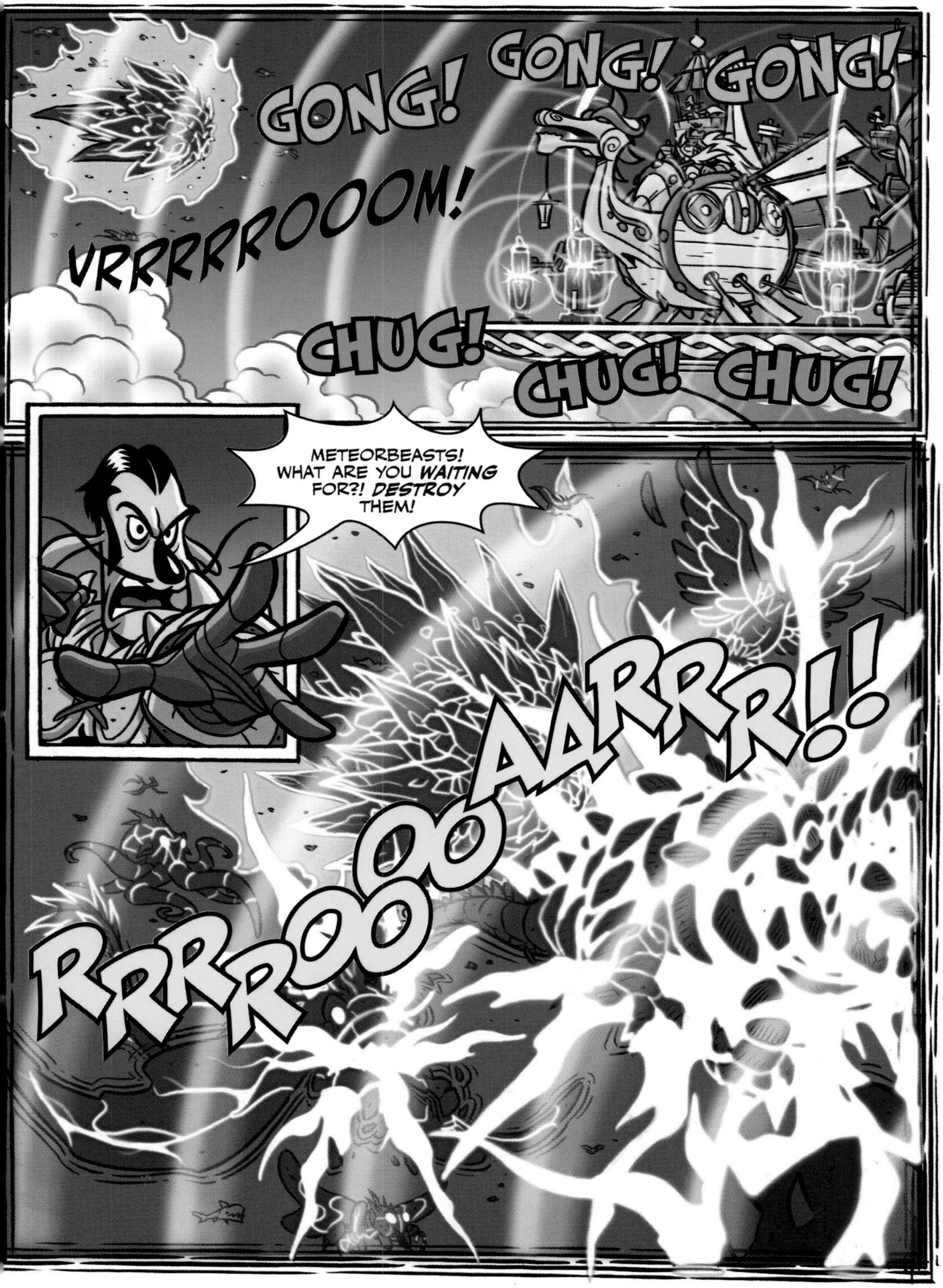
GONG! GONG! GONG!
VRRRRROOOOM!
CHUG! CHUG! CHUG!
METEORBEASTS! WHAT ARE YOU *WAITING* FOR?! *DESTROY* THEM!
RRRROOOOOAARRRR!!

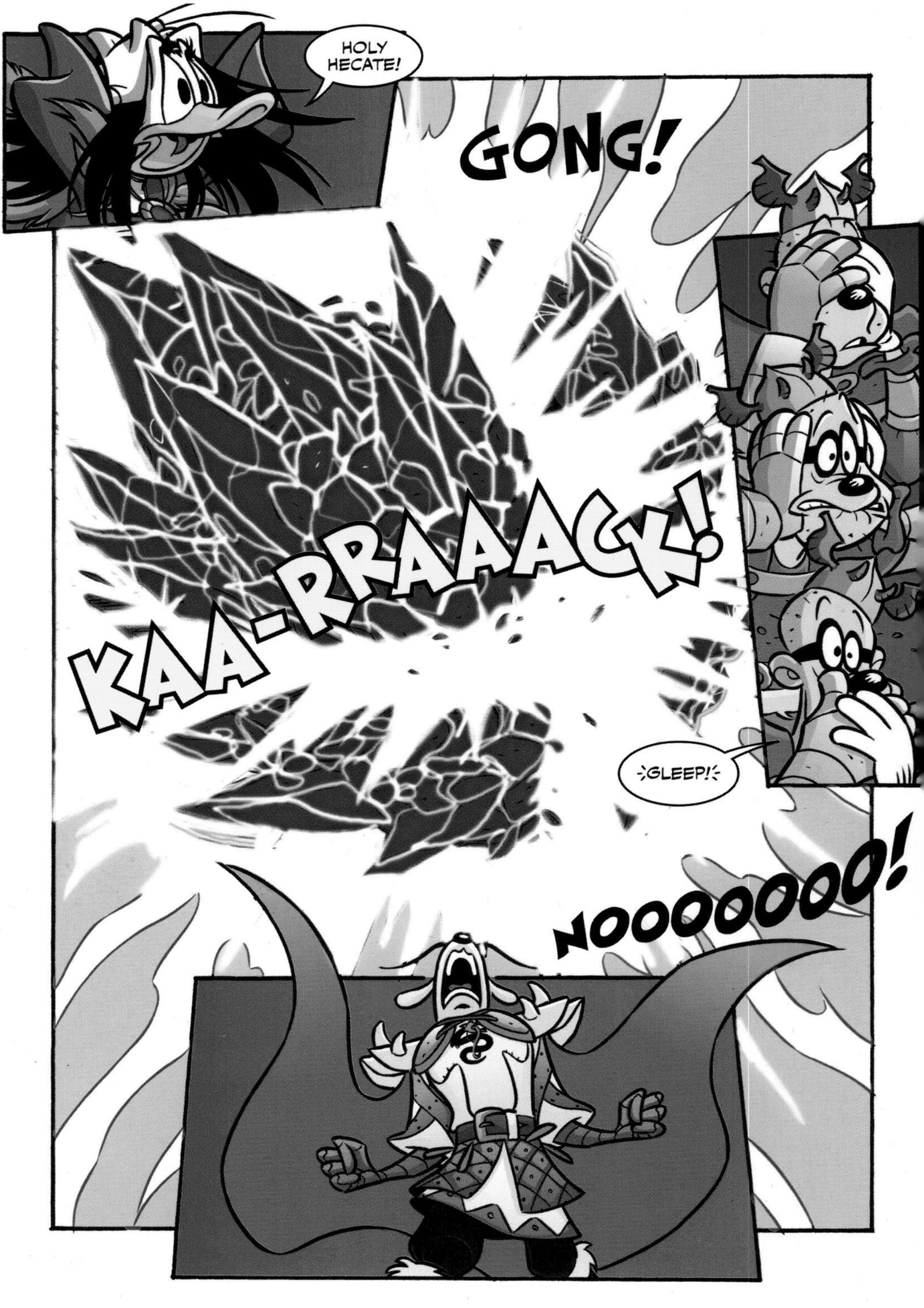
HOLY HECATE!
GONG!
KAA-RRAAACK!
-GLEEP!-
NOOOOOOO!

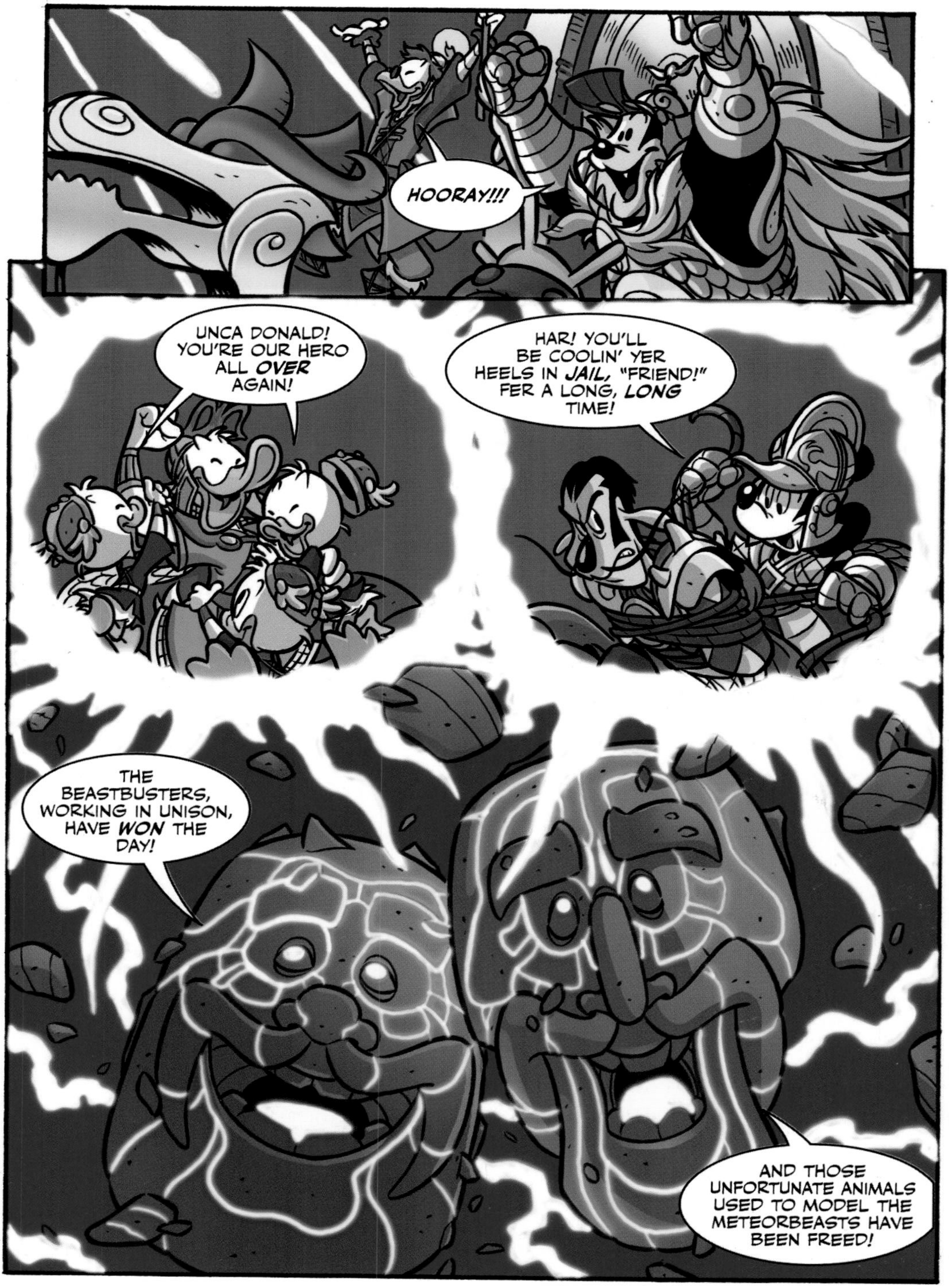
HOORAY!!!
UNCA DONALD! YOU'RE OUR HERO ALL OVER AGAIN!
HAR! YOU'LL BE COOLIN' YER HEELS IN JAIL, "FRIEND!" FER A LONG, LONG TIME!
THE BEASTBUSTERS, WORKING IN UNISON, HAVE WON THE DAY!
AND THOSE UNFORTUNATE ANIMALS USED TO MODEL THE METEORBEASTS HAVE BEEN FREED!

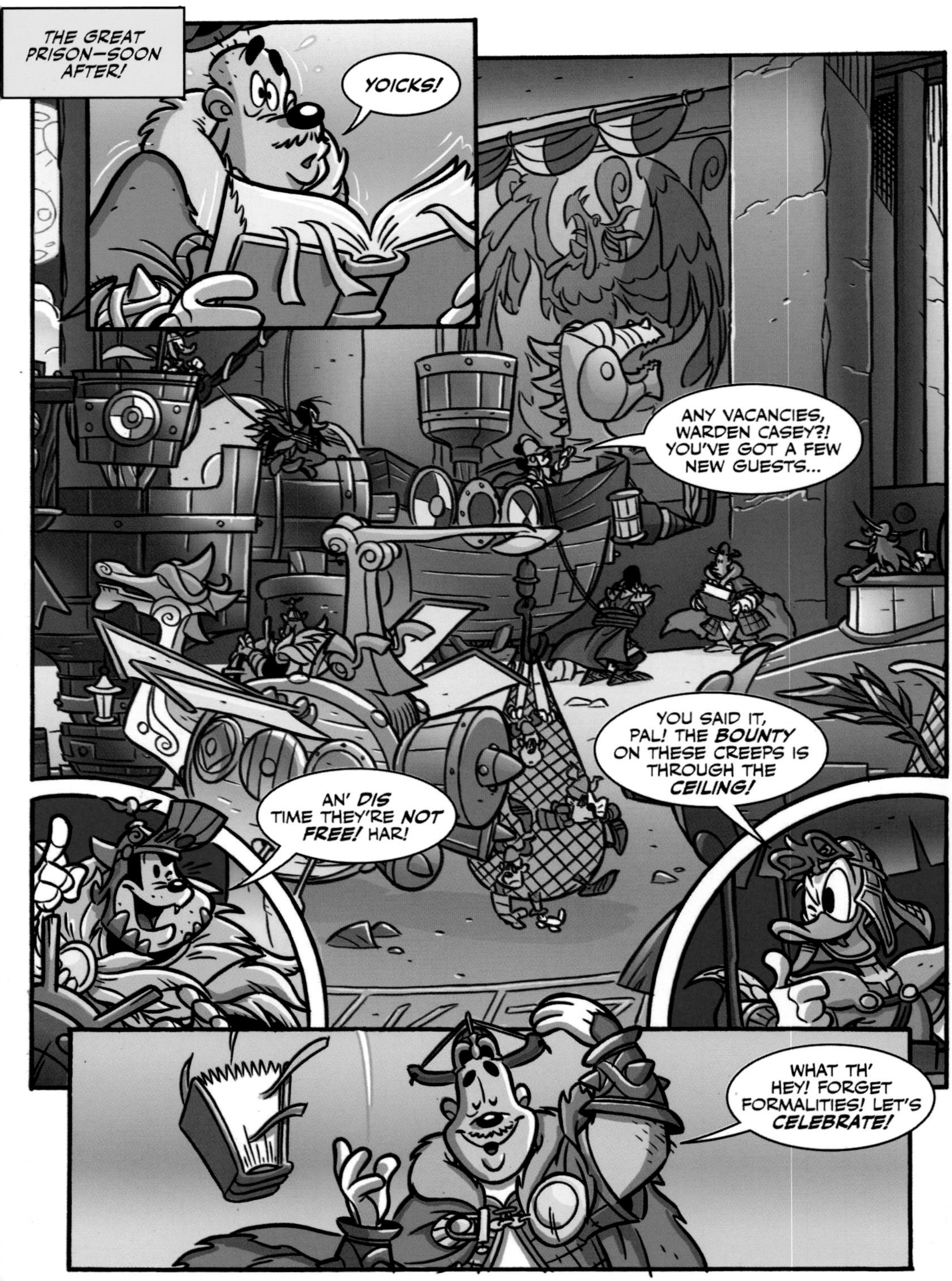
THE GREAT PRISON—SOON AFTER!
YOICKS!
ANY VACANCIES, WARDEN CASEY?! YOU'VE GOT A FEW NEW GUESTS...
YOU SAID IT, PAL! THE BOUNTY ON THESE CREEPS IS THROUGH THE CEILING!
AN' DIS TIME THEY'RE NOT FREE! HAR!
WHAT TH' HEY! FORGET FORMALITIES! LET'S CELEBRATE!

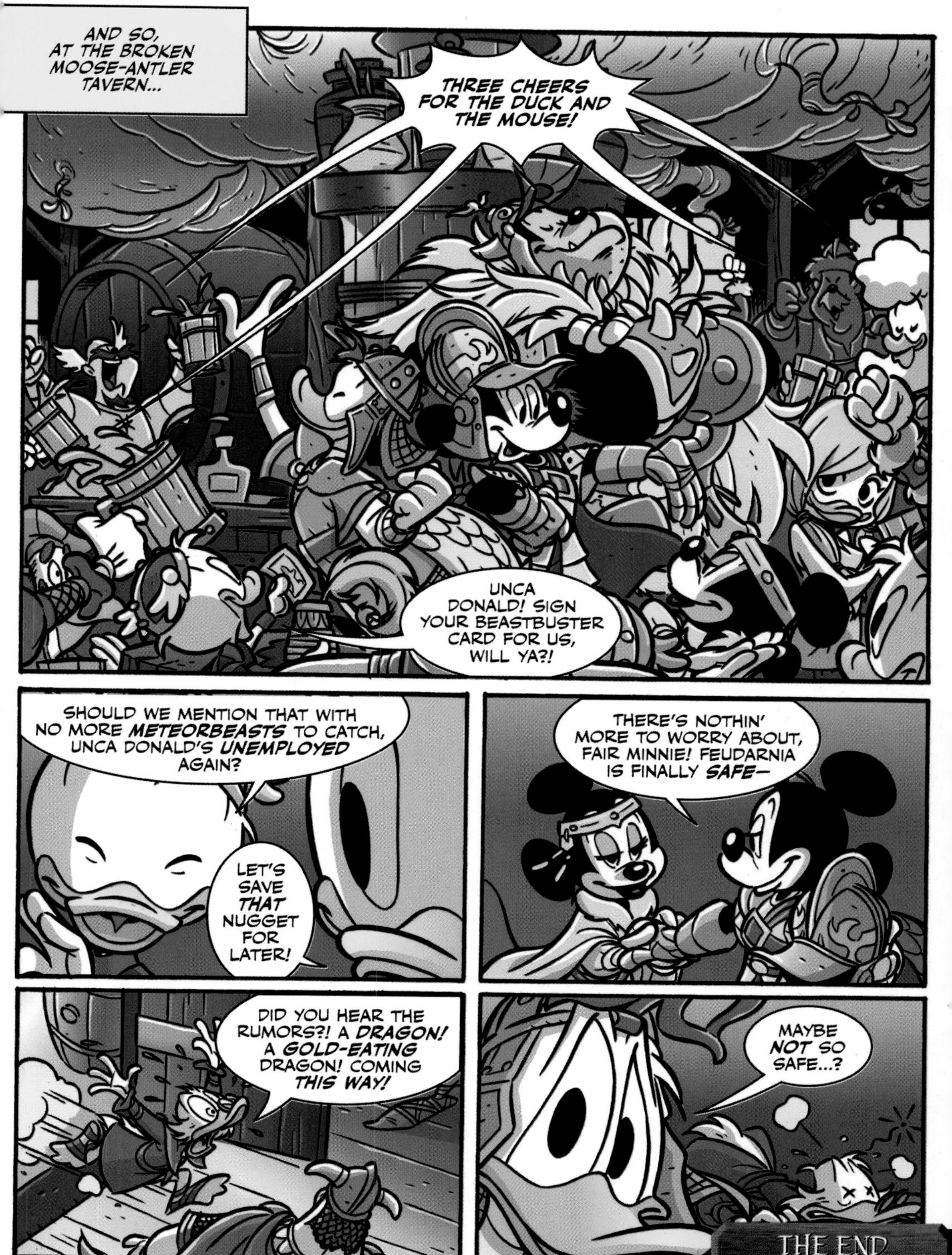
AND SO, AT THE BROKEN MOOSE-ANTLER TAVERN...
THREE CHEERS FOR THE DUCK AND THE MOUSE!
UNCA DONALD! SIGN YOUR BEASTBUSTER CARD FOR US, WILL YA?!
SHOULD WE MENTION THAT WITH NO MORE METEORBEASTS TO CATCH, UNCA DONALD'S UNEMPLOYED AGAIN?
LET'S SAVE THAT NUGGET FOR LATER!
THERE'S NOTHIN' MORE TO WORRY ABOUT, FAIR MINNIE! FEUDARNIA IS FINALLY SAFE—
DID YOU HEAR THE RUMORS?! A DRAGON! A GOLD-EATING DRAGON! COMING THIS WAY!
MAYBE NOT SO SAFE...?
THE END (FOR NOW!)

Art by Andrea Freccero, Colors by Ronda Pattison

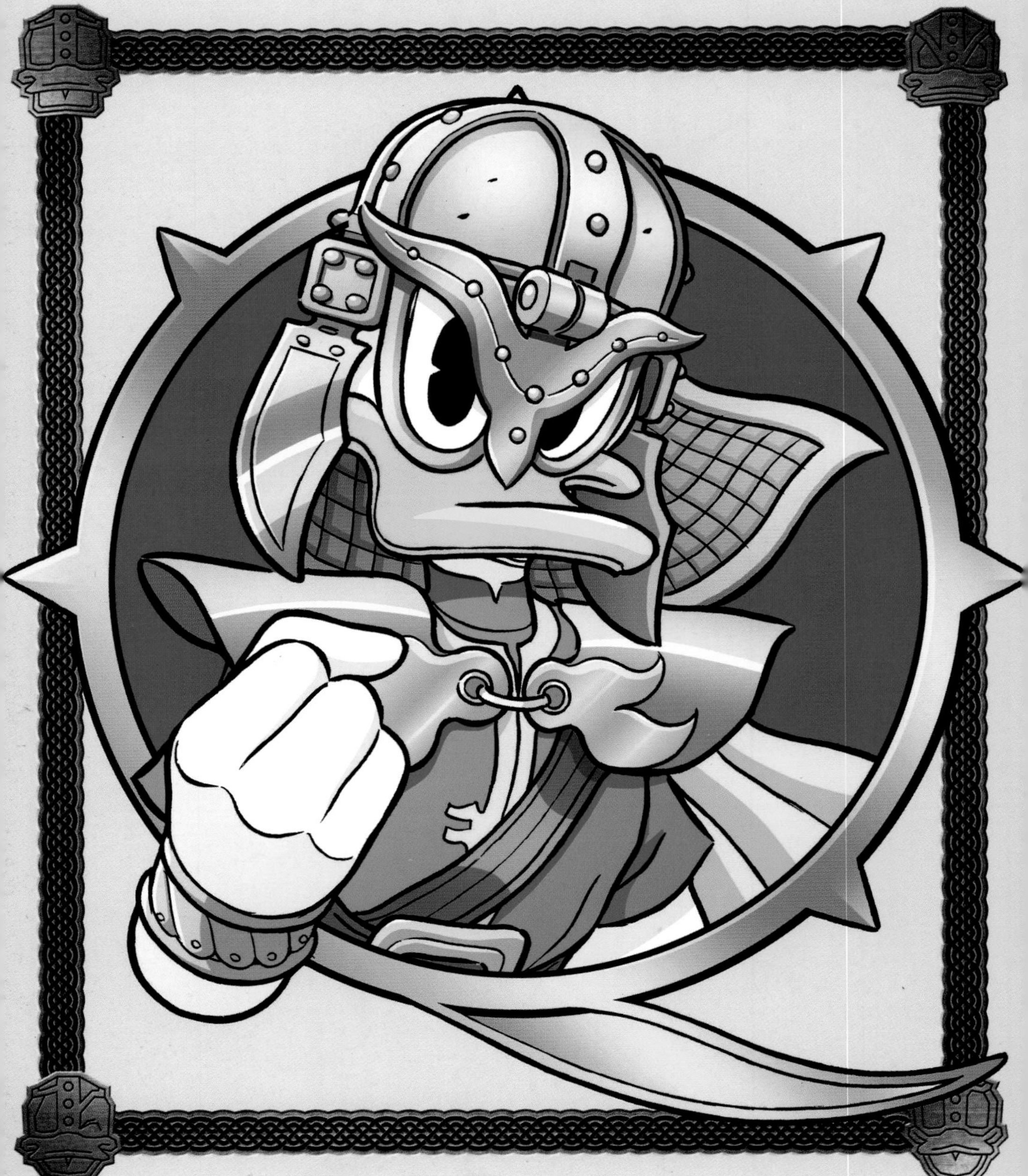

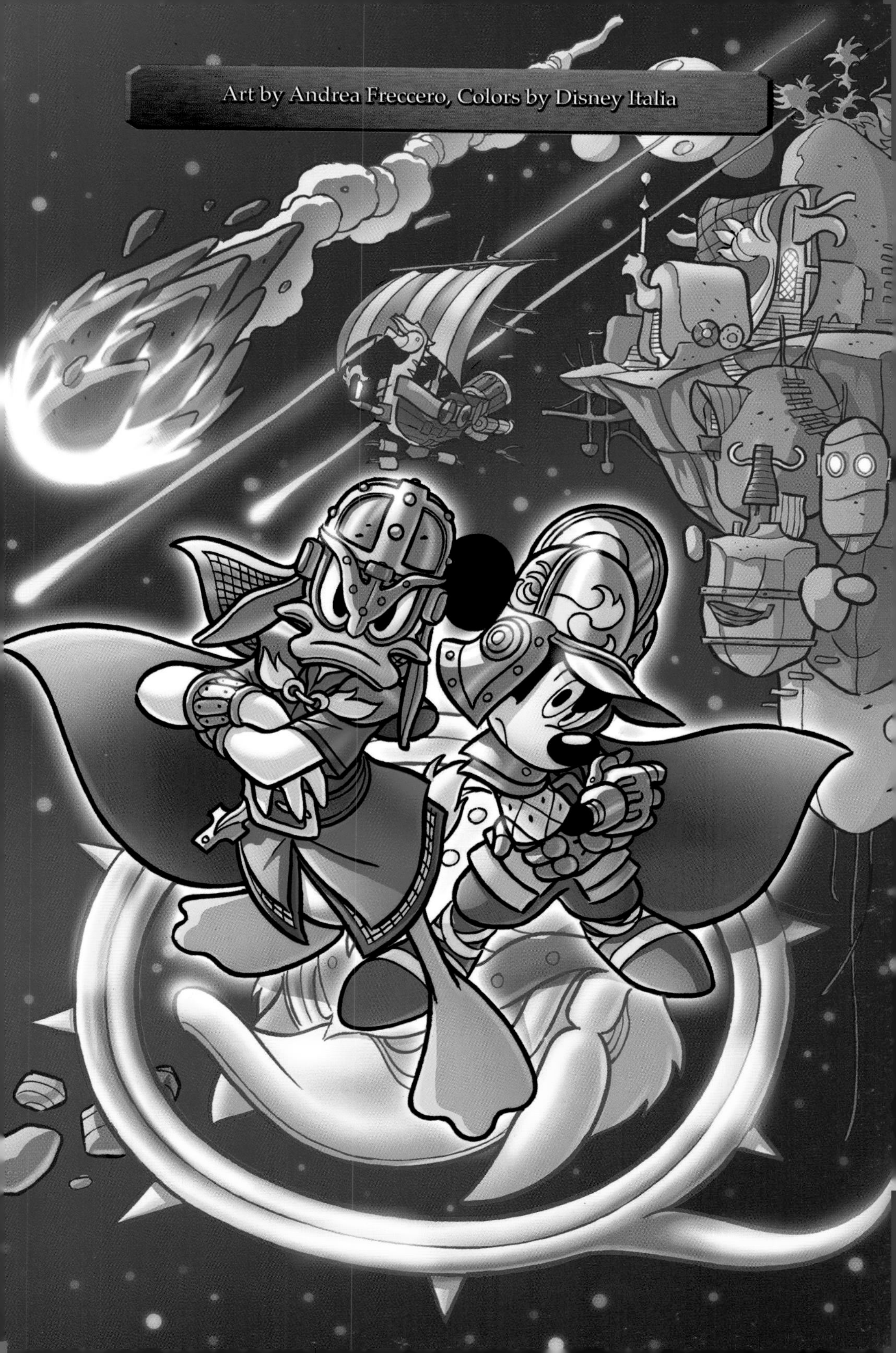

Art by Andrea Freccero, Colors by Disney Italia

Art by Andrea Freccero, Colors by Ronda Pattison

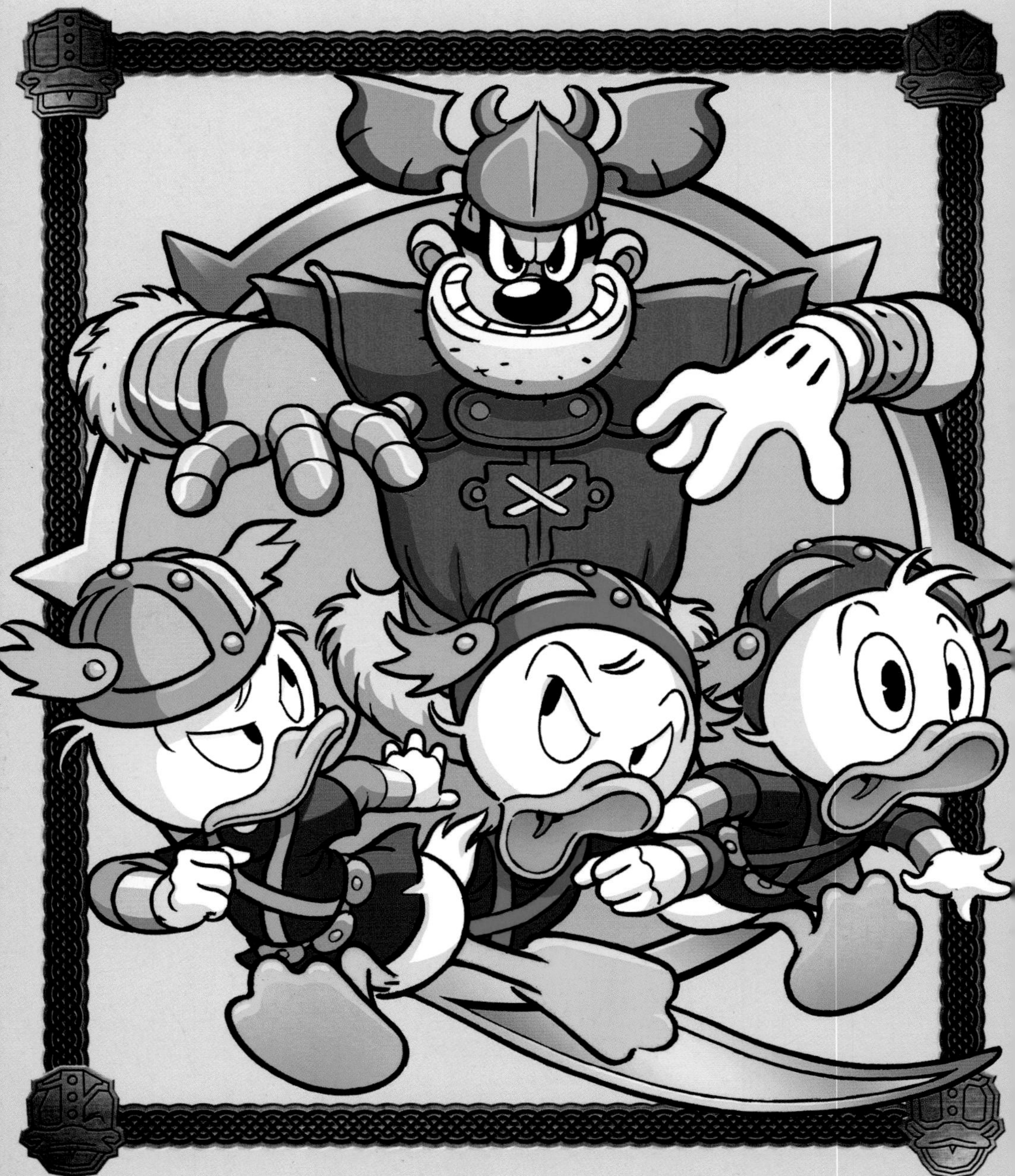

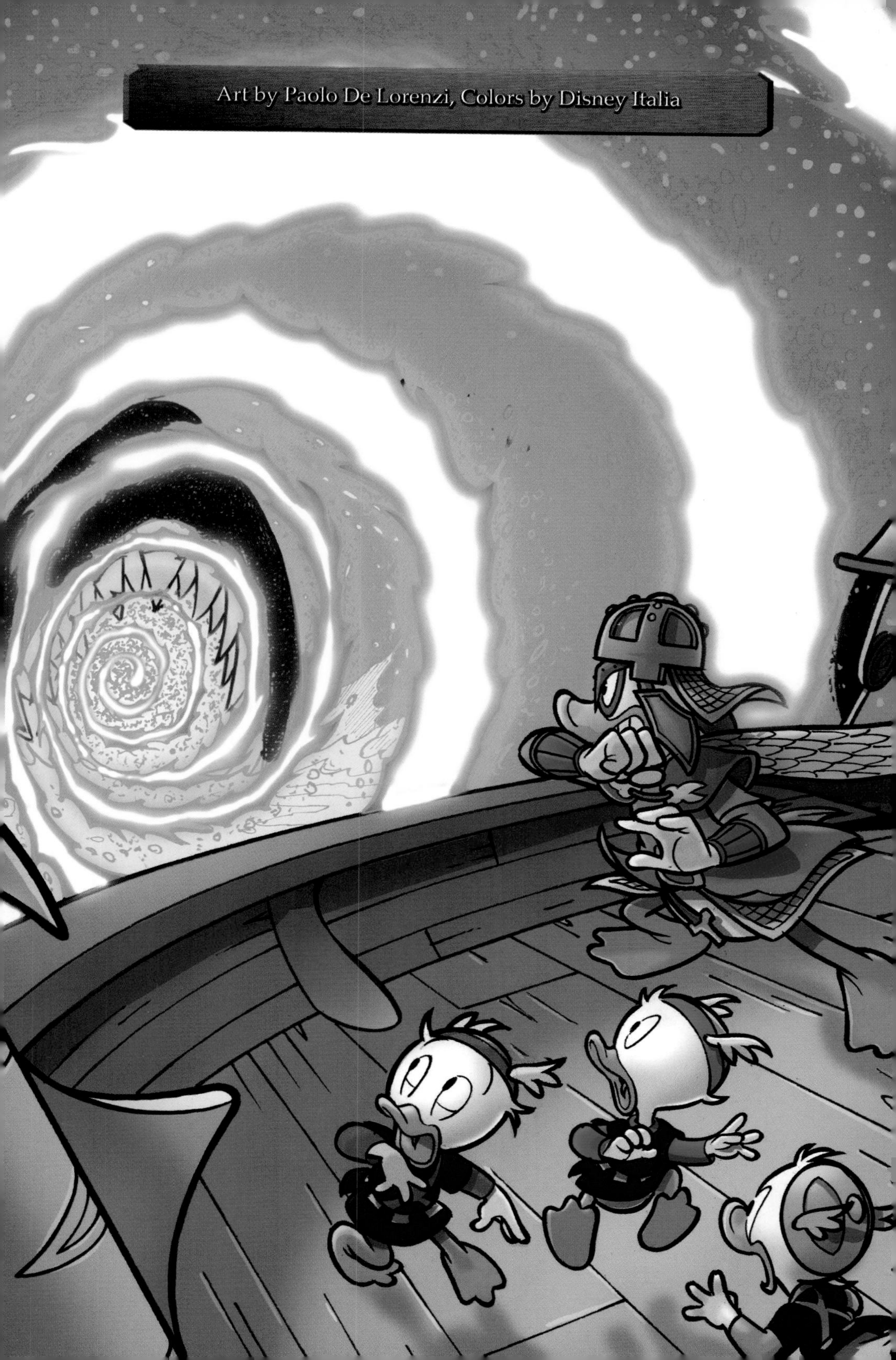
Art by Paolo De Lorenzi, Colors by Disney Italia

Art by Andrea Freccero, Colors by Ronda Pattison

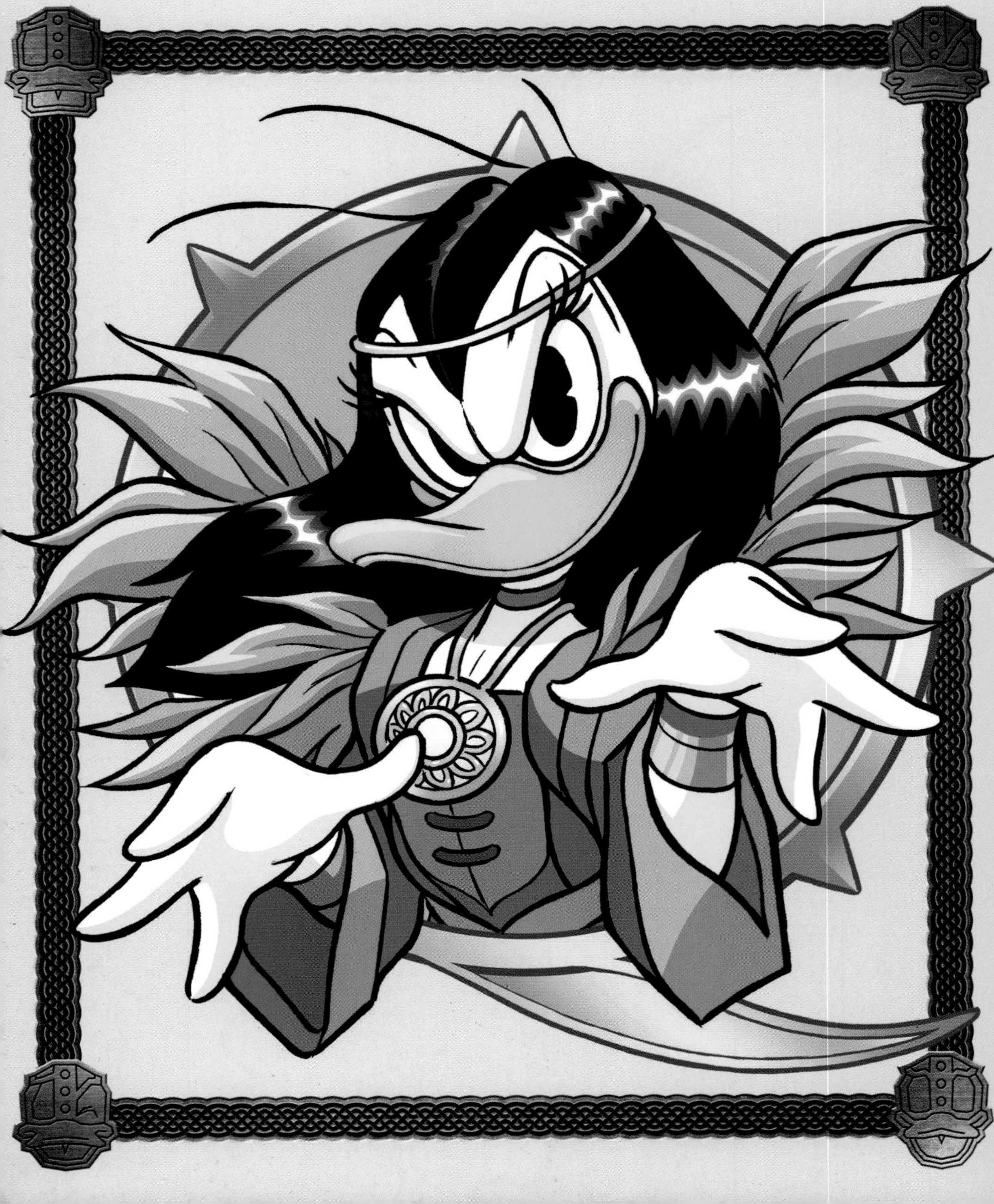

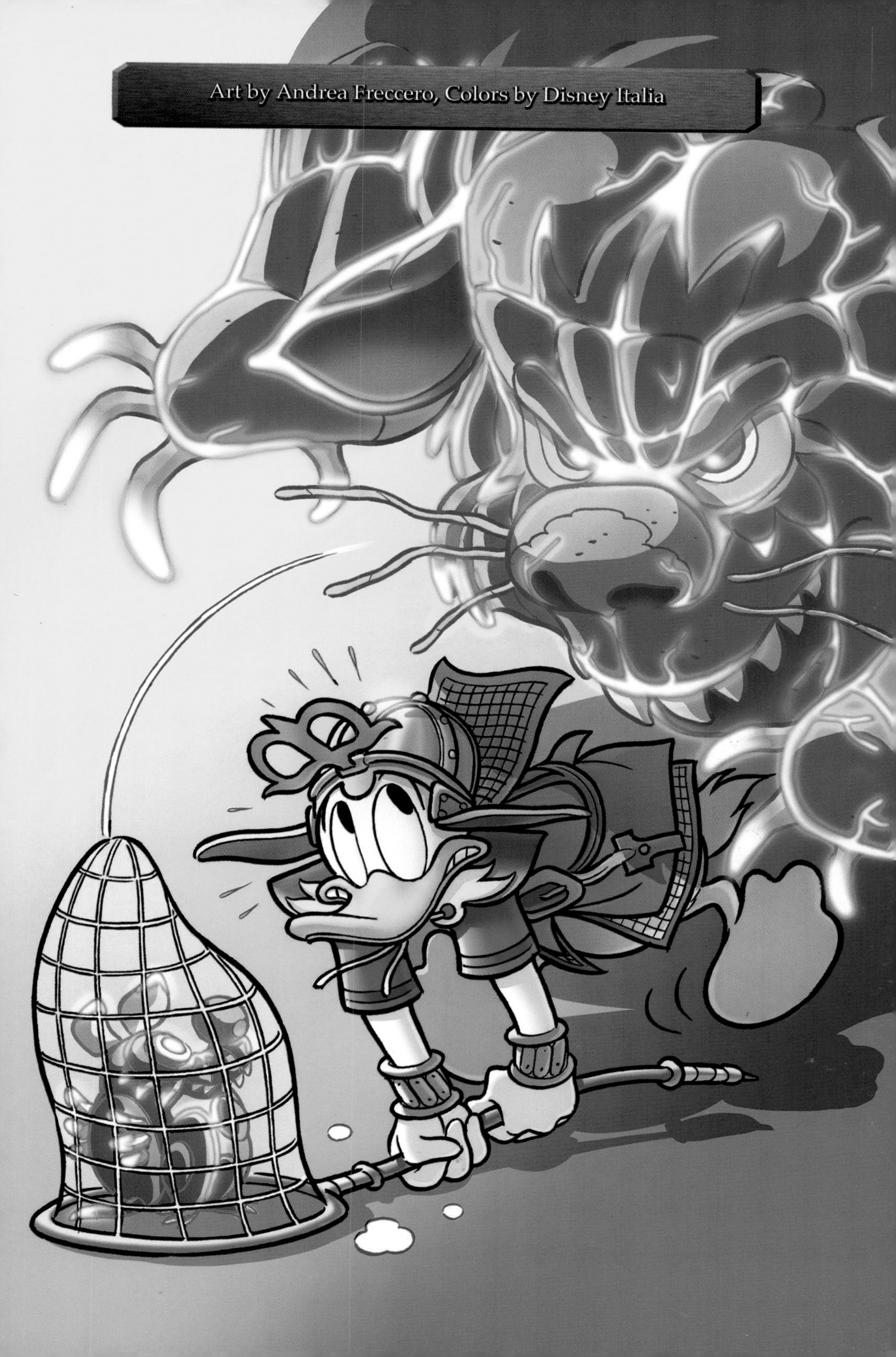
Art by Andrea Freccero, Colors by Disney Italia

Art by Andrea Freccero, Colors by Ronda Pattison

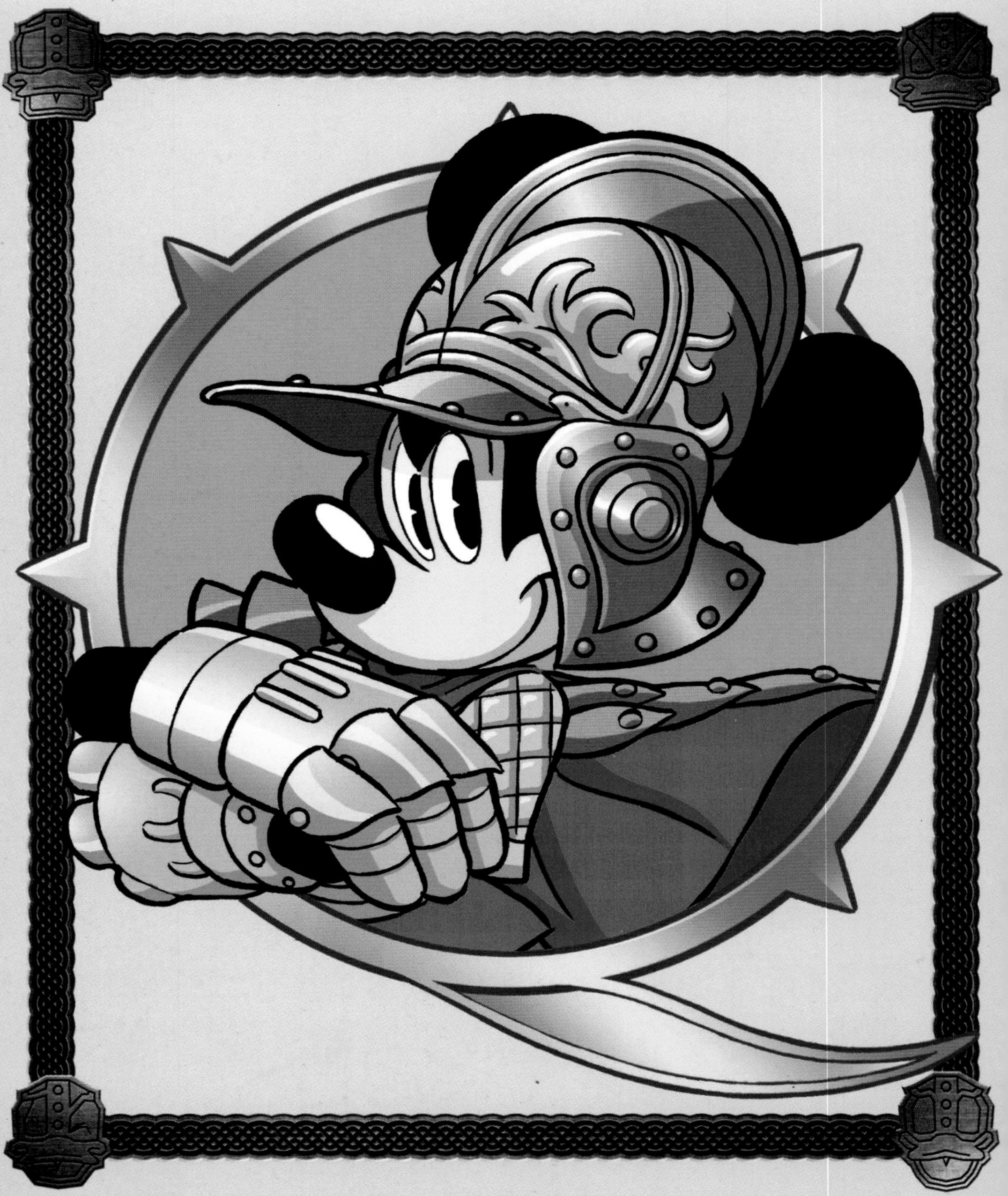

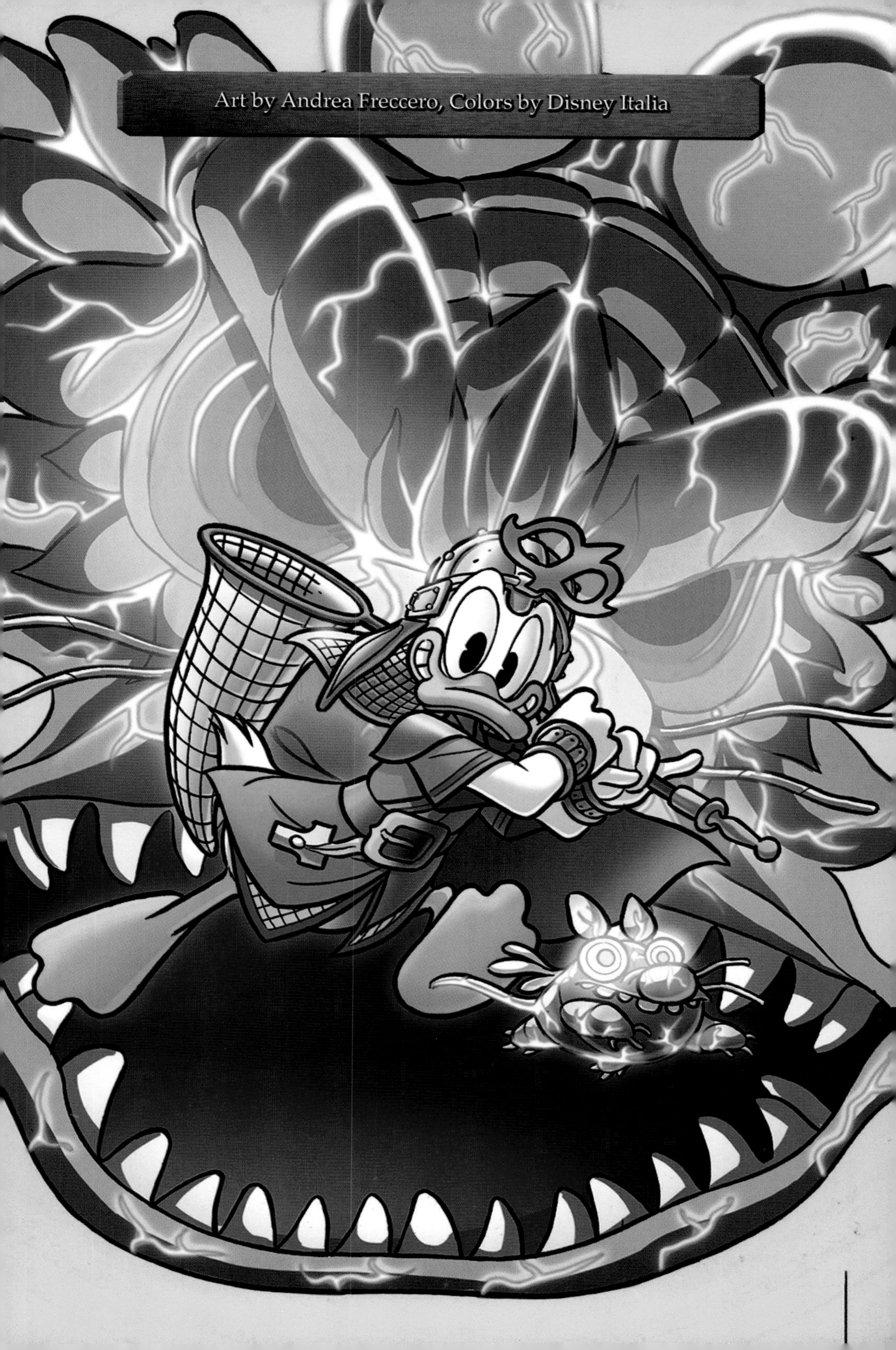

Art by Andrea Freccero, Colors by Disney Italia

Art by Andrea Freccero, Colors by Ronda Pattison

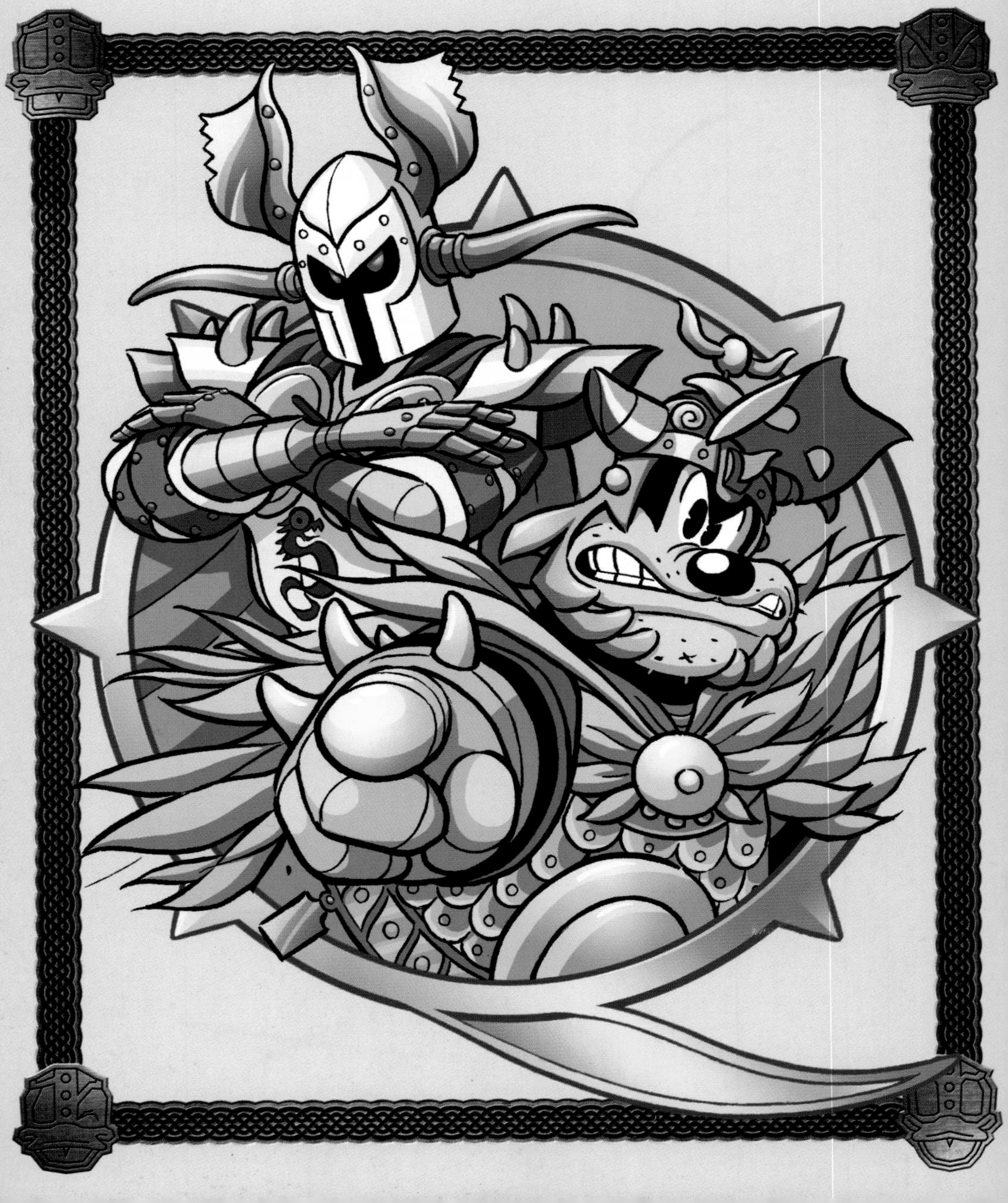

Art by Ciro Cangialosi, Colors by Disney Italia

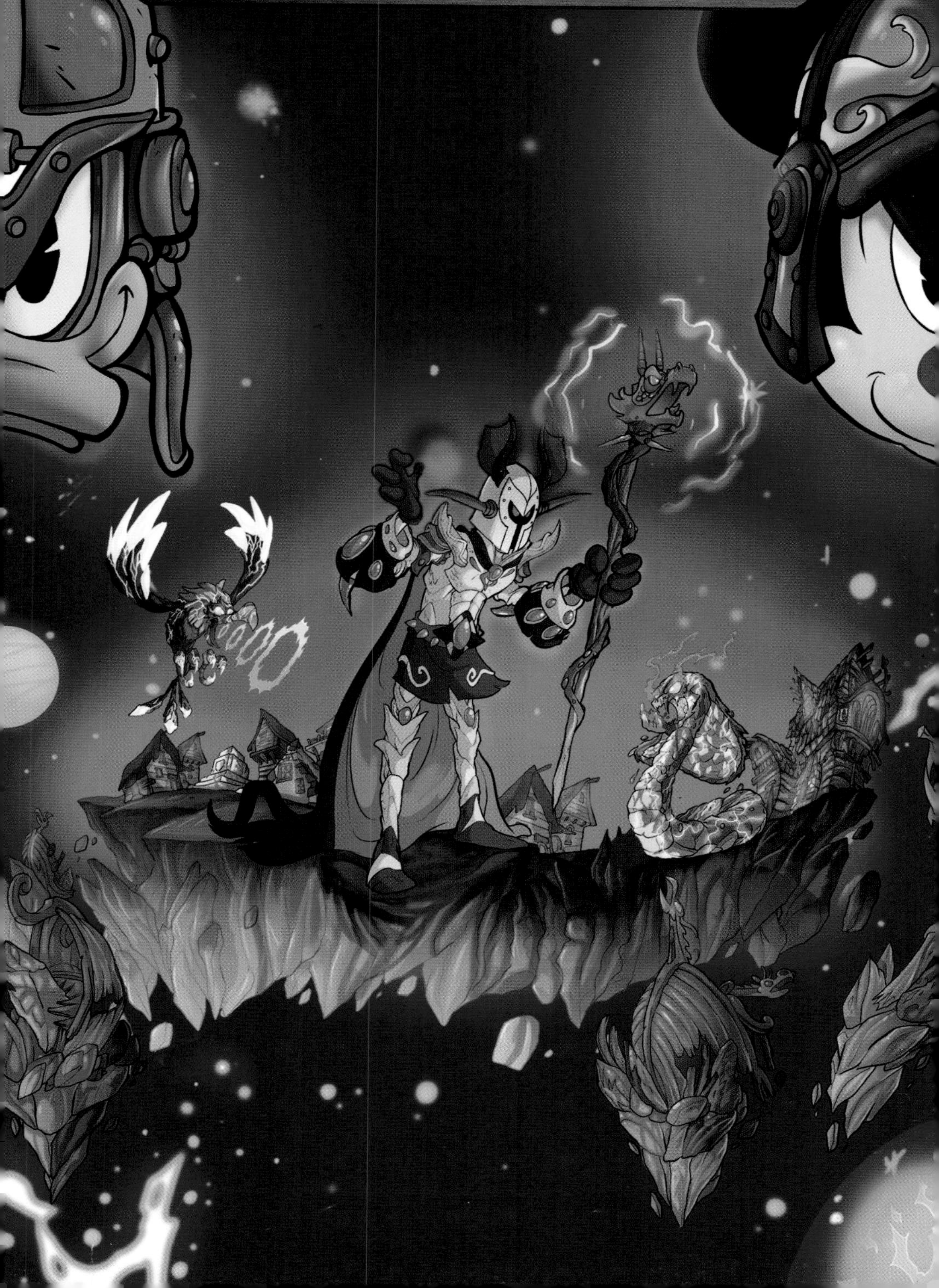

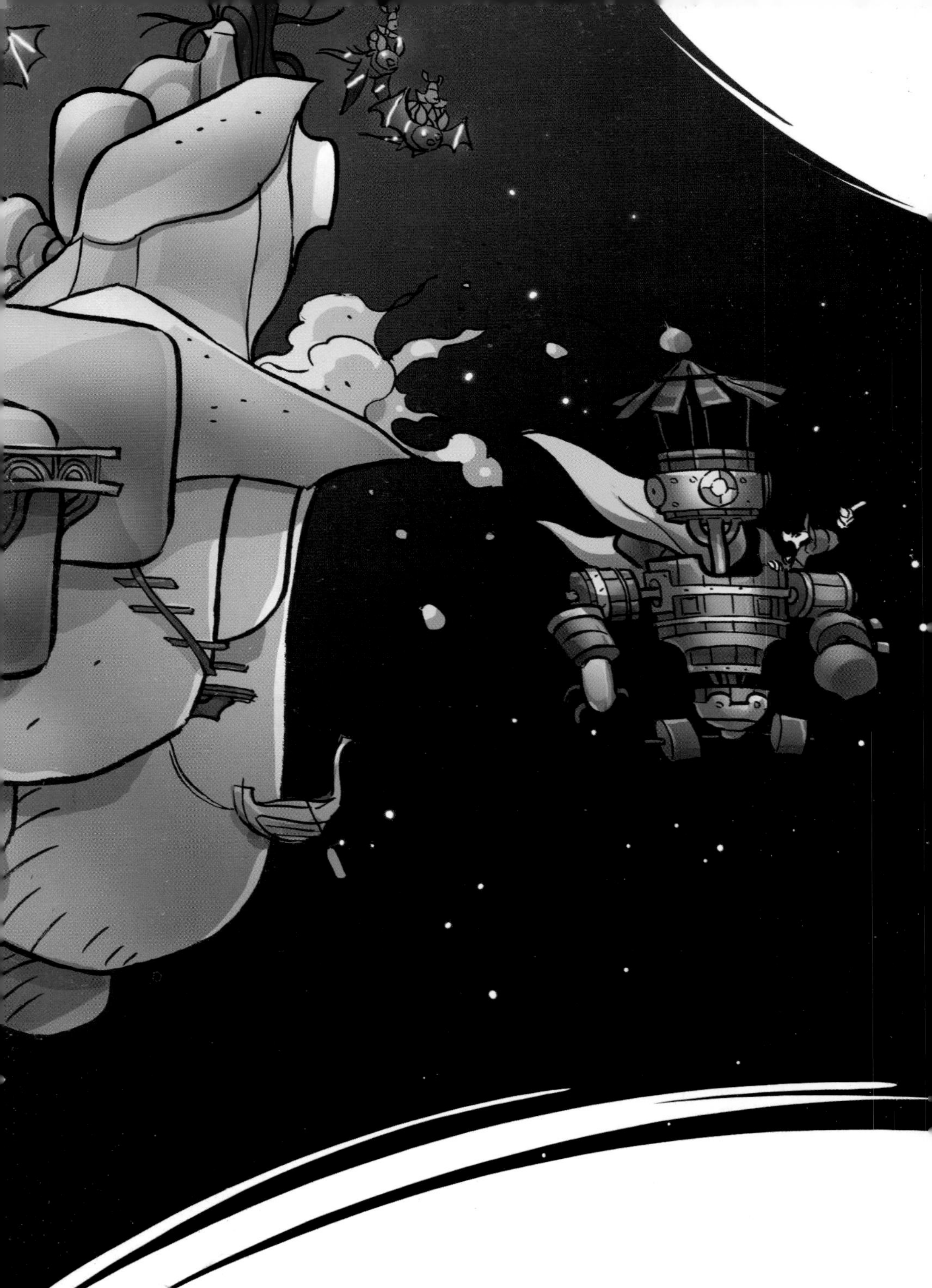